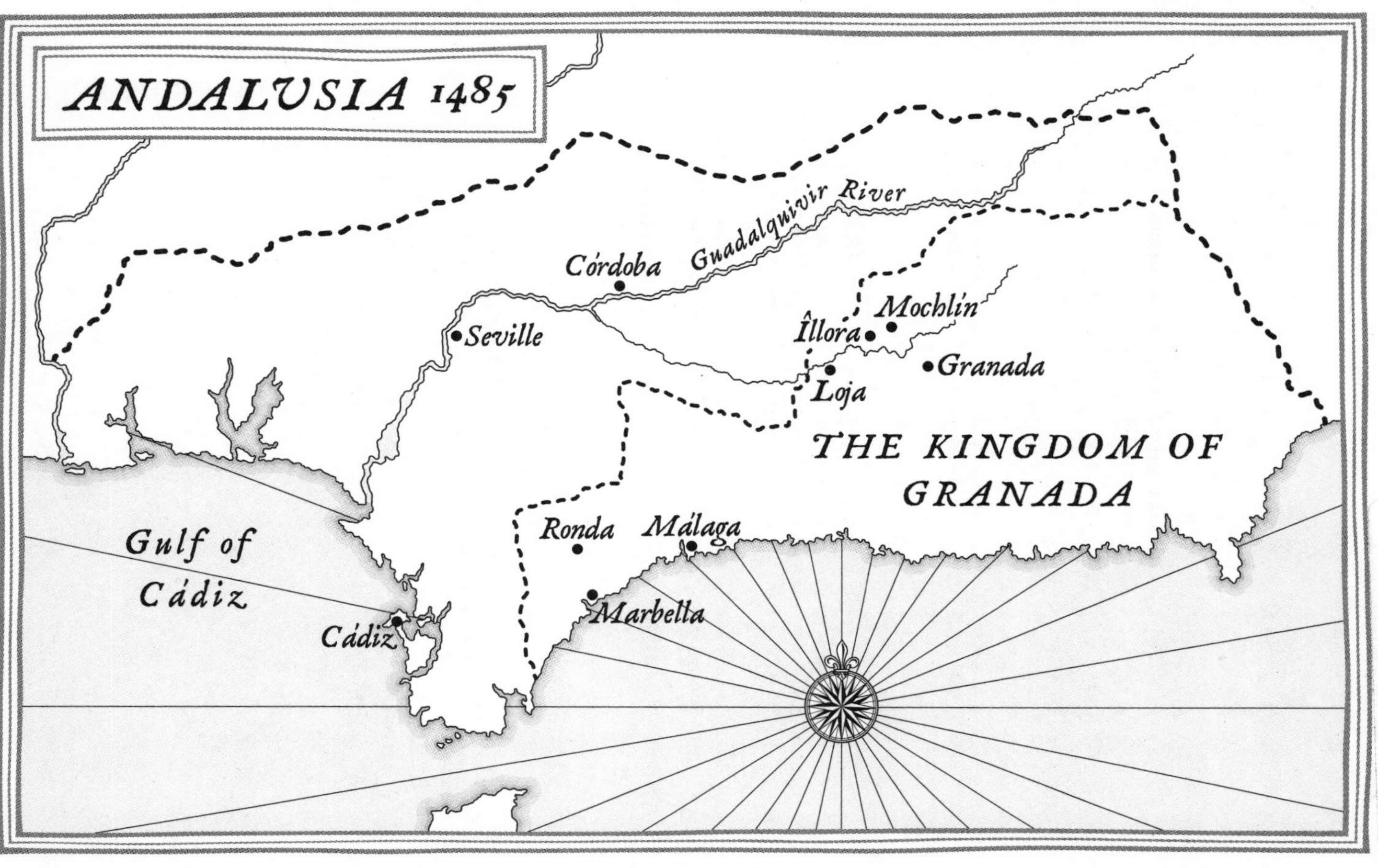
ANDALUSIA 1485
Guadalquivir River
Córdoba
Seville
Mochlín
Íllora
Loja
Granada
THE KINGDOM OF GRANADA
Ronda
Málaga
Marbella
Gulf of Cádiz
Cádiz

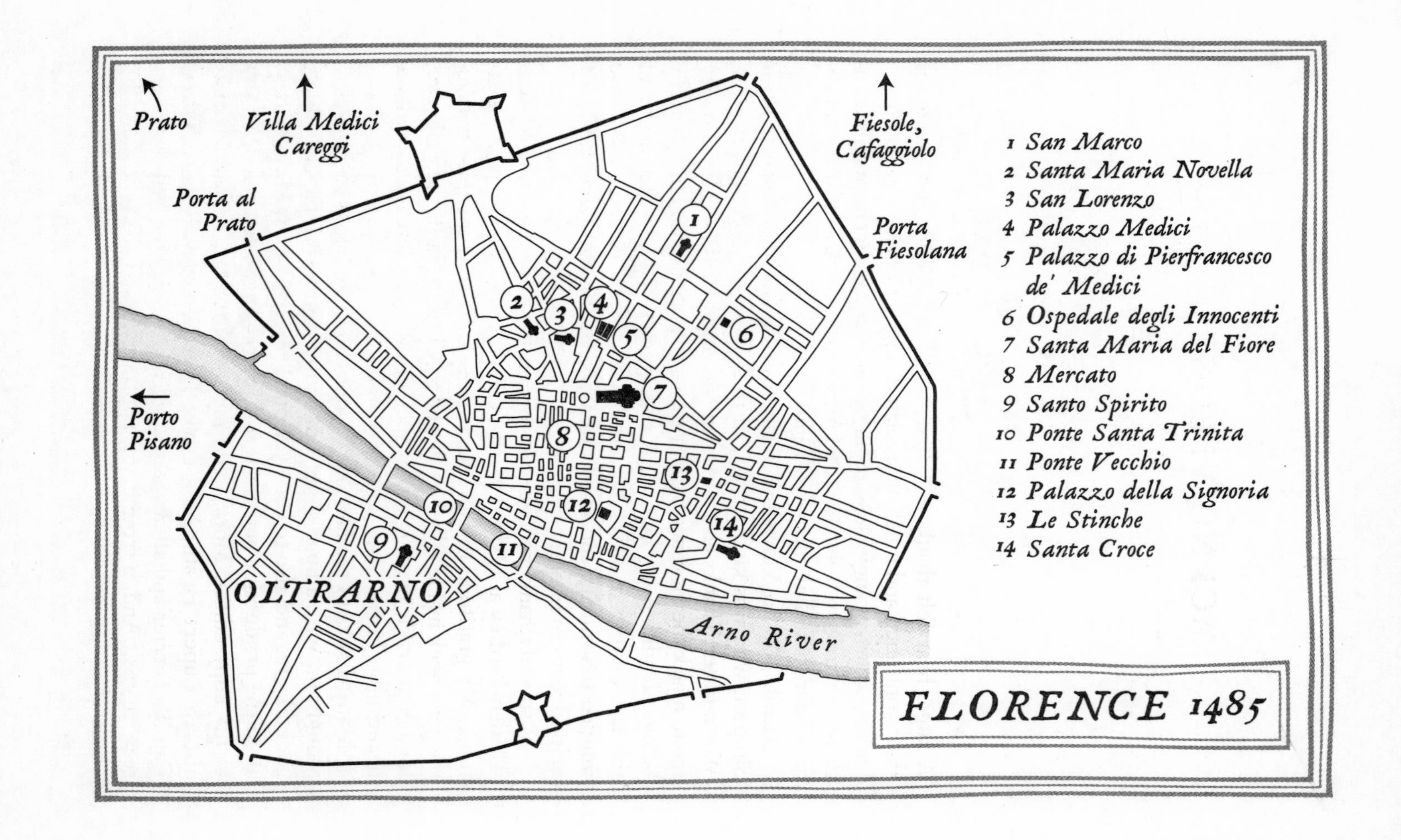
Prato
Villa Medici Careggi
Fiesole, Cafaggiolo
Porta al Prato
Porta Fiesolana
Porto Pisano
OLTRARNO
Arno River
1 San Marco
2 Santa Maria Novella
3 San Lorenzo
4 Palazzo Medici
5 Palazzo di Pierfrancesco de' Medici
6 Ospedale degli Innocenti
7 Santa Maria del Fiore
8 Mercato
9 Santo Spirito
10 Ponte Santa Trinita
11 Ponte Vecchio
12 Palazzo della Signoria
13 Le Stinche
14 Santa Croce
FLORENCE 1485

ACKNOWLEDGEMENTS

A huge, heartfelt thank you, first, to all my friends and family for their continued and much appreciated support as cheerleaders, pub-buddies, plot-wranglers, sounding-boards and huggers, with special thanks to Imogen Robertson and Alex von Tunzelmann for the timely reminder to 'follow the marsh lights'.

Thank you to Vincent Benham for the introduction to Mark Simpson who was kind enough to treat me to an incredible tour of Westminster. Thanks also to Helen and Anthony Riches for allowing me to hijack the Florence trip for research purposes and for generally being splendid. A big hug to my dad, Andy Young, for stepping in at the last minute to drive me around Andalusia (I don't think you minded too much), and thanks to Mark Griffin and David Boyle for helpful loans of books.

A special thank you goes to my historical consultant, Kirsten Claiden-Yardley at Oxford Heritage Partnership, for keeping me on track. My gratitude to Floriana at Riva Lofts, Florence, for helping me get a peek inside Villa Fiesole and to Claudio Nardi and Catherine for a memorable evening which opened a window into the soul of this beautifully elusive city.

Many thanks to the fantastic team behind the books at Hodder & Stoughton, with a huge shout-out to my wonderful, patient editor, Nick Sayers, and also to Cicely Aspinall, Kerry Hood, Alice Morley, all in the production and art teams, marketing, sales, publicity and to my copy-editor, Morag, and my proof-reader, Barbara. Thanks also to Rupert Heath, Meg Davis, Dan Conaway, Roberta Oliva, Camilla Ferrier and all at the Marsh Agency, and the brilliant overseas teams. And a round of appreciative applause to all the booksellers who have supported me over the years and, of course, to you wonderful readers!

Last, my love to Lee – for everything else.

I

The prisoner rose with the dawn. In the half-light, he poured water into a jewelled basin and splashed his face, smoothing back his dark hair. Stray droplets threaded down his chest where faded scars told stories of violence. The most prominent began near his shoulder and snaked in a knotted line to the palm of his hand, where it cut through all the other lines there: heart, life, fate.

After shrugging on his robes, the silk cool against his skin, he settled himself for prayer. The large chamber at the top of the tower filled with his chanted words, rising and falling like a song. The floor bruised his knees with each prostration, even through the softness of the mat. He prayed, as he always did, for God to grant him the strength to endure this day and to bless his family, wherever they might be.

When he was done, he moved to the window. Gripping the iron bars, he surveyed the slit of land his world had been narrowed to. To the east, the first shafts of sun were streaming through a bank of clouds in ribbons of light, gilding the tops of the trees that tumbled from the base of the tower into a valley, before rising up the other side in forested hills. It was late summer, but there was a sharpness to the air; a smell of change coming. Soon, those trees would begin their slow turn from green to bronze. Then, the leaves would fall and, finally, he would glimpse the river in the valley. In one sense he longed to see the water, desperate for something new in this vista. In another, he dreaded it. The sight of anything that moved through this place on its way to somewhere else – whether water, cloud or bird – pained him.

As the light spread, bathing his face, the prisoner closed his eyes and tried to free his mind, let it wing him home. But the pale sun and the scent of damp forest kept him tethered. After three years in foreign lands, even the faces of his family were hard to conjure in detail, like old paintings whose colours have faded. One visage, though, remained perfectly clear. He guessed that when all else had slipped from his memory it would remain: that hard jaw and aquiline nose, those steel eyes, clear and merciless. The face of his brother. The prisoner's hands tightened around the bars, but only for a moment. Even the deep well of his rage had become silted by time and silence.

Turning, he crossed to the table, where a stack of books awaited him, each a world into which he could escape the day. There were religious texts and grand romances, books on law and philosophy, poetry and war. His gaolers, seeing his appetite for them, brought a new pile each week. He wondered where they got them from. A library in the Grand Master's castle perhaps?

Some were old, bindings crumbling, the paper brittle, crackling under his fingertips. Others were pristine, boards wrapped in velvet. A few were in his tongue, but more were in French and Latin, Greek or English. Those languages he did not know, he learned, with the help of an elderly priest of the Order. Often, he paced the chamber as he read, trying to keep his limbs supple and strong. One day, God willing, he would need his strength again. One day, he might return to take back all that had been taken from him.

Settling himself on to a cushioned chair, he opened a book, smoothing the pages. Soon, the servants would come, bringing his meal, emptying the pot beneath his bed, thumping the pillows back to life. He liked to be deep in the words before they entered. He was halfway through the second page when he heard the scream.

The raw human sound tore through the silence, jolting him from the text. He rose, listening intently, hearing only the agitated chatter of birds. For a moment there was nothing, then harsh shouts sounded, followed by a familiar clashing of steel and the clap of wings as scores of birds lifted in fright from the trees outside the tower. Dropping the book, the prisoner darted to the window.

He could see nothing from this vantage except the tops of the trees, but more clashes and anguished cries told him the fighting was close. His heart pounded, blood pulsing, sharpening his mind. Through all these monotonous years, danger was a beast that had never left him, lurking ever near the surface, ready to rise. He knew his brother would finish him if he could. A well-paid assassin with a hidden blade, a drink laced with poison proffered by an unknown servant, an arrow lancing from a rooftop. He had expected them all.

Snatching up a silver candlestick, he tested it with a swipe through the air. It was hefty, but short. He needed something more defensive. A deep thudding reverberated through the walls of the tower, telling him the door was being broken down. Discarding the candlestick, he picked up a stool. Solid oak. A shield and a weapon. There was a splintering crash, shouts and more cries, some of which cut off abruptly. He imagined the attackers, whoever they were, moving through the guardrooms on the lower floors. He knew every inch of this tower for he had watched men build it, just for him. Tall and strong: a prison to last a thousand years, each stone settling heavy in his heart, every scrape of saw on wood a song of despair.

There were footsteps rising, heavy and purposeful. He slipped behind the door as voices echoed in the stairwell. He thought at first it was Latin, but as the men came closer he realised he didn't know the tongue. Still, it seemed akin, as though the words were different notes plucked on the same instrument. It gave no clue as to their intentions, however, and he gripped the stool tightly, heart thrumming. There was a rattle of keys and a snap of bolts. The door thrust open.

The moment he saw a figure enter – caught a glimpse of brown hair and a blue cloak – he attacked. The stool struck the man's shoulder with such force one of the legs broke. The man went flying, dropping the sword he was holding. As he fell, he cracked his head on the solid edge of the bed and crumpled to the floor. With a fierce cry, the prisoner swung again, but more men were piling into the chamber. Too many to fight.

One ducked his attack, then barrelled into him, catching him around the waist and throwing him to the floor. Another moved swiftly in to wrest the stool from his grip. He heard words, sharp and commanding, from an older man who was brandishing a broadsword, its blade slick with blood. The prisoner was hauled to his feet and marched towards the door. He glimpsed a young man, crouched beside the one he'd struck with the stool, now slumped on the floor unmoving, blue cloak tangled around him. The young man shook his head at his older comrade, whose jaw tightened, then he gestured with his sword, motioning them from the room.

The prisoner's feet slipped unsteadily on the narrow stairs as he was half pushed, half pulled down through the tower. He wasn't used to this much movement. In the guardrooms below furniture lay overturned around the bodies of four men. Blood arced across the whitewashed walls in violent sprays of red. Sprawled among three dead guards in their piebald tunics was a figure in a black surcoat and mantle, splayed like wings around him. His garments were embroidered with a forked white cross – symbol of the Order of St John.

The prisoner was bundled outside, the dewy grass soaking through his silk slippers. There were more men out here, some brandishing swords, others thick-barrelled guns, fuses smouldering in their hands. Several were wounded, leaning on comrades. Faces taut, the men beckoned the two holding the prisoner towards a small gate in the castle wall. A bell began to clang. Twisting round, the prisoner saw knights spilling from the castle all clad in their black surcoats, the white crosses on their chests bright as stars in the morning light.

He was forced through the gate, out into the trees beyond, thorns snagging his robes, twigs scratching his face. Some of the men hung back, forming a defensive line. As his captors brought him to a clearing in the woods, the ear-splitting crack of guns erupted behind them. There were dozens of horses here, stamping and snorting at the commotion, more men trying to calm them. The prisoner addressed his captors, first in his own tongue, then in Latin, demanding to know who they were, where they were taking him, but they ignored him, heaving him up into a saddle in front of one of their number.

Pinned to the pommel, he could only hold on as the man behind him kicked at the horse, sending it racing away through the trees, which opened on to a narrow track. As the clanging bell and the sounds of fighting receded behind them, the prisoner felt his heart lift with the sudden exhilaration of speed. For a moment, his fear forgotten, he gasped at the rush of wind and the sun on his face, the air grass-sweet and the jewel-blue glints of the river in the valley.

His world was all at once huge, opening before him.

2

The day was dying as the five men approached the city, passing close to the gibbet of Montfaucon, which towered over the road on its bald mound, two tiers high. Bodies, hanging from the beams like withered fruit, turned slow half-circles in the raw November wind, bones knitted loosely by wisps of clothing and ribbons of flesh, dry and brown as tanned leather. The air carried on its shifting currents the stale echoes of decay.

Jack Wynter's gaze was drawn to the hanging place, eyes moving over the ropes that had squeezed the life out of each man dangling there. He imagined the crowds, some silent, others roaring as the condemned were forced to mount the scaffold. The nick of hemp on skin, the tightening of the rope, the knot jammed up against the left ear. A last breath snatched. He wondered how many deaths had been witnessed here, the grass around the gibbet flattened by years of pressing feet. How many men strung up? Thieves. Traitors. The falsely accused. Left to hang – a warning and a promise – until their bones crumbled into nothing and their souls were left to wander. His mind filled with an image of his father, twisting on a rope in a far northern castle.

'Jack.'

He realised he'd slowed, the others moving ahead along the road.

Ned Draper nodded towards the city walls, looming beyond muddy fields. The large man lifted his voice above the wind that whipped his thatch of hair around his face. 'They'll be ringing the bell for curfew soon.'

Jack joined his companions, unclenching his fist, where the gold ring engraved with a caduceus – two serpents entwined around a winged staff – one of the last tangible pieces of his father left to him, had pressed hard against his fingers. He noticed Valentine Holt's dark eyes remained fixed on the gallows. Catching his gaze, the bull of a man spat in the dust before walking on, shifting his arquebus, swaddled in sacking, higher on his shoulder, his pack of powder and shot swinging against his back. Jack wondered if he too had been thinking about Sir Thomas Vaughan, or whether the gunner's thoughts were on his own neck, likely as not for the stretching had they stayed in England.

As Ned whistled, Titan left the pile of horse dung he'd been nosing in and bounded to his master's side, his white belly and legs caked with dirt. The little dog kept pace as the men lengthened their strides, heading for the walls of Paris.

They made it to the gates just in time, the watchmen preparing to heave the barriers closed as the bell clanged. Jack felt the guards' eyes linger on them as they passed through. Five men in travel-worn clothes with nothing but the packs they carried, battle scars and an assortment of weapons concealed beneath hoods and cloaks. He tensed, waiting for the shout at their back, the questions. Who were they? Where had they come from? Why were they here? But a mist of rain was blowing in on the bitter wind and the bell was calling the guards with the promise of fire and shelter now their watch was ended.

As they headed through the muddy streets beyond, Jack took point, eyes on the distant markers of Notre-Dame and the palace, glimpsed in gaps between timber-framed buildings. The two stone beasts faced one another across the Île de la Cité, towers rising like pale horns. The rain was falling harder now, soaking his cloak. He caught odours of their journey trapped in its weave: sour seas, cold earth, smoke from damp and cheerless fires. Ahead, two men ducked into an inn, the open door spilling a warm wash of firelight and laughter before it closed behind them.

Adam Foxley, strands of his greying hair stuck to his wind-reddened cheeks, nodded towards it. 'Looks as good as any we'll find tonight, no?'

'Agreed,' said David, gripping his brother's shoulder and stepping towards the inn.

'No.'

The Foxleys turned at Jack's call. Two sets of sharp blue eyes narrowed.

Adam, the older of the brothers by several years and thicker-set than David, but with the same letter branded on his forehead – a faded *F* for felon – gestured at the inn. 'We'll be wanting a bed. Why not here, before we're soaked to the marrow?'

'I want to see him first.'

Ned stepped in, rainwater dripping from his nose. Titan was shivering at his heels, fur plastered to his body. 'Come, Jack, let's be in. What difference will a night make? We'll go to him at first light tomorrow.'

Jack had held his impatience in check these past weeks, all through the delay at Dover, where they waited for the storms raging in the Channel to die down before seeking passage on a balinger carrying wool to the English enclave of Calais. He had held it in through their journey south to Paris, resting in the ruins of churches and farmsteads – old victims, perhaps, of the long war – to save the few coins they had left between them. But he was here now, so close, and could no longer press it down. 'You stay. I'll find you when I'm done.'

'No.' Valentine had hunched his shoulders around his thick neck and was clutching his pack of powder to his chest to keep it from the rain, but his slab of a face, peppered with powder burns, was set. 'We was agreed – we stay together.'

Jack looked over at him, surprised by his support. He saw at once that it wasn't sympathy in the gunner's eyes, but blunt self-interest.

Yes, they had agreed to stay together. The events of the past year had bound them all in fate and fortune. He had known these men since he was a boy. Ned, Valentine, the Foxleys – they had served under his father's command through the wars between the houses of York and Lancaster, marching with Sir Thomas Vaughan on the road to battle, following him into every bloody fray. It was they whom Jack had called upon for help two years ago when he'd returned from Seville, sent there with the map Vaughan had ordered him to guard with his life – home to find his father executed for treason by Richard, Duke of Gloucester, and his mother murdered. They had been the ones he turned to when he'd been left with nothing but questions and grief, and they had come, risking their lives in his quest for answers.

They had been with him when he entered the Tower to liberate the Duke of Gloucester's nephew, Prince Edward, the boy who'd been raised by Vaughan, his chamberlain. The boy who should have been king. With him when he spirited Edward from London in the hope the young prince could tell him his father's secrets: what the map, stolen from the Bristol merchant ship, the *Trinity*, showed, and who the men searching for it were – those who had killed his mother in pursuit of it. With him when he returned, broken and desperate, Edward wrested from his care and delivered into the hands of the new king, Henry Tudor, who would not have a prince of the blood free to challenge his rule.

Their actions had made them outlaws, any life they could have lived in England impossible with prices on their heads and Tudor – an avowed enemy – upon the throne. In helping Jack they had lost their homeland. None of them had been left with anything but what each carried to his name and Valentine wasn't about to let him seek out a possible future, in which they might all benefit, alone.

Jack owed them that.

'We go to the priest together,' finished the gunner, glancing at the Foxleys.

'If memory serves there are scores of inns across the river,' said Ned lightly, breaking the edge of tension. Tugging his hood higher, he clicked his tongue for Titan to follow. 'We'll drink with doctors and philosophers for a night.'

The Seine was swollen, its dark waters cascading between the arches of Le Pont Notre-Dame, the tangled flotsam of fallen branches, dead leaves and rubbish whirling around its piers. The bridge was congested, people hurrying between the rows of shops and houses that spanned its length, rain tumbling from overhanging eaves, the last traders slamming their doors shut. Once on the island, they wound through the riddle of houses and inns between Notre-Dame and the Palais de la Cité, the walls of which were pitted from the kingdom's long war with England, which had ended thirty-two years ago at Castillon, in a storm of shot and gunpowder, and English defeat.

As they made for Le Petit Pont, memories flared in Jack like dull sparks. He had walked these streets only months ago, back in the heat of summer, before the great Battle of Redemore Plain which had seen King Richard, the man who sent his father to the gallows, cut down by the blades of his own countrymen. Before Tudor seized England's crown. The memories were fitful, more like dreams. He had been burning then with fever, half mad with thoughts of vengeance and the agony in his scorched skin. He still bore the scars, his hands mottled pink and white beneath the dirt.

Often, even now, he would wake sweating and gasping, having dreamed he could smell smoke turning the air to poison, filling his lungs; fierce fans of flame buffeting him, his hair beginning to burn while he twisted on the floor of the hunting lodge, the knife stinging his skin as he tried to cut the ropes that bound him. Trussed like an animal and left to burn. By his own brother.

Harry Vaughan.

Just thinking the name sent a pulse of hatred through Jack and made his hands itch for his sword. The prince he had freed from the Tower, the map he swore to his father he would safeguard – Harry had taken both from him. And so much more besides.

Stumbling the endless miles from the smoking ruins of the lodge, it was here in Paris that Jack had been found and delivered to Amaury de la Croix. Only the priest had offered any relief: salves for his blistered hands, water for his parched throat and the promise of the answers he craved, if Jack brought him what Harry had stolen.

So, he had gone, back to England to seek out his half-blood brother. But he had failed. Now, the precious map was most likely under the control of Tudor, to whom Harry Vaughan had pledged his allegiance, inheriting their dead father's fortune. And the prince . . .? Jack didn't know for certain, but his gut told him young Edward and his brother, two princes locked in the Tower of London, were long past saving.

But, still, those questions were left hanging inside him and Jack needed answers more than ever, if only because they might offer him – all of them – a direction. That was what he'd been walking towards these past weeks, like a sailor searching for land after months at sea, desperate for some sign, some course to follow in this wild nothing of a life that was now his. He had no home, no family, no money and no kingdom. With his father and mother dead and, with them, any hope of the knighthood he'd dreamed of and trained for, he was just plain Jack Wynter. Bastard. Orphan. Outlaw.

Only the priest offered him anything more.

'We're here.'

At Ned's voice, Jack realised they'd entered the familiar street in the Latin Quarter that wound away from the river following the stinking Bièvre, an oily slug of water that emptied sewage into the Seine. A little way down, caught between two booksellers, was the bakery above which lived Amaury de la Croix. The shutters and door were closed, no sign of life beyond. Blinking into needles of rain, Jack stared up at the narrow building, whose upper storey jutted into the street, giving the impression the whole thing was about to fall on him.

'It's dark,' said Adam, brow pinching.

It was true – of all the houses in the street it was the only one where no firelight flickered behind the windows. Jack shook his head, unwilling to accept that Amaury might not be home. The man was ancient, with one hand and a limp. Where else would he be on a night like this, except perhaps at Mass? In which case, he would be back any time.

Hearing raised voices, Jack glanced down the street to where a group of young scholars were piling into an inn. 'Why don't you get us lodgings there for the night?' He turned to his companions. 'If the priest isn't home, I'll wait for him.' He met Valentine's narrowed eyes. 'He'll be more forthcoming, I believe, if I see him alone. I'll come as soon as I've spoken to him.'

'You'll ask him,' Adam Foxley said. In the soldier's gruff voice it was more statement than question.

'Yes.'

Slinging his pack from his shoulder, Jack passed it to Ned. The sad droop of leather contained most of what he owned in the world: a crusty blanket and pair of hose, a pouch of coins and the Book of Hours – a well-thumbed keepsake – taken from his father's deserted mansion on London's Strand. Jack kept hold of his father's sword, strapped to his body beneath the folds of his cloak, the broad blade concealed in an old scabbard Grace had given to him back in Lewes, the day they left for Dover. He guessed it had belonged to her dead husband.

'I'll save you a cup of wine,' Ned offered, his smile not reaching his eyes, which told Jack – *don't be long, don't forget about us.*

Jack watched them walk to the inn, Titan barking in expectation as the door was opened. Valentine paused and looked back at him, his squat frame silhouetted in the lantern-glow, his scarred scalp gleaming. As they disappeared inside, Jack headed for the side door in the building, which led into the lodgings above the baker's. He was relieved, but not surprised that it opened at his push, remembering the dwellings within all had their own locks and bolts.

The door opened on to a dank hallway, cracked flagstones and crumbling plaster walls, a set of wooden stairs leading up. Closing the door, Jack let his eyes grow accustomed to the gloom, rainwater dripping on the floor from his clothes. Sweeping back his hood, he climbed the stairs, the treads creaking beneath him. As he ascended, Adam's words echoed in his mind.

Back in Dover, storms hurling waves against the cliffs and tossing the boats in the harbour like toys, they had discussed how they might survive on the Continent. They could join a mercenary company – all of them were skilled fighters – but they would have need of more weapons and armour than they owned and hadn't the funds to buy any.

It was Ned who suggested Jack ask Amaury for money. None of them, not even Ned, knew the full extent of what the priest had told him about his father and the Academy, the brotherhood Amaury had recruited Vaughan into during his time in France as ambassador for King Edward IV; about the map from the *Trinity* and their vision for the strange new coastline inked across its margins.

We call it New Eden.

Jack had kept his silence, promised to Amaury, on that. But his men knew enough to know the map was valuable beyond the telling and that Vaughan had been somehow involved with the House of Medici: rulers of the Republic of Florence and one of the richest, most powerful dynasties in Christendom, with banks and businesses in almost every city from London to Naples. Jack knew, through all the months they'd followed him, they had really been following the ghost of his father and while Vaughan could no longer reward them for their loyal service maybe, they now reasoned, the men who had directed him from the shadows could.

He had reached the upper floor. Darkness shrouded the passage leading to a door at the far end, where a faint sliver of light bled around the frame. He headed towards it, footsteps quickening. As he reached it, he raised his fist to knock, then paused. The door was badly cracked around the lock, splinters of wood poking like bones from a shattered limb.

'Amaury?' His murmur was loud in the hush.

There was no answer.

Jack pushed the door, which bumped into something solid, wedged against the other side. He shouldered it open, the object scraping the floor in protest.

The long, narrow chamber with its slanting beamed ceiling was in gloom, the only light the last of the murky dusk seeping through the shuttered window. The place was a mess, things strewn across the chamber. The small bed where he'd been nursed back from his smoke-choked delirium had been overturned, the mattress torn, its straw stuffing ripped out; chests opened, their contents flung carelessly about, books and papers pitched across the floor. The object that had been wedged against the door was the priest's writing desk. All the shadows were still. No sign of life.

The shock of the room's ransack, and its clear abandonment, struck Jack almost as a physical blow. All these weeks he'd been tilting at this target he had never once thought what he would do if the priest wasn't here. They were down to their last few coins, with only their weapons left to sell. What would they do for food and shelter, winter coming on? Options flashed through his mind, none of them palatable. Would they be forced into begging in this foreign city, or become thieves and risk the gallows? *Like father like son.*

It wasn't just a question of money. As he picked his way through the debris to the window, things crunching under his boots, Jack felt the void inside him open wider – an emptiness filled only with restless ghosts. Could he go home to Lewes, back into Grace's arms? Play father to her children, start a new life? A new family? Try to forget all that had happened? All he'd lost?

The wild thought offered a moment of comfort, his heart poised, hoping. But it was swept away in a sobering instant. He couldn't go back. Go home. Home no longer existed and a sad life he would make for Grace; a sheltered fugitive, a danger to them both, haunted by that scorched patch of earth in the woods mere footsteps away, that had once been filled with a little wooden house and a garden of flowers, and his mother's laughter.

As he pushed open the shutters, the grey light intensified, along with the sound of rain clattering on the roof. Stooping to pick up a crumpled roll of parchment, he found it smeared with dried oak gall ink. Another was mottled with a substance that looked reddish in the half-light. Ink? Or blood?

Near the writing desk, Jack crouched to find a gnarled stick, snapped in two. He had an image of the old priest limping towards him with its aid. Rising, he stood there, the rain hammering outside, the last of his hope wilting inside him.

Amaury had answered some of his questions about the Academy, about what his father had been involved in and the dangerous game he'd found himself drawn into after the man's death – a game that cost his mother her life and ripped apart his world, challenging everything he thought he knew about the man he had once admired above all others. But the priest's explanations, coming at a time when all Jack had been able to think about was wrapping his hands around his treacherous brother's neck, now seemed incomplete, confusing; all that talk of a World Soul, Greek philosophers and pagan gods. All those things that sounded like heresy.

He needed more. Needed to know who his father really was and what that made him; his bastard son, so desperate to believe Vaughan's promises that he would make him a knight and open the door to a glittering life that he never stopped to question what dark paths his father might be leading him down. He had set out from Dover determined to follow in his father's footsteps, the need to understand his past and divine his future driving him on. Now, the path stopped dead before him. No way forward. No chance back.

Jack stared around the chamber, willing some answer – some sign – from the wreckage. As his eyes fixed again on the writing desk, he realised something was wrong. If the room was empty, abandoned, who had wedged the heavy desk in front of the door?

Alert, he turned, scanning the darkness. There. Hunched in front of the window. A shadow. He swore it hadn't been there before. As he went for his sword, the shadow rose and sprang at him with a cry. There was a flash of a blade slicing towards him. No time to draw his weapon, Jack dodged the wild swing of the knife and grabbed hold of the shadow's wrist, twisting it roughly aside. The figure screamed and dropped the blade, before ducking to sink its teeth into his hand. He shouted in pain and lunged with his free hand for the throat, squeezing until the teeth released and the shadow came up, choking and writhing. The figure, whip-thin with short, matted hair, was soaked through. He realised she had come in through the window.

'Amelot!'

The girl kicked out, catching him on the knee, although her soft hide shoes did little to hurt him.

'Amelot, *c'est moi*!'

She stopped struggling.

'*C'est moi*, James Wynter. *Jack*.'

For a moment, the girl remained in his grip, taut as wire, then all the fight left her and she slumped, fists falling to her sides.

As he released her, she backed away, touching her neck where his hand had crushed her. Her breaths rasping, she stared at him unblinking in the shadows. She was skinnier than he remembered, her hair a mess of sawn-off hanks, cut short like a boy's, only badly. The orbs of her eyes seemed the largest thing about her.

'Amelot, *où est* Amaury?' As soon as he asked the question, he remembered she didn't speak.

She turned away, shaking her head. Jack stepped towards her, impatient, wanting to press her, but she flinched back, wary as a spooked cat.

He held up his hands. 'I just want to know what happened here.' He spoke slowly, the French tongue taking a moment to come back to him.

After a pause, she seemed to settle.

'Someone did this?' Jack gestured at the room. 'Not you? Not Amaury?'

She nodded.

Jack glanced at the papers strewn on the floor, some of them flecked with dark splatters. 'Was Amaury here when it happened?'

Her head dropped forward. A smaller nod.

'Was he hurt?'

A sigh from her lips told him yes.

'Was he . . .?' His mouth tightened on the word, but he had to know. 'Killed?'

Her head shot up. She shook it fiercely and pointed at the door.

'Taken?'

Yes.

'When did this happen?' He rephrased it. 'Days?' No. 'Weeks?' Her frown told him she might not understand time. After a moment, an uncertain nod. So perhaps weeks, or at least not that long ago? He wondered how she had escaped harm. His gaze flicked to the window. Perhaps she had witnessed it from outside, or some other hiding place – watching, helpless, as the old man was overpowered. The haunted look in her eyes told him she had. 'Did you know those who took him? Did you recognise them?' A long, slow shake of her head. He scanned the papers again. 'Were they looking for something?' His mind filled with a dark web of coastlines and islands inked across yellowed vellum, the words of Hugh Pyke, murmured in the gloom of the Ferryman's Arms, echoing back to him.

If this showed a route to the Spice Islands? A way past the Turks? Then I would say it would be worth all the gold in the world.

'Was it the map, Amelot? Did they come for that?'

She nodded, then darted towards him to snatch aside his cloak, eyes searching.

'I don't have it. I tried to get it for him, but . . .' Jack trailed off. 'It is gone.'

Her shoulders slumped again.

'Have you searched for him? Tried to find who took him?'

A contemptuous hiss told him she'd been doing nothing but. Amelot paused, then swept her hand in a long, slow movement.

Jack took a guess. 'You think he was taken away? Out of the city?'

She nodded forlornly and made the motion again, as if to emphasise either distance or her own desperation. After a moment she crouched and began picking through the debris on the floor.

Jack turned away, thinking. The list of those who would want to take possession of the map was surely long, but those who would think to come here for it – to Amaury's lodgings? That, he did not know. But without knowing that how in God's name could he even begin to search for the priest?

His eyes drifted to the bed where he had sat, hands burned, heart broken, while Amaury asked him to retrieve it, his rasping voice strengthening with the promise that if he succeeded he would take him personally to the leader of the Academy. That there was much the man might choose to reveal to him. Lorenzo de' Medici: de facto ruler of the Republic of Florence and head of the Academy. The man known as the Needle of the Compass. The man his father had told him to seek in his last words, penned on the morning of his execution.

I pray you have found the answers I could not give you.
That the Needle has pointed the way.

Jack turned back, feeling a tug on his cloak. Amelot was holding a crumpled sheet of paper. As she passed it to him, he saw her fingers were black with ink. On the page was a crude drawing. He stared at it in the gloom. It looked like a large teardrop with two barbs coming off the bottom and two lines scored diagonally through the middle.

'What is it? Something to do with Amaury? With those who took him?'

Amelot nodded. As Jack frowned at it, she reached out impatiently and turned the paper in his hands. The symbol changed – became a pointed animal head with pricked ears and fierce slanting eyes.

He realised she had drawn a wolf.

3

In the vastness of Westminster Hall hundreds of candles were burning, casting a shimmering halo around the assembly of nobles, officials and foreign dignitaries who had gathered here in the royal heart of England. Beyond the sphere of light and warmth, January pressed its darkness against the hall's high windows. Outside, the Thames chopped at the harbour wall, where the barges of the guests were moored, flags and banners stiff with ice.

The revelry of Christmas was over. The Lord of Misrule had been dethroned for another year and Plough Monday had come and gone. Out in fields and pastures the work of carthorse and seed had begun, and what better way to celebrate new life beginning than with a royal wedding?

Earlier, within the hallowed magnificence of Westminster Abbey, King Henry VII had been joined with his betrothed in holy matrimony, the ceremony conducted by the Archbishop of Canterbury and witnessed by the peers of the realm. It was a union that had been promised many moons ago, across the sea in Brittany, when the king was a prince in exile – last scion of a bastard line of the fallen House of Lancaster – with war lying like a lion before him. He had come on the winds of summer, borne on French galleys, sword and banner raised against that beast, and with his victory the fragile hope of that marriage pledge had crystallised into victorious fact.

The long war that had ravaged England was over. He, Henry Tudor, was three months' crowned and his bride – a princess of York – now sat beside him, her mighty house tamed after all these bitter years. It was the end of civil strife, the ceremony declared. Two royal families, once torn asunder, now united in bands of gold and bonds of blood.

Peace, men said. Prosperity.

Yet even amid the celebrations, there lingered a sense of trepidation – that what had gone before might not be so easily forgotten. All around the hall this winter night could be glimpsed spaces where men should be seated. Fallen kings and princes cut down in their pomp, rebel lords who'd drenched the block with their blood, knights who had roared their last on fields of war: all of them were still here somehow, noticeable by their absence.

Harry Vaughan, however, had no eyes for ghosts. His gaze was reserved for the king, whom he caught in brief glimpses between the criss-crossing of kitchen servants bearing platters of eel flesh in wobbling jelly and stacks of crabs like giant pink spiders, hairy-legged and curled. When he'd first been led into the cavernous hall by the ushers, among the chattering multitude filing in from the abbey, Harry thought there had been some mistake. Flush-faced, he had turned on the page who had shown him to his seat, demanding to know who placed him here – down in the draught coming through the hall's doors, so far below the salt he could not even see it.

Why, the king, Master Harry, had come the wounding reply.

The anticipation Harry had felt for the evening's festivities had withered and died among his dinner companions: minor gentry and boorish officials, foreign merchants, London traders and their wives, drunk too quick on sweet Greek wine. He had dreamed of such a day as this all through the months in exile with Henry, all through the danger and uncertainty of that time: a day when he would sit in high honour and office in the favour of the king, just as his father, Sir Thomas Vaughan, once had. Tonight, that dream had turned to ash.

The servants parted and Harry craned his neck to watch as the king gestured to a page. The dark curtain of Henry's shoulder-length hair shifted to show his profile, the thin nose and mouth, the small chin that seemed to end too soon, cutting off his face abruptly. The king's gaze, cool and watchful, followed closely as the page leaned in to pour more wine into the goblet of the royal bride.

Elizabeth of York sat poised beside her husband, her abundance of hair, red-gold like her mother's, pulled back beneath an ornate headdress, which swept up in wings of silk from her head. Her skin was flushed, the stain spreading down her pale neck to disappear in the swell of her wedding gown, the indigo satin embroidered with hundreds of white roses. She wore no crown, for she was not yet his queen, but what she lacked in jewels on her head she made up for on fingers and throat, where rubies and star-bright diamonds glistered.

Despite his distance from the king, Harry hadn't failed to hear the eager gossip: that Henry had been courting his betrothed in secret at Coldharbour, his mother's Thameside mansion, and that his bride was already with child. Harry, along with the rest of the court, had studied Elizabeth during the vows, but had seen no sure sign of it.

Henry's mother, Lady Margaret, was seated left of her son, dressed in similar fashion to her new daughter-in-law in a mantle of regal purple. The small, sharp-eyed countess, aged just thirteen when she had borne Henry, her only child, did not now stray far from the son who'd been taken from her as an infant by Yorkist enemies and raised in foreign courts. Indeed, Margaret had walked into the abbey not two paces behind the royal couple, just ahead of her husband, Lord Stanley, whose treachery had turned the tide on Redemore Plain and who, in the bloody aftermath, had placed King Richard's fallen crown upon the head of his triumphant, battle-born stepson.

Further down the table sat Elizabeth Woodville, mother of the bride. Once a famed beauty – a commoner who had ensnared a king – she was now a pale echo of her handsome daughter. The recent years had not been kind to the queen-dowager, carving their grief in lines through her face. Her son by her first marriage and her brother, Sir Anthony Woodville, had been the first of Richard's victims, executed in a northern castle on false charges of treason, alongside Harry's own father. Next her son, Prince Edward – who, for a brief candle's flicker, had been king – locked up in the Tower with his brother. Richard, having concocted a story that their father, King Edward IV, had been married previously, declared her sons bastards, unsuited to the crown, which he had then taken for his own.

Most believed the tale that Richard had the two boys – his own nephews – quietly put to death. It was a rumour that had raised a rebellion against him, plotted in part by Lady Margaret and Elizabeth Woodville, but Harry was one of the handful of men who knew different. Looking at the queen-dowager, he wondered what she would do were she told the truth. That, perhaps, the man she had married her daughter to, irrevocably joining the houses of York and Lancaster, might not be quite who she imagined?

The thought took him back to Henry's coronation, just over three months ago, where he'd feasted in this hall with the king and all those who'd ridden through the wild summer of war alongside him; there to rejoice his crowning and be rewarded for their service. Among them had been another of the queen-dowager's brothers and uncle to her children, Sir Edward Woodville, who, for his part in the battle against King Richard, had been reinstated as Constable of Porchester and Governor of Portsmouth.

That night, amid the revelry, Harry had been startled to find himself cornered by the knight and probed about the fate of Woodville's young nephews. Unprepared, he had stumbled his way through the unexpected interrogation, hoping wine and candlelight would excuse the hot flush of guilt that had leapt into his cheeks. In the end, the knight released him, but the encounter had left Harry jangled and he'd been relieved when, arriving at the abbey that morning, he'd overheard one of the king's men say that Edward Woodville would be absent for the ceremony, gone abroad on a pilgrimage.

As servants crossed in front of him, breaking his view of the royal table, Harry turned his attention to the steaming piles of food now being deposited at his end of the hall, men and women welcoming them with loud appreciation and a rude clatter of knives. The heads of dead beasts lolled on platters as the bodies were cut into and soon the air was filled with the cracking of crab shells and the snap of bones.

Harry speared a slice of meat for his plate, but left the other guests to the rest of the feast. His appetite had died along with his hope of finding his way back into the king's good graces tonight.

'Have at it!' The man next to him, a fleshy, stinking fellow with a tumour of a nose, elbowed him. 'We common men feast like lords tonight!' He talked through a mouthful of meat. Feeling something wet land on his hand, Harry wiped it on his napkin. The man raised his goblet and bellowed, 'Long live the king!'

The cheer was taken up by others, echoing down the tables towards the distant royals.

As those around them struck up conversations, the lilt of foreign voices mingling with blunt local dialects, Harry reached for his goblet and drained it. The malmsey wine silked his tongue with sweetness and he wondered for a queasy moment whether it could have come from the same barrel the bride's uncle had reputedly been drowned in – another one taken by treason, the black imp that had carried off so many through the long season of war, including his own father, strung up on Richard's orders.

'Enjoy it while we can, I say.' The man leaned in again, nodding at the yeomen of the guard lining the walls in their green and white livery. 'Three hundred soldiers for the king's household? A man who makes himself an army expects trouble down the way.'

'Or prevents it by doing just that,' responded Harry tautly, lifting his goblet for a page to refill.

The brusqueness of his response didn't deter the man, who gestured with a crab leg towards the king. 'He'll need to get his seed in her quick. Make himself an heir with good Yorkist blood. Though some say he's already planted it, no?'

As the man chuckled and nudged him again, wine sloshed over the rim of Harry's goblet. Dark stains bloomed on the linen. He shook wine from his hand, cursing his lot. As if this placement wasn't insult enough, the king had sat him next to this fool? His eyes strayed down the tables again to where those men most in Henry's favour sat. Men able to catch the king's eye, raise a goblet, seek his approval. Men who had toiled alongside him all through those months in Brittany and France. Men like him.

Harry's fist tightened around his goblet. If not for him Henry Tudor might now be languishing in the Tower at Richard's pleasure, for it was his hand that delivered the information warning him Brittany was no longer safe, his word that had sent Henry fleeing into France where he'd found a king willing and able to finance and equip an invasion of England. An invasion that had won him the crown. Was the esteem in which his master had held him so fragile as to be tarnished by one God-damn failure?

Yet again, Wynter, that *bastard*, was getting in the way of his future. He should have stuck him with his blade and buried him deep, where the only thing he would have stunk up was the mud, but he'd left him to that fickle fire and the son of a bitch had survived. Now, Wynter had vanished and Harry had been unable to find any trace of him, much to Henry's evident displeasure.

The fleshy man was at his ear again. He opened his mouth to speak, but before any more words, or food, could bubble forth, Harry snatched up his knife and brought it stabbing down. The tip embedded itself in the table, a whisker from the man's hand. After a pause, the man laughed nervously and swigged at his wine in an attempt to recover some of his bluster, but he kept his hand off the table and his mouth shut for the rest of the meal, leaving Harry to nurse his drink in silence.

'Master Harry.' A page leaned in. 'The king requests your presence.'

Harry's heart leapt. He rose from the bench, but as he looked down the hall to the king's table, he realised Henry was no longer there.

'In his private chambers,' came the explanation.

Leaving his food untouched and his dinner companions to their drunken clamour, Harry followed the page, skirting groups of men and women who had risen to dance, the stamp of feet punctuated by raucous laughter.

Once through the doors, the din faded. The frozen air stung Harry's lungs, sweat drying cold on his cheeks. Frost crunched under his boots as the servant led him past the dark bulk of St Stephen's Chapel and the Queen's Chamber to the king's private apartments.

At the doors, two yeomen of the guard stood sentry. Harry halted at their command and waited while they checked him for weapons, hands reaching inside his cloak to briskly pat his velvet jacket. His nerves began to build. This was what he had wanted – an audience with Henry. But what kind of audience was this? The king had not begun his reign with acts of mercy towards those who had done him wrong. The skin of Harry's neck prickled in the cold. When the yeomen finally stepped aside, the page ushered him in.

Entering the Painted Chamber, he was assaulted by colour. It bled from everywhere at once – from the turquoise ceiling studded with gold bosses, to the vermilion and emerald of the stained-glass windows, and the garish murals of Old Testament scenes that covered the walls down the length of the room to where a huge, canopied bed stood. All of it was lit by a blaze of torchlight, the restless flutter of flame making the painted figures of angels and saints seem to shift and move. After all that malmsey wine on an empty stomach, Harry found the place unsettling. He breathed in the smoky air, trying to push down his rising queasiness. His eyes darted until they fixed on a figure, seated by a hearth.

'Come, Harry.'

He did as ordered. Removing his velvet cap, the best he owned, as he came before the figure, he bowed low. 'My lord king.'

Henry let him stay bent a pause longer than was comfortable, before gesturing to a stool opposite. 'Sit.'

Harry perched on the low seat, legs bunched awkwardly in front of him, cloak drooping on the floor. He licked his lips. His heart was thumping. Henry didn't rush to fill the silence for him, but merely studied him with his ice-blue eyes, one of which roved of its own accord and gave Harry the discomforting sense that the man was studying him from too many angles at once. The jewels that adorned the king's crown, cloak and fingers glittered madly in the firelight. Despite the heat coming from the hearth, Henry's lean face was pale, framed by his dark hair. The king would celebrate his twenty-ninth birthday at the end of the month, but to Harry, six years his junior, he had always seemed far older – something ancient in those roving eyes.

'God's grace upon you, my lord,' Harry blurted into the hush. 'Upon you and your bride. It was a grand ceremony and a – a truly marvellous feast. Your subjects sang your praises.'

Henry arched an eyebrow. 'Food and wine will rouse most mannered men to applaud their host. But only time will tell if their loyalty runs deeper than their bellies.' His voice was clipped, the inflections French not English. After twelve years in Brittany, the foreign tongue came more naturally to him than the language of his homeland. He took a sip from a goblet, his movements slow, measured. 'Am I to presume, Master Harry, that you have found no trace of your brother since we last spoke?'

Harry's jaw twitched. He wanted to correct the king – to remind him that Wynter was no *brother* of his – just some bastard seed of his father's spilled carelessly in a common whore. Instead, he shook his head. 'No, my lord. Despite my best efforts I have not.'

'Your best efforts.' Henry let the words hang there.

'I searched everywhere I could think to look, my lord, in London and in Westminster. I went to Lewes, but even his mother's house was gone. Burned down, I was told.' Harry didn't mention the foreign men he had sent to that little house in the woods two years earlier in exchange for a bag of gold – the men who had been searching for Wynter and who'd found his mother instead.

'If you had dealt with him when you had the chance, your efforts – such as they are – would not now be needed.'

An image flashed in Harry's mind. He was lying on the debris-strewn floor of his father's mansion, Wynter straddling his stomach, hands wrapped around his throat. Harry's fingers flinched towards his neck as he remembered the awful choking sensation, the rage-filled face looming above him as his half-brother squeezed the life from him. The memory set a fire in his blood.

Yes, he had failed in one task. But he had done everything else Henry had asked of him. He had brought him Prince Edward and had kept his silence after the boy was delivered in secret back into the Tower. He had said no word when Henry, on taking the crown, had publicly repeated the rumour that the two princes had been cruelly put to death by King Richard and he'd evaded those questions Sir Edward Woodville had had about his nephews as best he could. It wasn't his fault Wynter knew this to be a lie and was why Henry wanted him in his custody.

Sitting straighter on the stool, he met the king's gaze. 'I believe Wynter has left the kingdom, my lord. There is nothing here for him now, but a price on his head and the heads of his surviving companions. He is a nobody with nothing to his name. Even if he speaks about what he knows, who will listen? I doubt he will return to these shores, but should he ever do so, I *will* end him. You have my word on that.'

Henry studied him, only the pop of logs bursting in the fire to fill the silence between them. After a long moment, the king sat back. His expression had changed, the lines smoothing on his pallid brow. He motioned to the page who had escorted Harry to the chamber, lingering still in a shadowy corner. 'Wine for my guest.'

Harry watched the page head to a table by the gilded bed, decked for the wedding night with ribbons and bells. Later, the queen would be led in by her maids, who would undress her, ready for the king to be brought here by his squires to the rough music of lewd songs and laughter. Did she know the man she would lie beneath? What he was capable of?

As the page crossed to him with a goblet, Harry took it gratefully. The spiced wine soothed his dry throat. 'Thank you, my lord.'

'I have no need of your thanks, Harry. But your loyal service – that I do require.'

'You have it, my lord.' Harry sat forward, making sure the king could see the truth of this. 'Always.'

'Then, I have another task for you. One in which you might redeem yourself from the recent past.' Reaching into his lap, Henry picked up a long, thin object that had been lying there, hidden by the folds of his robes. 'You recognise this?'

Harry nodded, his gaze on the leather scroll case. He had taken it from Wynter when he seized the prince. Inside was the map those foreign men had been hunting for. The map his father had entrusted to that bastard over him – his true blood son. 'It was Sir Thomas Vaughan's.' His voice came out as a cracked murmur. He cleared his throat. 'It was my father's.'

'No, Harry, it wasn't. That much I have been able to ascertain.' Holding out his goblet for the page to slip in wordlessly and collect, Henry slid the roll of parchment from the scroll. 'I take it you viewed it for yourself, when you took it from your brother?'

Harry knew there was no point in lying. 'Yes, my lord. But . . .' He trailed off, not wanting to appear ignorant, but curiosity got the better of him. 'In truth, I could not see its value. It is just a map, is it not?'

In answer, the king unrolled it, opening it wide across his knees. In the firelight, the vellum was almost translucent. Inked outlines of huge continents and small dots of islands spidered across the parchment. At each corner was a cherub-like creature, cheeks puffed with wind. 'The map-makers I have consulted tell me they know of every land on this map. Every land, but this.' Henry touched his finger to one corner, far to the west in the vast expanse of the Atlantic Ocean, beyond Portugal and Thule.

Harry followed the king's finger as it moved down a long, uneven line that stretched away from a tiny cluster of three islands, before vanishing off the map. 'What is that?'

'Something new.' Henry leaned forward, his eyes intense. 'I have discovered that several years ago a Bristol merchant ship, the *Trinity*, was embarking on secret expeditions in the Western Ocean, financed by King Edward. Their mission was to seek whether there was truth to the rumours of other islands in those waters – islands of immeasurable riches. Hy-Brasil, perhaps?'

At that name, Harry had a memory of his father speaking of mysterious lands far out in the great ocean – lands where cities were made of gold and inhabited by strange, otherworldly beings, islands that vanished when sailors got too close.

'In the year before Edward's death, *Trinity*'s crew sighted what they claimed to be a new land. The man in charge of the expeditions was Thomas Croft, chief customs officer for the port of Bristol. I believe Croft had a map made from that last voyage. This map. That found its way, by chance, or more as like by design into the hands of your father.'

Harry thought that if all this were true the bag of gold angels those men had given him for information on Wynter's whereabouts had been a miserly offering indeed. But no mind. The map was here, in front of him, and the king seemed to be trusting him again. 'What task would you have me do, my lord? Do you wish me to travel to Bristol? Find out more from Croft and his crew?' He asked the question tentatively. More weeks away from the king's circle would further hinder his chances of courting his favour.

Henry sat back. 'No. When time allows, I will personally pay a visit to Croft.' He rolled the parchment, thin fingers spooling up the vellum until it fitted back inside the leather case. 'There is a Spanish knight here in London – Rodrigo de Torres – one of a company from the court of Queen Isabella and King Ferdinand who attended my coronation. He has spoken of a man who has captured the interest of Isabella – a sailor with a notion of a westward expedition to find a new route to the Spice Islands. Men have mulled such a concept for the past thirty years since the Turks took Constantinople, barring our paths to the riches of India, Cathay and Cipangu, but few have considered such a voyage possible. Until now. The sailor is reportedly seeking funding for the expedition.'

'And if he sails west he might find the land the men on the *Trinity* saw?'

Henry nodded. 'Whatever the land shown on this map is.' He held up the case. 'Whether the Spice Islands, or something new – something that lies between us and the East – the first sighting of it was by English sailors on a mission financed by the father of my bride. This land belongs to the English crown. I want to make sure it stays that way. To that end, Harry, I am sending you to Castile.'

'Castile?' Harry couldn't keep the shock from his voice. And he had thought Bristol seemed a long way.

'Your father was, I believe, ambassador to the courts of Burgundy and France. You will follow in his footsteps as my emissary in Spain. Rodrigo de Torres has agreed to introduce you personally to the king and queen. You will travel to Seville with him as soon as possible. I want you to work your way into Isabella and Ferdinand's trust. Do whatever you can to halt this sailor's progress and stop him getting that funding.'

Harry drained his wine to give himself a moment's cover as he thought. His father's possessions and estates – seized by the crown after his execution – had all been restored to him by Henry. But the mansion on the Thames and the dwellings scattered across Kent and Sussex, all in need of serious upkeep, were not the prize he hungered for. He wanted more: a place in the king's inner circle, a trusted man with the high offices, titles and benefits that might come with such status. All things his father had had under King Edward.

Spain might be a long way from the king's court, but he could see the seriousness with which Henry was treating this. Rarely had he heard the king speak with such passion. This mission had been granted to him alone – he would not have to vie with the officials all now crowding round to impress their new master. If he completed this task to Henry's satisfaction, who knew what the rewards might be?

'What is this sailor's name, my lord?'

Henry smiled, seeing that Harry had accepted. 'His name is Christopher Columbus.'

4

'Holy, holy, holy, Lord God of hosts, all the earth is full of your glory. Hosanna in the highest. Blessed is he who cometh in the name of the Lord.'

The congregation, swaddled in their fur-trimmed cloaks and packed into San Lorenzo's grand aisles for Sunday Mass, watched the prior, caught in glimpses through the rood screen, as he raised his hands to begin the consecration of the wine and the bread. All except Lorenzo de' Medici, whose gaze was fixed on the marble slab, inlaid with coral and blood-dark porphyry, on the floor before the high altar. Beneath that slab, in a tomb cradled within a pilaster that thrust through the crypt beneath, lay the remains of his grandfather, Cosimo de' Medici: great man of the republic, first among equals, founder of the Academy, and, to him, a blazing beacon of inspiration.

It was almost twenty-two years since his grandfather had been buried here, in the holiest place in this house of God, bones knitted within the fabric of the church where above met below, but Lorenzo could recall his funeral as clear as though he were looking back through glass. The grand procession of dignitaries weaving through the silent multitude on the streets. Men, women, children crossing themselves as Cosimo's body, draped in gossamer layers of white muslin, passed through their shifting masses.

Lorenzo had been fifteen then, thrumming with emotion as he walked at his father's side. His anguish at the passing of the old man had been tempered by the fierce pride he'd felt seeing the men of the republic – from the heads of the grand houses of Florence, the priors of the Signoria, officials and standard-bearers of the quarters and the members of the city's twenty-one guilds, to the poor wool-workers and artisans of Oltrarno, the rough-skinned farmers come from the Mugello and the merchants and sailors from the Porto Pisano – every one of them here to pay their respects to the man who had never needed the title of leader to tell them all he was.

'For of him and by him, and in him, are all things,' proclaimed the prior, lifting the chalice and the host, the eyes of his audience rising with them. 'To him be glory for ever.'

'Amen,' came the rumble of several hundred voices.

'*Amen*,' murmured Lorenzo, his gaze moving to the entrance of the sacristy on the left of the high altar, where his brother and father, uncle and great-grandfather were buried in magnificent tombs of their own. This whole church was a monument to his family, every curve of marble and embellished block of bronze, every stroke of gold leaf that brought the soaring figures of archangels and saints to glittering life across walls and ceilings, paid for by the House of Medici.

How far his family had come from their humble beginnings in the Tuscan countryside, their first money-changing business growing into a bank that had spread like golden seeds, new branches springing up in Rome, Venice, Naples, London, Cologne and Bruges, housing and providing the wealth of merchants and princes, kings and popes, all serving to nourish the great tree in Florence that had created them. Their power had grown with every florin dropped into their coffers, every alliance made and deal brokered, every election that had raised more Medici sons to the Signoria, the city's ruling council. Until, at last, they were supreme. It wasn't long after Cosimo's death that the people had begun calling him Pater Patriae.

Father of the Fatherland.

For a man who wore no crown, Lorenzo had become increasingly aware these past few years of the weight of the invisible diadem, passed down through his grandfather and father to him. He might have earned his own epithet – il Magnifico – but the name meant little without the power to uphold it, and that power had been eroded this past decade by the forces that had risen against him, threatening everything his family had built over the last hundred years.

He had defeated his foes with execution, imprisonment, bribery and banishment, but familial roots went down deep in Florence – deep as faith – and he knew some weeds would have been left in that soil. How much they had grown he did not know, but he had sensed something these past months: some stirring of discontent beneath the bedrock of his rule, faint murmurings within the Signoria, whispers in rival houses, unfriendly eyes in familiar places.

Lorenzo's gaze lingered on the door to the sacristy, where his beloved brother, Giuliano, lay entombed, cut down in his prime by the blades of their enemies. Soon, sure as day, there must come another reckoning. He could only pray the plans he had set in motion to secure the future of his empire would have chance to bear fruit before then.

'And taking the chalice he said to his disciples, drink ye of this for it is my blood and it shall be poured out for you.'

As the prior completed the Eucharist, Lorenzo forced his attention to the final prayers of the Mass, the voices of the canons lifting in harmony as they sang the Paternoster and the Agnus Dei. Afterwards, he paused to thank the prior, then made his way down the aisle, smiling, nodding, occasionally stopping to talk as he was hailed by distant cousins and business allies, local officials and fawning supporters. It took some time, but at last he was stepping into the bright January morning, pulling up the fur-lined cowl of his purple cloak, his children jostling to be out of the sombre setting where they could raise their voices and laugh again.

All around the city, bells chimed the close of Mass. People hurried across the piazza, breath pluming the air, most heading into the labyrinth of streets beyond San Lorenzo that led to the seething heart of the *mercato*. The hollow clop of clogs from a gang of wool-workers was accompanied by the jingle of bells tied in the hair of three whores, holding each other's arms as they picked their way across the rutted street, their laughter sharp and skittish.

The sky was blue and clear as stained glass, the air brittle. It was over a fortnight since Epiphany, when Lorenzo had led the city in a torchlit procession to the Christmas Cradle in San Marco – the initials of the three Magi still visible, scrawled in chalk over the doors of houses. In just two weeks it would be Carnival, but it remained unusually cold. A dirty crust of frost caked the stone-flagged streets and splintered sheets of ice had formed on the banks of the Arno and around the piers of the Ponte Vecchio, trapping the bloody clots of entrails tossed from the butcher's shops that lined the bridge.

'Father! May we have some?'

Lorenzo saw his youngest daughters and son, Contessina, Luisa and little Giuliano, named after his dead brother, had clustered at a stall selling candied quince and slabs of gingerbread, set up by the enterprising owner to catch the post-Mass crowd. Reaching into his purse with a smile, Lorenzo pulled out a handful of soldi which he passed to Lucrezia, at fifteen his eldest child. He watched as she skipped to the stall, followed by the rest of her siblings, all gabbling happily.

'You shouldn't spoil them. Not after Mass.'

His wife, Clarice, had moved from the circle of her friends to join him. The congregation was still spilling from the church, a few heading off, more forming huddles of conversation. A good number tried to edge towards Lorenzo, wanting to talk business, or politics, or petition him for some favour, while passing citizens, spotting him in their midst, came closer to gawp and point. Black Martin, Crooked Andrea and the rest of his bodyguards, dressed in their dark hooded cloaks, shielded him, waiting for his nod to allow any of the hopefuls through.

'It is unseemly, husband.'

In the stark winter sun, his wife's face was pallid. Her auburn hair was scraped back beneath a bulbous black headdress embroidered with tiny white pearls that looked like clusters of spider's eggs and her brow was furrowed with the three deep lines that always appeared with her displeasure: one of the children stealing a bite of food before grace was said, the too-loud laughter of a servant, the drunken gaiety of his friends at feasts.

Clarice – daughter of the House of Orsini, an ancient and noble family from Rome with vast estates across Italy and a private army – had always been this sober, even when they were sixteen and newly married. She would, he knew, have been happier wedded to Christ in a convent, but his shrewd mother had chosen her for her pedigree, not her charm.

'How can I not spoil them, Clarice? Look at them – how much they have grown. In just a season it seems.'

It was true. Dark-eyed Lucrezia, depositing the coins in the stallholder's hand, would be the first to fly. In just two months, when her dowry fund matured, she would disappear into the household of her betrothed, a wealthy political ally of Lorenzo's. Beside her was wilful Piero, on the cusp of manhood at fourteen, destined to inherit his empire. Behind him, dutifully waiting his turn, was Giovanni, eleven years old and chubby as a cherub, whose destiny, though he did not know it yet, lay in another direction entirely. And, there, arm-in-arm with Lucrezia, was Maddalena, thirteen and sweet as honey, her fate – should all go according to Lorenzo's plan – now entwined with young Giovanni's.

'They will soon be gone. Then who shall I indulge?'

'Nencia, I should expect.' Clarice spoke this in a murmur so no one else could hear – even though all of Florence knew of his dalliance with the peasant girl from the Mugello. The softness of Clarice's voice didn't take the bite from her words. Not waiting for a response, she turned away and called to a nearby group of men. 'Angelo.'

A handsome man with a hooked nose and softly sculpted face, framed by shoulder-length brown hair, looked round at her voice.

Clarice pointed to the stall. 'They are to buy one piece each. And the younger ones can share.'

'Of course, signora.'

Giving Lorenzo a look as if she had won this particular game, Clarice returned to her friends. But his gaze had already moved to the young man now walking to the stall.

To Lorenzo, and all his companions, he was Poliziano, but Clarice refused to call him by the familiar name, despite the fact he had lived in their household for over a decade, teaching their children in turn. Now, tutor to Giovanni and professor of Greek and Latin at the University of Florence, a post Lorenzo had secured for him, Angelo Poliziano was one of his closest friends.

The young man had been beside him that fateful day eight years ago, the Sunday after Easter in Santa Maria del Fiore – the day of blades and chaos – when Giuliano had gone down screaming under the swords of their rivals, the Pazzi, and blood had been spilled in the house of God. It was Poliziano who had dragged Lorenzo into the sacristy when the back of his neck had been slit by the dagger of a priest; Poliziano who lifted his hair and closed his mouth over that wound, sucking out any poison that might have laced the blade, while their friends hauled furniture in front of the door to halt the assassins.

Clarice had given him seven healthy children, after the loss of three in their early years, and, despite her demeanour, commanded his household well, at the head of an army of administrators, cooks, nurses, servants and slaves. But there was no love grown between them on this stony ground, nor would there ever be. For that, Lorenzo had always looked elsewhere.

He watched Poliziano divide gingerbread between his younger children. After making sure Clarice wasn't looking, the young man knelt with a grin and handed each of them a piece of candied quince in compensation. Lorenzo felt a sudden urge to go to his friend and confide in him, to tell Poliziano everything he'd been keeping from him these past months. But he had agreed with Marsilio Ficino, his old mentor and confidant, that he should maintain his silence. The fewer people who knew his secrets the better – and safer for them all – at least until there was hope his plan would work. Lorenzo thought of the man now hidden in the heart of his palace. How long might it take to turn him? How long before he would feel sure ground beneath his feet again? See a clear road ahead?

'Lorenzo de' Medici? Signore?'

A man was approaching across the piazza. On first glance, Lorenzo took him for a beggar – his coarse, filthy clothes, dark hair tangled to his shoulders, a thick beard covering a hard jaw beneath a nose that looked as though it had been broken a few times. But, as the man came closer, searching the crowd outside the church, Lorenzo saw how tall and well-built he was – hollow-cheeked, yes, but nothing like the emaciated wretches who thronged the streets of Florence, in whom the rot of true poverty had set in. Then, he saw the great sword protruding through the folds of the man's threadbare cloak.

The blade was in a plain leather scabbard, but Lorenzo caught a flash of silver and the red glint of a large jewel at the pommel. Black Martin – so named for both his hair and his temperament – saw it too, shouting to his fellow bodyguards, who immediately closed ranks around Lorenzo, unsheathing their blades with a unified rasp of steel. There were a few startled cries from the crowd.

'Leave this to us, signore,' urged Martin, encouraging him towards the Palazzo Medici, a short distance down the street.

The stranger had halted, eyes on the armed men arrayed before him. He held up his hands. A gesture of peace. 'I must speak to the signore.'

He spoke Latin, rather than Tuscan and his accent had the bluntness of a northern land. English, Lorenzo thought.

'Please, it is important.'

'Remove your sword,' ordered Black Martin. 'Slowly.'

Clarice was already with the children, hastening them towards the palazzo. Poliziano hung back for Lorenzo, who was moving to join them when the man called out again.

'I've come from Paris. I have a message he must hear. It concerns Amaury de la Croix.'

At this, Lorenzo turned back. Pushing through his guards, he went to the man. Some of the crowd was dispersing. Others were lingering, hoping perhaps to be noticed for their bravery, or else keen for gossip. 'What message?' he asked, slipping into the Latin tongue.

The stranger's eyes alighted on him. He stepped forward eagerly. 'Signor Lorenzo?'

It was one step too close for the guards. Black Martin lunged, grabbing him.

'I mean no harm!' The man was struggling now as another guard tried to take his sword.

As the stranger grabbed the offending guard's hand in a fierce grip around the wrist, Lorenzo caught sight of the gold ring on his finger – bright against the dirt – a disc engraved with two serpents entwined around a winged staff. It was a twin of the one that adorned his own hand.

Jack flexed his shoulders. The guards had bound his hands behind his back and his muscles were starting to cramp. The two either side of the doorway eyed his movements warily, although what they thought he could do, disarmed and trussed to the chair, was unclear. Settling, he scanned the chamber – a study it seemed – furnished with a desk and a daybed piled with cushions, chests inlaid with ivory and a brass candelabra. Cupboards with carved doors lined some of the walls interspersed with silk tapestries, but although richly appointed, the study was by far the smallest and humblest of the rooms Lorenzo de' Medici's guards had marched him through.

A hulking block of stone from the outside, dominating the street near the Church of San Lorenzo, with barred lower windows that made it look like a prison, the interior of the Palazzo Medici had been a glittering surprise. Jack, bundled in past guards and scores of men seated on benches, some clutching papers, had seen marble pillars flanking a grand inner courtyard, open to the sky, from which arched doorways led off and a wide staircase swept up. In the centre, perched atop a plinth in a well of sunlight, a strange bronze statue of a man, naked but for a hat and sword, looked down on him as he was escorted into a cavernous chamber lined with paintings. Jack caught the coiled mass of a dragon's tail and the barbed chaos of a battle before he was ushered into an adjoining room dominated by a curtained bed and decorated with gilt-framed mirrors. He'd glimpsed his untidy reflection being marched across them, then his captors were pushing him through the red sweep of a curtain into the study, where, despite his protestations, they removed his sword and twisted his father's ring off his finger, then bound him to the chair.

Despite the uncomfortable position and his rough handling, it was a blessing to be seated in a warm room on something other than flagstone or floorboard. Jack had arrived in the city only yesterday and the miles still throbbed in his feet, the soles of his boots worn paper thin on the long road from Paris. Faint noises drifted in from the street beyond the shutters, along with smells of food. He tried to ignore the hunger that clenched his stomach into a knot. He hadn't eaten properly in weeks and the desire for a good meal had become maddening, picking at his mind in the empty hours of the days, filled either with the slow drudgery of travel or the fitful rests between.

His eyes flicked to the doorway as he heard voices coming closer. Boots clicked on tiles. Anticipation and apprehension built in him, until the red curtain was swept aside and Lorenzo de' Medici entered. In a tongue Jack didn't know, he addressed the two guards, who ducked out through the swag of silk. The lack of footsteps told him they remained just outside. Drawing up a chair, Lorenzo settled opposite him.

Up close, the man known as the Needle of the Compass – a prince in all but name, who was called the Magnificent and whose fame spanned as much of Christendom as his vast financial empire – was not at all what Jack had been expecting.

He wore a long scarlet robe buttoned high at the neck, with boots of leather peeking from beneath its folds, but his clothes, although exquisitely tailored, were plain in comparison to those of many of the peacocks Jack had seen strutting around the English court. Beneath the layers of silk, he discerned the muscled bulk of a fighter and on Lorenzo's neck, just above the collar, an ugly scar disappeared beneath his hair. A few inches to the left and Jack reckoned the wound would have sent him to the grave. His hair, dark and parted in the centre, framed a broad, sallow-skinned face with a wide, squashed nose and thin lips. But although Lorenzo de' Medici couldn't in any way be considered handsome, there was something nonetheless alluring about him – something charged and crackling beneath the surface of those eyes.

His unwavering gaze discomforted Jack. He felt Lorenzo's scrutiny as a thing hot and alive, boring its way into him. 'Where is my ring?' he asked to break the silence. 'My sword?' The black-haired guard who had wrested them from him had disappeared after he'd been tied up. He'd cursed himself for having brought the precious items here, but had wanted them as proof he was who he claimed to be.

'In my care,' answered Lorenzo, switching into Latin.

His voice came thick through that squashed nose, but Jack understood him well enough. His own Latin, rarely used since the schooling his father had paid for, had been a little rusty, but after weeks on the road, staying in monasteries and talking to the monks, it had mostly returned to him.

'But since you are in my house and my custody – you will answer my questions. Who are you?'

'My name is James Wynter. My father was Sir Thomas Vaughan, trusted man of King Edward IV and chamberlain to his son, Prince Edward of York.'

Recognition – and perhaps eagerness – flashed in Lorenzo's eyes, but neither his tone nor his expression changed. 'Vaughan? From what I know, his son's name is Harry.'

'My mother was with him before he married,' Jack said tightly.

'I see. You have a message regarding Amaury de la Croix?'

Jack knew that if he didn't start from the beginning he would only have to travel back there and so he began, not with what he'd discovered in the priest's lodgings in Paris, but with that summer day, over two and a half years ago, when a stranger from England had come to Seville to tell him his father had been arrested for treason. The same day he had fought Estevan Carrillo in the dust of the olive grove – such a foolish grudge that seemed now – and spilled the nobleman's blood on that ground.

He told Lorenzo how the stranger tricked him and tried to take the map Thomas Vaughan had entrusted to him. How his father had ordered him to guard that map, but told him nothing of its origins or importance. When he explained this trickster was working for Sir

Anthony Woodville – a man his father had thought was a friend and a fellow member of the Academy, who intended to betray him and take the map for his true master, Pope Sixtus – Jack saw the first emotions begin to shift across Lorenzo's broad face: surprise, understanding, anger. He looked again at the scar on the man's neck, recalled Amaury telling him Sixtus had authorised the attempt on Lorenzo's life.

When Lorenzo remained silent, he continued, speaking of how he'd returned to England, hoping for answers, only to find King Edward was dead and Thomas Vaughan and Anthony Woodville had been executed by the king's brother, Richard of Gloucester, who, after locking Edward's sons in the Tower, had taken the crown for himself. His tone gritted, forcibly measured, he told Lorenzo how he'd found his home in Lewes burned to the ground, his mother murdered at the hands of Pope Sixtus's men, come hunting for the map in the wake of Woodville's death. As he spoke, his mind filled with memories of Carlo di Fante, slumped beneath him in the flooded alley in Southwark and the man's monstrous companion, the masked giant, looming out of the shadows in the Ferryman's Arms. His fists clenched behind his back as he thought of that masked brute who had so easily, so *remorselessly* admitted to the murder of his mother – thought of Harry, his own blood, who had sent them to her house in return for a fistful of gold. Pope Sixtus was dead and Amaury said Carlo di Fante had breathed his last in that Southwark alley, but Harry and his mother's killer, they were out there still.

Forcing these thoughts away, Jack described how, during the chaos of an uprising against King Richard and with the help of his father's men, he had broken Prince Edward from the Tower and spirited him to France, but that, by then, Henry Tudor had fixed his sights on England's throne and sent Harry to hunt down the young prince. He finished with a curt account of his brother's attempt on his life and how he'd come to find himself in the care of Amaury de la Croix.

'So the map from the *Trinity* was taken by your brother? Vaughan's own son?' Lorenzo's tone was tight. 'Where is it now?'

'I believe Henry Tudor has it.'

'But you saw it for yourself? There was land to the west?'

'Yes. A coastline. Beyond Portugal and Thule.'

Lorenzo sat back. 'Then it is out there,' he murmured. 'Plato was right. Atlantis. Beyond the Pillars of Hercules, out in the Western Ocean.' After a pause, he met Jack's eyes again. 'And the prince?'

Jack shook his head and watched the furrows in Lorenzo's brow deepen. 'My men and I left England when Tudor took the throne. Prices on our heads. I went to tell Amaury what had happened.' Jack paused, but decided not to reveal just yet how he had been driven from Paris by his need for answers and the vital funds for him and his men. He wanted to gain Lorenzo's trust first, in the hope he might satisfy both.

'Amaury sent you here?'

'No. We found his lodgings ransacked. Amaury had been taken. His – companion – believes those who took him were looking for the map.'

'When was this?' Lorenzo's tone was sharp, but more with impatience than surprise or concern.

Jack suddenly got the feeling the man might know more about all this than he'd let on. 'We arrived in Paris in late November. I believe Amaury had been gone for several weeks. My comrades and I made the decision to travel here, to inform you.' He thought of the dispute back in the tavern in the Latin Quarter that had raged between him and his men before he'd won his way.

Lorenzo was up now and pacing, his face a closed book, hiding his thoughts.

Jack watched him, not speaking of the journey south from Paris, the winter rains and the hardships he and his companions had suffered, their friendships pushed to breaking, the sickness that had carried David Foxley to death's door and trapped them in a monastery near Dijon until Christmas was behind them and, before them, the mountain passes closed by snow, forcing them to take the sea route from Aigues-Mortes – through waters patrolled by the Turks and roamed by pirates of the Barbary Coast – to the Port of Pisa.

Lorenzo turned back to him. 'You say you think Amaury was taken for the map. Do you know, then, who his captors were?'

'No. But his companion was able to—'

'Companion? You mean the girl?'

'Amelot. Yes. You may know she is a mute, so she hasn't been able to give many details, but she indicated there were four of them and described a badge one of them wore. It was silver – a wolf's head.'

Now, Lorenzo's expression left nothing to the imagination. Recognition dawned across his face.

'You know it?' Jack pressed.

Crossing to one of the trunks that lined the wall, Lorenzo opened it and drew out a dagger with a jewelled handle. As he approached, Jack flinched, but relaxed when Lorenzo stepped in behind and cut his bonds with expert slashes of the knife. Jack flexed the life back into his fingers.

Lorenzo laid the dagger on the desk and planted his hands either side of it. After a pause, he glanced at the doorway, beyond which his guards remained stationed. When he spoke, his voice was low. 'Amaury de la Croix wrote to me in the summer, telling me not to lose faith. That he had located the map from the *Trinity*'s voyage – a voyage authorised by King Edward, but funded by my bank – and had sent a man he trusted to retrieve it. You,' Lorenzo added, meeting Jack's eyes. 'He said that when it was in his possession he would bring it to me himself.' He shook his head. 'I trust Amaury as my grandfather did. But he is not a young man, nor a strong one. I feared for him on that journey. Not wanting to lose, again, the map your father pledged to secure for us, I sent one of my men to Paris to bring it here. But my man never returned and I heard no further word. I had been praying that bad roads or weather had delayed him.'

'Could your man have been the one who took Amaury?'

'No.' Lorenzo's tone was assured. 'But he might have been followed. Intercepted. It is possible Amaury's letter could have been read by eyes other than mine.' His voice lowered further. 'I sensed it. Enemies stirring in the shadows.' He clenched his hand, knocked his knuckles against the table. 'But here? In my own household?'

'You think Amaury was taken by someone from the city?' After the initial surprise, Jack realised this made sense. He remembered Amaury saying the manuscripts he hunted down and translated for the Academy – their Gathering – were sent by messenger to Florence when completed. In his questions about who might know where to find Amaury he'd not suspected the very people the priest worked with. The revelation gave him hope. If Amaury's abductors were from this city, then his decision to travel here was indeed justified. 'And the badge? The symbol means something to you?'

'The Court of Wolves,' Lorenzo murmured. He straightened, eyes elsewhere. 'I must speak to Marsilio. There is much at stake.' He glanced at Jack. 'I thank you for bringing this to my attention, James Wynter. You are free to go.'

'Free?' Jack rose, the severed ropes falling from his wrists.

Lorenzo called out and his guards ducked in. One, seeing Jack on his feet, went for his sword, but Lorenzo stopped him. He spoke calmly, gesturing to the door. Though Jack did not know the words, the meaning was clear. He was to be escorted out.

He found his voice. 'Signore, before my father was executed, he wrote to me. In his last words he said you would give me the answers he could not. Amaury promised me the same, if I brought him the map.'

'But you failed. You did not get the map.'

'Failed?' Jack felt a tide of emotion rush in, almost overwhelming him. The road to Florence had been long indeed, but one foot in front of the other was nothing compared to the hardships he'd suffered in his greater journey to this point. The danger that had dogged him, the confusion and uncertainty that had shrouded him, the grief that had shattered him.

He saw himself: racing through the trees that encircled the little house in the woods where he'd grown up, his vision filling with a horror of blackened, twisted timbers, smoke still tainting the air. His mother's name tearing ragged from his throat. The sorrow in Grace's eyes as she told him Sarah Wynter was gone. Later, his helplessness, as he realised if he had come home sooner, mere days, he might have saved her. She had stood no chance against Carlo di Fante and that masked brute, but he might have. If only. *If only.*

'*Failed?*' Jack repeated, his voice cracking on the word. 'With respect, signore, I could have done no more. My friends – my father's men – and I did all we could to protect the map and the prince. You have no idea what we sacrificed. One of those men died helping me!' An image flashed in his mind: Hugh Pyke's head on a spike on London Bridge. 'All of us are outlaws in England. We've lost everything!' His voice was rising. The guards looked as though they were preparing to step forward, but kept their eyes on Lorenzo who remained impassive. 'My home is gone. My mother dead. My father too. I have nothing left, signore!'

'So it is money you have come for then? Compensation?'

Jack felt his cheeks warm at Lorenzo's dispassionate tone. Was that condescension he saw in the man's eyes? He realised, standing here in a palace fit for a dozen kings, that Lorenzo de' Medici could not possibly understand just how little he and his men now had.

How had he thought this meeting would be so different? How had he imagined it so wrongly, every step of the way here promising Ned and Valentine, Adam and David that they would get their reward for what they'd lost? Promising Amelot, who had joined their company, that he would find her master. How had he believed that the questions thrumming in him – tormenting him – would at last be answered? That he would be able to lay the ghosts to rest? Build himself a new life out of the ashes of the old?

Now, the beacon they had all been walking towards, flickering on the horizon, had winked out – and at his own breath. What a trusting fool he was. Hunger had emptied his mind as well as his belly. He should have bargained for the information he had.

'It isn't just money, signore. I need to understand who my father was. What he believed in. What he was working towards. Your Academy? New Eden? I need to know. Was all I did – all I *lost* – in service to him . . .' Jack shook his head, hating the desperation in his voice but unable to mask it. 'Was any of it worth it?'

'Your father's sword.'

Jack faltered. 'Signore?'

'I will return your father's sword to you, as payment for your service. It is a valuable piece.' Lorenzo gestured to his guards, who stepped forward to seize Jack's arms.

Jack felt the world threaten to sink beneath his blistered feet as the guards forced him towards the curtain. 'And my father's ring?' he blurted, twisting to Lorenzo. 'Signore!'

'Is not yours to wear.'

With that, Jack found himself marched back through the opulent chambers, out through the courtyard with the bronze statue, past the gold and the marble, and all the glittering wealth. His sword, in its battered old scabbard, was thrust into his hands and then he was out in the street with the beggars and the sewage, the cold snatching his breath.

5

The Spaniard had been gone for some time and Harry was beginning to worry.

He glanced at the three men – one secretary, a servant and a groom – who had accompanied him from England, now resting on the dockside, mopping their brows in the heat. Around them, piled on the harbour wall, were the chests that had travelled with them from the Port of London, filled with Harry's personal effects and a costly array of gifts for Queen Isabella and King Ferdinand: gold plates, beeswax candles, ivory hunting horns, cloaks of fine Flemish cloth, jewelled daggers from Nuremburg and furs from Novgorod. There were even two hunting hounds, picked from the royal kennels by King Henry's Master Huntsman, although one had been terribly sick on the voyage and was now flopped on the floor of his cage, panting shallowly. Harry prayed the sorry creature recovered in time for his audience. The presentation of a dying dog to the Spanish monarchs would not prove an auspicious beginning to his role as English ambassador.

'I need to stretch my legs,' he told his secretary, nodding to the trunks. 'Watch them. And give that damn dog some water, will you.'

'Of course, Sir Harry,' answered Peter, an earnest, keen-to-please young man King Henry had chosen for his knowledge of the Castilian tongue.

Sir. The title felt to Harry like a new cloak: shining and exquisite, but perhaps still a few sizes too big. Henry had knighted him just before he left England – a hasty ceremony with little fanfare, nothing like Harry had imagined it would be, the king's blade upon his shoulders and his cool voice in his ear as he embraced him, reminding him what he was expected to do in return for the honour.

Wiping the sweat from his face, Harry headed along the harbour, passing into the shadows of the square-sailed caravels – some of them up to six hundred tons – moored at the docks near a gleaming tower with walls that looked to be made of gold. It was February, but felt like June, the Spanish sun prickling his skin, still wan from the English winter.

The harbour was busy, galleys being loaded. There was a crane clawing lengths of timber from the bowels of a large cog and customs officials moved through the bustle, talking to captains, checking cargo. He heard many tongues – French, Latin, English. Others he did not know.

A brisk breeze blowing across the river laced the air with dust and carried smells of smoke, rotting fish and a sweet scent Harry couldn't place – a spice or perfume? His legs felt unsteady, the ground still seeming to tilt beneath his feet, but he was grateful to be back on terra firma. Around the northern coast of Spain, he had been as sick as the dog, every ominous creak of timber telling him the ship was about to crack apart. He'd been on boats before, but never had he experienced such seas – mountains of water lifting the galley to terrifying heights, before hurling it down the other side, waves exploding over the bowsprit.

The ordeal had lasted days until, finally, they edged around the southern coast of Portugal into the Gulf of Cádiz. Even then the crew remained watchful and wary, looking south across the Straits of Gibraltar towards the dark ramparts of the mountains of the Barbary Coast, where Harry heard a savage brood of pirates lurked, waiting to take cargo for plunder and sailors for slaves. He'd been told the threat from the Moors across the water had grown since the king and queen had declared a vigorous renewal of the centuries' long *Reconquista* – their aim to conquer the Muslim Kingdom of Granada and take back control of the last Christian territory held by the infidel in Spain. The relief on board had been palpable when the galley had entered the wide mouth of the Guadalquivir and sailed upriver towards Seville.

Just beyond the gold tower, where a line of ramshackle taverns began, Harry got his first glimpse of the city proper. The riddle of red rooftops, stark white walls and tiled domes shimmering under the midday sun seemed an impossible maze. A place that might be filled with wonders, or dangers. A place he could lose himself if he wasn't careful. All at once, the gratitude he felt for having simply made it here alive dimmed in the face of his task. Would the king and queen accept him into their court? How would he gain their trust? Enough to prevent them from granting any funds to this sailor, Columbus? Enough to stop the man's plans for a voyage west? He thought again of Henry's voice whispering in his ear, the king's blade heavy on his shoulder.

Do not fail me.

Harry glanced back the way he'd come to where his men were still waiting with the chests. It was almost two hours since Rodrigo de Torres had headed to the royal palace to announce their arrival and arrange transport for the baggage and a suitable escort. Where was he?

Hearing wailing cries, Harry turned back to the dockside. Following the sounds, he came upon a row of people kneeling on the harbour wall. There were a few young men among them, but most were women and girls, some rocking as they cried, roped one to another all along their line. They were an arresting sight.

In London, Harry had seen people of different colours, pale like himself to ruddy, sallow, olive and tanned. But he'd not seen skin like this before – a deep brown-black, like oak gall ink. He moved closer, drawn by their strangeness, to see more being herded down the gangplank of a caravel. Some were girls, barely out of childhood. A few clung to one another as they were pushed along by men who hurried them with rough shouts and, if they were too slow, the flick of a stick to their legs.

A voice sounded at his ear. Harry turned to see a man looking questioningly at him. He shook his head and used a few of the Castilian words Peter had taught him on the crossing to say he didn't understand.

With a knowing laugh, the man switched easily into English. 'I said they will be in the market tomorrow. Come early if you're looking for strong ones. Come later if you want a good deal.' He dropped his voice and nodded to a man who was moving down the row of kneeling girls, studying each in turn before chalking something on a board. 'We took a lot of young ones this haul. The price will be lowered by the afternoon.'

Slaves, Harry realised – these men were slave traders. 'Thank you,' he muttered.

The man nodded and headed over to join his companions, inspecting their miserable cargo. Harry had heard the trade was booming in some parts of Christendom, although he'd not known anyone in

England who owned slaves. His eyes tracked south down the river towards the gulf, where those Barbary pirates waited. He felt queasy as he thought of being taken, bonded to a stranger in a foreign land. No wonder the sailors had been fearful. Praise God he had made it here.

'Sir!' Peter was hurrying towards him. 'Don Rodrigo has returned.'

Leaving the men to corral the weeping women, Harry set off with Peter to where the Spaniard was waiting.

From what King Henry had told him and from what Harry had learned direct from his travelling companion, Rodrigo de Torres was a hidalgo – one of the lower noble class – born of an affluent family in the province of Jaén, which had been wrested from the Moors over two hundred years earlier. One of his ancestors had been instrumental in the capture of the province and had been rewarded with a coat of arms and a parcel of land, which successive generations of the family had turned into a prosperous estate with acres of olive groves and its own presses. Rodrigo, who had grown up serving Queen Isabella as a squire in the royal guard, had succeeded his father upon his death three years ago and had become a favoured vassal of the queen. He was a young man with a confident manner and coal-black eyes that Harry had noticed would burn with a zealous fire whenever talk turned to the Moors.

'Señor de Torres,' he greeted, looking past Rodrigo for the expected host of royal officials come to greet him and the beasts to carry his bags. As his gaze alighted on a company of five coarse-looking men, two of whom led bandy-legged mules, Harry felt a flush of indignation. His father's talk of his arrival as ambassador to the royal courts of France and Burgundy had sounded so dignified, so grand: musicians and high stewards to usher him in, wine and delicacies to welcome him. 'Did you speak to the king and queen? Did you tell them I am here?'

'Queen Isabella left the city three months ago to give birth to her daughter,' Rodrigo said, his accent making music of the English words. 'At present, she and the king are in the north.' Rodrigo smiled. 'Do not be troubled, Sir Harry. I have a house here in the city.' He gestured to the men leading the mules, beckoning them down to the pile of chests. 'My men will bring your belongings. I will send word to the queen. Inform her of your arrival. You may stay with me until you get your audience.'

Harry fought to keep the bitterness from his voice. 'You were gone so long, I thought you would surely return with better news.'

'On the contrary, my friend, I have excellent news. In my absence, the tide of the war has turned.' Rodrigo's black eyes smouldered. 'Many more strongholds of the enemy have fallen to our forces.' He grasped Harry's shoulder. 'Come, one of my men is waiting to give me a full report. God willing, this very year we will wipe the infidel stain from our lands.'

Jack scanned the riotous masses, the din of drums assaulting his senses as the first of the wagons rolled towards him, winding up the street from the cathedral, the rust-red dome of which mushroomed over the city. A loud boom rattled the shutters of buildings and shuddered through his chest, sparks flashing amber across the pallid sky. The air was thick with the smell of sulphur. He had thought at first that people were firing guns into the crowds, until Valentine Holt had told him they were toys.

Flowers of Cathay the gunner had called them – black powder stuffed into paper tubes with a lit fuse, shot skyward on arrows. Jack had been with his father under King Edward's banner at the Battle of Barnet, aged thirteen; deafened by the roar of cannon, choking on the smoke. He had seen, first-hand, what shot and the devil's powder could do to a mass of men. It seemed irreverent to use it as a plaything.

'Here they come,' called David, gripping Adam's shoulder to peer over the heads of the crowds that pressed in around them in an oppressive stew of body odours and bellowing voices.

Earlier, forcing their way through the crush, they'd spotted a set of steps outside a baker's that would give them a slight vantage, but as the crowd swelled they'd been pushed further back until now the five of them were pressed up against the shutters of the shop front.

The wagon approached, accompanied by the throb of drums. As it trundled past, Jack saw the back of it had been decked out like a forest. Among painted trees with green and brown ribbons for leaves, furry-legged satyrs and nymphs in diaphanous gowns cavorted. The crowd cheered, men hooting at the girls who danced in circles around the leering satyrs, staggering as the wagon's wheels jolted over the cobbles. High above, people leaned from balconies to watch, most of them women in glittering gowns, jewelled and aloof. A second wagon trundled in the wake of the first, this one occupied by a blindfolded Eros, poised with bow and arrow, wings of turquoise satin splayed behind him, young boys in white singing at his feet.

Last week, arguing over the details of their next move in the cheapest lodging they'd been able to find – a rundown tavern near a row of wool-washing sheds that emitted an eye-watering stink – they'd met a German merchant who knew English well enough to tell them all about Florence's forthcoming Carnival: a wild celebration of the change of season from winter's darkness into spring; the different guilds and confraternities who commissioned the wagons, the route the procession would take, the taverns to avoid unless they wanted overpriced piss-water and pox-riddled whores. The whole parade, the merchant said, would end at the Palazzo Medici, where performances would be held for the entertainment of the Medici family and the city's dignitaries. This would, they had decided, provide the best opportunity to gather what they needed to implement their plan. It was the first time since Jack had returned from the palazzo empty-handed that they'd all agreed on anything.

Jack's eyes strayed down the street to where the imposing palazzo thrust above most of its neighbours. Outside, an enormous tiered dais had been erected, blocking the street. It was packed with hundreds of men in sumptuous robes and fur-trimmed capes, elaborate hats and jewelled belts. Servants threaded among them, bearing drinks and food. Over them all was raised a scarlet standard, displaying a shield of gold emblazoned with seven red balls. Jack, who'd glimpsed the symbol throughout the palazzo on his brief visit, had seen it many times since, engraved and embossed on buildings across Florence – the Medici coat of arms, like a stamp of ownership on the city.

He rubbed absently at his finger where his father's ring had made a white band. It was almost a fortnight since he'd lost it to Lorenzo de' Medici's keeping, but his hand still felt naked without it. He had returned to the palazzo the day after the man dismissed him and the day after that, waiting in line with the host of men who thronged the benches at the palace entrance, but his requests for another audience had been denied.

'Eyes on her, boy,' Valentine warned in his ear.

'They are,' Jack retorted, bridling at the apellation. Valentine and the Foxley brothers might each be about old enough to be his father, but at twenty-seven he was long past boyhood. Forcing his gaze from the palazzo, he scanned the crowds around the dais, now edging back to make way for the wagons lining up outside the palazzo. He searched the sea of feathered caps and silk mantles until he picked out a flash of grey and a crop of short brown hair. He held Amelot in his sights for a moment, then she was gone again, swallowed by the throng.

'Lose her and we lose our chance,' Valentine reminded him.

Jack said nothing, but thought how the gunner had changed his tune. Valentine had been against Amelot coming with them from the start, demanding to know what use the mute girl was. Besides which, though she might dress as a boy, she was a woman – *and God knows women be bad luck and trouble in a company of men*. But when, in Aigues-Mortes, after a fruitless week searching for a vessel whose price they could afford to take them to Pisa, the girl had dropped a pile of purses on the floor of their lodgings like a dog bringing birds to please its master, her value had at once been clear.

'Didn't know they'd be celebrating you in this parade, Holt!' Ned shouted over the din, nodding to the next wagon, which was occupied by a bald and bloated Bacchus squatting on a swathe of green velvet, several lambs tethered, bleating unhappily, around him. As he swigged from a jug of wine that washed red down his belly the crowd roared its approval. Grinning, Ned dipped two fingers in his ale and offered them for Titan to lick. The little dog, unnerved by all the bangs and flashes, was nestled in his coat.

Valentine growled something into his tankard, but Jack didn't catch it as the press of people in front of him parted like the twitch of a curtain and Amelot slipped through.

Her pinched face was flushed, her tawny eyes bright and alert, whether with nerves or excitement he couldn't quite tell. From beneath the folds of her grey cloak she pulled five purses, the strings of which had been cut by the dagger Ned had given her. Adam and David stepped in closer, shielding her from view as she handed them to Jack. Two were of worn leather, but three were more ornate, including one of purple velvet decorated with a pearl.

Jack stowed them in the bag he'd strapped to his body beneath his cloak. 'Be careful,' he cautioned as she turned to go.

Amelot narrowed her eyes at him in response, before stealing into the throng, visible here and there as she weaved her way back towards the dais.

'There're more guards now,' David observed, nodding at the crush around the platform.

Jack saw four men in the same blue tunics emblazoned with a black viper they'd seen others in this area wearing that morning, all of them armed and watchful. They were moving slowly through the rowdy hordes, keeping a close eye out. He hoped Amelot had seen them. They had been right in their estimation – the crowds here offered the richest pickings – but that meant more protection. 'Perhaps we should call her back?'

'No,' said Valentine gruffly. 'We've not enough.'

Adam nodded in agreement, his sharp blue eyes meeting Jack's. 'The barge leaves in two days. If we don't have the funds we'll not be on it.'

Jack didn't answer. What could he say? The others were set on this plan now and he could either go along with them or remain in the city alone. He'd done what he could to find out more about this Court of Wolves Lorenzo had spoken of in connection with the badge Amelot indicated had been worn by one of Amaury's abductors, but with scant understanding of the Tuscan dialect all he'd been able to discover was that it was some kind of duelling company. He could see no more trails to follow. Not if Lorenzo wouldn't see him.

Ned, sharing a cup of sour wine with him last night by the tavern's smoky fire, had told him to give it up. 'Jack, you did what you came for. You tried. But you must see we have to move on?'

He couldn't blame them for their haste to be gone. He had led them here for nothing; made them believe Lorenzo de' Medici would open the door to all their futures. Instead, the man had slammed it in his face. What could he do now but follow the course his companions had settled upon?

Spain – that was the direction they had chosen, after days of debate. The holy crusade against the Moors in Granada offered opportunities to five skilled fighters, fresh from war in England. A chance at honour and plunder. They had secured passage on a vintner's barge that would take them down the Arno to the Port of Pisa, where they would hunt for a ship to take them west, but as well as funds for the journey they would still need the requisite armour and equipment in order to offer their services.

Jack had felt guilty, using Amelot in this way. He hadn't yet told the girl what Lorenzo had intimated – that Amaury might have been taken by someone from this city. Perhaps, when she'd done what they needed her to, he should. Then she, at least, could make a choice, whether to travel on with them, or remain and search for her beloved master. He had brought her all this way, after all, partly hoping she might yet be able to reveal more about who had taken the priest, partly not wanting to relinquish his last connection to Amaury – to his father and his secrets.

Jack thought of that snow-sullen afternoon a year ago outside the hunting lodge near Dijon, Prince Edward watching him chop wood for the fire, the boy's breath pluming as he spoke of a conversation he'd had with Vaughan.

Sir Thomas once told me the Turks are not our true enemy. That we – and the Muslims and the Jews – are all fighting for the same thing. Only the world does not yet see it.

Jack had been unable to countenance such sentiment coming from the mouth of his father – or any Christian. It was thirty-three years since the Ottoman Turks had broken as a devastating wave upon the city of Constantinople, jewel of the western world and gateway to the east. But time had not dimmed the loss, which saw Christendom cut off from its life's blood of trade routes and its ancient foe entrenched on its doorstep. Stories of horror had filtered through from the few survivors: Turks pouring in through breached walls, soldiers fleeing their posts to protect their families, the blood flowing as rivers in the streets, the looting and defilement, the murder of thousands and the enslavement of tens of thousands. God, men said, still wept for that day.

But, when Jack found himself in Amaury's lodgings, the priest had confirmed his father's stance, telling him the Academy believed that before the Flood mankind had been united, one brotherhood under God, connected by what Plato described as the World Soul. He'd claimed the waters that engulfed the world in the time of Noah had erased this understanding, scattering all knowledge and dividing that soul into many broken shards of faith. It was the dream of Cosimo de' Medici, founder of the Academy and Lorenzo's grandfather, to search for that lost knowledge and gather it together, in the hope this would unite mankind and its divided faiths, saving it from a path to darkness and destruction.

Jack had said nothing of this to the others, partly to keep his word to Amaury, but mostly because these men still worshipped his father.

They wouldn't accept Vaughan might have been some sort of defender of the hated Turk, or a believer in a dream that sounded like heresy.

He had tried to tell himself this new future would not be much different to how he'd lived much of his adult life: roads to war and camaraderie around campfires, seeking the next fight and a master's favour, finding solace in a flagon and a whore's bed. But it was different. *He* was different. The thought of taking that barge down the Arno, to Spain and the fight against the infidel, made him feel as though he were turning his back on everything: from his ambition, harboured since boyhood, to become a knight and wash clean the stain of his bastard blood; from the answers he'd been seeking and all he'd lost in pursuit of them.

His companions didn't seem to comprehend his need to delve deeper into his loss, Ned murmuring that he was chasing ghosts.

They're gone and buried, Jack. Nothing you find will bring them back. You're just fingering a wound.

But why would they understand? They had lost their homeland, at least as long as Tudor remained on the throne, but for veteran mercenaries, itinerant, rootless, this was not disastrous and home could be found elsewhere. Whatever family they had each known had been lost or abandoned long ago and what remained seemed enough for them. David and Adam had each other, their sibling bond so strong they rarely needed words – just a glance or a flicker of a smile – to know what the other was thinking. Ned had Titan, who gave him all the adulation he could want and Valentine had his gun, an iron and fire extension of himself, which seemed to make him more than content.

But he'd had a home. A mother who loved him. A father he'd once worshipped. They were gone and – Ned was right – couldn't be returned. But how could he let them go with all the questions that remained? How could he let them sink down inside him, settle in his soul, if he didn't know whether he should grieve for them or blame them? Remember fondly, or forget?

These past days Jack felt as though two doors had opened within him. One led with his companions to war and the promise of its spoils. One led into darkness, into which his father's footsteps had disappeared. If he turned from that door he knew it would always remain open, the shadows within restless, its airs never still. But to turn from the other would leave him truly alone, his last friends in the world – the closest thing he had left to family – gone for good.

Jack focused on the wagons and the roar of the crowds, David's grin and Valentine's bulk to either side of him, Titan's anxious barks. Ned was right. He had to move on.

A new murmur was rippling through the crowd. A low shudder of excitement, or fear. Another wagon was approaching, this one larger than the others. Painted black, it was drawn by four beasts, the like of which Jack had never seen before. They looked like oxen, only bigger, with hunched backs and curved horns rising from monstrous heads. On the cart he saw figures dancing and swaying, their limbs swaddled in white and grey cloth painted to look like bones. The skeletons leaned out as they sang, fingers stretching towards the spectators, who shrieked and shied from their touch. At the back of the wagon, standing on a plinth surrounded by tombstones that jutted like broken teeth, was a man in black robes and a white mask, holding aloft a scythe.

Jack's mind stirred with memory.

A face white as bone. Death it was, I tell you.

The words conjured an image of his mother's killer. That cracked leather mask covering half a face, pale against the dark, those twitching hands, reaching out. Jack flinched as Ned grabbed his arm.

'There!'

Following his gaze, Jack saw the four guards in their blue tunics moving purposefully through the crowd. With them was a tall man in a cloak of purple velvet, who was gesturing agitatedly at something. Jack thought of the purse of the same fabric, now stowed in his bag.

'Where is Amelot?' Ned said. 'Can you see her?'

Jack scanned the masses around the dais. '*Damn it!*' He pushed his way forward. 'I'll find her.'

'I'll come,' said David, pressing in beside him.

Jack entered the crowd; a shifting tide. Elbows dug into his back, feet stepped on his. A hand slipped inside his cloak, fingers trailing across his hip towards his groin. It was gone before he could react. He smelled rancid breath, sulphur, a heady musk of sweat and perfume. A man shoved him, then laughed in his face as he turned. He'd already lost sight of David, the press surging him on, closer to the dais, as Death rolled in behind.

Rising on to his toes, his height giving him an advantage over most of those around him, Jack spied the guards, some distance ahead. They were still moving in, but had slowed, two scanning the area, the others turning people by the shoulders. He couldn't see Amelot, but the girl, short and slight, was easily lost in this multitude. He glimpsed David's coarse grey hair. His friend, who had got ahead of him, wasn't far from the guards, turning in a circle, the brand on his forehead standing out on his pale skin. Thoughts flickered through Jack's mind: Amelot caught, him and the others rounded up, a foreign gaol and a flogging, or worse. A few years ago he'd been ascending the lofty path to knighthood. Now it seemed he might reach no higher platform than the pillory.

Feeling a hand tug hard at his cloak, he spun round. It was Amelot. Seeing her agitated expression he thought she'd seen the guards too, until she grasped his arm, small fingers pinching his skin as she urged him towards the dais. He called to her in warning, but she was gone again, slipping into the mêlée. Cursing, he forced his way through behind her, the sky exploding above them with bangs and sparks.

He caught up with her not far from the platform, in the midst of a boisterous group of well-dressed young men, swaying at one another's shoulders and singing, cups of wine held aloft. As he grabbed the girl's shoulder, trying to pull her back, she pointed frantically at the dais, the tiers of which rose up before them, packed with hundreds of dignitaries, thronged beneath the Medici's scarlet standard. Her eyes were wide, urgent.

'What is it?' he shouted.

Amelot gripped her arm, down near the wrist then let go. She did this several times, until finally Jack realised. She was indicating a missing hand.

'Amaury?'

She nodded and pointed at the dais again.

'He's here?' Jack said, stunned.

She shook her head furiously.

Then, Jack knew. Not Amaury, but those who had taken him. 'Who, Amelot?' His eyes were raking the crowds on the dais now, desperate as hers. 'Who is it?'

Jack was distracted as one of the young men singing beside him swayed too far and toppled over in a sprawl of limbs and laughter. As the man's cheering companions bent to help him and the crowds parted, he heard a harsh cry rise above the drunken jeers. The man in the purple cloak was pointing in his direction. The four guards, fixing as one on Amelot, lunged through the mob.

Cursing, Jack thrust Amelot ahead of him, steering her towards the tall buildings that bordered the street. People growled in protest, reluctant to move, some pushing him back. Behind, the shouts of the guards intensified. Jack used his elbows, feeling like he was fighting his way through a thicket. Any moment, he expected the mass to close in and halt him completely. Amelot was just ahead, struggling in the crush. Behind, more shouts were rising. Twisting, Jack saw someone arguing with the group of young men. It was David. As he watched, his friend shoved one of the men in the chest, who retaliated with a clumsy punch that David dodged neatly. A few of the others were moving in to aid their companion, their mass shifting, blocking the path of the guards. Glancing over his shoulder, David caught Jack's eye. *Go!*

Jack pressed on, making it to the buildings where, a few yards along, an alley opened. Grabbing Amelot's hand he dragged her down it, their feet skidding in stinking pools. But even as they ran, forced from the Carnival crowds and the men on the dais, hope burst inside Jack, bright as the Flowers of Cathay.

Fortune had granted him another chance.

6

'Thank you.' Jack accepted the goblet from the elderly servant who stooped to hand it to him. The wine was cool, refreshing after the hours spent sitting on the bench at the palazzo's entrance with a host of other men, all of whom had been seen before him. Only when day was fading into a chill purple dusk and the guards were changing shifts, had he finally been ushered through.

The servant glanced at Lorenzo de' Medici, settled opposite Jack in a chair with carved arms and legs like a lion's paws.

The signore nodded. 'Thank you, Papi.'

As the man shuffled from the bedchamber through the red swag of curtain that led out from the study where Jack had been questioned on his first visit, Lorenzo turned his attention to him. His face looked drawn, the light of the candles casting his skin in a jaundiced hue. 'So, Master James, I have granted you my time. What is this crucial information you assured my guards you have?'

Jack recounted what had happened at Carnival, avoiding mention of what he and his men had been doing there – the purses heaped on the mattress in their lodgings afterwards, Valentine grunting appreciatively as Ned counted the contents, David grinning as he accepted a cup of ale from Adam, fists and cheek bruised from the altercation with the drunken men. Instead, he concentrated on Amelot's recognition of one of Amaury de la Croix's abductors. Lorenzo said nothing for a moment, merely took a sip of wine. But Jack caught the interest that flared in his eyes.

'This man? What did he look like?'

Back in the tavern, flushed from their sprint through the alleys, Jack had prompted Amelot to describe the man through a painful process of elimination – furious shakes of her head and vehement nods. She intimated he had dark hair, was neither very young nor very old and of normal height and size, but other than this there seemed to be nothing remarkable about him. Jack, seeing Lorenzo's disappointment at this, pushed on swiftly. 'But I'm certain she would recognise him if she saw him again.'

'*If*.'

Jack, unsure whether the cool tone was doubt or disbelief, felt his chest tighten as Lorenzo shifted in his chair, looking as though he were about to stand. 'Is there another such occasion planned? Perhaps, were she to attend, she might be able to point him out?'

'More than four hundred men were with me that day. Lords of the Signoria and dignitaries from a multitude of houses. Officials and leaders of confraternities. Professors and lawyers. Friends, family, servants.' Lorenzo set his goblet down. 'This is a populous city, Master James. What you suggest could take months.' His eyebrow arched. 'And who, I wonder, will feed and house you in that time, given your assertion of poverty?'

'You said yourself, signore, you believe those who took Amaury may have intercepted his letter to you. Surely that could only have been someone with access to your household?'

Lorenzo held his gaze, a hint of warning in those dark eyes, but he had settled back in his chair, hands curled over the carved arms. 'That number is not inconsiderable, as you would have seen.'

It was true: as well as the men who had, one by one, been granted their audience with the signore in the suite of rooms on the ground floor of the palazzo, Jack had watched an army of people entering and exiting through the day, guards in black and servants in grey, kitchen staff with barrows and young men in outlandish fashions. Still, he pressed on. 'You have no suspicions at all?'

Lorenzo grunted. 'In Florence a man of standing wears suspicion as his shadow. My family and I have not gained our position by being trusting fools.'

'Of course,' Jack assented. 'But when we first met you spoke of enemies – stirring in the shadows? It made me wonder if you suspected someone?'

Lorenzo pressed his fingertips together. 'Not someone, no.'

Jack waited in the silence.

'But there have been incidents over the past few years that have sprung to my mind since we spoke. Papers going missing from my private study, business deals undermined with privileged information, political allies shifting their allegiance unexpectedly. All occurred in isolation and I dismissed each as misfortune at the time. But since you told me Amaury was taken . . .?'

Jack seized the opportunity he felt open at Lorenzo's plain talking. 'The badge one of them wore. Might that not narrow the field?'

'You are assuming the men who took the priest and those who ordered it are one and the same. If someone with access to my private chambers did indeed read Amaury's letter and was inspired to act upon it, they could have used those men as tools by which to take him.'

'But find the tool and you might find the hand that wields it?' Jack watched as Lorenzo's hand strayed back towards his goblet. 'I have heard the Court of Wolves is a duelling company?' The twitch in Lorenzo's jaw told him he'd struck a nerve.

'Yes.' Lorenzo took up the goblet, but didn't drink. 'It was established around a decade ago. A minor fraternity made up of retired *condottieri*. Mercenary captains,' he explained at Jack's frown. 'Skilful, brutal men grown rich and powerful in the arena of war. At first it was inconsequential, I'm not certain it even had a name back then, but over the past few years, as peace has settled over our restive states and mercenaries have found themselves less occupied by the blood trade, the company has grown considerably in size and reputation. Now, men other than soldiers look to join its ranks – ambitious sons of wealthy families, seeking camaraderie, excitement, business opportunities. Seeing its growing prominence, I tried to enrol my eldest son, Piero.' Lorenzo's brow pinched. 'They maintained they declined him because of his young years, but when I attempted to join, I, too, was rejected.'

Jack was surprised. Despite the fact Lorenzo wore no crown, he would have thought the man's affluence and power would have made him impossible to refuse. The hint of weakness made him bolder. 'The company troubles you, then?'

Lorenzo's eyes flicked back to him. 'I am the guardian of this republic. Any father who does not know what his children are involved in might have cause for concern.' He returned the goblet to the table. 'Their elusiveness has frustrated me, yes, but I have not been *troubled* by them. Not until you told me what the girl saw in Paris.' He laced his fingers. 'Of course, it is entirely possible Amaury's abduction has nothing to do with the company as a whole. As with any brotherhood in Florence, a man might be a member but remain under his own agency, with ties to family and business that are as important and compelling as any loyalty he owes to a fraternity or guild. But . . .' Lorenzo paused, looking towards the curtained door as footsteps echoed beyond.

Moments later, an old man entered. He was small and wizened, like a grape left too long in the sun. The pleated cape he wore over his black robes only partially disguised the hunch that crooked his back, causing him to walk with a stiff-legged limp. As he removed his cap, releasing a shock of white hair, and bowed to Lorenzo, Jack saw a tonsure marked him as a man of God.

'Signore,' the man began, then halted, noticing Jack with a questioning frown.

'This is James Wynter,' Lorenzo explained, maintaining his Latin for Jack's benefit.

'Sir Thomas Vaughan's son?' murmured the priest, revealing to Jack that they had spoken about him.

'Master James, this is Fra Marsilio Ficino.'

Jack went to rise to greet the priest, but Marsilio had already turned away and was addressing Lorenzo in the Tuscan dialect. He sat still, watching the two of them converse, Lorenzo gesturing occasionally, the priest nodding thoughtfully then replying. All the while their eyes darted to him, telling him he was the subject.

Finally, the priest inclined his head to Lorenzo, then, with a last glance at Jack, turned towards the door. As he replaced the cap, Jack caught a flash of gold and saw that a familiar ring engraved with a caduceus – the staff of Hermes – graced his wrinkled hand. Marsilio Ficino, like Amaury and his father, was a member of Lorenzo's Academy. He touched his own finger, marked with the pale trace of a band.

'The hour grows late,' observed Lorenzo, rising when Marsilio had gone. 'I have other matters I must now attend to.'

Jack stood with him. Was that it? Was he about to be dismissed again? He fought for something to say, but Lorenzo beat him to it.

'Fra Marsilio believes there is merit to your suggestion the girl be used to identify this man.'

'Yes?' ventured Jack, chest tightening in anticipation.

'If there is, indeed, an enemy within my household they must be rooted out. Besides which, Amaury is not only a friend, he is also privy to a great deal of knowledge, which I cannot allow to be used against me. But I must think upon how best to orchestrate this. I will grant you a stipend to cover lodgings for the month, but I expect you to keep the girl in the city.'

Jack felt the headway he'd made slipping from him. In his keenness to use what Amelot had seen to his advantage he'd made her the indispensable one. What was he now but her guardian? And what might he command as a reward for the service of a mute girl? Little, he suspected, of what he'd travelled here for. Even if Amelot spied the suspect again, once she had pointed him out there would be nothing stopping Lorenzo from dismissing him. His mind raced as Lorenzo motioned him to the door, searching for something to turn the man's attention back to him, make himself of value. 'What if I were to join them?'

'Join them?'

They were almost at the door. Beyond, the hall led to the inner courtyard and the doors to the street. 'You say the Court of Wolves was established by men of war? I trained under my father, served King Edward in battle. I have the qualifications.'

'And, as I also said, it now favours young men of the noble classes. Those with money and influence. Those with the right – pedigree.'

Jack's blood stirred. 'My father was one of England's highest ranking officials. I may be his bastard, signore, but I have lived in his world. I know it well.'

'Florence is not England. More than just miles separate our nations.'

'I learn quickly.' Jack pressed in, seeing Lorenzo hesitate. 'No one in the city knows me. If I was accepted into their company I could hunt down those involved in taking Amaury, yes, but I could also perhaps discover whether or not you have reason to be troubled by them. Why they refused entry to you and your son? What do you have to lose by this course?'

Lorenzo's dark eyes glittered. 'The real question you want answered, Master James, is what do you have to gain?'

Jack nodded after a pause, holding his gaze.

'Money,' Lorenzo said. 'For you and your men?'

'And answers, signore. The answers my father promised I would find here. The only legacy he left me.'

*   *   *

'He has told you nothing? Nothing at all?'

'We have tried everything to make him talk, monsignore, I assure you.'

'And I can assure you, *sir*, that His Holiness will be extremely displeased by your feeble attempts.' Battista di Salvi held the knight's gaze in his steel glare. 'Why did you not send word to Rome, the moment the prisoner was taken?'

'We hoped to find and return him to our custody before it was necessary.'

'A failure on all counts, then. Well, you can inform your Grand Master the agreement will not now be honoured.'

'Monsignore, I—'

'You wish to offend His Holiness further?'

The knight bowed, chin dropping towards the splayed white cross that emblazoned his black surcoat.

'I thought not. Now, let us see if we can draw something of use from the wretch.' Battista peered into the cell, his grey eyes narrowing. 'My companion may be an abomination of nature, but he is well versed in such matters.' He glanced round at the figure, waiting on the fringes of the guttering torchlight. 'Are you not, my hideous friend?'

Goro stepped forward, out of the shadows of the dank passage. As he did so, he noticed the knight move back, giving him more room than he needed, the man's eyes lingering on his face. Inured to such intimate stares, Goro ignored him and focused instead on the cell, the door of which was hanging open, a foetid smell seeping from within. For a moment, he felt as though he were somewhere else: in the stinking bowels of another dungeon, a chorus of cries and whimpers stinging his ears, a young man before him, drenched in blood and smiling like the devil.

'Well? What are you waiting for?' Battista's voice bit at his back.

Clenching his jaw against the vision, Goro ducked his huge body through the door and entered the cell. The man inside, chained to the wall, naked but for a pair of torn and filthy hose, lay crumpled in a pool of his own urine. The acrid stink permeated the cramped, lightless chamber, spiking Goro's nose. A beard straggled from the man's chin and his hair was matted with blood. His face, arms and torso were a mess of bruises, old and new, his skin waxy between the livid wounds, oily with sweat in the sickly light of a single torch burning on the wall. His eyes were wide, fixed on Goro as he entered, his giant form almost filling the cell. The man's breaths came in shallow bursts, his sunken chest heaving.

Slowly, allowing the man to take in every movement, Goro reached for his belt and drew a stiletto dagger from its sheath. The blade was long and thin, the handle decorated with three crosses of milky mother-of-pearl. A gift from Carlo di Fante, it was Goro's most prized possession: the last thing he had left of his beloved master, killed by the English whoreson in that alley.

He turned it in the light so the chained man could see its length and keenness. The man blinked rapidly, breaths quickening, but he made no sound – none of the usual pleas for mercy or promises to do or give anything Goro had heard over the years. He wasn't surprised. Despite the monsignore's barbed criticism, he knew the Knights of St John would be more than capable of drawing a confession out of most captives. This man, clearly, was a professional, although that much was evident from the knights' description of the company he'd been part of, liberating the prisoner in a daring dawn raid on the castle. It seemed the knights had been fortunate to even take this man alive, his comrades leaving him for dead in the prison tower, where he'd been found barely conscious, bleeding from a head wound.

Goro heard Battista's voice come from further down the passage, the two men leaving him alone to work. He caught his name and guessed the monsignore was talking to the knight about him. The voice nipped at him, that salty tone now all too familiar. He pushed the cell door closed, blocking it out. Turning to the chained man, his hand tightened around the dagger. He would relish this task today.

First things first, though. The captive had clearly seen many fists and blades during his incarceration here. It was time to give him something new to be frightened of. Slowly, Goro reached up and unhooked the mask – white leather over moulded steel – that covered half his face. As he pulled it away, he watched horror leap into the man's eyes.

When he was done, hours and screams later, Goro ducked out of the cell and shambled down the passage, head bent beneath the rough-hewn ceiling, a smell like warm copper coming off his sticky hands. He found Battista talking to the knight in the guards' room.

The monsignore rose as he appeared, the large gold cross he wore around his neck inlaid with green jewels glinting in the lantern light. His grey eyes took in the blood on Goro's clothes. 'Well?'

'He and the others were paid to take the prisoner. He was never told by whom. But he said where his company was from.'

'Where?'

'Florence, monsignore. They came from Florence.'

7

The walled garden was haloed with light. Candles, trapped in glass and strung from the branches of trees, glittered like stars. The evening air, fragrant with herbs, was still warm from the day, the sky, framed by the high walls of the palazzo, peacock blue. Over the splashing of fountains came the murmur of conversation, punctuated by the clink of glass as servants ladled wine into goblets.

Stepping out among the first guests, Jack accepted a vessel a servant handed to him, twisting his head as the stiff collar of his shirt scratched his neck. He felt constricted, self-conscious in his new clothes. Each button on the doublet of sky-blue damask that matched his hose was a pearl inset in a shell of gold. He suspected, if he sold the garment, he could live like a lord for a year.

Earlier, in Lorenzo de' Medici's private suite on the palazzo's opulent first floor, he had stood before a mirror while Papi, the elderly servant who'd been with the signore since boyhood, fussed over his attire. By the time Papi had finished, Jack hardly recognised himself. The man in the glass looked nothing like the vagabond who arrived in Florence five months ago. Now, he was clean-shaven, his dark hair trimmed and combed, sleek with perfumed oil. The hollows of his cheeks had filled out, as had the muscles of his chest and arms from his dawn duels with Ned on the banks of the Arno, and his skin was darkened by the June sun. With the fog of secrets that had risen to shroud his father, he'd been unable to guess whether Thomas Vaughan, had he lived, would have made good on his promise to see him knighted. But standing there in the magnificence of Lorenzo's chambers, staring at his noble twin, Jack could dream he had.

Hearing raised voices, he glanced back through the doors that led into the inner courtyard. More guests were arriving, men greeting one another effusively, embracing and kissing cheeks and lips. No English reserve here. Guards met them in turn, taking daggers, servants stepping in with goblets of sweet wine to ease the transfer of arms. One of the things Jack had learned in his moments with Lorenzo over the past few months was that the man did not give his trust easily and, then, only if he had some exchange of power in return.

Over them all towered the bronze statue of David. It was an odd thing, David's naked body almost womanly in its proportions, coquettishly poised with a sword in his hand and a foot perched on Goliath's head. Two boys were chasing one another around its base – Lorenzo's sons, Piero and Giovanni, dressed in doublets of rose-gold damask, their laughter high. A handsome young man stepped in to chide them with an indulgent smile, grasping Giovanni, the younger and chubbier, playfully by the shoulders. Yesterday, in the guise of his new persona, Jack had been introduced to him – Angelo Poliziano, Giovanni's private tutor, close friend of Lorenzo and member of the Academy.

As the newcomers spilled out around him, Jack moved deeper into the gardens down paths lined with marble statues, some pristine, others ancient, in search of familiar faces. He found his men loitering in the shadows near the back of the courtyard, looking as awkward as him in their new attire as they gulped their drinks and eyed the flamboyant guests. Moths tilted at candles in the trees above them.

'Prince Jack is it now then?' remarked Valentine Holt, looking him up and down. 'Don't fret,' he grunted at Jack's warning stare. 'We know our parts, *Sir* James.'

They looked at least, he thought, neat and well groomed, as would be expected of the men of an affluent knight abroad on business. While Valentine and Adam, clad in tunics of oil-stiffened leather, were masquerading as his bodyguards, Ned and David were his clerks, in robes of blue wool with hats to match, all loaned by Lorenzo. David had kept his beard, but the grey tangle had been shorn close to his jaw and a pair of thick-rimmed spectacles completed the scholarly look. His hair, clipped in a low line along his eyebrows, hid the brand on his forehead. Ned, with his imposing height and build, still looked intimidating, but if that made people more wary, less likely to question him, that was no bad thing. All of them were well versed in Jack's story, but with their knowledge of the language still limited he didn't want any mistakes.

'You must move around,' Jack advised, switching into French for Amelot, who was tugging at a thread on the hem of her new tunic. 'Get a good look at everyone.'

She was dressed as his page, her brown hair cut short around her ears, but these past months she had changed from the wild thing he'd found in Paris. Despite all her efforts to appear as a boy nature was starting to make that more difficult. The blade-sharp contours of her face had softened and keen eyes would surely soon notice those buds at her chest, however tight she bound the lengths of dampened linen to hide them. She made Jack think of the bronze David in the entrance hall: a figure caught somewhere between two sexes, neither one nor the other. He wondered sometimes what had made her turn from her womanhood – an act both strange and forbidden – but since Amaury had told him almost nothing about his mute companion he doubted that unless they found the priest he would ever know.

'If she spies her man do we tell you, or Signor Lorenzo?' David wanted to know, his blue eyes large behind the curved glass of the spectacles.

'Tell me. Don't draw any attention.' Jack glanced at Ned as he spoke, eyes shifting meaningfully to Amelot. He had no idea how she might react if, as hoped, she spotted the man she'd seen at Carnival, but with the undertaking he'd been tasked with this evening they couldn't afford to make a scene.

Ned placed a hand on the girl's shoulder. 'I'll keep her with me.' His gaze shifted as more people flowed out into the gardens, voices rising. 'Go. Do what you need to do. We're with you.'

Seeing the others nod, Jack felt himself settle. It had taken time to convince all of them this charade was worth abandoning their plan to head for Spain, at least for now, but in the end the potential reward offered by Lorenzo had convinced them. Now, he just needed to make good on his promise he could make this work.

With a fortifying sip of wine, he moved into the swelling crowds. Lorenzo had told him he would make the introduction this evening, but that didn't stop Jack's eyes flicking over mantles and doublets in search of badges. Over the buzz of conversation delicate notes drifted from the plucked strings of lutes. He glimpsed Lorenzo's wan-faced wife, Clarice, talking with a group of women dressed in richly embellished gowns and jewelled caps, the gems that adorned their necks and fingers flashing with every movement.

Her eldest daughters, Lucrezia and Maddalena, were perched on the stone lip of a fountain. An older girl he didn't recognise was seated between them, framed by the glittering cascade of water. Her hair, thick and dark, was plaited neatly around her head, bound in place by silver braid. Several coiled ringlets had been teased free to frame a delicate face with high cheekbones and a sharp nose. She wore a dress of grey samite, embroidered with black falcons. It was pulled in tight at the bodice, accentuating the swell of her breasts. Her eyes narrowed as she caught his stare and she tossed her head, the ringlets dancing. As Jack moved on, he heard a peal of girlish laughter behind him.

There, where the crowds were starting to congregate, was Lorenzo, regal in a blood-scarlet mantle, clasping hands and smiling as men jostled one another to greet him at this, the first party of the summer season. During his time in the city, Jack had seen how deeply ingrained Lorenzo was in all aspects of the republic. He shaped and led the Signoria, entrenched his followers within the guilds, enlisted his sons in the confraternities, decided how churches would benefit from funds, and governed the affairs of the grand families – Florence's elite – agreeing marriage contracts and business mergers, who would or wouldn't be elected to public office, who could punish a rival and how. A large number of notaries and secretaries, many of them lower-class men from the Santa Maria Novella quarter – one of the city's four districts, dominated by the Medici – who had grown up in awe of their powerful patron, were employed to keep ears and eyes open, bringing him word from every corner of the city. Bees carrying pollen back to the hive. Only the Court of Wolves, it seemed, remained out of his long reach.

Marsilio Ficino was close by, talking to Angelo Poliziano, his white hair sprouting wild from beneath a cap, the lines that carved his face deepened by shadows. Jack had only met the stoop-backed priest a few times, but Fra Vito – a monk and a friend of Lorenzo's, who'd been teaching him Tuscan at the nearby monastery of San Marco – had told him all about the renowned scholar, astrologer and philosopher. Along with Lorenzo's grandfather, Cosimo de' Medici, Marsilio had promoted and encouraged the spread of humanism: a philosophy that viewed the world through the eyes of ancient Greece and Rome, shaped by newly discovered writings of Plato, Cicero and Aristotle, which had travelled west some thirty-three years ago with scholars and priests fleeing the Turks advancing on Constantinople. Marsilio had translated many of these texts. As Fra Vito put it: if Cosimo was one of the fathers of humanism, Marsilio Ficino was its midwife.

Marsilio glanced in his direction. As he locked eyes with Jack his furrowed face hardened. The only one of Lorenzo's household other than Papi who'd been apprised of the plan, the priest had been candid in his misgivings about whether he was up to the task. Lorenzo had dismissed the older man's doubts, but he hadn't let Jack forget the confidence he was investing in him, telling him the trust Sir Thomas Vaughan and Amaury de la Croix clearly had in him was the basis of his faith, while warning him not to take it lightly.

Turning from Marsilio, Jack felt his nerves tighten. That afternoon, watching servants roll wine barrels up from the cellar, smells of spice-rubbed meat drifting from the kitchens, he'd felt eager for the evening to come. All these months shut away for the most part in San Marco or in the lodgings in the Fig, a tavern near the *mercato* Lorenzo had installed him and his men in, he had been preparing for this. Now, he just felt daunted by the prospect of what he'd agreed to. Lorenzo's voice echoed in his mind.

Keep to your story, whomever you speak to. Become the lie. You are the bait on the hook. If it is to be taken, no fish in this pool can see the ruse.

Holding out his goblet for a servant to refill, Jack steeled himself, thinking of what he had been promised in the bargain. Gold – enough of it for him and his men to start new lives wherever they wished; Ned already musing about travel and adventures, David trying to convince Adam to buy a tavern with him, Valentine enthusing about Italian guns. For him, though, money came second to the answers Lorenzo had agreed to give him. No coin could buy back what he'd lost, but maybe – released from the questions that kept him tethered to the past – he could look to the future and what his place in this world might now be?

More servants were drifting through the crowds, passing around silver plates piled with what looked to Jack like the chrysalises he used to find in his mother's herb garden.

'Sir?' said one, proffering the platter.

He took one of the orange cocoons warily. It was warm, full of something that oozed out over his fingers. Seeing other people stuffing them into their mouths, he followed suit. The pod was filled with some sort of minced meat, laced with flavours he couldn't place. He took another before the servant could take the tray away.

'Delicious, aren't they?'

Jack found himself faced with a stocky man with a craggy face and intense dark eyes. He guessed him to be only a few years older than himself, perhaps over the cusp of thirty, but too young certainly for the hair loss that had stripped his head bare. His scalp, bald as a baby's, glistened with sweat. Jack had to swallow the cocoon almost whole to answer. 'They are.' He smiled guiltily, holding up the other.

'Lorenzo's cook is famous for his zucchini flowers. I believe half the grand families of Florence have tried to bribe him for his recipe. Without success.'

Jack nodded, picking out the key words to understand the gist of what the man was saying. Although Tuscan's roots were Latin, its flowers were distinctly different. After four months of intensive study, he knew the language broadly, but its nuances would take a lot longer. It had been a year in Seville before he'd felt confident understanding Castilian.

'By your accent I take it you are Lorenzo's guest? The Englishman?'

Jack inclined his head. 'Sir Ja— James Wynter.' Although he was growing accustomed to calling himself by this name, he still sometimes faltered. He'd given himself the alias Jack as a boy – named after a young robber in Lewes who'd escaped the gallows – in a vain rebellion on learning the lie of his parentage. He had begun using it again in Seville and, after more than four years, it was discomforting to be known again by his birth name, the sound of it quick to conjure thoughts of his mother. 'Word travels fast here.'

'Fast as rumour in a hive,' answered the man wryly, accepting his grip. 'I am Amerigo Vespucci.'

Jack snatched the name from the personal histories of notable guests Lorenzo had coached him on. A Florentine by birth, son of a rich lawyer, Amerigo had worked for some years as a clerk in the Medici household, but was now employed by Lorenzo's younger cousins, who resided in the adjacent palazzo.

'I was hoping we would meet. I'm always pleased to make new acquaintances from abroad. My masters' – Amerigo gestured to two young men standing close to Lorenzo –'Lorenzino and Giovanni di' Pierfrancesco de' Medici, have begun looking to expand their interests overseas.'

Jack had been told the two brothers had been taken in by Lorenzo when they were children after the death of their father, head of a secondary branch of the extensive Medici family. Lorenzino, the older of the two, with a round, sallow-hued face and rather bulbous, frog-like eyes, had hold of his brother's arm and was whispering in his ear. Giovanni, still in adolescence, with curly hair the colour of cinnamon and an arrogant tilt to his head, was scowling, trying to pull from his brother's grip.

'So, Sir James,' Amerigo continued with a smile, 'you have come here to learn the Florentine way of life?'

'Indeed. My father believes such knowledge will be beneficial for when I inherit his business. The signore has had dealings with my family and was generous enough to invite me to stay.'

'Your business is wool, so I am told? I hear your father is favoured by your new king, Henry Tudor? That he has secured preferential rates for exportation?'

Jack stuffed the second zucchini flower in his mouth to avoid an immediate answer. Lorenzo had invented these details about a noble father with affiliation to Tudor and a business in the wool trade – the lifeblood of Florence, which had nourished many of its grand families, including the Medici – as a reason to explain his honoured status here and to attract the men whose interest they hoped to entice, but he hadn't expected to be interrogated quite so soon on the ins and outs of this fiction.

When he nodded, mouth still full, Amerigo smiled. 'Well, there is no better place to understand Florence than in the court of il Magnifico.'

Jack was thinking how to steer the conversation away from himself when a man with white-grey hair and dressed in the sober black of the Dominican's habit approached. For a moment, he thought it was Marsilio, then realised his mistake. This man was younger, with an upright bearing and a composed, thoughtful face.

'Ah!' Amerigo smiled. 'Sir James, allow me to introduce my uncle, Fra Giorgio Antonio Vespucci.'

Looking closer, Jack realised he'd seen the man before, glimpsed through the window of Fra Vito's cell in San Marco, into which he slipped most mornings while it was still dark and the monks were at prayer. Fra Giorgio, from what he'd been told, had worked for Cosimo de' Medici as a scribe, translating manuscripts for the Academy. Later, after Lorenzo took in his cousins, the friar had become their private tutor.

'Amerigo, I believe Master Giovanni could benefit from your presence.'

Jack saw that the curly-haired adolescent had relinquished his older brother's grip and was talking to Lorenzo, gesturing animatedly at his cousin. Jack caught a few raised words – spoken too fast for him to catch the meaning – but it was clear Giovanni was irate.

'A little too much sun and wine,' observed the friar with a smile at Jack, although his pale blue eyes were tight beneath the neat fringe of his tonsure.

'Excuse me, Sir James,' said Amerigo. 'We will speak again.'

Grateful for the distraction, Jack downed his wine, watching as Amerigo cut in with a nod to Lorenzo and circled an arm around Giovanni's shoulders, drawing the younger man away. Jack saw Lorenzo's expression harden, but the look was gone in an instant and he was smiling at the next guest who stepped in to fill the gap. Clearly, everyone wanted their moment with il Magnifico.

Taking more wine from a passing servant, Jack was scanning the shadows for Ned and Amelot when an arm slipped through his and a voice sounded in his ear.

'A little drama for our entertainment.'

Starting in surprise, Jack spilled wine down the front of his doublet.

As he cursed, a slender young man with laughing grey eyes and wavy hair the colour of honey stepped in with a gasp of concern. 'Oh! Excuse me!' Pulling a silk cloth from the sleeve of his russet doublet, over which he wore an exquisite cape of pleated gold, the man went to dab at the spreading stain.

'It's all right,' Jack said, pushing his hand away and shaking wine from his fingers.

The man dangled the cloth for him to take, then snatched it aside. 'You can have it if you talk to me in your own tongue,' he said in English. 'You are, Sir James, yes?' He didn't wait for an answer. 'It has been so long. You must teach it to me. I fear I've forgotten every word!'

The lie was plain to them both, the man's speech perfect.

Most of the people Jack had met in Florence didn't like to speak anything other than Tuscan. Lorenzo was particularly proud of his language and vocal in his dislike of Latin, which he claimed was rigid and pompous, neither fit for love nor poetry. 'You've been to England?' he asked, accepting the cloth as the man pressed it into his palm.

'Oh, once,' the man replied airily. He frowned thoughtfully. 'Or was it twice?'

As he waved a dismissive hand, Jack caught a flash of gold. There – on one finger – a gold disc engraved with two serpents. Another man of the Academy. For a moment, out of sight and earshot of Lorenzo, Jack had an urge to ask if he had known his father. Would this man speak of Thomas Vaughan's secrets? Maybe he could learn everything he wanted, right here and now? No need to play this role he'd offered himself up for to get what he wanted from Lorenzo.

'Well, who can remember such things?' said the young man, breaking the moment. He grinned at Jack, arching an eyebrow. 'It is the girls I recall. Are the – what do they call them – the *stews*? Are they still there on Bankside? The Rose? The Swan?'

'They are.'

The young man shook his head, half closing his eyes. 'There was a woman in the Rose. Fortune, she called herself. I tell you, Sir James, she had a tongue that could—'

'Pico!'

Leaping round at the voice, the young man clapped to see Angelo Poliziano approaching, holding two goblets. 'Ah! You come just in time!' With a wink at Jack, he plucked the goblets from Poliziano's grip, handed one to Jack and kept the other for himself. 'Oh, don't look at me that way, my dear. You know me well enough by now. This is Sir James. I spilled his wine.'

'We've met.'

Jack nodded as Poliziano turned his gaze on him, the sudden switch back to Tuscan throwing him.

'Isn't he charming, Poliziano?' The young man stroked Jack's arm, smiling.

'I doubt he has even introduced himself, has he?' Poliziano addressed the question to Jack, but kept his eyes on the young man.

The man let out a merry burst of laughter. 'Indeed, I have not! Sir James, forgive my rudeness. My name is Giovanni Pico della Mirandola.' He gave a theatrical bow. 'And I am at your service.'

Jack doubted his sincerity, for now he had a name he knew the young man was Italian nobility – the son of a lord. Lorenzo counted him among his closest friends, but from all Jack had been told of him – that he'd studied at the universities of Padua, Paris and Florence, was a master of philosophy and a formidable orator who apparently spoke twenty languages – he had expected someone in the winter of his life. Giovanni Pico della Mirandola, with his angelic face and cleft chin, appeared barely out of adolescence.

'Now, do excuse us, Poliziano.' The young man slid his arm through Jack's insistently. 'There are many people Sir James must meet.' As he led Jack away, he grinned. 'Goodness, he will make me pay later!'

Jack glanced back to see Poliziano thrust a hand through his hair, before turning on his heel and vanishing down one of the paths. 'Giovanni, I—'

'Please, call me Pico.'

For the next hour, unable to extract himself from Pico's tight hold, Jack found himself swept up in a whirl of faces, names and conversations with artists and poets, heads of families, men of government, lawyers and silk merchants.

The garden was now packed with people. More food was being passed around – spiced sweetmeats and sugared almonds, saffron biscuits and balls of dyed red marzipan on golden shields, in imitation of the Medici coat of arms. Jugglers performed tricks with knives and fire, and music competed with voices that grew louder as the wine flowed.

At one point on his way through the tumult, Jack saw Ned and Amelot moving among the throng, an incongruous couple. He arched a questioning brow at his friend, who shook his head, telling him the girl hadn't yet seen the man from Carnival. Then, Pico was presenting him to another artist – Jack caught the name Sandro – whose works apparently graced most of the palazzi in the city.

The young man seemed to delight in introducing people in Tuscan, then gabbling away to Jack in English in front of them, telling him all their bad habits – the illicit affairs they were engaged in, the fortunes they'd lost in gambling, the telltale rash of pox he'd glimpsed in the bathhouse – while the poor souls smiled along in polite ignorance. If Lorenzo was magnetic, drawing men in, Pico was the opposite – a blazing star or a crackling fire. Something wild, uncontrollable.

Among the crowd, Jack glimpsed more caduceus rings and many other symbols besides – falcons and lions, keys and crosses – stitched on tunics, engraved in badges and embossed on pouches. In many ways, the gathering was reminiscent of the royal banquets and parties he'd attended as a page with his father in England. But, here, he had to remind himself that, with the exception of a few men like Pico, these weren't kings and lords, but bankers and merchants, descendants of men who had worked their way up from nothing, building empires out of wool and spices. To be among them, to see their status, conferred not by title or blood, but by their own endeavour, stirred something in him. Florence, perhaps, was a place where the indignity of his birth – a fact that had dogged him all his life – might be irrelevant.

He was starting to enjoy himself – the cool sweet wine, the flattery and attention, all these eminent men and beautiful women calling him *sir*, the glimpses of himself in mirrors, looking like a lord in his new silks – when a harsh voice sounded behind him.

'Sir James.'

Turning, dizzy from the wine and Pico's incessant chatter, Jack saw Lorenzo. Beside him stood a man with short black hair and a neat beard framing an angular jaw.

'If I may tear you from Pico's company, allow me to introduce Signor Marco Valori.'

'A pleasure to meet you, Sir James.'

As the man held out his hand, his cloak parted and Jack caught a flash of silver. There, pinned to the man's doublet, was a badge. It was fashioned in the head of a wolf.

8

Jack grasped the young man's hand, noting the telltale calluses along the ridge of Marco Valori's palm from the chafing of a sword hilt, the strength in his grip. 'I am pleased to meet you,' he murmured, feeling the intensity of Lorenzo's gaze lingering on him.

'Our host tells me you are from London?' said Marco, as Lorenzo departed, taking the effervescent Pico with him.

Jack nodded, eyes on that badge, winking in the flame-light. 'I am.' Gathering himself, he set his wine down on the edge of a fountain, from which rose a bronze Old Testament Judith, dragging back the hair of Holofernes to bare his neck for her sword. There was an inscription around the base:

Kingdoms fall through luxury, cities rise through virtues.
Behold the neck of pride, severed by the hand of humility.

'Signor Lorenzo mentioned that your family, like mine, is in the wool trade?'

'Cloth, to be precise,' Marco corrected. 'My family are members of the Calimala, not the Lana.'

'Calimala. Yes.' Jack kicked himself. He'd been told this – and that the cloth importers and wool-weavers were rivals, each proud of their different trades and their place within the city. Of Florence's twenty-one guilds, the Arte della Calimala claimed to be the oldest, but the Arte della Lana, the guild of the wool-weavers, had risen to vie for position as one of the most powerful. 'My apologies.'

Marco smiled, a cleft appearing in his cheek, making him look boyish. 'The Calimala, the Lana, the Arte della Seta, the Vaiai e

Pellicciai. Four guilds, all involved in the same business. And we wonder why visitors to our city become confused.'

Jack smiled along with him, but glanced across the milling crowds, searching for Ned and Amelot.

'I am told you are here to learn more about the trade?'

'Yes, in preparation for when I take on my family's business.'

Marco nodded sympathetically. 'I know my time will come too. But for now I am content to enjoy my freedom. Tell me, Sir James, are you able to take pleasure in sport? With your friends?' The dimpled smile was back. 'With women?' Marco sipped his wine. 'Or do you wear a husband's chains?'

'My wife died, bearing a child.' The lie came easily, all part of his new history. Lorenzo had said these men, well travelled and worldly-wise, would know it unusual for an Englishman of his age and status to be unmarried. By contrast, he'd been told, while it was common in Florence for girls to marry young, men would shirk the bond for as long as possible, content to live at home, playing at boys deep into adulthood. Jack thought he had detected wistfulness in Lorenzo's tone, since he himself had been pressed into marriage with Clarice in adolescence.

'My apologies,' Marco said solemnly. 'Forgive me.'

'It was some time ago. Another life.' Jack thought of Grace – her hand slipping from his. He had turned one last time on the road out of Lewes to see her still standing there, watching him go. Did she think of him or had her father married her to another man twice her age and half her worth?

He returned to the present as Marco asked him how England fared under its new king. He seemed genuinely interested, but less obviously eager than Amerigo Vespucci, less willing, perhaps, to step on to Lorenzo's territory. Jack answered his questions as best he could, but his mind felt foggy from the wine and he couldn't take his gaze off that wolf's head, watching him through slanted eyes, Lorenzo's voice in his mind.

I will open the door. But you must walk through it.

As Marco broke from his questioning to take a fresh goblet from a servant, Jack seized his chance. 'That is an interesting badge. Your family's crest?'

Marco glanced down. 'No. The symbol of a company I belong to.'

'A guild?'

'More a fraternity.' Marco smiled, then drank. 'I must commend you on your aptitude with our language, Sir James. How long have you been in the city?'

'My father insisted I learn, back in London.' Jack nodded to the badge, determined to keep the conversation on track. 'In England we consider wolves a bane. Ill luck and trouble.'

'Not so for Romulus and Remus.'

Jack thought of the story: the twins, cast into the Tiber by a member of their own family, found and nurtured by the wolf. 'I suppose so,' he admitted.

'By suckling the she-wolf the brothers survived to become the founders of Rome.'

Marco cocked his head. 'And do wolves not possess other commendable qualities? The unity of the pack. Strength. Fearlessness.'

'You are soldiers, then?' Jack knew the answer, but he needed to get Marco to open up – show him a way in.

'Not all of us have served in war. But, yes, we are adept in arms.'

'I fought in my father's command. In the wars between York and Lancaster.'

There was interest in Marco's eyes at this, but just then someone in the crowd hailed him. He raised his goblet with a nod.

Jack plunged in, not wanting to lose his attention. 'I should like to hear more about this company of yours. Tell me, can any man join?'

Marco's smile remained, but the interest vanished from his eyes. Jack knew he'd lost him.

'Sir James, it has been a pleasure. Please excuse me.' With that he was gone, slipping into the press.

Jack seized his goblet and went to drink, then tossed the dregs into the fountain, cursing his incompetence.

'He isn't the one.'

Jack turned to see Ned had emerged from the crowd. 'He isn't?'

Ned shook his head. 'Amelot doesn't recognise him.'

'Lorenzo said the company has many members. More, he suspects, than he even knows of. The chance of him being one of those who took Amaury was slim.'

'How did you fare?' Ned asked, studying his expression.

'It was a start,' Jack said shortly, not wanting to admit he'd made a mess of the introduction. Was there a way back? Might he try again?

He scanned the throng of people, seeking Valori, but fixed instead on Lorenzo, who was talking intently to a man with an extravagant mane of grey hair and a hard, rugged face. The man was shaking his head, his flushed face stormy. His voice was loud, thick-tongued with drink. People were turning to stare, others moving to get a better look. Someone stepped in, tried to soothe the man, but he shrugged them off, stumbling as he did so. Lorenzo seemed calm, holding up a hand to halt his bodyguard, Black Martin, and the others who had appeared, but Jack noted the tension in his shoulders and his wide-footed stance – the stance of a man who expected to have to defend himself.

'Did you arrange another meeting? Are you in?'

Jack glanced at Ned, still looking at him expectantly. 'Wait here,' he told his friend, not wanting his scrutiny right now.

'Where are you going?'

Jack didn't answer, heading for the arched doors that led into the palace. He needed to get away from the whirl of voices and faces, clear his head, think how best to approach Valori again. Ahead, in the archway, was a young woman in a silvery-grey gown. He had seen her earlier, sitting with Lorenzo's daughters at the fountain. Her eyes were fixed in Lorenzo's direction. After a moment, she broke her stare to glance quickly around her, then slipped in through the doors and disappeared.

Excusing himself through a press of men, all craning their heads towards Lorenzo and the man now arguing with him, Jack entered the archway in her wake. The inner courtyard was cool and dark, David rising into shadow. Just a few servants moved between the pillars, ghosts in their featureless woollen robes, empty trays stacked in their arms. Outside, through the main entrance, Jack saw grooms standing talking, waiting with horses for the wealthier guests to leave. Heading for the wide marble staircase, he caught a shimmer of silver and saw the young woman disappearing up the first flight. There was a sweet smell lingering in the air, a scent that took Jack back unexpectedly to a warm winter's day in Seville. Orange blossom.

After a pause, he began to climb. The woman wasn't a member of Lorenzo's immediate family, all of whom had been pointed out to him, and her fine clothes told him she wasn't a servant. A governess perhaps, or a friend of the family.

On the first floor, a passageway stretched in either direction. One way led past the dining room to the bedrooms of Lorenzo's children and the chambers of household officials, the other to Lorenzo's private set of rooms where he had changed for the party. Jack moved on, climbing the stairs that ascended past the kitchens, stores and servants' quarters on the third floor, then up to the fourth. Earlier in the week, Lorenzo had installed him and Amelot up here in a small chamber, which opened on to a terrace, affording a breathtaking view over the rooftops of Florence that inspired a rare smile of joy in the mute girl, who'd made herself a nest in the chamber's empty storeroom.

Exploring the palazzo over the past few days, Jack had found himself in a bewildering maze of interconnecting suites and antechambers, shadowy mezzanine levels, grand corridors lined with statues, dusty stores and a private chapel where Lorenzo prayed daily, displaying a genuine piety, despite the Academy's unorthodox ideas. While the first three floors were devoted to opulent reception rooms and living quarters, most of the top floor was occupied by an enormous armoury, siege engines and weapons gathering dust in the gloom, and the Medici Library, which he'd not yet been permitted to glimpse, but which he guessed would be filled with the thousands of books and manuscripts Cosimo and Lorenzo had collected over the years – their Gathering of the knowledge of the world, scattered in the time of the Flood.

By the time he reached his room, through the hushed dark of the palazzo, the noise of the party fading behind him, his head was already clearer. After splashing his face with water from a jug left by a servant, he felt positively fresh, but the question of how best to recapture Marco Valori's interest remained.

He was making his way back down, lost in thought, when he saw the doors to Lorenzo's private rooms were ajar. Pausing in the passage Jack heard faint footfalls within. Papi? Or Lorenzo himself? Perhaps the signore would have some advice as to how he should proceed? Turning from the stairs, Jack knocked. No servant opened the doors and he guessed they were all downstairs, attending to the guests. Tentatively, he entered the *Sala Grande*.

The hall was lined with benches built into the walls, backed with walnut panelling. Paintings were hung the length of the room, many of Hercules: battling a snarling lion, striking writhing heads from the Hydra, shooting his bow at a storm of monstrous birds. It was lit by a feeble glow filtering through the windows on the courtyard side. The hum of the party came muted through the shutters. At the far end, the door to Lorenzo's bedchamber stood open, the buttery glow of candlelight spilling out.

'Signore?'

The creak of a floorboard was the only answer.

Entering, Jack scanned the magnificent bedchamber, eyes moving over the gilded mirror where earlier he'd watched his visage change as Papi dressed him; across gilt-framed paintings and marble busts, an imposing canopied bed heaped with silks and perfumed pillows and a daybed draped in glossy pelts, the set of wooden steps that climbed to a mezzanine level obscured by shadows where Papi slept. He could see no one, although the candles fluttered as if disturbed, sparking off countless crystal pitchers, jade goblets and gemstone ornaments displayed in cupboards, shelves and alcoves that made the chamber look like a mine seamed with precious veins. At the far end, another door led into Lorenzo's private study, which only a handful of men seemed permitted to enter. Jack hadn't seen inside.

The door was closed. As Jack approached, he heard a noise come muffled through the door. It sounded like someone singing. But the song was strange, the words rising and falling over one another, sometimes off-key. More a chant than a song. He didn't recognise the language. It sounded like a man, but was too faint for him to be sure. He moved closer, curiosity drawing him.

'What are you doing in here?'

Jack whipped round to see Marsilio Ficino behind him. 'I – I thought I heard Signor Lorenzo,' he blurted, his face warming under the priest's baleful stare. 'I was hoping to speak to him about Marco Valori.'

'Signor Marco has left,' said Marsilio, glancing at the closed door to the study, eyes narrowing.

'Left?' Jack's heart sank.

'The party is coming to a close. The signore is downstairs, saying goodbye to his guests. But,' added the priest gruffly, 'I am sure he will be keen to hear how you fared in your conversation.'

'Of course,' murmured Jack, following the priest out into the *Sala Grande*.

Before they reached the double doors, he caught a whiff of something sweet and realised he could smell orange blossom, faint in the air of the chamber.

9

Passing through the shade of a gatehouse tower, the company re-emerged in the sun's white glare. Ahead, the bridge Harry had glimpsed on their approach to Córdoba stretched before them, its massive piers butting into the broad expanse of the Guadalquivir, whose course they had followed from Seville. Mills churned along the banks, spray glinting from the wheels like sparks from whetstones.

Don Garcia, the official who had met them on the road that morning with six royal guards, turned with a smile for Harry, spreading his hand to the bridge. 'Built by Romans,' he called, clenching his fist. 'Very mighty.'

Ahead, beyond another fortified gate, the city walls reared, encircling a forest of spires and towers, beyond which rose a ridge of hills, simmering in the heat.

'Which is the palace?' Harry asked Rodrigo, riding beside him on a piebald courser.

'There,' his travelling companion answered, pointing to an imposing group of sand-coloured buildings looming behind crenellated battlements, just along the river. 'The Alcázar.'

Harry fixed on the buildings with a surge of anticipation. He had been waiting four months for this. After celebrating the birth of their sixth child, a daughter, Princess Katherine of Aragon, the monarchs had been remarkably itinerant in their courtly affairs. Harry had sent a message to Henry Tudor, informing the king of his arrival in Seville, but with Rodrigo gone for several weeks attending to business in Jaén there had been little for Harry to do but linger in his host's house; hiding from the scorched heat of the days, wandering the streets in the airless evenings, trailing from the din of the docks to the hush of the alleys that wound through the former Jewish Quarter, whose inhabitants had been given the choice to convert to Christianity or leave the city. Any *conversos* – those accused of returning to their faith in secret – were now subject to the public ordeal of the auto-da-fé and the purifying fires of the Inquisition.

Bored, restless, he had occupied himself with food, gorging on dates, salt-sweet meats, sugared almonds and spiced wines. Peter had had to find a tailor to let out his doublets and lengthen the laces of his hose. He'd even taken to dipping his morning bread in the piquant olive oils he found in the market, until Rodrigo returned and chastised him for the habit, warning him only Moors and Jews ate the oil, which was used by the Spanish for soap, and that the Inquisitors were always on the lookout for telltale signs of the enemies of Christianity that lurked among them.

Harry dug his heels into Nieve, the placid white mare Rodrigo had loaned him, eager to be about his business at last and calm the worries that had nipped at him in the wait. King Henry's orders had never strayed far from his thoughts. Neither had the unpalatable prospect of failing the man.

Ahead, at the city gate, guards were shouting at people to move aside, nodding in respect to Don Garcia and his party. Harry smiled to himself as he saw merchants dragging braying mules out of the way and men and women hastening left and right to let their company pass. This was more what he'd been expecting from his new role.

Once through, they turned left, following the Alcázar's walls, until they entered another gateway, guarded by men in red and black livery with gold-pommelled swords. The carts – one loaded with the chests that had accompanied Harry from London, two others filled with the belongings of Rodrigo and his men – trundled in behind, wheels rattling on the flagstones. In a sandy courtyard, Don Garcia invited them to dismount, calling for grooms to see to their horses and servants to bring refreshments.

Leaving his secretary, Peter, to deal with the chests, Harry stepped into a patch of shade, taking a goblet that was proffered. There was a damp, perfumed cloth, too, to wipe the dust and sweat from his sun-stinged face. Around him voices rose, streams of Castilian out of which he could pick only a few words. Peter had been teaching him, but Harry had never settled easily into schooling and had cut short most of the lessons, irritated by Peter's patience, which he took for condescension.

'Sir Harry,' Don Garcia called, motioning him through the crowd. 'Don Rodrigo.'

Draining the wine, Harry thrust the empty goblet at a servant. Rodrigo moved in at his side, a keen spring in his own step. The hidalgo was not here merely to introduce Harry to his mistress, the queen, but to commit himself to the war in the Kingdom of Granada now the new season of campaigning had begun. It was said King Ferdinand had already marched east into the Nasrid emirate in the early spring. To this end, Rodrigo had brought weapons, armour and the ten men: three knights, caballeros they were called, four infantrymen, two servants and a groom, who would accompany him to the front line.

They followed Don Garcia into another sun-dazzled courtyard, this one filled with orange trees, trilling birds flickering in and out of their green depths. A channel of water cut between colourful mosaics, leading to a bubbling fountain. An arcaded passageway beyond brought them into the palace proper, its cool stone hallways a blessed relief. They passed officials, well dressed and imperious, hurrying servants and a few dour-faced men in black robes Harry recognised as Inquisitors. He had seen processions of them in Seville, leading condemned men and women in the painted robes and pointed hoods of heretics from their austere castle across the river to the auto-da-fé. The black stains of Islam and Judaism, that ever threatened to seep into the blessed shroud of Christianity, could only be cleansed by those fires.

At the end of a vaulted passage, the ceiling painted with intricate configurations of stars and crescent moons, was a set of doors studded with iron. Outside, two guards stood sentry, eyeing them as they approached. There was a bench along one wall, where Don Garcia gestured Harry and Rodrigo to sit while he spoke to the guards. He returned after a moment with a relaxed smile which Harry, who'd remained standing, found instantly irritating.

'Please, sir, rest your feet. Her Highness has been engaged all morning with visitors. They have been crowding in to see her since her arrival here. You will be summoned when she is finished with her guest. I will have your gifts brought here.'

Harry sat reluctantly, watching Don Garcia head off. Hadn't he been kept waiting long enough? Rodrigo, already seated, was brushing horse dust from his doublet. Harry glanced towards the studded doors, hearing a raised voice on the other side. After a pause, he stood and paced, stretching his saddle-stiff muscles. The guards followed him with their eyes.

The raised voice behind the doors belonged to a man, the tone hard, grating out the words. The language was Castilian, but although the speaker was slower, more deliberate with his words – as if it weren't his first tongue – Harry still only caught the odd phrase. Something about time? Something taking too long? A female voice cut in. Now, the words were fast, a forceful torrent. When she'd finished the man spoke again, his voice lower, as if he'd been chastised. There followed other voices, mumblings and murmurs, then the thud of footsteps approaching. The doors opened and a man strode through.

He was an arresting figure, well over six feet tall and brawny as an ox, with a ruddy, sun-worn face and a messy crop of white-blond hair. The man met his gaze, his ice-blue eyes narrowing, before he marched away down the passage.

'He looks as mad as he sounds, does he not?' murmured Rodrigo, appearing at Harry's side.

'Who is he?'

'The one I told your king about. The sailor with the dream.' Rodrigo smirked. 'Or, as we call him, Cristóbal Colón el Loco.'

Harry turned quickly, but the man had gone. In his place, Peter had appeared with Don Garcia, leading a train of servants bearing the chests. *God damn!* Why hadn't he taken the time to study Castilian? He might have just learned something useful. He realised he would have to start paying more attention to Peter if he was to accomplish his task here. The thought that he'd wasted so much time doing nothing but filling his stomach and had fallen foul at the first opportunity made his palms sweat.

'Sir Harry Vaughan? Don Rodrigo?'

A man in a fur-trimmed robe and jewelled collar was standing expectantly in the doorway. Forcing his attention from the passage Christopher Columbus had vanished down, Harry stepped forward, steeling himself.

The chamber was shadowed and airy, a cool haven. Patterned tiles decorated the floor and parts of the walls, while at the borders of the ceiling bands of pale stone had been carved into complex whorls and knots. Harry had seen similar work on many of the buildings in

Seville, a legacy, he'd been told, from the time when the Moors had ruled over their vast caliphate of al-Andalus. Over the last four hundred years that territory had been steadily eroded by the forces of the *Reconquista*, until now only the Kingdom of Granada remained. Other than this decoration, the room itself was surprisingly bare, certainly in comparison to the Painted Chamber back in Westminster Palace. There were no tapestries or gilt-framed paintings, no grand bed or statues. It made Harry think of a shell, beautiful, but empty.

Along one side of the room were several desks, littered with the paraphernalia of administration: rolls of parchment, stacks of paper, inkwells, seals. Robed figures clustered around them talking quietly, while others sat, scratching away with quills. A few glanced at Rodrigo and Harry, then returned to their tasks. Ahead, on a raised dais, the steps of which were flanked by more armed guards, two thrones stood beneath a canopy of gold. The back of the canopy was embroidered with red lions and gold castles on a shield, capped with a crown and mantled by a black eagle: the royal arms of Castile and Aragon, united fifteen years ago by the marriage of Isabella and Ferdinand. One of the thrones was empty. On the other sat a woman.

Queen Isabella I of Castile was a surprise to Harry. The commanding female voice he'd heard through the door – and all Rodrigo had told him of the queen – had painted in his mind a picture of a tall, darkly formidable woman. The figure on the throne was short and rather plump, with rosy cheeks and a neat little bow of a mouth. From the encirclement of her simple gold crown her auburn hair – telling a tale of her Lancastrian ancestry – fell in tresses almost to her waist, covering her wine-red mantle and gown, both stiff with brocade. Around her neck she wore a gold cross, with a single red jewel at the centre.

As Rodrigo approached the dais, removing his cap and bowing low, Harry hastened to follow suit. Rodrigo spoke for a few moments. When his eyes flicked to him, Harry realised the introduction had been made. Now, it was his turn. Henry Tudor slipped into his mind as he stepped forward. He could almost feel the king's hand on his shoulder, long fingers pinching his skin, one cold eye on him, the other roving as if seeking his thoughts.

'My lady,' he began, tremulous, and cleared his throat. 'I bring greetings from His Grace, King Henry of England, to you and Lord Ferdinand.' Harry paused as Rodrigo translated for him. 'His Grace thanks you most sincerely for the gifts you sent upon his coronation. In return, he sends you these offerings in the spirit of friendship.' Harry looked to Peter and his servant, Hervey, who were setting down the chests at the foot of the dais on Don Garcia's instructions. As Peter bowed and opened the lids for the queen to inspect their glittering contents, Harry was relieved to see everything seemed intact after the jolting journey. The only things missing were a pretty, jewel-handled dagger he had slipped quietly in among his own possessions and the two royal hunting dogs. One had expired soon after their arrival in Seville and the other had become so morose at the death of its companion, pacing and howling around Rodrigo's courtyard, Harry had decided to omit it from the presentation.

Isabella gave the chests a cursory glance, but her focus was back on him almost immediately. Harry found her unwavering stare unsettling. He wasn't used to being looked at so intently by a woman. His mother had died when he was a boy and other than the nurses and governesses who'd raised him, his only real experiences of women were his weepy young sister, Ann, to whom he'd never been close, and the blank-eyed whores he'd pleasured himself upon in the stews of Bankside.

Isabella spoke after a pause, addressing Rodrigo but keeping her gaze on Harry. When she was done, Rodrigo translated.

'King Henry has sent you to be his emissary in our court?'

'If it pleases you, my lady,' answered Harry, gesturing to Peter, who swiftly tugged the papers, decorated with Henry's seal, from the bag he carried.

The official who had led them into the chamber took the documents from the secretary. After scanning the papers, the official nodded up at the queen, who spoke once again through the voice of Rodrigo.

'We have more need, Sir Harry, for men of war than men of diplomacy, as we advance upon the last of the infidels' territory.'

Harry's chest constricted. Was the queen going to send him home? Deny him the role of ambassador? He had been told this was a risk, but hadn't for one moment entertained the thought that it might actually happen. All these months and all he had to show for it were a thickened waistline and a peeling nose? And just when he'd come close enough to Columbus to touch the man? If he was sent home now, failing to accomplish yet another of Henry Tudor's orders, he might as well throw himself into the ocean on the way.

At once, he was back in England, three years ago, standing, dazed and silent, as the lawyer read him the Act of Attainder.

By the charge of treason, Sir Thomas Vaughan has lost the right to pass on property and titles to you, his heir. Your father's estates are hereby forfeit to the crown.

That had been a black day indeed, the world tumbling away from under him with a lurch and a drop as all he'd ever dreamed he would be was snatched from him with his father's last breath.

Henry, who rewarded him at his coronation with the restoration of his inheritance, hadn't openly threatened him, but Harry knew the man well enough to sense the king's warning, implicit, the day he'd set sail from the Port of London. *I made you, Harry*. His tone and eyes had said. *Just as I can unmake you*.

And this time, if he lost estates and title, there wouldn't be some ragged band of rebels for Harry to join; some bold uprising on which he might scrabble his way to fortune on the blood and bodies piling up around him. There would be nothing but poverty and ignominy. He'd be disgraced; worse than a scoundrel, a beggar or a bastard. Worse than – *Wynter*.

He went to speak, but his mouth was dust dry.

Isabella cut into his silence. 'Others of your countrymen have harkened to our cause these past months and we have welcomed their bows and swords for the fight. Indeed, one such company has recently joined Lord Ferdinand at Loja.'

After translating, Rodrigo paused then said something to the queen. He looked meaningfully at Harry. 'I told Her Highness that you, too, have distinguished yourself in battle.'

Harry nodded quickly. 'Yes. I – well – I fought alongside Henry Tudor when he took England from King Richard, my lady.'

This wasn't true. While Henry faced down Richard's forces on Redemore Plain, Harry had been delivering young Edward, struggling and pleading, back into the Tower to join his brother, where they would meet their fate. He thought of Sir Edward Woodville, their war-scarred uncle, cornering him in the revelry of the king's coronation, torch-fire in the man's eyes, the drunken roars of jubilant men grazing Harry's ears as he stammered like an idiot through Woodville's questions about what had happened to his nephews and why he hadn't been at Redemore Plain.

But he *had* spent months in Tudor's company in Brittany and France while the war was being planned, and before that had fought in

Buckingham's rebellion; albeit a rebellion that had failed and seen them scattered into the depths of a Cornish winter, half starved and hiding in caves. 'It would be a great honour for me to serve you,' he added, thinking of Rodrigo telling him how he'd risen from a squire to become one of the queen's favoured vassals. Perhaps, in a similar position here in her court, he might come to earn her trust? Enough to fulfil his mission here? She certainly hadn't sounded pleased in her conversation with the sailor. It might not take much to sway her opinion against him? He felt suddenly buoyed up by the thought. 'My sword is yours, my lady,' he added, bowing deeply.

At Rodrigo's translation, the hint of a smile flickered at Isabella's red lips.

'I was going to say, Sir Harry, that despite our need for warriors our friendship with England is also important to us and you are most welcome in our court. But if you wish to join me and my husband in our holy conquest, then your sword will be gratefully accepted.'

Isabella added something to Rodrigo that the man did not translate. Instead, he bowed low and, when he raised his head, Harry saw the hidalgo's coal-dark eyes were shining.

Isabella addressed Don Garcia, who gestured them towards the doors. 'Please, my lady wishes you to rest, take food and drink. She asks that you join her tomorrow at her prayers; that God may bless your alliance and this new season of her righteous campaign.'

Harry found himself being escorted through the doors. Glancing back, he saw Isabella talking with her official. He wished he'd been able to ask about Christopher Columbus, but this, clearly, was not the time. At least he'd been accepted, although for what, exactly, he wasn't quite sure.

'Now, you shall enjoy true Castilian hospitality,' Rodrigo said as they followed Garcia down the passage.

Harry noticed that the light in Rodrigo's eyes had not dimmed. 'What did she say to you, at the end?'

'She told me a company will be leaving in the next fortnight, carrying supplies to the royal camp at Loja. And that very soon I shall have the opportunity to avenge my father's death.' Rodrigo gripped his shoulder. 'We will both have the chance to honour ourselves. Welcome, Sir Harry, to God's war.'

10

The Ponte Vecchio seethed with people. They inched between the shops that lined its length in a sluggish stream, disturbed by eddies of movement as, here and there, someone struggled against the tide. Between the statue of Mars, rising behind him, and the bridge's far end, all Jack could see were shuffling bodies. They clammed around him, an oppressive mass of nudging elbows, spit-flecked coughs and sour sweat. Calls of traders sounded, butchers leaning from their doors to announce the price of pigs, freshly slaughtered; copper sting of blood on the air, a slop of guts swirling in the river below.

It was still early, but already it was hot. Not the scorched heat Jack had known in Seville, or the blushing warmth of England and France, but muggy, the air thick, clouded with insects. As a line of perspiration threaded down his cheek, he swiped it away, not taking his eyes from the blue silk cap, banded with gold, that bobbed several bodies ahead.

That morning, poised in the shade of a shuttered shop, gaze fixed on the arched doors of Santa Croce, he had alighted on the gaudy hat only briefly, almost dismissing it, eyes scanning the men and women pouring out through the doors, the church bells hammering in his ears, before the man wearing it emerged from the crowd and, beneath its bright brow, Jack had recognised the face of Marco Valori, his angular jaw framed by a neat dark beard.

The relief he'd felt on seeing the man had escaped him in a sharp breath and Ned had turned expectantly.

'What? Do you see him?'

Ned had straightened as Jack motioned to the young man making his way across the piazza, then turned and whistled down the alley the shop bordered, attracting Adam's attention. 'It's him! Get her set.'

'Don't lose him,' Ned had murmured, as Jack had stepped out into the molten gold of the early morning.

Jack had no intention of doing any such thing.

It was a month since he'd been introduced to Marco Valori at the party and failed to make any inroad into the Court of Wolves; a month of restless lingering and fruitless planning, listening to the grumbling of his companions in the stale dusk of the Fig tavern, unable to sleep at nights in the hot little room at the top of the palazzo, airless even with the door open on to the terrace, trailing the streets with Amelot, hoping the girl would spot the man she'd recognised in the bustle of the city's twisting streets. But with no sightings of Amaury's abductor and no sign of Marco at either his family's wool-washing factories or the church Lorenzo had told him the young man attended for Mass, Jack had started to panic.

These past weeks, he had only been granted fleeting glimpses of Lorenzo: sweeping through the inner courtyard followed by a flock of clerks and notaries, at the end of a corridor talking intently with Poliziano, disappearing through the doors of his private chambers with Marsilio Ficino. It seemed there were many things to occupy Florence's ruler: elections in the Signoria, the recent marriage of his eldest daughter, Lucrezia, and the city's greatest celebration of the year – the Feast of St John the Baptist – which had surpassed even the riotous merriment of Carnival, with tournaments, banquets and a wild horse race through the streets. But, after their last meeting, Jack had been left in no doubt that if he didn't make progress soon, Lorenzo would tire of allowing him and his men to live at his expense and find another way into the secretive company to hunt down whoever had taken Amaury and had – perhaps – infiltrated his household.

His host wasn't the only one growing frustrated with the wait. Just last night Valentine had mentioned Spain again, offhand in another conversation, but, still, it had made Jack's nerves tighten. All this time, learning the language, embedding himself in the city and the fiction of his new life? If turning from what he had come here in search of had been unpalatable back in February, it now seemed impossible. He'd walked too far down this road to be dragged back to take a different, unwanted, route that would lead to another life entirely, away from what he'd been promised if he succeeded here. Even now, his dreams would throw him, sweating, from fire-bruised hells, and every unbidden memory or thought of his mother or father was tangled with the questions that kept him trapped in a past grown murky and confusing; everything that made him – *him* – thrown into doubt.

Heart hammering with weeks of pent-up anticipation, ignoring the anonymous crowds that pushed against him, Jack kept his focus fixed on Marco Valori crossing the bridge just ahead of him, eyes drifting only briefly to the slight figure in grey, who'd been trailing Marco closely since he'd passed out of the shadow of Mars, and was now only one pace behind.

Ahead, a man halted abruptly, catching someone passing with a call. As they paused to talk, they became rocks around which the tide parted grudgingly. Jack cursed, losing sight of Marco in the shift of bodies. He pressed forward, ignoring the muttered gripes. Suddenly, someone stepped into his path; a glitter of tawny eyes, the stretch of a hand and the wink of a blade disappearing beneath grey folds of cloak. He grasped hold of the purse Amelot stuffed into his palm as she slipped past. At the same time Jack caught sight of the blue hat again, slightly to his right now, but still close.

'Hey!'

A few people glanced round at his shout, but the girl was gone, leaving no sign of who or what Jack was yelling at.

'*Thief!*'

More people turned at this, including Marco Valori, just as Jack lifted the purse.

The young man's eyes alighted on it and widened. 'You!' he shouted angrily, starting forward. He pulled up short as he reached Jack, brow pinching in confused recognition. 'Sir . . .?'

'James,' Jack added for him, discouraged by what little impression he'd clearly made on the man at the party. He held out the purse: soft blue leather, its cut strings dangling. 'Is this yours? I saw someone snatch it. I had no idea it was you.'

'Who?' urged Marco, eyes flicking over the people now squeezing around them.

'I tried to catch him, but he dropped it and ran.'

Marco, an angry flush colouring his cheeks, was still staring past him as if thinking to go after the thief, but the purse extended in Jack's hand and the press of people dissuaded him. Amelot had chosen her moment well. 'A pox on the son of a bitch,' Marco murmured, before turning his attention to Jack. 'Sir James, of course. From

London.' He took the purse with a tight-lipped smile. 'Thank fortune you were here.' He tied the strings to the front of the decorated belt that pulled in his brocaded doublet, close to a gold-handled stiletto. 'How are you faring in the House of Medici?'

The question was exactly what Jack had been hoping for. The bait, thanks to Amelot's light fingers, had been taken. Now to reel him in. 'To be honest, Signor Marco, since fortune has brought us together, I would appreciate some advice.'

'Oh?' said Marco, eyes flitting in the direction he'd been walking. 'Well, I'm—'

'It's about my host,' pressed Jack. 'It's about Signor Lorenzo.'

Marco's gaze sharpened on him. 'Yes?'

Jack tensed in expectation, but kept his expression neutral, glancing at the stream of bodies shuffling around them. 'Is there somewhere we might talk?'

After a moment, Marco nodded. 'I haven't broken my fast yet. There's a place in Oltrarno I frequent. Will you join me?'

As Marco led the way through the crowds, Jack felt his anticipation pull tighter, knotting in his chest. That sharpness in Marco's eyes had roused him.

Lorenzo had hoped the lies they had spun around him – a young nobleman on a sojourn in Florence, with a father in the wool trade and royal connections – would be a tempting enough prospect for the Court of Wolves, many of whose older members had made their fortunes in wool, before rising export rates in England had begun to curtail such opportunities. But although other men, like Amerigo Vespucci, had sniffed keenly around him at the party, drawn by the story, Marco had seemed only politely interested. In deciding how to approach the man again, Jack had opted to take a different tack.

Ahead, across the river, the red dome of Santo Spirito rose above the haze that shrouded the cramped and dirty district of Oltrarno. Earlier, when the bells had rung to end curfew, the eleven gates in the city's vast ring of walls – five miles around and set with forty-five watchtowers – had rumbled open and men and women of the outer districts had filed in, heading for the cloth factories, drying barns, tanneries and workshops of their masters. The narrow thoroughfare that ran alongside the Arno was filled with the rattle of cartwheels and the clop of clogs. Marco strode along it to a row of tall, narrow buildings, their façades dappled by the sunlight dancing off the river.

One door was open into a shadowy, vaulted interior. Outside it, a round, red-faced little man in an apron stood talking to someone by a bench. At the sight of Marco he smiled broadly. Nodding his comrade farewell, the man gestured them enthusiastically towards the bench. 'Signor Marco! Good day to you. Come, come! I will bring wine. And food, yes?'

'Please, Tommaso.'

As the man bustled in through the door, Marco sat on the bench, his doublet fanning out around him. The silver wolf badge pinned above his heart glinted in the sunlight. Jack sat beside him, trying to keep his gaze away so as not to afford it any importance.

'So? What advice are you seeking, Sir James?'

Jack paused as if considering his next words, which he'd been running through his head for weeks. 'At the signore's party we talked briefly about our fathers – the responsibilities we would inherit as their sons?' He went on at Marco's nod. 'I am honoured to know I will bear my father's mantle, but, in truth, it weighs heavy on me. I miss my friends. My comrades-in-arms. I did not realise how much until that night – hearing you speak of your company. The strength and unity of the pack?' He shook his head, feigned chagrin. 'I apologise if my questions seemed impertinent.'

Marco waved the apology away as Tommaso hurried out, carrying a cracked glazed jug from which he poured two goblets of wine, beaming as he handed them to Marco and Jack.

Jack continued as the man disappeared inside. 'I was just hopeful of finding a friend here. Someone to watch my back.' He waited when the portly man reappeared, humming as he brought a tray laden with cheese, black cherries and figs bursting with ripeness.

'This is good, Tommaso, thank you,' Marco said when asked if they needed anything else. 'Go on,' he prompted Jack, plucking a cherry from the tray. Two gold rings adorned his fingers, one displaying a knuckle-sized ruby.

Jack caught sight of his own hand as he lifted his goblet to drink. The white band left by his father's ring had disappeared in the Italian sun. In some senses he welcomed its fading. It felt like a clean start: a way to come at his father anew, look upon him with clear eyes as he sought the truth about the man who had sired him.

'Signor Lorenzo has been extremely generous to me as his guest and I do not wish to sound ungracious . . .' Jack let another pause do its work. 'But I do not know if I should put my faith in him? I am well aware that he hopes to gain business from my father, of course. That is why he has agreed to host me. But can I trust him with my father's company? The company I am to inherit? I have heard things that make me wonder.'

This wasn't far from the truth. Although the Medici family were clearly honoured as princes in the city, their arms and images everywhere, Jack had sensed wariness, even hostility among some citizens; a cold mutter from a shopkeeper when asked where he was staying, a narrowing of the eyes or sudden silence from a formerly garrulous innkeeper or butcher.

Marco spat a cherry stone into one of the napkins Tommaso had left, then dabbed at his lips. He took up his goblet, swirling it contemplatively. 'You would do well to be wary in this city, Sir James. There are many wolves here.' He drank. 'Some may fit your English perception better than others.'

'Should I be concerned? I mean, about the soundness of the signore's promises? His word?'

Laughter rose from a group of young men on the banks nearby, washing wool in the river. There was a sour tang on the air from the horse urine the fleeces had been soaked in.

Marco looked out over the green water, his eyes – a deep, almost indigo blue – narrowing as they filled with sunlight. 'Tell me, Sir James, in your time at the palazzo, have you noticed if your host is experiencing any troubles?'

Jack's heart skipped at this. What did Marco mean? Could he be talking about Amaury? The intercepted letter and the priest's abduction? 'Troubles?'

Marco's voice remained light. 'Any difficulties in his businesses? With his finances? Any uncertainties at all? You must know the Medici were forced to close their bank in London some years ago?'

Jack nodded, thinking of the *Trinity*'s expeditions, ordered by King Edward and funded by the Medici bank on Lombard Street; a loan that was never repaid.

'And Naples? What do you know of the signore's imprisonment there?' Marco took another cherry when Jack shook his head. 'Eight years ago there was an attempt on Lorenzo's life. It was carried out by the Pazzi, an old banking family – long-time rivals of the Medici – who wrested control of the papal accounts from Lorenzo and moved to overthrow him.' He chewed the fruit, then spat out the stone. 'The Archbishop of Pisa was involved in the plot, as were two priests. The whole affair was sanctioned by Pope Sixtus.'

Jack thought of the scar on Lorenzo's neck. Had the pope merely sanctioned it? Or had he orchestrated it as Amaury had implied back in Paris?

'Lorenzo survived, but his brother, Giuliano, was killed. Lorenzo pursued the assassins – had them hauled naked through the streets and tortured mercilessly before they were hanged. Even in death their bodies were defiled. After that he hunted down virtually every male of the family line and executed them. Anyone accused of aiding the attempted escape of the Pazzi, or sheltering them and their fellow conspirators was rounded up, imprisoned or banished. All their assets were taken, their coats of arms erased from the city. When the pope discovered what had been done to the archbishop and the priests, he excommunicated Lorenzo, putting Florence under interdict. Seizing all Medici assets in Rome and the Papal States, Sixtus declared war on the republic, aided by his ally, King Ferrante of Naples.

'The war was protracted. Trade suffered, companies – whole families – collapsed. In the end, Lorenzo gave himself up to the King of Naples. He spent months in Ferrante's custody, an honoured prisoner. Hoping to win his freedom he showered the king with luxuries; put on lavish banquets, organised festivals and tournaments, gave alms to the city's poor. It is not known how much he spent in his efforts to appease the king, but it was rumoured to be much of the fortune his grandfather and father amassed.

'In the end, Ferrante made peace with Florence, but more because he did not want to fight a war on two fronts. By then, the Turks had begun massing in the south and their fleet threatened Naples.'

Jack remained silent, his father's words coming to him in the voice of Prince Edward.

The Turks are not our true enemy. We are all fighting for the same thing. Only the world does not yet see it.

He forced the memory away as Marco continued.

'Sixtus had to back down in the face of the menace and Lorenzo returned to Florence, hailed a hero. But what many do not know was that during his time in Naples, vast sums of money vanished from the coffers of the republic.'

'You think Signor Lorenzo used money from the city to bribe King Ferrante?'

Marco shrugged and ate a piece of cheese, but his expression told Jack all he needed to know.

'But even if he did, his plan worked.' Jack gestured to the city, buzzing to life around them, people hastening about their day after Mass. 'The war ended and Florence seems to be thriving. As does the signore. I've seen his wealth for myself. It is beyond the telling.'

'Sometimes even the smallest crack can bring down a mountain.'

'You worry he has weakened Florence?' Jack studied Marco's expression. No, that wasn't it. 'Weakened himself?'

There was a twitch in Marco's lips – a rapid, involuntary tic. Gone in an instant. 'Florence has suffered through many wars. For now, we enjoy peace, but how long will it last? What good are walls and watch-towers if our leader is enfeebled? We cannot allow ourselves to be vulnerable. Left open to exploitation from our enemies.'

Jack was hearing the words, but he wasn't really listening. The lie had been exposed by Marco's own mouth, as if it had been the thing that wanted to jump first from his lips. Lorenzo's possible weakness didn't worry the man. It *interested* him. Jack's eyes strayed to the wolf's head on his cloak as Marco chewed one of the figs.

Mercenary captains. Ambitious sons seeking new opportunities.

The door he'd been standing before these past weeks had cracked open. Now, he just needed to walk through it. 'In truth, I cannot say for certain if Lorenzo is experiencing any difficulties.' He waited before taking the final step, careful not to seem too keen. 'But I could perhaps find out?'

Marco drained his wine and tossed the napkin on the tray, before digging into his purse for coins.

God damn it! Jack searched frantically for a way to backtrack.

'I must be about my day, Sir James. No, no . . .' Marco said forcefully, as Jack's hand went to his own purse. 'If not for you that filching bastard would have these. Please, stay. Enjoy the rest of the meal.' After dropping a generous handful of coins on the napkin, he looked down at Jack. 'Many of my brethren have left the city for the summer, heading for their residences in the country. But when the cooler air returns, so will they. I believe they may be interested in meeting you. Until then, my advice would be to keep your own counsel in that house. Trust your instincts.' Marco inclined his head. 'You will hear from me, Sir James.'

11

After a brief stop at the Fig to make sure Amelot had safely escaped the scene of her crime and to tell Ned and the others he'd secured Marco's interest – keeping the young man's account of Lorenzo to himself – Jack returned to the palazzo.

Slipping past the ragtag beggars clustered near its entrance and the daily queue of guildsmen, officials and businessmen keen for an audience with il Magnifico, he passed the guards' inspection and entered the shaded sanctuary of the inner courtyard. Sweat trickled down his face and his hair curled damply at his brow. He should wash before he went to Lorenzo's chamber. Besides which, he wanted a moment in the cool solitude of his room to think.

Since Marco Valori had left him Jack's mind had been churning. On the one hand he was keen to see Lorenzo – tell him he'd succeeded in snaring the man's attention. On the other, he felt deeply uneasy. Amaury de la Croix had painted one picture of Lorenzo de' Medici, but Marco's words had added new, darker detail to the image: tortured priests and the brutal erasure of an entire family, excommunication and the theft of public money.

There are many wolves in this city.

Jack already held a seed of doubt about the man his father had served in secret, planted back in Paris when Amaury spoke of the Academy and Lorenzo's personal vendetta with the pope – successor of St Peter, God's instrument on earth. Now, that seed unfurled, tendrils of distrust curling through him. Did this mean all his fears about his father could be founded? That the man he had revered – had set his life and heart upon – was no more than a thief and a liar, and, worse, a heretic and sympathiser of the Turks? And, if so, were Carlo di Fante and the brute who killed his mother in their attempt to secure the map for Sixtus somehow in the *right*?

No, that was intolerable.

But, as he climbed the marble staircase, faintly aware of voices and the scrape of furniture coming from somewhere, one question refused to leave Jack's mind, the ruse by which he'd captured Marco's interest solidifying into something real and significant. Could Lorenzo de' Medici be trusted?

Heading past the family's dining room and the suites of Lorenzo's sons, a wet-nurse's chamber and a linen cupboard he'd heard Piero de' Medici threaten to shut a tearful Giovanni in – promising his younger brother he'd end up like an insubordinate servant, locked in there and forgotten – Jack was approaching the staircase that would take him up to his room, when he smelled it. Orange blossom. At the same time, he heard two female voices, one young and anguished, the other older, soft with reassurance.

For a few days after the party he had thought of the young woman he'd seen disappearing up the stairs; the creak of footsteps beyond the doors to the *Sala Grande* and the bated silence that had followed his call, that sweet scent hanging in the air and the strange chanted song coming through the locked study door. But she had faded from his mind in his preoccupation with Marco. Now, as he turned the corner of the passage, he saw two figures lingering outside a door.

One was Lorenzo's daughter, Maddalena. He'd heard the girl was soon to celebrate her fourteenth birthday, but she still looked more like a child than a woman: plump of cheek and fair, more akin to Giovanni than the dark-eyed Lucrezia or the raven-haired Piero. Her face was blotchy from crying. The other figure had her back to him, but Jack could tell it was her. The young woman was dressed in a gown of stiff navy silk. A simple padded headdress netted her hair, a few dark wisps of which floated free at the base of her neck, which was long and slender, the bones of her spine leading like pale stepping stones down beneath the line of her gown.

'Hush now, Maddalena,' the woman murmured, as the girl dug the heels of her hands into her eyes. 'I promise you have nothing to fear. Lucrezia is happy. She has told you so.'

'What if he is unkind? Or ugly. I know he is older. As old as my father! I cannot—' Maddalena cut off abruptly as she caught sight of Jack making his way down the passage towards them.

The young woman looked round sharply, meeting his gaze. Jack nodded politely as he passed them, but both girls merely followed him with guarded eyes. As he continued, he heard a murmur and a rustle of skirts, followed by the thud of a door. When he looked back, they had vanished. He had wondered if the woman might be a governess or tutor. But she wasn't part of the horde of domestic staff whose faces and roles he had become familiar with, and she seemed young for such a position – not many years older than Maddalena herself. He thought of that perfume, lingering in Lorenzo's rooms. Might she be something else? Something Clarice de' Medici did not know about? He'd heard rumours Lorenzo had a lover, out on one of the Medici estates.

Jack was approaching the stairs, lost in thought, when a man's voice came to him, harsh on the quiet.

'You must talk to him. Demand to know what he is hiding.'

Acerbic, brisk, the voice was instantly recognisable. Giovanni Pico della Mirandola. Jack had glimpsed the enigmatic young man only once since the night of the party, early in the morning when he was walking the halls unable to sleep: Pico slipping from the palace, hair dishevelled, eyes shot with drink or lack of sleep. Jack paused, eyes on the door to Angelo Poliziano's room.

Another voice – distinguishable as Poliziano's, but too low for Jack to hear what was said – responded. Glancing round, making sure no one else was in the passage, he moved closer, blinking as he entered a shaft of light that lanced through a gap between the door and the frame. He pressed his face to it and saw a sliver of room beyond: the corner of a bed, crumpled sheets, a window, the shutters open.

'. . . and you know him well enough, Pico. Lorenzo does not bow to pressure. He will tell us in his own time. If, indeed, there is anything to tell.'

A shadow passed in front of the door, blocking Jack's view.

'You are his friend – his *dearest* friend. By Christ, Poliziano, he owes you his life! The truth is a poor cousin to that debt.'

The shadow shifted and the room came into view again. Now Jack could see Pico standing by the bed, a sinewy shadow, silhouetted in sunlight. The young man was naked.

'The Academy hasn't met in months,' Pico continued, pacing. 'Why does he avoid us?'

'We are meeting in—'

'Yes, yes,' Pico retorted impatiently. 'But why so long? And when did you last set foot in his sanctum? Months ago? It seems only Marsilio is permitted in there these days.' Pico swiped something off a table. A goblet. 'They have a secret I tell you.'

Were they talking about him? Jack wondered. Or were they sensing Lorenzo's guardedness, now he feared an enemy in his household? The shadow passed again, then Poliziano appeared. He wore black hose tied at the front with blue laces, but was bare-chested. His hair trailed wet around his shoulders, threading glistening lines down his back. 'You need to go,' he murmured. 'I can hear the household has woken. We have to be more careful.'

'So I'll use the window.' Pico's tone was now light, teasing. 'Like I do when you're sleeping.'

Poliziano wrested the goblet from his hand. 'Besides, you've had enough.'

The young man tutted, but let him take it. 'Save your chiding for your pupils, would you, my dear.'

'We must keep faith, Pico. Trust him, as we always have.'

'How can I when everything has stalled? All our plans, our hopes. This world we pledged to build together – what has become of it? New Eden remains a dream. A dream that grows more distant by the day.' Pico reached up, tugged a strand of wet hair behind Poliziano's ear. 'We must set a fire under him. You and I. He cannot be allowed to forget what we have started.'

So gripped was he by their words, Jack only noticed Papi when the man called his name. He jumped back from the door, red-faced, to see the elderly servant frowning questioningly at him.

'Sir James,' Papi said warily, 'the signore has been asking after you. He wishes to see you in his chambers.'

The *Sala Grande* was alive with activity. Servants moved between the bedchamber and the great hall, bearing baskets stacked with clothes and linens, and coffers and chests that they hauled to a pile near the doors. Porters stood waiting, sleeves rolled up ready. Household officials organised and directed.

Jack, entering with Papi, saw Lorenzo in the midst of the chaos speaking to Bertoldo, his chief steward. Seeing him, Lorenzo hooked a finger and beckoned him to approach. Jack went to him alone, glancing around at the activity. Above him, Hercules snarled across the canvases, battling one foe after another.

'Look again, Bertoldo. It must be in there. I saw it only last month.'

The steward, a diminutive man with watery eyes and a bristling moustache, inclined his head.

'Bertoldo.'

The man turned back. 'Yes, signore?'

'I will want it for the meeting.'

Watching Bertoldo hurry towards the bedchamber, Jack felt a spark of anticipation. Pico and Poliziano had mentioned a meeting. Was the Academy coming together? Here?

Lorenzo turned his attention to him. 'Come.' Leading Jack to the other side of the hall, out of earshot of the servants, he halted by one of the tall windows overlooking the gardens. 'I am leaving for my villa in Fiesole.'

'Leaving?' Jack knew the Medici family had villas scattered throughout Tuscany, but it was the first he'd heard of any move.

'Some of my staff will depart this afternoon. My family and I will follow in the next few days. I was due to leave in a week or two, but there has been a report of plague in the market. The pestilence can spread like fire in this heat.'

'May I ask how long you will be gone, signore?'

'I will return when the air cools.'

Jack thought of Marco Valori telling him the men of the Court of Wolves were leaving the city for the summer. He guessed it must be a privilege of the rich.

'But I wanted to make sure that you understand my absence does not excuse you from your efforts.'

'Of course, signore. In fact, I was on my way to speak to you.' Jack, speaking about his encounter, was gratified to see Lorenzo's hard expression shift.

'Valori said his brethren would be interested in meeting you?'

'Yes, signore. When they return from their estates.'

'Did he say anything else? Give you any sign he knew of Amaury's abduction?'

Jack paused. In his brief report, he'd omitted Marco's interest in Lorenzo's vulnerability and that the young man's suggestion of a meeting had come on the back of his own offer to find out more about any troubles in the House of Medici. But Marco was just one man, not the company as a whole. Who knew what personal history might have coloured his view of the signore? Besides, he'd learned his lesson not to give Lorenzo everything and risk receiving nothing in return. 'He just had more questions about my father's business in England.'

'And the girl? I take it she has seen nothing of the man she saw?'

'I'm afraid not.'

Lorenzo's jaw tightened. He looked back at the lines of servants, carrying chests to the pile. 'Then, if that is all—'

Jack jumped before he could think, the doubts and questions that had risen in him at Marco's words and the conversation between Pico and Poliziano made all the more pressing with Lorenzo's impending departure. 'Signore, is the Academy meeting soon?'

Lorenzo's eyes were on him, narrowed and searching. 'Who told you that?'

He was caught now, his face growing warm under the man's scrutiny.

'Do not hover on wings, Sir James. Speak.'

'I heard Pico and Poliziano talking about it on my way here.'

'Pico is here? Now? With Poliziano?'

Jack flushed deeper, the image of Pico's nakedness, the crumpled sheets, that affectionate gesture, all telling a discomforting tale. He knew there were many men in this city with such proclivities; had discovered this soon after their arrival, Ned and Adam returning, grim-faced and early one evening from a whorehouse a mischievous innkeeper had sent them to.

'*Men, Jack,*' Ned had confided in a whisper after several ales. '*The place was crawling with men!*'

'Aren't they always?' Jack had asked, laughing at his mortified expression.

'No, Jack. I mean – *all* men. Men and boys! Some even painted like whores, by God! Men *lying* with men. Ah, my eyes!' he'd groaned, clapping his hands over his face.

There were other places they soon heard of: hidden alleys down near the river in Oltrarno where men of all ages and classes ventured after sundown, a bathhouse where the steamy dark concealed any manner of sins, a butcher's on the Ponte Vecchio run by two brothers where, at night, another kind of meat could be enjoyed. There were laws against it that threatened execution – let alone what the Church thundered about it – but it seemed nonetheless to run as a current, wild and alive, beneath the city.

Well, he was in it now. 'Pico was speaking of a secret he thinks you are keeping,' Jack admitted. 'Something you're hiding from them.'

Lorenzo's eyes darted towards his bedchamber, but they were back on him again in an instant. 'Did he say what this secret was?'

'I wondered if it might be me – if Pico had seen through our deception? But I'm not sure. Either way, he seemed agitated.'

'And Poliziano?' Lorenzo's voice was tight. 'What did he have to say about it?'

'He said they should trust you.'

Lorenzo pushed a hand through his hair. He looked as though he were about to say something further when his gaze fixed on two figures approaching through the bustle of servants. One was Papi. The servant was escorting a man with grey hair, dressed in a black habit. For a second Jack thought it was Marsilio Ficino, then realised it was Giorgio Antonio Vespucci, the friar from San Marco – Amerigo Vespucci's uncle.

'God damn,' murmured Lorenzo. 'He is early.'

'Signore,' greeted Giorgio, as Papi ushered him over. The friar bowed and kissed Lorenzo's hand, his tonsure gleaming in the sunlight.

'Fra Giorgio.' Lorenzo glanced at Jack. 'Have you met my guest? Sir James?'

'Yes, indeed. Good day to you, Sir James.' The friar looked round at the servants, piling the chests by the doors. 'You are departing already, signore?'

'Yes, a little sooner than planned. I wanted to talk to you about Lorenzino and Giovanni's tutelage while I am gone.'

Giorgio nodded, smiling placidly as he turned back. 'This heat! You must be keen to get to Fiesole. Amerigo, I know, is eager to spend some time in the clean air.' The friar's pale eyes flicked to Jack. 'I presume you will be attending the feast, Sir James? My nephew was hopeful of another chance to speak to you about affairs in England?'

Jack shifted uncertainly.

Lorenzo answered before he could say anything. 'Of course. I am sure there will be an opportunity.' He met Jack's gaze. 'Now, Sir James. If you would excuse us?' Placing a hand on Giorgio's shoulder, Lorenzo led the friar away.

As Jack turned to go, he caught sight of Bertoldo outside the bedchamber talking to Papi. The steward was shaking his head, face taut with concern.

12

More horses had died in the night, littering the scrubby ground around the hastily established campsite in the shadow of a spur of rock. Swarms of flies clouded the air above them as the grooms worked to drag saddle cloths from under the heavy, limp bodies. Hearing a cry, Harry looked up, shielding his eyes from the sun, flaming over the eastern mountains. Carrion birds were wheeling in slow circles on the currents.

'You see why Andalusians say there is no such thing as summer – only hell?'

Harry turned at Rodrigo's voice. The hidalgo had already donned his gambeson and breastplate, the deep curve of which caught the sun's red fire. There was a cross carved into the iron. His sword, a spiked mace and a dagger hung from his belt. Rodrigo's face was sun-bruised; stubble crusting his jaw, dirt from the road ingrained in his skin. Harry guessed he looked much the same, only redder.

'Better get moving,' Rodrigo advised, eyes flicking to the packs and blankets crumpled on the ground by the ashy remains of the fire that had guttered through the night. 'Don Carlos's men found footprints, not far from our camp. Ten or more sets.'

'Moors?' asked Harry, looking over to where Don Carlos, the leader of their company, a seasoned captain in Queen Isabella's royal guard, was talking to his men. As he watched, several split away, shouting orders. The camp was stirring to life quickly around him.

'A scouting party most likely. Don Carlos aims to reach the king's camp by dusk.'

One of Rodrigo's band, a stocky man with a scar-lined face, approached, boots crunching on the powdery rocks. He was called el

Barbero – the barber – apparently on account he liked to take heads. With an offhand glance at Harry, he addressed Rodrigo, before heading over to where the others were saddling their horses.

'We're in the vanguard today,' Rodrigo told Harry.

'I heard,' Harry answered, pleased that some sense was now starting to form out of what had mostly been streams of nonsense. Turning, he called for Tom, his groom, but the young man was already hunkered under Nieve, tightening the mare's girth strap.

The camp took scant time to pack up, no man wanting to linger in the wilderness now word had spread that the enemy might be alert to their presence. Men swallowed down a meagre breakfast while they set about their tasks: royal captains ordering lancers and *jinetes* – the light horsemen – to form up in their companies, hidalgos and caballeros pulling on helmets, while servants fastened the buckles of their armour, infantry steeling themselves for another gruelling march, hands blistered from the shafts of pikes, carters greasing the axles of the carts that transported the cannons, grooms loading packs on to the backs of the horses and mules that would bear their loads of grain and wine through the day's savage heat.

In no time at all they were off, leaving the detritus of broken belts, lice-infested blankets, misplaced trinkets and the corpses of the animals who'd expired from exhaustion to litter the plain. Behind them, the carrion birds circled lower as, ahead, the land rose, taking them towards the crags and mountains that emerged from a milky haze, growing clearer and more daunting with the sun's rising.

An hour into the march and it was sweltering; the sun in their eyes, haloed by a white aura. An hour later it was unbearable. Mules plodded, heads hanging, hooves skidding on the broken ground. Out from Córdoba they had travelled through hills and fertile plains, green and gold with olive and almond groves. Now, all was bare rock and spiky plants, incessant flies and birds of prey. The only sign of civilisation was the ruin of a fort on a distant peak, jutting like a broken tooth from the mountains' jaws. Infantrymen trudged in silent columns behind their captains, leather brigandines dark with sweat, the forest of spears and pikes jolting in time to their footsteps. Carters cursed as the wheels of wagons carrying artillery rocked into ruts on the twisting, ever upward path. And, above them all, a cloud of dust rose like a gritty yellow banner, announcing their presence.

Harry, riding with Rodrigo's company in the vanguard behind Don Carlos's men, felt the sweat pouring off him like water. His dark hair, lighter at his temples, was plastered to his scalp and dripping into his eyes. His palms inside his gloves were sore and his arse had made a soupy puddle of his hose.

The armour he'd been forced to buy in the market in Córdoba hung heavy on his frame, chafing him even through the padding, sawing red lines into the skin of his armpits and around his thighs and calves, where the buckles of the cuisses and greaves were fastened protectively tight. His servant, Hervey – a red-haired, taciturn man, who'd been in Henry Tudor's company since Brittany – was au fait enough with armour to get him into it quickly and easily, but Harry guessed it would take some time yet for he himself to become accustomed to it.

Much of his experience of warfare had been spent as a rebel, down at times to the shirt on his back. He'd worn armour in his training and in his father's command in France with Ned Draper and the others of Thomas Vaughan's company, but not a full suit of plate like this. He had tied the helm – too much of a restriction – to the saddle, but wished he could shrug the whole steel shell off him. The risk, though, was too great, now they were in enemy lands.

Enemy lands? How had he allowed himself to be here?

There had been a lot of Christian blood spilled in these mountains, Rodrigo had told him. They had made some important gains this past year, towns Harry had never heard of falling to their forces: Ronda, Marbella, Coín. But many of these victories had come at either a high cost to their men, or because the Moors themselves had been in disarray, the Nasrid emirate divided between the forces of the elderly emir, Abu'l-Hasan and his war-seasoned brother, Muhammad al-Zagal – and the emir's ambitious son, Boabdil, who had risen in rebellion against his father and uncle four years ago, setting himself up in the city of Granada, even agreeing an alliance with Isabella and Ferdinand to suit his interest in defeating his own kin.

Despite his initial triumph at the recent gains, Rodrigo had become more cautious on the march, describing the fight to take back the wild territory as a long game of chess: the Christians seizing border fortresses, precipitous mountain towns and coastal villages, the Moors – experts in the terrain and masters of ambush – wresting others back in turn. As the Spanish moved east, deeper into the frontier, each stronghold became more strategic, more vital, but, so too, their own pieces became more exposed for the taking. It was a game that had been going on nearly five years, with the greatest prizes yet to take: Loja, Málaga and – the endgame – the city of Granada itself, capital of the Muslim emirate.

Stones skittered away, tumbling from the high path the snake of horses, mules and men was slowly winding around. Men twitched at the dart of a bird or the clatter of falling rocks, heads snapping round, hands reaching for crossbows or swords. Harry sagged in his saddle, swallowing back the burning in his parched throat. His tongue felt like a dried-up slug, sticky in his mouth. There was a gnawing pain in his head. The world swam in his vision, everything white, sun-blasted. He felt himself jolt – like one of the falling dreams he'd had as a boy, waking his sister with his shout. He fell forward, breastplate knocking against the pommel of the saddle. Nieve stumbled. Coming to with a start, Harry realised he'd let the weary mare wander off course. Beside him, the ground fell sharply into a boulder-strewn ravine.

'Careful.' Rodrigo was at his side, grasping the reins and pulling Nieve back towards the rest of the company. Twisting in his saddle, he sought out Harry's men, a short distance back with his own servants and grooms. 'Bring wine!'

Plucking a skin from the pannier of one of the mules, Peter sent Hervey hastening up the line. The servant's face was scarlet, his nose peeling. With his bright orange hair, he looked more like a carnival mask than a man. Harry took the skin and drank deep. Watered wine sweetened with honey. Inclining his head to Rodrigo, letting the man know he was in control, he took up the slack on Nieve's reins. As his mind came back into focus, he thought how close – how *easily* – he could come to death out here.

Two days ago on the march an infantryman had caught his foot in a rock and had fallen badly. He'd come round screaming, the broken bone of his leg splintered through his hose. Don Carlos's physician had set it and the man had been carried, whimpering and sweating, on a wagon for the rest of the day. But by the next morning he was white and shuddering. Last night, Harry had watched from his dim campfire as the man's captain and friends had gathered round him. Murmured words of prayer and the brief flash of a dagger, and all that was left by morning a pile of raised earth and a cross made of broken sticks.

'Better?' Rodrigo asked as Harry drained the skin.

Harry nodded, but his mind answered to the contrary. *You fool, you shouldn't even be here.*

Back in Córdoba, after pledging his sword to Queen Isabella, Harry had imagined himself staying in her court, working his way into position as a favoured dignitary, much as his father had in the courts of Burgundy and France. He would amuse the queen with tales of England, enjoy the shaded gardens of the palace, the exquisite wine and meats of a royal table, while turning her against Columbus and thus winning the favour of Henry Tudor, making amends for his failure to hunt down Wynter. He would return to England triumphant, take up the place he deserved at Henry's side, adorned in the mantles of trust and power; no more lingering on the sidelines, hoping for crumbs of honour, no more hiding in corners intimidated by men like Edward Woodville.

Harry had been bluntly disavowed of such notions the following day, however, when Isabella thanked him for his offer of service and Rodrigo had begun discussing the company they would leave for the front line with in a fortnight.

Realising he'd been taken at his word, his sword, barely blooded, put into service against the Moors, Harry had attempted to suggest he remain with the queen to cement the ambassadorship, but Rodrigo – the eager son of a bitch – insisted he could not pass up this honour: a chance at holy crusade, in a Christian country no less. Besides which, he could not rescind his gallant offer to Queen Isabella.

Harry's only consolation was that Columbus himself had not remained in the queen's court either, but had departed for Seville. The man was, from what Harry had been able to glean, now working with a slave trader there, the queen having agreed a stipend to keep him in Spain while she considered his radical proposal for a voyage west to seek the Spice Islands. It seemed, at least, the sailor's plan would not be implemented any time soon. Other than that, Harry's only hope for this journey into hell was that he was heading for the camp of King Ferdinand – and the only other person who could help him execute Henry's order and bring him to the future he had imagined for himself.

By late afternoon they were high in the mountains. The sky was searing blue. The air rippled, thrumming with heat. Rodrigo had become pensive. He'd stopped speaking to his men and rode apart from them, brow creased with some inner conflict. When Don Carlos gave the order for a rest – cavalry dismounting with groans to stretch aching muscles, infantry laying down pole-arms to gulp from skins, or relieving themselves against wind-withered trees – Harry watched the hidalgo walk away up a shallow slope that stretched from the path to a long ridge above them.

He glanced round, hearing a guttural voice. El Barbero was looking at him as he tore sinewy strips off a lump of salted meat. The scar-faced soldier repeated his words, tipping his head towards Rodrigo. Harry didn't understand all of what the man had said, but he did catch one word he now knew.

'His father?'

The Barber nodded.

Harry's gaze returned to Rodrigo, who was kneeling on the hillside, hands clasped in prayer. He knew the man's father had died three years ago, somewhere in these mountains, cut down in the bloody chaos of a rout when the Moors under Muhammad al-Zagal had ambushed the Christian forces on their way to attack Málaga, seizing a huge amount of plunder and livestock, killing thousands of men and taking many others as slaves. The brutal victory had reinforced the Muslim warrior's epithet, the Valiant. Watching Rodrigo pray, Harry wondered if they might be close to where that attack had happened.

As they set off again, men and beasts stirring sluggishly to life, he sat straighter in his saddle, eyes flicking across the ridge above them, hand resting near the pommel of his sword, next to which hung the jewel-handled dagger he'd slipped from the offerings Henry had sent to the monarchs. A gift to himself.

The sun was sinking, flushing the western slopes of the mountains and sending shadows stealing down the eastern sides, when they heard it: a low rumble, indiscernible at first over the din of wheels and hooves, but becoming clearer, louder, a wave of thunder rolling towards them. All at once, Don Carlos was yelling and men were drawing swords and fixing quarrels in their crossbows. Infantry rushed to surround the pack-animals with their cargo, levelling halberds and pikes. Rodrigo's sword flashed free, as he roared for his men to form up around him. Harry wrenched his own blade from its scabbard, pulling on the reins to control Nieve as the horse reared. The air was full of panicked shouts.

The rumbling was louder, the ground trembling, stones skipping down the slopes. Suddenly, the Barber bellowed, pointing his sword up the hillside to their right. Harry and Rodrigo twisted round to see men appearing on the ridge above them, silhouetted by the sun. The tips of their spears blazed like torch flames. Others of Don Carlos's company, seeing the danger, were whipping round, pointing crossbows towards the ridge, but now the rumbling had become the drum of many hooves and hurtling down the path towards them came scores of horsemen. Harry's heart hammered in his chest. His stomach clenched with that familiar terror he'd felt before, faced with battle. A couple of crossbow bolts shot upwards, premature and badly aimed, triggered by fear. The horsemen were approaching, slowing now. Suddenly, Don Carlos was roaring again, rising in his saddle.

Others took up his cry, sending it down the line. Harry blinked in bewilderment as, around him, men began lowering their weapons. Were they surrendering? Without a fight? He thought of the black slave girls he'd seen roped on Seville's dockside and others he'd seen since in the markets, inspected like cattle by prospective masters. His insides felt like water. Now, absurdly, some of the men were smiling, laughing even as they sheathed their weapons. 'What's happening?' he hollered at Rodrigo.

'It's our forces.' The hidalgo grinned. 'It's the king's men!'

Less than an hour later, the sun now set, the heat seeping reluctantly out of the air and a faint wisp of cool to prickle Harry's tight skin, they were winding down from the heights to enter a valley. After all the grey, it was surprisingly verdant, two rivers running through it. Down on the flatter ground beside one of the rivers was a massive encampment: a great sprawl of tents, wagons, men, paddocks for animals and several huge structures that looked like wooden towers, in various stages of completion. Campfires were burning and smoke hung in shifting layers.

Some distance beyond the camp, just visible in the deepening shadows, was a large walled town, clinging to the side of a bald, grey mountain. No – not clinging – rooted, like some bony, obstinate growth. Beyond the walls, that rose sheer across the riverbanks, set with round watchtowers, was a mass of rooftops, towers and slender spires. Loja.

Harry had never seen anything like it. On high ground opposite the town, where the river cut through the valley at its narrowest point, were rows of artillery set on platforms and giant catapults, a line of angular beasts, silent and waiting. Loja's walls were scarred and several of the towers were chipped, but only in the way a tree might be battered by a storm – a few branches lost, but the trunk still standing firm.

Soon, they were entering the encampment, heading for a red and gold pavilion at the centre. Men came to greet them, voices lifting in welcome, eyes on the mules carrying fresh supplies. Most were bearded, dirty and sunburned. All looked exhausted, hungry. Harry smelled sweat and wood-smoke, animal dung and the pungent stink of latrine pits. Dogs barked and cooks, bent over fires, turned to watch the weary train pass through.

Ahead, from out of the wings of the pavilion, strode a tall, dark-haired man with olive skin and the shadow of a beard. Harry guessed him to be in his early thirties. Over black, dust-stained hose, he wore a brigandine of stiff plates covered with red velvet, studded with silver-tipped nails. A great sword was strapped to his hip, hanging from a belt embossed with golden crosses. Although he wore no crown, Harry knew at once that he was the king, a host of men following obediently in the wake of his long-legged stride. Behind the monarch, outside the tent, a banner displayed the royal arms of Castile and Aragon, the splayed-winged black eagle glaring one-eyed from the expanse of cloth.

Don Carlos slipped from his saddle to greet Ferdinand. Bowing low, the captain kissed the king's proffered hand. Harry slid gratefully down from Nieve's back, handing the reins to Tom. Men crowded around, greeting one another and bowing to the king. Their voices were just a jumble of sound to Harry. He was too tired to even try to understand them.

'I will introduce you,' Rodrigo called to him as he patted his horse affectionately on the rump, sending it away with his servant. But, before he could, someone shouted his name.

The hidalgo looked round, his face lightening at the sight of a middle-aged man marching towards him. Over a brigandine, the man wore a black cloak lined with white leather, pinned over one broad shoulder to fall in folds down his back. His hair, turning silver at the sides, was cropped close to his skull. He had a square face and deep-set dark eyes that seemed to hold a hostile intensity, at odds with the broad smile of greeting on Rodrigo's face.

'Don Luys!' Rodrigo embraced the man tightly.

Harry wondered if they were family, so close they seemed as they stepped back to talk, still gripping each other's shoulders. He stood there, uncertain, waiting for Rodrigo to finish, while around him men talked. He'd lost sight of the king among the milling crowd.

'Harry? Harry Vaughan?'

He turned to see a tall, rangy man approaching, bright blue eyes narrowed in questioning surprise. His auburn hair had been bleached almost to the colour of straw and a ginger beard covered his angular jaw, partly hiding a scar, red and fresh, the stitches still knitted through his skin. But despite these changes, Harry recognised him at once. The man was Sir Edward Woodville.

13

Five days ago, in the back room of a ramshackle inn overlooking the *mercato*, where patrons with fistfuls of coins crammed nightly around pens in the cellar to cheer the dogs that ripped one another apart, a man was said to have died vomiting blood, boils rupturing on his neck, his fingers black with rot. Rumours of plague spread rapidly, the chief official of the quarter ordering the inn sealed up. It now stood empty, boards nailed over its windows and doors, ominously lifeless in the midst of the market's clamour, a corpse in a crowd.

Jack, making his way across the noisy square, caught the acrid stink of vinegar, splashed on by those hoping to ward off the dreaded vapours. Most people gave the inn a wide berth, as if the building itself might bear the contagion, save for a small group of flagellants who had gathered outside, white hoods covering their faces, robes split up the back so they could strike at bare flesh as they prayed. Passing them, Jack felt Amelot draw closer at his side. The girl flinched with every flick and crack of their whips, eyes on the men's skin, glistening red-raw in the sullen light.

One morning several weeks ago, airless and stuffy as this one, Jack had entered his room in the palazzo to find her bent over a basin of water scrubbing at her clothes, naked from the waist up. She had hissed like a cat, crouching to hide herself as he'd backed out mumbling an apology, but not before he had seen the scars. They decorated her pale back: long pink lines criss-crossing her shoulder blades, shorter, deeper ones carved between her ribs, ugly jagged ones stuttering across the bones of her spine and down beneath the rolled waist of her hose. So many there was hardly a patch of skin left unmarked.

The wounds looked old to him, but Amaury had said Carlo di Fante's masked companion had tortured Amelot in London and Jack had been left to wonder if any of that mutilation could be down to him. If the girl could talk, what might she be able to tell him about his mother's murderer? Might the bastard have spoken about his other kills to threaten her? Might Amelot even know how his mother died; what torments she had suffered in her final moments at his mercy? Sarah Wynter had been a beautiful woman. Jack had known that since he was a boy; catching the way men looked at her with sideways glances, noticing the purse-lipped jealousy of women. Questions of what that brute could have done to her – questions that scalded him with images that left him coiled with rage – had become more frequent these last few days, since Marco Valori had spoken of Lorenzo's past.

Steering Amelot from the blood-streaked flagellants, Jack headed down one of the alleys that wound away from the market. Rats scurried through rubbish, ignored by toothless old men with leather skin conversing in doorways and youths crouched around gambling boards, kissing their fists before casting the die. The innkeeper of the Fig gave his usual effusive greeting as Jack passed through, no doubt keen for word of his hospitality to be passed on to il Magnifico. Up a zigzag of stairs, Jack and Amelot climbed to the top floor. They heard Titan barking as they approached the door.

The four men had, with what little they owned, tried to make the cramped lodgings in the eaves their own. Valentine's apostles, filled with black powder, were stashed in one corner with his arquebus, the scarred wood of the stock carved with words: *God's Messenger*. On a shelf, warped with age, Ned had set out his prized collection of stones and shells, some gathered from the banks of the Thames, others dug from the mud of the Seine and the Arno, while Adam and David's crossbows – gifts from Thomas Vaughan for the brothers' service during the wars between York and Lancaster – were stowed under the pallet they shared. Valentine and Ned slept in the other bed, and Titan had a hair-matted blanket beneath the window. The place smelled of unwashed bodies, old cooking odours and dog.

'Jack?' Ned greeted him with a surprised smile. 'Well, you've come in good time. David just went to get food.' He appraised him as he entered, noting Jack's russet and gold-trimmed doublet – another loan from Lorenzo – with a click of his tongue. 'You look more the part every day.'

'Looks be deceiving,' muttered Valentine from the table he was sitting at, rocked back on a stool, arms crossed behind his head. He glanced at Amelot, taking in the small pack she carried on her back, in which Jack had stuffed her cloak and blanket. 'What's this?'

'She's staying here, with you.' Jack bent to ruffle Titan's ears as the little dog skipped around his feet.

'Like hell—' began Valentine, the stool thudding down as he sat forward.

'Just for a few days,' Jack cut in, rising. 'I need you to take this,' he added to Ned, pulling his father's war sword from its scabbard. As the great blade caught the light, the Latin inscription along its length flared to life.

As Above, So Below

'I've been summoned to Lorenzo's villa, outside the city at Fiesole. He's holding a feast there in a few days. He's making an announcement.'

'About what?' Adam asked, rising from his pallet, folding his muscled arms.

'I'm not sure. But some of the city's highest dignitaries have been invited, so I assume it's important. Keep it safe,' Jack pressed, as Ned reached for the weapon. He felt reluctant, handing it over, but he didn't want to leave it unguarded in his room and couldn't take it with him, the inscription tying the blade – and him – to the Academy.

Ned accepted the sword carefully and laid it on his pallet, pushing Titan away when the dog came sniffing at it. 'How long will you be gone?'

'I don't know.' Jack knew little of what to expect from Lorenzo's invitation, except the man wanted him at Fiesole partly to keep up the pretence of his role as honoured guest and, partly, to get closer to Pico. His confession that he'd overheard the conversation between the young man and Poliziano seemed to have given Lorenzo the idea Jack might be useful in finding out what, exactly, Pico thought he knew or suspected about his private business, in the wine-infused atmosphere of a feast. *He likes you*, the signore had added, making Jack think with discomfort of Pico, naked with Poliziano beside the crumpled bed. 'Not long. I hope.'

'So,' said Valentine, elbows on his knees, his bald head greasy with sweat. 'We fools are to stay in this plague heap, while you plays at lord of the manor?'

'Valentine—' Ned began.

'You heard the same tale as me,' said the gunner, turning his black eyes on Ned. 'Them guards shutting up that house not an arrow's flight from here. Only a rumour of plague,' he continued, addressing Jack, 'but they shut it all up – nails and boards – the people still inside. No mind if they was sick or fine.'

'What do you want me to do? I cannot see off the pestilence.'

'No,' cut in Adam, 'but you can get us out of this city. Get us on our way.' He was less riled than Valentine, but his blue eyes were keen. 'A new life. That's been your promise, Jack, all these months.'

'And that's in progress.' Jack felt irritation nipping at him. He was used to Valentine's crustiness, but recently Adam, too, had become more insistent in his questions and demands. He wished David hadn't been the one to go for food. The man, who usually sided with him, was able to calm his brother in these altercations, ending any argument before it began.

'Progress, my arse,' spat Valentine. 'Them men *might* be interested in meeting you. *When the air cools?*' the gunner mimicked. 'If the signore's truly so troubled why don't he just end the company? He's got the might to do it. Round them up? Interrogate them? Find who took the priest.'

Jack shook his head, thinking of Lorenzo's response to this same question, the signore describing the Court of Wolves as a web stretched taut across the city, with threads in all the grand houses and guilds. *It cannot simply be disbanded. Not without a struggle.* 'All you have to do is wait, Valentine. You've got lodgings, a generous account for food, wine and whatever else you want. It's more than most men can say.'

'And if you fail?' Adam cocked his head. 'If Lorenzo turns on his word? What then?'

Jack said nothing. Since meeting Marco that question had been swirling more and more in his own mind.

'Then we're back where we started,' Adam answered for him. 'Food in our bellies, yes, but no coin in our fists. All those crusading in Spain, filling their purses with infidel gold? That could be us. It *should* be us.'

Valentine grunted his agreement.

'Why fight a war?' Jack demanded. 'When we're on a promise from the richest family in Christendom?'

'The Medici didn't get rich by being generous. They got rich by tricks and by the dagger. You're a fool if you don't see that.'

'Come, let's take some air.' Ned clasped Jack's rigid shoulder. 'This place is hotter than the devil's pit and Titan's clamouring to be out.' The dog, lying on the pallet by the sword glanced up at his name, but didn't lift his head from his paws.

After a moment, Jack took his gaze from Adam. With a last glance at Amelot, who was huddled in the window, staring over the rooftops, he crossed to the door.

Ned slapped at his neck as they headed out, walking down the alley to enter the din of the *mercato*, where fears of the Great Pestilence hadn't dissuaded citizens from their usual fight for space at the stalls, shouting over one another as they haggled with traders. 'Christ alive! How much more of me can the little bastards eat?' The large man was covered with insect bites. One, on his elbow, had swollen into a pus-filled blister the size of a plum. A physician had given him an ointment, but it apparently smelled so foul the others had forbidden him from using it. 'Don't mind them, Jack. They're just twitchy in this heat.' Ned's eyes flicked towards the boarded-up inn on the other side of the square.

'But I'm in now, with Marco,' Jack responded, tugging at the stiff collar of his tunic. He felt as though he were being suffocated.

'You must understand, Jack. We were raised for war. To sit idle isn't in our natures. Even beyond the battlefield each of us had purpose.'

'All our endeavours these past years. The map? Prince Edward? We might not have been successful, but you cannot say we didn't have purpose.'

'Then we did. But this is your mission now. You've not told us what Amaury told you in Paris – not allowed us to truly understand your reasons for coming here. I know you gave the priest your word,' he went on before Jack could speak. 'We came because we thought it would be in all our interests. Now . . .?'

They moved deeper into the market, in the centre of which was a grand pavilion, where butchers bellowed the prices of their cuts and flies swarmed around gutted carcasses dangling from hooks. Spiralling out from the pavilion were scores of other stalls, selling vegetables and books, hats and shoes, bolts of every colour cloth. The smell was overwhelming: a sweltering stew of body odours, animal dung, pungent cheeses, overripe fruit, newly tanned leather and smoke from roasting spits. The whole place was frenetic with movement, even the bruised sky where swifts shrilled and swooped.

'Titan!' Ned summoned the dog from a bloody pool beneath a fishmonger's stall. 'What about the map? Has Signor Lorenzo said anything about the land it shows?' He glanced at Jack. 'I mean, if Pyke's brother-in-law was right, back in Southwark? That it could be the coastline of Cathay or Cipangu . . .?'

'It's gone, Ned. In Tudor's hands.'

'The map, yes. But we know there's *something* out there.'

Jack heard Amaury's rasping voice.

We believe something else lies between Christendom and the shores of Cathay and Cipangu. Between Occident and Orient. Plato called it Atlantis. We call it New Eden.

Ned shrugged in his silence. 'I just wonder if we're seeking our fortunes in the wrong place?' He held up his hand as Jack went to argue. 'I'm with you. I'm just saying, if getting in with Marco and this company goes nowhere, we might find ourselves something even greater out there?' He gestured in a vague westerly direction.

Jack thought of the glint in Ned's eyes as he had traced the contours of that inked coastline in the candlelit gloom of the Ferryman's Arms; the hoarded shells he'd seen his friend – one arm crooked behind his head – turning in his fingers at night sometimes. Lodestones to adventure. Since he'd known him, the man had talked of travel and distant lands – always wondering what was over the next horizon, feet tapping to be off. Jack envied him. If he could walk free now, out of this city, looking forward, never back, he would. 'You know who you are, don't you, Ned?'

'How do you mean?'

'You know where you come from, who you were born to and what you were born into.'

'I suppose,' Ned agreed dubiously. 'I'm just me.'

'I've never known who I'm supposed to be. I was born thinking my father was an innkeeper in Lewes. That he died before my birth. It wasn't until I was older that I heard the rumours. People said James Wynter was a drunk and a cripple, who'd hanged himself when he caught my mother—' Jack bit back the words. 'That he wasn't my blood at all.' His eyes narrowed with memories: fists pummelling him down into the dirt, the taunts and kicks, laughter sharper than blades.

Bad-blood! Low-born! Bastard!

'When I discovered Thomas Vaughan was my father, I thought I knew why I didn't belong. I was meant for something else – another life entirely. When he took me into his command to serve with you and the others, I thought I'd found my place.'

Ned was nodding. 'But then he was called to Ludlow, to raise the king's son.'

'And his own – a brother I never knew – who grew up hating me. All those years, my father kept me close yet separate, as if at a window, able to see the life I could have, but never able to touch it. When he came to me with the map I believed, at last, he would let me in. Then he was gone. Strung up on Gloucester's orders. I still don't know who he really was. What he believed in. Did he knowingly put my mother in danger? Allow her to be sacrificed? Did he use me too?'

'By my faith, Jack, I cannot believe that. Whatever secrets he held in his heart, Thomas Vaughan was a good man. He could not know what would happen to your mother.'

'He never even knew she'd died. Nor her him. His last will came when she was already gone.' Jack blew through his teeth. 'It's as though I'm at sea, no land in sight. I know whatever Lorenzo tells me will not bring my family back. That it won't change the past. But maybe those answers will let me see a shore to swim to? Until then, I cannot know what direction to travel.'

After a moment, Ned nodded. 'Then we'll swim together. Not that I can,' he added with a crooked grin. 'I'll have to hold on to Titan. Walk with me to the river, Jack?'

'You go.' Jack motioned to the market. 'I need food.'

As Ned headed off, Titan trotting beside him, Jack was turning towards the roasting spits when a cool voice sounded at his back.

'I thought your name was James?'

Jack started round to see a young woman staring questioningly at him. It was her – the woman he'd followed the night of Lorenzo's party. Up close she seemed even younger than he'd first thought. Sixteen? Seventeen at most. There was a smattering of dark freckles over the bridge of her nose and the high bones of her olive-skinned cheeks, which most women of standing – which clearly she was by her clothes – would have whitened with lead. Her hair was swept back beneath a gauzy blue veil, held in place by silver braids. A silver pendant, fashioned in the shape of a bird, hung on a chain around her neck. Tiny holes needled artful patterns along its back. He caught a trace of orange blossom; a whisper of sweetness among the market's reek. 'Signora?'

'Your clerk,' she said, eyes following Ned. 'He called you *Jack*?'

How long had she been watching him? More importantly, how much English might she know? Had he given himself away? 'It's a nickname,' he told her, switching back into Tuscan, smiling politely to cover his concern. 'But you have me at a disadvantage, signora. I do not know your name?'

'Laora.'

He repeated it, making sure he'd heard her correctly over the clamour of the market. 'Are you Maddalena's governess?'

She laughed lightly. 'No. My father used to work with Signor Lorenzo. I grew up with Lucrezia and Maddalena. They are as sisters to me.'

'So you are a friend of the family?' he questioned, remembering that night, the glimmer of her gown disappearing above him. Had he been right in his suspicion – that Lorenzo might have more than one mistress beyond his wife? As he studied her, thinking how young she seemed, an image came to his mind of Lorenzo – sallow-faced and squash-nosed – drawing her to him.

Laora stiffened at his close attention. 'Yes, a friend,' she said briskly. 'Why do you ask?'

'I saw you,' he said, relieved the focus of the conversation was now on her and determined to keep it there. If she was Lorenzo's lover, she might know more about the signore than anyone. His secrets. His plans. 'The night of the party? Going upstairs alone?'

Her poise cracked and she looked suddenly frightened. Then, she straightened with a toss of her head. 'I was going to Maddalena's room. She was upset.'

Was that a lie in her flushed face? Before Jack could press her, a grizzled woman wrapped in rags approached – one of the *miserabiles* who haunted the streets here, many of them widowed or abandoned. Laora turned from him to dig in her purse, but Jack caught the slight tremble in her hand as she placed a coin in the woman's outstretched bowl.

'Signor Lorenzo has been in negotiations for Maddalena's marriage,' Laora continued, returning her attention to him as the woman shuffled off. 'To the son of Pope Innocent. He's more than twice her age and Lorenzino di' Pierfrancesco says he's a perpetual drunk.'

'The pope has a *son*?' Jack's surprise eclipsed his suspicion. He swiped a trickle of sweat from his cheek. The heat was growing heavier. Flies buzzed him.

'A bastard. Franceschetto Cybo. Only the Holy Father proclaims he is his *nephew*.' As a group of people pressed in around them to reach a fruit stall where the trader was carving watermelons into juicy pink smiles, Laora moved on.

As Jack followed her, he noticed that the material of her gown, although exquisite, was faded in places. Now he thought about it, he realised it was highly unusual to see a lady of her standing on her own in the streets, especially in the *mercato*. Any noble women he'd seen here were always accompanied by a flock of attendants. 'Do your father and mother not mind you being out alone?'

'My father is away on business.' There was a bite to her tone. Laora paused at a stall selling old clothes, the musty odour of them clagging the air.

'Your mother?'

'She is dead.'

Jack felt the weight of those words, but before he could say anything Laora pulled a patterned headscarf from a ratty pile on the trestle.

'How much for this, Pia?'

The woman behind the stall, sleeves rolled up to show slim arms covered with a down of black hair, glanced over with a smile. 'For you, signora, two denari.'

'I come here all the time,' Laora told him, stuffing the scarf into her purse and handing the young woman the coins. She gave a small smile as she looked around her. 'All these people. So many stories. So much life.'

She reminded him a little of Grace; that same self-assured poise. But she also reminded him of Amelot. Some old echo of pain in those hazel eyes.

Laora had paused in the shadow of the column that marked the centre of the market, a voluptuous statue of Abundance atop it, holding aloft her cornucopia overflowing with flowers and fruit of stone. The base of the column was slung with chains. Jack had heard an unlucky sodomite might occasionally be shackled there for a vicious flogging by the Officials of the Night, who oversaw public decency and were keen to show citizens that the laws would be enforced, despite all evidence to the contrary.

Laora squinted up with a sigh. 'It is so hot!' She was turning to him, about to say something more, when the air filled with a piercing shriek of birds.

Black clouds of them rose into the sky from roofs, domes and spires; from everywhere at once. Dogs began barking. Chickens flapped and squawked in their cages. All around people stopped mid-barter, mid-rummage, staring at each other in confusion.

'What—' Jack sensed a tremor in the ground beneath his feet. He'd felt something similar once before, on the field of battle, braced behind his father and Ned and the others, the Lancastrians' heavy cavalry thundering towards them. He turned, searching for horsemen.

The bells of nearby churches were beginning to ring, but not with their normal clanging: more as if the tremor was running up the walls to shudder through them. The quaking intensified. Stalls juddered, goblets and candlesticks toppling. Shutters on buildings clattered madly in their frames, as though the houses were being shaken by some enormous invisible force. People were shouting, traders grabbing at falling wares.

A stall selling pans collapsed with a crash, the iron pots rolling off in all directions. It sparked a panic among some of the crowd, several of them running for the nearby church, as if for sanctuary. A heavy-set man knocked into Laora, sending her flying. Jack, stumbling across the trembling ground, went to help her. As he took her hand he heard a sharp crack behind him, like the report of a gun. Someone screamed. Whipping round, Jack saw a thin fissure snaking its way up the column, which was swaying on its base, the chains rattling wildly. Hauling Laora to her feet, he pulled her away as the horn in the hand of Abundance broke off, chunks of stone smashing down.

A moment later and the quaking began to lessen, rolling away beneath the city, until it had gone completely. For a second there was nothing but eerie silence, then the dogs all began barking again and people starting shouting, helping one another up, calling for friends and misplaced children.

'Are you hurt?' Jack said, turning from the pile of stones at the foot of the cracked column to look at Laora. He realised he still had hold of her hand, so tight he was probably crushing it. He let go.

Her veil had snagged in the fall and was hanging from its braids. She reached up and tugged it free, shaking her dark hair loose. 'That was worse than last time!' She let out a stilted laugh, but her hands were shaking.

'This has happened before?'

'A few times. Fra Girolamo Savonarola has proclaimed it is God showing His displeasure at the sin here.'

Fra Vito had spoken to Jack of Savonarola, a Dominican friar who had built a reputation for forceful sermons, haranguing citizens and their leaders for the vices in their city. He thought of Pico and Poliziano. As Laora turned to brush the dust and straw from her skirts, he saw her gown had slipped from her shoulder. There was a large bruise darkening her skin; reddish purple outlines that might have been made by pinching fingers. Had he done it? No, the bruise looked older, fading to green at the edges. 'You are hurt?'

Following his gaze, she pulled her gown up quickly. 'No. I'm fine.' She turned to one of the alleys leading out of the market. 'But I must get home.'

'I'll walk with you.'

Passing out of the crowd, they entered the alley, several skinny street children racing ahead of them, whooping as they held aloft spoils snatched from the chaos: a candlestick, a leather shoe, a cooking pot. Jack thought of Ned and the others, but none of the buildings he could see looked damaged and he guessed they would have escaped unharmed.

They were halfway down, Laora hitching her skirts out of the muck of night soil and refuse, when Jack heard it – a chanting somewhere high above them. He stopped, cocking his head to listen. He didn't recognise the language, but the sound was familiar. After a moment, he realised where he'd heard it before. It was the same as that strange singing he'd heard coming from the depths of Lorenzo's private study the night of the party: an off-key chant, half spoken, half sung.

Laora looked back at him. 'What is it?'

'That singing?' Jack stared up at the building it seemed to be coming from. It was unremarkable among its neighbours: cracked stucco, peeling paint on the shutters, a precarious-looking balcony tilting towards the one opposite, almost blocking out the sky. At the top, a set of shutters hung open.

She followed his gaze. 'The Muslim prayer?'

'What?'

'A slave, I would imagine. My father used to keep several in his household. He forbade them from praying, but I used to hear them in their room sometimes.' Laora closed her eyes, angling her head back as the notes of the chant climbed and tumbled. 'Strange, is it not? How beautiful the language of the infidel is?'

'Beautiful?' murmured Jack, the word utterly at odds with everything he knew of the enemies of Christendom.

Laora flinched as a spot of rain dashed her cheek. It was followed by another, then another. Huge droplets that promised a deluge. She turned to him. 'I will leave you here, Sir James. Our paths are not the same.' She paused for a moment. 'Thank you for . . .' Her eyes flicked back towards the market. 'Thank you.'

Before he could say anything, Laora turned and hastened away. Jack stayed there, listening to the chanting of the Muslim prayer, faint above the rush of rain and curses of people hurrying past him, pulling up hoods.

After Constantinople fell to the Turks, their armies had spread through the islands of the Aegean, to Bosnia, Kaffa, Albania. They made it all the way to Venice, but were turned back from Rhodes by the Knights of St John. A truce was finally agreed, at a heavy price, and when Sultan Mehmet, the Conqueror of Constantinople, had died five years ago, Christendom had breathed a sigh of relief. But even on the crossing from Aigues-Mortes, Jack heard one of the crew, who'd lost an eye in an attack by a Turkish ship, talking to Ned of the armies of Islam, gathered at the doors to the east, watching the kingdoms of the west war among themselves, waiting like carrion crows around a dying citadel; scenting blood on the air.

Lorenzo had slaves, most of them female, two of them black, like those he'd seen in the markets in Seville. He didn't know if any were Muslim, but he supposed they could be. Still, that didn't explain what a slave would be doing in Lorenzo's inner sanctum, where only a few men – Marsilio, Papi and Bertoldo – were permitted. Praying, no less?

More people were streaming from the market, pushing past him. Jack entered the tide, the rain soaking him as he wound his way through the labyrinth.

It was morning. The thin blade of light that carved a white line across the cellar floor told him so. He stirred slowly, joints creaking painfully, each breath drawing a rattling wheeze from deep within his lungs. As he sat up on the pallet, the coarse blanket slipping from him, he was taken by a fit of hacking, the coughs exploding in his chest. A graveyard cough, his father would have called it.

Not long now, son. Not long now.

It was strange how many people from his past had returned to speak to him. Some came in memories or dreams, but others seemed to be here with him, conversing about his situation, offering unhelpful suggestions or telling him morosely he would die down here. It was his father, who died when he was a boy – how many lifetimes ago? – and King Louis of France, for whom he'd worked for some years as a translator, who were the most talkative.

He combed his hand roughly through his white hair, his tonsure long grown out and a wispy beard sprouting from his chin, then rose slowly, stretching with a wince. After relieving himself in the bucket, he set off through the dusty shadows, using the damp walls and stone pillars to steady himself.

The expansive cellar was stacked with barrels, most of which were empty. There were some old crates and broken chests in one corner, also empty, and sacks of mouldy grain that lured the rats. There were hundreds of them down here in the dark, scuttling from his limping walk. Sometimes, on colder nights, he would wake to find himself crawling with them, drawn by his warmth. After his initial revulsion, he had come to enjoy their company. He had even named a few of them. One had a missing front paw that reminded him of himself.

'Hello, old boy,' he would say whenever he spotted him. 'Off on another hunt? Perhaps you might find me a manuscript?'

Then he would find himself giggling uncontrollably, with no idea of why he'd started laughing in the first place.

Memory, he had discovered, was a fluid, changeable thing. Sometimes he forgot how he had come to be down here and it might be hours before he remembered – the door of his lodgings bursting inwards, men pouring in, him pushing the girl towards the window.

Go! Flee!

Then the long, painful journey, most of it spent huddled in a wagon, only snatches of the changing world beyond the monotony of the hooves: misty forests and brown fields, rising hills and snow-crowned mountains, winter's breath freezing his bones.

After his initial interrogations, at the hands of the man with the wolf badge free with his fists, his captors had grown surly and silent. Then, when he'd been bundled out of the wagon – a glimpse of sand-coloured buildings, one grand one in the centre, castle-like, gardens stretching into vineyards and forested hills – the questions had begun anew. Mostly it was the Wolf Man, as he'd named the one with the badge, who asked them. So many questions, coming in endless loops – usually in French, although he understood their native tongue – until they became a song that played constantly in his mind.

The map you wrote to Lorenzo de' Medici about – where is it now?
Who was the man you sent to retrieve it?
What does it show?
What is New Eden?
What are Lorenzo's plans?
Tell us!
We will let you live.

Oh, the lies! Even the Turks who had held him in their foetid prison all those months hadn't promised him that.

He had reached the blade of light that shone on the floor near the back of the cellar, where the walls became rough-hewn, more cave-like. Dust-motes sparkled. It was still here. He hadn't imagined it. He stepped into the bright shaft, sighing at its warmth on his face.

It had appeared two days ago, after the tremor, when the walls had shaken and he'd thought the whole world was collapsing around him: a thin fissure cracked through the stone roof. It was then he'd discovered this part of the cellar must extend beyond the foundations of the building because, in that gap, when the shaking stopped and the dust settled, he had seen a narrow slice of sky. Later, sweating with effort, perched precariously on a barrel, he'd pressed his eye to the crack, heard birdsong, felt droplets of rain. It had been like life. Like drinking life. But it wasn't wide enough – nowhere near wide enough. Only his soul would be able to slide through it.

As he stared up at the fissure, he felt King Louis at his shoulder, his knowing eyes and thin smile, one of the hunting birds he loved so much perched on his head.

What will you do, Huntsman? Become air?

'I will wait for another tremor, my lord.'

Ah, yes! Then maybe the building will come crashing down on your head! That will make you thinner, for certain!

Amaury de la Croix shook his head, forcing the mocking voice away to focus on the sliver of light. Eyes closed once more, face turned up towards its faint warmth, he made himself a promise to keep alive. Keep alive a bit longer. No more talking to dead kings.

14

'Shall we begin, signore?'

Lorenzo, seated at the centre of the gathering, nodded at Marsilio Ficino's question, motioning him to stand.

The priest rose, fingers on the edge of the table to steady himself, the hunch of his back keeping him bent. The tufts of white hair sprouting from his tonsure formed an ethereal cloud around his head. In his free hand, he gripped a book. The bindings were cracked, the pages soft, jaundiced. It had begun life as a series of ancient texts, smuggled out of Constantinople before the city's fall, hunted through the Balkans by Amaury de la Croix and delivered to Cosimo de' Medici. Translated by Marsilio from Greek, these texts had been brought together in one body of work, the *Corpus Hermeticum*: a work – its words whispering down from the dawn of the world – that had shaped and directed the Academy.

A pair of spectacles was balanced on Marsilio's nose. His creased face screwed up around the rims as he lifted the book closer. The other men in the chamber settled into silence as he began to read.

'O Hermes, philosopher king, priest of the ancients; Hermes the Thrice Great, you who dwells within the heart, who first taught tongues to speak, messenger of the gods, bearer of light and bridger of worlds, you who see the hidden paths and know the fate of all, guide us this night and always on the path to wisdom. Light our way to knowledge and, through it, the divine.'

Listening to the words, which he'd heard recited countless times before, Lorenzo cast his gaze around the seated men. Candlelight burnished their faces and glowed in the crystal goblets set out on the table with platters of food. His servants had readied the meal, but the men would serve themselves tonight. No other eyes or ears were permitted in the chamber, which stretched into dusk beyond their circle. The shutters were closed, the last of the sunset seeping through the gaps, a slow-dimming fire.

When he had first arrived at the villa, the air in here had been stale, hazy with dust. Now – the servants having cleaned the floors and cracked open shutters – it was sweet with the perfume of cypress trees.

The villa, just below the village of Fiesole, perched high on the hillside overlooking Florence, was his favourite. Coming here, riding the winding road from the city up into the fragrant hills, made him feel like he was travelling back into boyhood; walking shaded paths through the newly planted olive groves with his grandfather, listening to him speak of his dreams for the world, feeling that charged hum inside him at the old man's words that made him feel anything was possible.

Careggi, which had been his grandfather's preferred dwelling, was too rustic for his liking, and Cafaggiolo, out in the hills to the north, had passed to his cousins a year ago. He was still regretful about losing the extensive property, where he'd spent many summer days in the fields with Nencia, flushed and warm beneath him. Now, Fiesole felt like one of the last sacred spaces of childhood – of family – left to him.

It was here that he'd first sat with the men of the Academy listening to the same words Marsilio read now: among them the sculptor, Donatello, who had fashioned David for the palazzo courtyard; Giorgio Antonio Vespucci scribbling down their words; Amaury de la Croix, called the Huntsman for his skill in rooting out ancient texts, returning with another precious manuscript; Marsilio Ficino ready to translate it; Toscanelli, the old astronomer who theorised about the possibility of reaching the Spice Islands by sailing west and who, in the winter of his life, hearing rumours of the land sighted by the crew of the *Trinity*, declared that Atlantis, the island Plato proclaimed was destroyed by a terrible conflagration, had returned, as prophesied.

They had debated long into those nights, sometimes till dawn, reading passages from Petrarch and Cicero, hot with passion and conviction, their words building new worlds from the old, breathing life into lost empires, as they talked of ushering in a golden age, where the beliefs and values of humanism and her arcane sister, Hermeticism

– mistress of alchemy, astrology, sorcery, of the ancient ways – might spread beyond the bounds of Florence. Lorenzo had listened, the radical, sometimes heretical nature of their speeches slowly turning into inspiration inside him; that the world did not have to be this way. That they could construct it anew, away from the influence of the Vatican, the old house that walled them in for so long, the rotten core of which he had seen for himself. That God's voice might echo truer in other, purer chambers.

'With reason,' continued Marsilio, 'not with hands did the Maker – author of all things – create the world. Down to Earth, to contemplate his creation, He sent man, who dies and is yet deathless, rising again through Nature's wheel. It is thus God's will that we strive to contemplate the divine. That we seek to understand Him and all His works.'

As the priest cleared his throat and paused to sip his wine, Lorenzo's focus returned to the twelve men – artists, philosophers, scholars, astrologers and poets – seated around the table, some with eyes closed in thought or prayer, others nodding at Marsilio's words. In the years since the deaths of his grandfather and father, Lorenzo had built his own Academy, seeking out new blood, enlisting men closer to his own age; those with the same fire in their souls. But he wondered now, had he let in an enemy?

Lorenzo realised that Poliziano was staring at him. The young man sat forward as their gazes locked. He tilted his head, his brow knotting, asking him silently, *What is wrong?* In the upheaval of the move from the city, Lorenzo had mostly avoided the man. He knew he would have to face him soon. But what then? How long could he keep these secrets from his dearest friend, now he knew Poliziano suspected something? Lorenzo's eyes flicked to Pico, seated to the right of Marsilio, his former tutor. The young man seemed preoccupied tonight, his grey eyes distant, fingers tapping at the arms of his chair.

'And so He filled a cup with knowledge and sent it to the Earth that men might drink of it and be wise.' Marsilio glanced over at him as he read this passage.

This was the moment they usually paused in the reading from the *Corpus Hermeticum* to fill the chalice with wine and pass it around the table, each man taking a sip, cementing their bond and their intent. But, tonight, there was no cup. The space in the centre of the table where it would have stood seemed to shout its absence. Lorenzo had told the others it had been temporarily misplaced in the move.

Despite Bertoldo scouring his study, the cup had not been found. Lorenzo could swear to have seen it not long ago, in its place on a shelf near his desk, a king among a host of other glittering ornaments. The gold chalice, which had inspired the rings they all wore – its stem entwined with two serpents twisting up to the cup, which was cradled with wings, its rim encrusted with sapphires, rubies and diamonds – had been left to him by his grandfather, who'd told him it had been unearthed from the ruins of a temple near Athens. Used in the very first meeting of the Academy, it was not only one of the most valuable of Lorenzo's possessions, but the most prized.

It was almost a year, now, since he had barred all but Marsilio, Bertoldo and Papi from his study; forbidding his children from sneaking in and playing with his treasures like they used to, making certain it was locked whenever he was absent, taking more of his meetings in the ground-floor suite. When Jack first arrived, informing him of the fate of Amaury and alerting him to the possibility of a traitor in his household, Lorenzo had sent up a grateful prayer that this provision – made for another reason entirely – had perhaps kept him safer than he'd realised. In all that time, nothing else had gone missing and there had been no further issues in his business affairs that hinted at possible infiltration. Maybe the chalice really had been mislaid? But its loss nagged at his mind, whispering that his fears were right: someone in his own household was against him. Perhaps someone in this room.

'Hermes Trismegistus, uncloud our eyes and guide us in our searching, reveal the path from the cave of ignorance that we might ascend into the light of knowledge. As above, so below. Amen.'

Lorenzo stirred as the priest sat, closing the book and removing his spectacles. Thanking Marsilio, he looked around the room. 'Welcome, brothers. It gladdens me to be back in your company after our long absence. Affairs within the republic have kept me busy, but I join you today eager to continue our discourse.' He spread a hand to the feast on the table. 'And may we fill our bodies as we fill our souls.'

A few of the men nodded appreciatively as they reached for the goblets and platters.

'Brothers,' Pico cut across them, standing.

'Pico—' Poliziano said, his tone full of warning.

Lorenzo held up a hand to quiet him. 'What is it, Pico?'

'Before we begin, signore, I should like to address the chamber.'

Lorenzo caught the gaze of Marsilio. He had told the old priest what Wynter had overheard – that Pico suspected he was keeping something from them. He could tell by the priest's expression that Marsilio was thinking the same as him. Was Pico about to challenge him? Demand to know what he had been hiding? If he denied the young man the chance to speak that would only serve to heighten suspicions. Besides, what more might he learn about what Pico thought he knew from his own lips? 'You have the floor.'

'The signore is right,' Pico began. 'Our absence from this gathering has been long indeed. In that time, within our hearts and minds, how many weeds have grown in place of flowers? How many candles have dimmed?' The young man raked the circle with his gaze, coming to rest on Lorenzo. 'Signore, with respect, I fear the Academy is losing its way.' He motioned to Marsilio, watching him in silence. 'When the texts of the *Corpus Hermeticum* were delivered to Signor Cosimo, the fire of our truth was ignited. Those texts revealed what our founder had already glimpsed through the Gathering: that all faiths, though diverted into many streams, spring ultimately from the same source – a perfect river, flowing through us all and through mankind to God – the World Soul of which Plato himself wrote. We saw, too, how that soul was darkening, corrupted by the avarice and ignorance of our clergy, the tyranny of kings and the warmongering of the Turks. And we saw how these broken, muddied waters, all flowing still towards God, were polluting paradise.

'In the decades since, the Academy has fought to uphold and spread our beliefs. We have seeded followers in the hearts of the kingdoms of the west to whisper our truths into the ears of kings and princes. We have gathered the ancient knowledge, scattered in the time of Noah, that we might uncover the lost wisdom of the ages, the better to touch the face of God. We have pursued dialogue with men of other nations and faiths to foster understanding of the World Soul and the dangers to us all if mankind continues its aimless drift down these streams to darkness.'

Marsilio shifted on his chair to frown up at his former pupil. 'Pico, must a man lecture the architect of a house on its structure? The signore is well aware of what his family has built and why. As, indeed, are we all.'

Pico inclined his head to the priest, before his grey eyes flicked back to Lorenzo. 'I apologise, signore. I merely wished to laud the brilliance of our past in order to question the impotence of our present.'

'Impotence?'

'When the sailors on board the *Trinity* claimed to have seen land in the Western Ocean and Toscanelli told us he believed Atlantis had returned, we talked – passionately, determinedly – of finding it. We dreamed of building a New Eden, away from the reach of enemies who seek to destroy us and halt our aims. Sixtus may be dead, but already his successor, Pope Innocent, calls for a new crusade against the Turks. Now we risk, once again, becoming crushed between the jaws of two mindless, gnashing beasts. Signore, to my eyes we are no closer to seeking New Eden or to establishing our place in the world than we were when we, as brothers, last met.'

Lorenzo noted the surprised glances between the men at Pico's oratory – brazen even for the heated debates they often entered into in their circle. He also saw the slow nods of agreement from some.

'If I may, Fra Marsilio?' said Pico, leaning over to slide the *Corpus Hermeticum* out from under Marsilio's hand. He skimmed the text. 'Here,' he said, lifting the book. 'We are told to go forth into the world. To light the dark places with the light of our truth. That same command was passed down from Hermes to Plato and Moses and, on, to Christ Himself.' He placed the book down. 'Do we now only read the words, not follow their tenets? What mute disciples are we?'

'Only if those men have minds to listen, Pico,' Marsilio reminded him. 'Many still have ears full of clay. First, we must teach those who are already listeners in the wilderness.' He gestured to the men around the table. 'Bring the cup to them, that they might help us shape and change the world. Then, others will begin to understand.'

'Why not send our wisdom out into the world, cast it like a net to lure like-minded souls?' Pico bent down and rifled in the bag that was slung over his chair.

'Pico.'

Ignoring Poliziano, Pico pulled out a handful of papers, curled and ink-stained. He held them up, showing them to Lorenzo and the others. 'I have begun writing a thesis – an oration if you will – inspired by our beliefs. I wish to publish it. Perhaps, by way of it, we may draw more disciples to our cause?'

Several of the men began speaking at once.

'Now is not the time,' Lorenzo said, cutting across them all. 'You are right, Pico. There are indeed storms on the horizon. It is why I have pulled back from our advance.' Resting his elbows on the arms of his chair, he steepled his fingers under his chin. 'We have been weakened these past years, by events beyond our control. We cannot sail, reckless, into those tempests. Caution is needed now, if we are to continue our legacy. Pope Innocent must not see us as a threat, as Sixtus came to.'

Lorenzo faltered, wondering whether to go further – tell them his plan, so they understood what was at stake? Tell them, too, that an enemy had taken Amaury de la Croix and there was, perhaps, a spy in his household? He glanced at Poliziano, hating the distance growing between them – a distance he knew he'd created by his secrets. But suspicion crept in again, curling dark around his indecision. He heard his grandfather's voice. *Never show your hand until you are ready. Know your enemy before he knows you.* Already, he had suffered one betrayer: Anthony Woodville. If one of these men was against him and he revealed too much, it could put everything at risk. His plan, if it came to light too soon, would not only provoke the wrath of Rome, but Christendom itself. The wrong thing, said to the wrong person, had the power to bring his whole empire – everything his family had built – crashing down.

Pico shook his head, flushed with frustration. 'Signore, forgive me, but we know you are keeping things from us.' He looked from him to Marsilio. 'Both of you. Hiding away in your study, speaking behind closed doors and—'

Lorenzo stood, his chair screeching on the floor. Several of the men started. 'Leave your papers and go, Pico. I will speak to you tomorrow.'

'Signore—'

'I am your leader, within these walls and without. You will obey me.'

After a long pause, Pico laid the curled and ink-stained papers on the table. Flame-faced, he pushed back his chair and strode from the room. The bang of the door echoed around the chamber.

Lorenzo snatched up the papers and held them over one of the candles. The edges turned dark, before hissing alight. He held them there until a flame leapt up to consume them. Dropping them on the table, he scoured the men. 'Does anyone else wish to challenge me?'

He saw, then, that Poliziano, eyes on the burning papers, was stained with the same shame and knew that Pico had told him what he was planning – and his friend had not warned him.

Marsilio laced his hands on the table. 'Let us start this meeting anew. Poliziano, perhaps you could pour the wine?'

As the chamber filled slowly with the sound of voices, Lorenzo sat, eyes on the smouldering papers, Pico's words turning to ash.

Sometimes, he wondered at the choices a man made in his life: what a chaotic road had been laid behind him of carefully made plans and rushed decisions, rapid shifts and backtracks. Where might that road have led him if any one of them had been different? Sometimes, the thought left him light-headed, as if he were looking out over an abyss, no road laid before him, all the choices yet to make and the weight of those already made pushing at his back.

15

Men called it the thunder of God. The ear-splitting bursts from the cannons ricocheted through the valley, the mountains volleying every explosion back as a series of answering echoes. The air itself – hot as hell even with the early morning's cover of cloud – the ground, the sky: everything seemed to shudder with the fury of each barrage. Smoke billowed, accompanied by flashes of fire, the rushing hiss of fused powder and the shouts of men, readying to prime the weapons for another shot.

Harry, watching the assault with a host of men on the edges of the royal camp, could only imagine what the Spanish gunners, stationed on the hillside opposite Loja, must feel with every chest-shattering boom. The guns the supply train had dragged from Córdoba – a mixture of fat-barrelled bronze cannons and slender iron serpentines – were lined up alongside those already in position. Lashed to movable platforms that controlled the line of fire, they had joined with the others in violent chorus, launching their deadly shot of iron, lead and stone at the town.

Harry had heard the guns called various names, which Rodrigo had endeavoured to translate: bombard, mortar, falcon. There was even one called an organ, made of three tubes that fired lance tips, no doubt lethal to any man exposed on the battlements, although he'd not seen this one used yet. The enemy remained elusive, ensconced behind their scarred but indomitable walls, just the odd flicker of movement on the walkways, occasional high-pitched screams when a cannon found a mark, and sometimes, in the hush between bombardments, the eerie wailing of their prayers. Occasionally, a puff of smoke from a tower-top, a great boom, and one of the Moors' own, much lighter, guns would answer the Spaniards. But the king's artillery was protected by stout wooden screens, buttressed with earth, and, so far, Harry hadn't seen any of the enemy's cannons do any real damage.

There was an explosion of stone as a projectile smashed through the side of a tower, pulverising a section of it. Rubble rained down with a distant roar. It was greeted with ferocious glee by the men around Harry. El Barbero, his face twisted with a vicious grin, turned to Rodrigo, yelling something Harry didn't catch. Harry noticed the hidalgo's hands were clenching and unclenching as he watched the assault, as though he wanted to be the one to do the damage; to crush skulls and bones, not stone.

'They are making good work of it today!' Harry shouted.

'By the might of our guns and by God's will, the infidel will fail!' Rodrigo responded, his black eyes glittering.

'The king will be pleased.' Harry faltered as Rodrigo returned his intent gaze to the barrage of the cannons. 'Perhaps he will see me today? If all goes well?'

Rodrigo glanced distractedly at him. 'Patience, my friend. You will get your audience soon enough.' Another triumphant roar of men swept his attention back to the town, where another section of the broken tower had been struck. The hidalgo's lips peeled back in a savage smile.

Harry gritted his teeth. He had been in the king's camp for over two weeks now, but although he'd been formally introduced to Ferdinand and accepted as England's ambassador, the king – cordial, respectful – had been too preoccupied with the siege of Loja, and all the comings and goings of men and reports from other companies in the region, for a proper audience, or the niceties of diplomatic relations.

Harry felt the days turning as if by the handle of a vice, the passing of time tightening the anxiety inside him. Columbus's proposal might not have progressed much further than the queen's mild interest, but if he was to be certain of preventing the man from securing any funding or real support from the monarchs – scuppering his chances of launching any serious expedition west – he would need to have wound his way much closer into the royal circle than these fringes he found himself lingering at. King Henry had conceded the mission would take time, but just how long Harry would have to remain here to complete it was unclear.

'Impressive, isn't it?'

Harry turned sharply to see Edward Woodville at his shoulder. In the clamour he hadn't noticed his approach. Harry's heart thumped harder. He had been startled, the day he arrived at the king's camp, by the sight of the English knight in this foreign place. But before he'd had a chance to ask how he had come to be here, Woodville had left with a company of Spanish lancers on a special assignment. It was something Rodrigo had called a *tala*: the burning of crops and destruction of farmsteads, crippling the enemy's ability to supply their increasingly isolated towns, forcing them east into the Vega of Granada, corralling them like animals. The company had returned four days ago, trailing a stale odour of smoke and driving a whole herd of cattle before them, the beasts now penned near the camp; living plunder. In the knight's absence, Harry had been left to wonder, and then to fret, over his presence.

He had heard at the king's wedding that Woodville was abroad. But here? The coincidence had made him question whether Henry could have sent him too. Tudor had a fondness for competition among his men, using it to gauge strength, loyalty, ambition. Harry had seen him employ it in many arenas, from the tennis court and jousting field, to his household and court. The thought that the king might have sent Woodville with the exact same mission as himself had nestled in his brain where it had festered. He knew well what it was to have his place – his future – thrown into turmoil by a usurper. More and more, the memory of following his father to that house in the woods outside Lewes had played in his mind: the soul-deep shock as he'd watched his father embrace a woman who wasn't his mother and laugh with another son.

Edward Woodville squinted as he surveyed the distant cannons. 'Impressive indeed.'

It was bright, even with the cloud cover. A brightness Harry found got stuck behind the eyes, where it needled the brain. 'I hear the king is most pleased with the success of your mission, Sir Edward. Congratulations.'

The knight smiled placidly. 'It was easy pickings.'

The man's modesty nettled Harry. Even in just the few days he'd seen him in the camp, he'd not failed to notice how admired Woodville was by King Ferdinand, who'd given the knight a tent almost as grand as his own and, yesterday, had presented him with a pair of golden spurs in honour of his accomplishment. Harry had watched, teeth gritted. Ferdinand, in their brief first meeting, had welcomed his pledge to fight, but the courtesy made Harry feel supremely foolish when he'd discovered Edward Woodville had brought with him three hundred men, most of them Welsh archers, who'd already earned much admiration for their skill from the Spanish.

'I hear you've been asking questions about me.' Woodville's easy smile remained, but his blue eyes were now fixed on Harry.

'I was merely curious what brought you here,' Harry replied, cursing inwardly. He'd thought he was being careful in the probing he'd done in the man's absence – getting Peter to try to unearth what his purpose here was. 'I wasn't expecting to find a fellow Englishman.'

Woodville maintained his gaze, but his sunburned face relaxed a little. There was dust caught in the bristles of his red-blond beard and a smudge of soot on his cheek above the scar, the stitches of which were beginning to be pushed out by skin. 'My brother, Sir Anthony, fought the Moors in Portugal, years ago. He always spoke of going back, to finish God's work. But then . . .'

Harry nodded. There was no need to finish the sentence. Sir Anthony Woodville had been with his father, escorting Prince Edward to London for his coronation, when they had been arrested by Richard of Gloucester and sent to their deaths – an act that had left Richard free to take custody of the prince and seize the crown.

'After Henry's coronation I made a pledge to honour his wish. So I came here.' Woodville pulled a gold chain from the stiff neckline of his brigandine, on which hung a cross. He touched it to his lips. 'A crusade for my brother.' There was another harsh cheer as a second tower beyond Loja's walls took a hit. 'I'm told you are here as King Henry's emissary. A knight now, too?' Woodville stowed the cross. 'I must admit, I was surprised to hear it. I never knew Henry held you in such esteem?'

'My father was an ambassador for King Edward. In the courts of Burgundy and France.'

If Woodville noticed the offence in Harry's tone, he didn't show it. 'Of course he was.' He laughed wryly. 'I wonder what Sir Thomas and Sir Anthony would think of us now? We men of York – our fealty sworn to a Lancastrian king? What a strange course Fortune's wheel can turn.' He blew through his teeth at another air-splitting series of booms from the Spanish cannons. 'By God, even more thunder than Richard's forces had arrayed against us at Redemore Plain.' His smile faded, those blue eyes sharpening again. 'But I suppose you wouldn't know that, Sir Harry. Being as you weren't there.'

Harry's mouth felt dry. He swallowed as Woodville continued.

'You never gave me an answer – no clear one at least – at our Lord Henry's coronation, when I asked you where you were. I always wondered at your absence from the battle, given how close Henry kept you after you warned him Richard was trying to make a deal with the Bretons to have him delivered to England. I wonder even more now, with your new position of authority. What other task did Henry have you doing last summer? What could have been so important that it kept you from the war? A war Henry needed every man he could muster for?'

Harry's head filled with an image of Prince Edward – Woodville's nephew – screaming as he was bundled on to a horse in the clearing of the woods near Dijon, where they'd found the hunting lodge, the fire taking hold behind as they rode away. The blood was pounding so hard in his temples it took him a moment to realise that the guns had fallen silent and the men around him were starting to move. The bombardment of Loja had paused. It would start again after prayers and food. He was opening his mouth to speak, not even knowing what words – excuses, lies – were about to come forth, when Rodrigo interrupted them.

'Sir Edward,' the hidalgo greeted respectfully, before turning to Harry. 'Shall we break our fast?'

'Excuse me,' Harry murmured to the knight, shamed by the weakness in his voice, but now desperate to be out from under Woodville's piercing gaze.

'Of course. No doubt we will have other opportunities to talk, Sir Harry.'

'What is wrong?' Rodrigo asked, as they headed across the grass, parched by the sun and flattened by the constant traffic of men, beasts and equipment. 'You look as pale as milk.'

'Nothing. It's just the heat.'

Rodrigo chuckled. 'You English never handle it well. Come, you need food and shade.' He glanced back at the beleaguered town, the air gritty with dust from the destruction, his face set. 'We will all need our strength before long.'

The evidence of that was plain as they walked through the camp. In one area, clear of tents, animal pens and fires, the wooden towers Harry had spotted on his arrival were now near completion.

Carpenters were still at work on two, the clanking of hammers audible now the guns had fallen silent. The Spanish called them *bastidas*. The towers, set on wheeled platforms, were hollow in the middle, with a ladder inside that climbed to the top where a hatch opened like a drawbridge. They had been built to the size of Loja's walls and, when moved to the base, would allow men to scale them within the defensive cover of the tower. Each was coated with leather soaked in vinegar to proof against fire, its astringent smell sharpening the air. Harry didn't envy those who would be the first out of those hatches, over the wall and into the teeth of the enemy.

Around them, men crouched by fires, digging bowls into pots of stew. The different companies were almost impossible to number. Along with Ferdinand's own troops, there were several magnates: dukes and counts, all commanders in their own right with armies under their authority. There were nobles like Rodrigo: vassals of the queen or squires in her royal guard, and other hidalgos not so closely affiliated with the monarchs, many with their own bands of men. Some were very rich, others poor. There were caballeros and the knights of the Holy Brotherhood, and several prelates, who seemed more like warrior princes, wearing armour with as much pride as the cross. And there were thousands of tan-faced, coarse-mouthed men: farmers and workers called to serve as infantrymen, camp followers, foreign mercenaries and the *homicianos*: murderers, rapists, thieves, released from gaols with the promise of pardon in return for service.

Harry, wondering how on earth this fragmented body functioned as a whole, had heard enough from Rodrigo to know that sometimes it didn't. There was a suggestion that something in its disparate nature had led to the rout in which his father had been killed. Still, although, as in any army, each man had come for his own reasons – duty, honour, prestige, boredom, plunder, absolution, revenge – all seemed to share one common goal: to wipe the infidel from the soil of Spain.

'Don Luys!' Rodrigo hailed the man Harry had first seen him greet on entering the camp.

He'd been told he was another hidalgo, highly favoured by Queen Isabella, and – according to Rodrigo – as a father to him, but other than that Harry knew little, Don Luys preferring to keep to his own company.

Don Luys was wearing his black robe lined with white leather and his usual hostile expression. He and Rodrigo spoke fast and fluid, Harry catching snippets of words, helped by gestures that formed the vague sense they were talking about the morning's bombardment and the coming assault on Loja. As they talked, Harry searched the shifting crowds of men for any sign of Edward Woodville, half fearing the knight might have followed him.

His heart had slowed, but his thoughts were still racing. His worry about Woodville's presence seemed, at least on the face of it, to have been assuaged with the knight's claim he had come here under his own volition, on crusade. But it had now been replaced by greater concern. Woodville, it was clear, was not at all satisfied by his answers at the coronation. But he couldn't tell the man the truth: that he, Harry, had not only delivered Woodville's own nephew to his death, but by that action had helped establish the reign of a Lancastrian king, ending all hopes of the House of York and those who had served it. If Woodville discovered this, Harry reckoned his fears about failing Henry or the danger posed by the Moors would be the least of his troubles.

He was drawn back as Rodrigo, in mid-conversation with Don Luys, motioned to him. Luys gave Harry a cursory glance, eyes hardening. He shook his head, lip curling in a scowl. After a few more words, they grasped one another's hands firmly, then Don Luys stalked off, his leather-lined cloak swinging from his broad shoulders.

'Were you talking about me?' Harry questioned, as they walked on. It was frustrating, not knowing what men were saying about him. He really must pay more attention in Peter's lessons.

'I asked if Don Luys wanted to join us for food.'

'He didn't?'

Rodrigo glanced at him. 'Do not take his demeanour personally. He is not fond of Englishmen. Believe me, even Sir Edward's charms will not win his favour.'

'Why?'

'His son was killed by one.'

Harry saw some spark in Rodrigo's eyes – a momentary flash of pain or anger – then it was gone and the man was gripping his shoulder.

'Come, let us eat.'

But, as they approached their tents, they saw an agitated crowd gathered outside the king's pavilion. Moving closer with Rodrigo, Harry saw the king's physician and other servants rushing out, bearing bowls, pliers and armfuls of linen. Surrounded by the growing knot of people were a dozen or so men. Several were wounded, some badly, lying on the ground and being tended to, their faces ashen. There were horses nearby, mouths and nostrils white with foam. As the saddle was removed from one beast it collapsed. Grooms struggled from the nearby river, hauling buckets of water to splash over the animals.

King Ferdinand was crouched beside one of the wounded, whom his physician was inspecting. The man was shuddering, his face, contorted with pain, an oily grey. The physician had cut away his bloodstained gambeson and pulled up his shirt to reveal a deep puncture wound in the man's abdomen, packed with what looked like small wads of cloth, seeping yellow pus. The whole area was dark and swollen. Feverish red tendrils snaked out from the wound; telltale signs of infection. Harry caught the king and the physician exchange grim, knowing looks. After placing a hand on the man's trembling shoulder, the king rose to speak with a group of men who had arrived, among them the Marquis of Cádiz, a veteran of the war, here with his own army.

'Wolfbane,' murmured Rodrigo, eyes on the man now whimpering in pain as the physician poured what looked like wine over the wound. 'It grows in the mountains,' he added, glancing at Harry. 'The Moors dip their arrowheads in a mixture of it. It infects any part of the body it pierces. It's a wretched way to die.' He turned to question a man beside him, then relayed the information to Harry. 'They were part of a scouting company. A band of enemy archers attacked them last night, not far north of here.' His teeth clenched. 'They lost ten men.'

'Don Rodrigo.'

The hidalgo turned quickly at King Ferdinand's voice. 'My lord?'

The king, the marquis and other officials were ducking into the pavilion. Rodrigo looked back at Harry. 'I'll find you when I'm done, Sir Harry. Tell my men I want them ready to move out. I imagine the king will have orders for us.'

'Orders?'

'Lord Ferdinand will want retribution. If we are so honoured, we will be his sword.'

With that Rodrigo strode towards the pavilion, leaving Harry alone in the milling crowd, the cries of the wounded in his ears and a creeping stench of death in the stifling air.

16

From up here the city seemed serene, gleaming in the amber haze, cradled on all sides by steep hills punctuated with the dark exclamations of cypress trees that ascended into distant mountains. To Jack, it looked like a vast cloak of russet and gold lying crumpled in the valley, decorated with precious stones, the cathedral's dome a great jewel in the centre, the Arno a snaking green ribbon, pinned by its four bridges. He'd only left it that morning, riding out from the Porta Fiesolana, but already the sweltering heat, the oppressiveness of the tight alleys, the eye-watering stench of tanneries and wool-washing sheds, the constant clamour of carts and people and animals, the ceaseless hum of flies, all seemed hard to imagine.

Here, high on the hillside, the air was fresh with pine and grass. Jack felt as though he could breathe again. It was still sultry, although evening was well on its way, the sun flaming like a torch as it descended, the sky turning from turquoise to cobalt, the pin-prick glimmer of stars in the east – but the breeze through the olive groves and the burble of fountains served to temper it. No wonder Florence's wealthy left for the summer, escaping to their villas in the hills and valleys of Tuscany, leaving the poor to do their best to ward off the sicknesses that thrived in the heat of the city. He thought of Ned and the others, trapped down there in that stinking maze.

Hearing the clatter of hooves, Jack turned to see more guests arriving, urging their horses down the tree-shaded lane towards the grand buildings of the villa, built on two levels on the steep slope, with stables, outhouses, gardens and olive groves descending in stepped tiers of land. The heads of the company rode richly caparisoned horses and were sumptuously dressed, with a train of liveried guards and pages following in their dust. Two of the men wore jewelled collars over the scarlet and black robes of the Signoria. From what Jack had seen of the other attendees arriving through the afternoon it seemed half the elite of Florence had been invited to this feast. He wondered again what announcement Lorenzo would be making.

Grooms hastened from the stables to greet the guests and servants appeared bearing wine. Black Martin and Crooked Andrea were there too, ready to remove any weapons. Jack turned for the steps, thinking he should change his clothes for dinner, when he saw two young women emerge from the lower villa, arm-in-arm. As they paused by the dismounting riders to pat one of the horses, he recognised them as Maddalena de' Medici and Laora.

Anticipation fizzed through him. It was several days since his encounter with Laora in the market, when the earth had shaken the city to its foundations, but the young woman had remained in his thoughts; her face tilted up, eyes closed, the words of the prayer tumbling down with the first drops of rain.

Strange, how beautiful the language of the infidel is.

Later that day, and the next, he had loitered in the hallways of the palazzo, near to the closed doors of the *Sala Grande*, watched by coy nymphs and glitter-eyed satyrs from the wooded depths of gilt-framed paintings, wondering how he might conjure some pretext for Papi to allow him to enter – get closer to the locked study, maybe ask the elderly servant whether Lorenzo had Muslims among his army of anonymous staff? But, then, Marsilio Ficino had returned from his brief stay at Fiesole, attending to some business of Lorenzo's, and the chance had vanished.

He had told himself it was most likely just a slave at prayer between tasks he'd heard that night. But all the threads in his hands – his father's words about the Turks, Marco Valori's warnings about Lorenzo, the bite in Pico's voice as he told Poliziano the signore was hiding something – had tied themselves in knots and he could no longer separate the significant from the irrelevant. Laora, though, had lingered in his mind; that scent in the dusk of Lorenzo's rooms, the air hushed, held like a breath, the tremble of her hand and the flush in her cheeks when he told her he'd seen her that night, slipping upstairs. If she had been in Lorenzo's chambers, for whatever reason, might she, too, have heard that chanting? Might she know the source? Be able to help him untangle his thoughts?

Determined to speak to her, Jack started towards the steps that led up from the garden, but Laora saw him first. She seemed to stiffen at the sight of him, then leaned in to Maddalena and said something in the girl's ear, before extracting herself. Jack watched as she descended the uneven steps towards him, hitching the skirts of her gold gown, which ballooned from the tight bodice, making her look like a burnished bell in the last of the shimmering copper light.

She approached with a cautious half-smile, part greeting, part question, her shadow thrown long across the grass, birds flickering from the box hedges at her passing. 'Sir James, I did not expect to see you here tonight?'

'Nor I you, signora,' he said, removing his hat and inclining his head. Up close, he noticed her gown was frayed around the hems and there were a few beads missing from the ornate cap that covered her hair, but despite these flaws she looked as regal as any noble lady he'd seen at the royal court in England. The kind of woman a man would win a tournament for. Jack realised he had stared a little too long. 'No more tremors in the earth?'

Laora smiled, the tightness in her eyes disappearing. 'No. The world seems calm.' She looked out over the city, her sharp features softened by the sun's smouldering glow. 'I forget how beautiful it looks from up here.'

'I was just thinking the same.'

'I used to play in these gardens, when I was a child.' A shadow passed across her face, but then that poised smile was back in place. 'So, you are here for the grand announcement?' She coloured a little at his expression. 'Oh, you do not know yet?'

The only instruction Jack had been given, arriving at midday with servants bringing supplies from the palazzo, was to be groomed and ready after sundown. Lorenzo had told him he would be seated next to Pico and that he should converse with the young man, get him to open up. *It shouldn't be difficult. Pico rarely tires of talking about himself. I want to hear what he thinks he knows.* Jack studied her. 'But you know, signora?'

Laora glanced around, making sure they were still alone. 'The signore plans to announce that the proposed marriage between Maddalena and the pope's son has been agreed. Maddalena told me earlier in confidence,' she confessed.

Jack nodded, hiding his disappointment. Part of him had hoped the feast might have something to do with the Academy, since he'd heard the company was meeting. Still, maybe Pico could be coaxed, with enough wine, to speak of things that might be of use to him too?

'First Lucrezia, now Maddalena,' Laora murmured. 'Soon, it will just be me on my own.'

Jack had another image of Lorenzo, pulling her to him. It was all very well playing the part of a nobleman with other men: he'd seen that role played out enough times for himself in his father's company. But, with a woman? Grace had been a daughter of the local Justice of the Peace. Given her place within the Medici household, Laora might as well be a queen's lady-in-waiting. How could he possibly get to the meat of the matter – ask if she was close to the signore? Close enough to know his secrets? 'To be honest,' he began carefully, 'I am surprised you aren't married already.'

'And what of you?' Her eyes flicked to him, voice sharpening. 'Have you left your wife alone in England, Sir James, while you enjoy Signor Lorenzo's famous hospitality?'

Jack was taken aback by the change of her tone. 'My wife is dead.'

Laora stared at him, then clasped her hands as if in prayer. 'Please, forgive my discourtesy, Sir James. I did not mean to offend you. I am sad to be losing my friend to a husband's bonds.' She reached out, touched his arm lightly. 'But that is nothing compared to your loss.'

Jack shook his head, the regret in her eyes making him feel worse for the lie. But his attempt to brush away the subject only seemed to deepen her sympathy.

'When did your wife pass?'

Now she was closer, he could smell the blossom: sweetness with a bitter bite. A memory – lavender and thyme, summer light and his mother's hands, deep in dark soil, worms turning from her touch.

'Some time ago.'

'Do you have children? A family?'

'No children. My family . . .?' Jack looked away, the pain now real. 'They're gone.'

Laora followed him with her gaze until he looked at her again. She nodded, her hazel eyes, fixed and knowing, on his.

The silence between them was filled by the clang of a hand-bell as one of the cooks summoned the servants to the kitchens for the final preparations.

'Laora!'

She turned distractedly at Maddalena's call. 'I must go, Sir James.' She inclined her head. 'I will see you at dinner.'

He watched her leave with a curse in his mind. If he was to find answers here he would need to be bolder.

An hour later, at the silvery tinkle of another bell, Jack headed downstairs from the room he'd been allocated. He was wearing the sky-blue doublet Lorenzo had lent him for the party in June. There was a faint stain on the front where Pico had made him spill his wine. In the mirrors he passed he looked like an actor moving across a stage; the rich garments his costume, the lines in his head devised by someone else. Laora calling him *sir* and all the expensive clothes in the world could not make this pretence real. Once his business was done – even if Lorenzo kept his word, gave him what he wanted – he would become an outcast again, with tainted blood and nothing to his name. *What are you doing here?*

The reception room – more a grand hall, with tapestries to line the walls and a painted ceiling decorated with gilt bosses – was radiant with candlelight. Incense smoke puffed from pewter burners. Long tables covered with cloth of gold had been set out in a horseshoe, so the guests could view one another. Between polished cutlery and goblets, silver basins had been filled with perfumed water for guests to wash their hands. Ushers, tunics decorated with the Medici arms, were showing people to their places.

As Jack passed the windows, the open shutters of which let in the night air, he saw hundreds of flickering lights down in the shadows of the valley. Florence had become an earth-bound constellation. He sat in the place the usher gestured him to, men and women filing in around him, skirts rustling, chairs scraping, voices lifting.

Jack recognised some from the night of the party, or from brief glimpses in the palazzo. There were Lorenzo's cousins, Lorenzino and Giovanni di' Pierfrancesco de' Medici, dressed in matching blue hose and black doublets with ballooned sleeves, slashed to show blue silk beneath. They sat opposite him, Lorenzino looking imperiously around, his large eyes glassy in the candlelight. Giovanni, catching Jack's gaze, leaned in to whisper in his older brother's ear, before smirking and tossing back his cinnamon curls. Moving in beside them was their clerk, Amerigo Vespucci, nephew of Fra Giorgio, folding his thick-fingered hands on the table, the bald dome of his head gleaming. Here was Angelo Poliziano, slipping past with a brief nod, to sit at the end of the table at the head of the horseshoe, pushing back his brown hair, his expression inscrutable.

Jack looked to the doors, wondering when Pico would make an appearance, to see Marsilio Ficino enter, presumably just arrived from the palazzo. The old priest shuffled, stoop-backed, to take the chair at the other end of the head table. Soon, most of the other seats had been filled, leaving only the chair beside Jack and the middle of the top table empty. Jack caught one of the ushers who was passing. 'Is Signor Giovanni Pico della Mirandola here?'

'I'm afraid he has taken ill, signore. He will not be attending this evening.' As a bell was rung, the usher looked round. 'Excuse me.'

The man hurried off, disappearing through the double doors that were closed behind him, leaving the chamber to echo with polite murmurs as the guests greeted one another and craned their heads to see who else had been invited.

After a moment, the doors opened again and in swept Lorenzo de' Medici. The signore wore a scarlet robe, buttoned high to the neck. Nodding to the company, who rose to greet him with a shuffling of feet, he made his way to the centre of the top table. In his wake came his wife, Clarice, dressed in a gown of green velvet, a black padded headdress jigging with each step. Following was her daughter, Lucrezia, with her new husband, one of Florence's powerful silk manufacturers, with a grand palazzo and a workforce of hundreds. Jack saw the telltale bulge beneath the embroidered band of Lucrezia's dress that told him the girl was already with child. Behind came Lorenzo's two eldest sons, Piero, proud and erect, and chubby-cheeked Giovanni, grinning behind his hand at all the attention. Last were Maddalena – dwarfed by her voluminous gown, a gem-encrusted cross at her throat – and Laora. She met his gaze briefly as she followed Maddalena to sit in honour with the Medici.

Lorenzo remained standing. 'Welcome, all of you.' His harsh, nasal voice filled the chamber. 'I am honoured to be your host here in my home. Family. Friends. Men and women of our city.' His eyes alighted on Pico's empty chair; a flicker of irritation, then he was moving on. 'Please,' he said, motioning to the servants, waiting at the wings of the hall. 'Pour the wine, for there is much to celebrate.' He continued as they moved in, bearing jugs of jade and crystal. 'For seventeen years I have borne, proudly, the mantle of guardianship over our noble republic, as my father, grandfather and great-grandfather before me. It has been my deepest honour and greatest joy, even through turmoil and trouble, hardship and strife. Its citizens I count as family and nothing is more important to me. Family is the blood and bonds that bind us, the mutual pain of loss and the shared pleasure of success.' Lorenzo waited for the servants to finish pouring, then lifted his goblet. 'We – each – are nothing without it.' He fixed on his cousins as he said this. 'To family.'

Lorenzino raised his goblet in answer, Giovanni joining him a moment later.

'It is thus with pride and with honour that tonight I announce the expansion of my family – of Florence's family. This coming year, my daughter, Maddalena, will celebrate her betrothal to Franceschetto Cybo, nephew of His Holiness, Pope Innocent VIII.'

The announcement stirred a mixture of reactions. A few people nodded, clearly having expected this. Others appeared pleased or impressed, while some smiled wryly at the careful use of the word nephew. Jack caught a man beside him murmur to his companion.

'It seems everyone but his own children may call His Holiness, *Father*.'

Maddalena kept her eyes down as Lorenzo and the rest of the room drank in her honour. Jack noticed her small hand was entwined in Laora's.

'Furthermore, this new accord with Rome has ushered in the prospect that my son, Giovanni, may soon be granted a cardinal's hat.'

This revelation elicited gasps of surprise, all eyes turning to the chubby-cheeked eleven-year-old. As the guests began murmuring, Jack kept his gaze on Lorenzo, not missing the small smile that played at his thin lips. No wonder the man was pleased. If his son became a cardinal it would put him in line to the papal throne.

Jack's eyes moved to the scar on Lorenzo's neck, from the attempt on his life authorised by Pope Innocent's predecessor, Sixtus. He had seen how much the signore involved himself in all aspects of the day-to-day business of the republic, but he'd not realised until now just how far forward his gaze seemed to be focused; a man moving a piece on a board, but thinking many steps ahead.

Jack recalled Amaury speaking of corruption in the Church; a spreading cancer, he'd claimed. Did Lorenzo mean to cure that poison by seeding his own son in the heart of the Vatican? What other long games was he playing? And what small, expendable piece might he be within them?

After the guests had drunk to the announcements, servants carried in the food. There were spiced peacock tongues and kid roasted in cherries, zucchini flowers in honey and saffron-flavoured cream. Angelo Poliziano was called to say grace and, as the company tucked in, two musicians plucked softly on lutes, although the melodies could barely be heard over the clatter of dishes and the buzz of conversation among the guests, all talking among themselves at Lorenzo's announcements and the fates of his two children, now entwined with the most powerful house in Christendom: the House of St Peter.

Jack sat alone in the midst of the chatter, Pico's empty chair beside him. He felt out of place and foolish, eating in silence while these illustrious guests talked around him – a beggar at a table of kings. He glanced over at Laora, seeing if she would catch his eye, but she was focused on comforting Maddalena, who was pushing her food around her plate, her stern-eyed mother murmuring intently in her other ear.

By the time the plates were being cleared away, the hum of conversation had risen, the wine flowing. Lorenzo was turned in his chair, talking with the priors from the Signoria. Other people were shifting their places, moving to talk to friends and acquaintances. Jack caught snippets of friendly banter mixed with more serious exchanges about business or politics. He was wondering if he might be able to extricate himself, retreat to his room, when the chair beside him scraped back.

Amerigo Vespucci smiled as he sat, his teeth stained dark with wine. 'Good evening, Sir James. My uncle told me you might be here.'

'Master Amerigo,' Jack answered with a guarded nod. Was the clerk going to drill him again on his family's non-existent wool business? He had neither the patience nor the energy.

'I've been meaning to seek you out since our first meeting. Tell me, are you gaining a deeper understanding of our city? Finding inspiration to take back to London and your father's company?'

Jack's spirits sank. 'I am.'

Amerigo studied him. After a moment, his dark eyes flicked to Lorenzo. 'I understand.' He raised his goblet with a dip of his head. 'You do well to be guarded about your affairs with the signore.'

No doubt he did, thought Jack, when it seemed everyone in Florence was guarded about everything. Despite all the talk of the noble republic, of the strong bonds of family that bound them, all he was starting to see was a city of secrets, envy and distrust.

'But your wool business isn't what I wanted to talk to you about.'

'No?'

'I wanted to ask if you have heard of a man called Cristoforo Colombo? A sailor?' When Jack shook his head, Amerigo looked disappointed. 'Ah, I thought if your father exports wool through Bristol or Southampton you might have come across him.'

'Who is he? I may have heard of his deeds, if not his name?'

'He's from Genoa apparently. I heard of him recently while seeking new business opportunities for my masters in Spain.' Amerigo looked at Lorenzino and Giovanni as he spoke. 'It is said this sailor believes that by sailing west from Portugal he can reach the Spice Islands. He is currently seeking funds from the monarchs of Spain for such a voyage.'

Jack's interest was sparked. Amaury had spoken of this sailor. What had the priest said? That if the man attempted such a voyage he would surely find New Eden first?

There are factions who would carve up the world for themselves, careless of the cost. We are on a path to darkness, all of us.

'I've been trying to find out more about him,' Amerigo continued. 'But all I know is that he crewed for a Genoese company shipping supplies of mastic to England, that he spent time in Lisbon and may have worked the seas off Thule on a fishing vessel.'

'What interests you in him?' Jack asked. As he thought of the map and that strange new coastline seen by the Bristol sailors of the *Trinity*, he felt a shift inside him. He wasn't just some actor playing a role; or a nobody no one wanted to talk to. There was real power in his own truth. That map had been in his hands, entrusted to him by his father. It had endangered him, yes, and had led directly to his mother's death, but the fact was – for a time – he had been in control of something desired and fought over by some of the most powerful men in Christendom. Didn't that mean something?

'What interests me?' Amerigo said with a surprised bark of laughter. 'Imagine – a new route to those islands, just over our horizon? No need to challenge the Turks? A path, all our own, to the greatest concentrations of spices, perfumes, silks, pearls, gems and gold in the world? Any man who succeeded in finding it could become richer than the pope!' He took a gulp of wine, as if to temper his fervour. 'One of my uncles is commander of a fleet of ships that patrols the waters off our coast. Several of my cousins are also seamen. The ocean runs like blood in the veins of my family, but my father, a lawyer, wanted me to follow in his footsteps.' Amerigo set the goblet down, slowly twisting it on its base. 'All my life I have dreamed of horizons and those who have sailed into them, undaunted.'

Jack thought of Ned, turning those shells in his hands. *We know there's* something *out there.*

'Marco Polo,' continued Amerigo, 'Prester John, the Vivaldi Brothers, Prince Henry of Viseu, navigating his way down the African coast. Imagine what you would feel being the first man to set foot on a land not yet known? Like Adam, at the dawn of the world, no?' His dark eyes reflected the glitter of candlelight.

Amerigo's intensity was infectious. Faint skeins of stories his father had told trailed Jack's mind: of the golden cities of the far east, of lands with mountains made of gems, the air dusted with the perfume of a thousand spices, of men like Prester John disappearing into the depths of Africa, seeking new roads to the Orient, rumours they were now kings of other worlds. 'Have you heard of Antillia?' he asked Amerigo, forgetting himself. 'The Island of the Seven Cities? It is said to disappear whenever sailors get too close. Or Hy-Brasil?'

As the man went to answer, eyes lighting up at the question, Lorenzo's voice sounded, harsh above the hum of voices. 'Master Amerigo, perhaps you ought to spend your time focusing on your own business? Or, more importantly, the business of my cousins, which is what you are employed in my household for. Not idle gossip or children's stories.'

The hall had fallen silent, the only sounds the footsteps of a servant and the slosh of wine in a glass. All eyes were on Amerigo. Jack saw the man's hand had turned white around his goblet.

After a pause, Amerigo cleared his throat and rose. 'Of course, signore. Forgive me.'

The silence dragged on. Finally, Lorenzo threw down his napkin. 'Let us take some air. Sweets will be served shortly, with wine from my grandfather's store.'

The company clattered back to life, men groaning as they stood, patting their stomachs, ladies taking the moment to dab perfume behind their ears. Amerigo was one of the first up heading for the doors, the goblet still gripped in his fist. Jack followed, keen to be out in the fresh air, realising just how close he'd come to speaking of things he shouldn't.

As he passed through the doors, he saw Lorenzino di' Pierfrancesco had slipped out with Amerigo. The two men were walking down the passage, heading for the torchlit gardens.

'What was that about?' Lorenzino asked Amerigo.

'Nothing. It was nothing.'

Lorenzino's voice lowered, but Jack caught the words. 'All that talk of family? I do not know how you can even stand to sit at his table, my friend, after all he has done to yours.'

'Sir James?'

Jack turned to see one of the ushers.

'The signore would like to speak to you.'

He lay on the floor, panting. Smoke curled into his nose and mouth; poisonous, searing streams, filling his throat and lungs. His wrists and ankles worked uselessly against his bonds, the ropes rubbing his skin to blood. He was trying to grab a knife that had fallen somewhere close by, but his fingers just scratched at dirt. Heat buffeted him, the roar of flames at his back unrelenting. Then, everything fell silent.

His hands and feet were free. He sat up. A strange song was rising and falling. A chant? A prayer? There – in the shadows – a young boy, appearing and disappearing in the smoke. The boy's eyes were closed. He was singing.

There were three ravens in a tree, they were black as black could be.
One bird turned and asked his mate, where shall we our breakfast take?
Down in the long grass in yonder field, there lies a knight slain 'neath his shield . . .

He recoiled as the boy's eyes opened. They were empty – two orbs filled with nothing but darkness. The boy stretched out a hand, pointing. He turned, heart thrumming. The world behind him was still on fire. The hunting lodge where he'd been struggling, moments before, the woods beyond, the sky – all of it was burning. But in silence. In the midst of the fire he saw a figure, hunched and huge, a devil in the flames, crouched over a body. A white mask covered one side of its face. The body on the floor was a woman. His mother. The creature had one hand wrapped around her throat. As he tried to run forward, to save her, the savage heat forced him back. He could do nothing but watch as the figure reached up and lifted the mask, revealing the face of Lorenzo de' Medici.

Jack jolted round, tangled in the damp sheets. He lay there, swallowing at the dryness in his mouth, sweat trickling down his face. After a moment, he sat up. He'd had the dream many times, but had not seen the boy before. The song was familiar though: a favourite of Prince Edward's. Sometimes, the man in the mask was his father, other times it was Harry. Lorenzo was a new face for the horror.

The room was in darkness, the air close. Tugging off the clinging sheet, Jack rose, the bare boards cool beneath his feet. He crossed to the window and pushed open the shutters, the cool air a blessing. He closed his eyes. Too soon. The image of the masked figure pinning his mother in the flames was still imprinted in his mind. He gripped the sill, the stone solid beneath his fingers.

Back in Lewes, three years ago, his clothes still dusted with ash where he'd rushed into the charred ruin of his home, yelling his mother's name, Grace had tried to comfort him, telling him the coroner said it would have been quick – the smoke, not the flames. But that was before she found the body of old Arnold, his father's lawyer, strangled in his home by Sixtus's brutes; before Jack had come face to face with the masked man who admitted to his mother's murder; before Amaury had told him that same man had tortured Amelot.

Jack had often thought of his mother's terror – the pain those men could have inflicted in their interrogations. But, after coming so close to burning alive at the hands of his own brother, his mind had seized on the one truth he did know: her remains had been found in the heart of a fire. And, now, those visions of her death, powered by his own experience, had become even more potent. Had she been alive when the flames took hold? Felt the furious heat stripping the air from her lungs, burning her hair, melting her skin?

He focused on the piping of night birds in the cypress trees that surrounded the villa, a motionless army of shadows. The sky above him was black, star-glistered, but a faint blue tinge in the east over the distant mountains spoke of dawn. Apart from the birds, everything was silent. He glanced back at the bed, but didn't want to retreat to its dishevelled dampness, risk a return to the dream. Besides which, he was wide awake. How long before the household was up and about? Hours, he suspected, given how late the party had gone on: long after he'd retreated to his room, lying awake in the dark, listening to hoots of laughter and drunken singing, stumbling feet and the shattering of a glass, the soft rising cries of a woman in pleasure.

Going to the stool where he'd discarded his clothes, he pulled his boots on over his hose and struggled into his shirt and doublet. Enough of this room, stale with his sweat. He would walk the gardens and watch the sunrise, enjoy the sweet air before he was sent back down to the city, which would no doubt be shortly, given Pico's absence and Lorenzo's displeasure at his carelessness. The signore had questioned him intently on what he and Amerigo had spoken about and whether he'd revealed anything he shouldn't have. Jack had answered distractedly, his thoughts on the murmured comment he'd heard Lorenzino make to the clerk. What, he wondered, had Lorenzo done to Amerigo's family?

Another thread for the knot.

The villa was hushed and still. Statues filled the ends of hallways with suggestions of figures, making Jack halt and stare into the darkness to check for movement. He didn't fancy bumping into Black Martin or any of the others if they were patrolling. He had spoken only rarely to Lorenzo's bodyguards, but had the impression they would all likely strike first, then ask questions.

Down the next flight of stairs, he paused. Below, the passageway was brighter, candlelight bleeding from somewhere. Hearing voices, he descended cautiously. Once down, he followed the guttering light along the hallway towards the reception hall, beyond which was the door to the gardens. Odours of spiced meat lingered, trapped in the air. He'd not indulged his appetite at the feast and his stomach growled at the smell. One of the hall's double doors was ajar. The voices were louder now. Servants? Jack wondered if he might get some leftover food.

Reaching the doors, he peered in. The hall stretched into a dull gold dusk, lit by melted stubs of candles sputtering in their holders. Sitting alone at the top table, bathed in shifting shadows, were Lorenzo and Angelo Poliziano.

'It seems a lifetime, no? Since we talked like this.' Lorenzo sounded tired, his voice heavy with drink. His head was propped on his hand, elbow on the table. 'Do you remember those nights? When poetry dripped like honey from our tongues? And dreams took flight before us?' He swept his free hand in an arc through the air, sending the candles aflutter. 'Soaring. Wondrous.'

'Lives have seasons, my friend.' Poliziano's tone was soft. 'They change.'

'But not ours, Poliziano. Surely not ours?' As Jack watched, Lorenzo reached out and touched the younger man's cheek. 'If that was summer then let us go back. This winter freezes my heart.'

Footsteps echoed. Jack started back as the two men looked towards the doors.

'That will be the wine,' he heard Lorenzo say. 'Just one more drink. For me.'

'For you, signore.'

Jack saw a shadow on the passage wall, coming closer. Hastening to the door that led to the gardens, he gingerly slid back the bolt and slipped outside, closing it quietly behind him.

Keeping to the shadows, he moved away from the house, the murmur of voices through the open shutters fading behind him. Preoccupied, he descended the steps to the lower buildings, across the wide darkness of the lawn, past the stables and down to the lower gardens where he and Laora had talked. Phantom trees crowded the shadows, a green bite of pine in the air. The trill of nightingales accompanied him as he headed for a stone bench among the roses and box hedges.

Sitting, he glanced back up towards the villa, which loomed against the sky, the windows of the hall glowing faintly like golden eyes. His mind filled with the image of Lorenzo and Poliziano bathed in candle-light, heads so close they were almost touching. Men were more familiar here than they were in England, but even so, the moment had seemed weighted with more than mere brotherly affection. More secrets. More questions.

He fixed instead on something tangible – the distant mountains, clearer now in the lightening sky. Beneath, in the valley, watch-fires burned low on the towers of the city walls. Beyond, spires and domes of churches rose, ghost-grey in the blue of early dawn. In the hush, Jack's thoughts returned to the dinner and his conversation with Amerigo. Their talk may have been cut short, but the man's feverish words had sparked something in him, a fire set flickering in the corner of his mind.

Amerigo and this sailor he'd spoken of might be interested in the wealth of the Spice Islands, but the men of the Academy believed something else lay between here and there. Their New Eden. Worth more to them than gold or riches. He had been concentrating on finding out why this lost land was so important to them. So important, his father had stolen the map from the *Trinity* and sent him away to Seville with it, unaware of the danger he carried. So important, the pope ordered those men to retrieve it, at the cost of his mother's life. Important enough for Harry to deliver it, along with Prince Edward, into the hands of Henry Tudor. In its brief time in his care, the map had changed his life completely. Even though it was gone, Jack felt it was still somehow with him, inked under his skin like lines of fortune, their fates entwined. Maybe he shouldn't be focused on the why, but the *where*?

Lorenzo had offered him a sizeable sum in gold, if he succeeded in entering the Court of Wolves and helped him root out whoever could have read that letter and taken Amaury. Enough gold to go anywhere he and his men wished. Jack saw in his mind that coastline; oak gall on vellum, disappearing off the edges. Saw his father's words, written in the hours before his death.

I pray you have found the answers I could not give you.
That the Needle has pointed the way.

Might the map itself have been a legacy? A legacy his father, in entrusting it to him, had intended for him? And, even though it was lost to him, could the simple knowledge – that something was out there – be enough to obtain that inheritance?

Kings of other worlds.

He was distracted by voices and the crunch of footsteps. Looking back towards the villa, Jack saw the flare of a torch on the sides of the building, the shadows of men moving in it. He heard the gruff tones of Black Martin. Closer, there was a rustle of leaves, footsteps thudding softly towards him, muffled breaths. Movement to his right. A figure appeared and dropped down behind a bush, a bag swinging from his shoulders. Even in the gloom, Jack – hidden by the rose bushes – recognised him. It was Pico.

The young man, clearly not so sick after all, was dressed in black. Pico crouched there for a moment, eyes on the guards moving in the pool of torchlight above. As they rounded the corner of the villa, voices fading, he slipped away through the gardens, heading for the steps that led down through the olive groves to the road below. Jack kept his eyes on the slim figure, descending quickly between the aisles of trees. After a pause, he rose and followed.

17

They made their way south into the mountains, streamers of flame gusting from their torches. It was late August and the men said the weather would soon be turning, but Harry could see no sign of it yet. Out here in the wilderness, far from Loja's verdant valley, the sun had burned away everything, leaving a crusty scab of a landscape, choked with dust, rivers just lifeless dribbles, grass withered and brown. It didn't seemed like they would have a job to do at all, until on the third day, just after dawn, they came down through a rocky defile and the land opened before them on to a wide plain, awash with a golden sea of wheat.

Don Carlos, whom the king had set in charge of the *tala*, ordered a group of knights towards a series of buildings clustered around a mill beyond the crop fields. As they spurred their horses away, cutting arrows through the corn, Don Carlos relayed commands to the rest of the company. Rodrigo and his men, Harry among them, were sent to the eastern edge of the fields in charge of fifty infantrymen, all brandishing torches. Another band went west and one north, the foot soldiers holding the flaming brands aloft to keep them from the corn, waist height in places, the stalks beginning to bend with ripeness.

After the long rest in the camp, Harry found Nieve unusually sprightly, the plump white mare trotting eagerly at pace with Rodrigo's piebald courser. A haze of corn dust rose around him, speckling his armour like ash. 'It seems a waste to burn it all.'

'The longer we stay in the field at Loja, the more exposed to attack we become.' Rodrigo's black eyes swept the crops as he spoke. 'By destroying their food supplies we lessen the enemy's ability to come at us in any strength of numbers.'

'I just wonder if we could take it for ourselves?'

'It would take too long and too many men to harvest and transport it. There is too much risk.'

Harry detected a flatness to the man's tone. Rodrigo, he knew, had been disappointed to have been assigned to the *tala*. In the wake of the attack on the king's scouting company, it was the war-seasoned Marquis of Cádiz who had been granted the honour of heading north to hunt down the enemy archers and pay them back in blood, while Don Carlos and his forces were sent south, following reports of an abundance of corn two days' ride away. Harry had been secretly relieved to have been assigned to the less hazardous task, but his relief had been short-lived when he discovered Edward Woodville would accompany Don Carlos with a number of his men.

The narrowness of the mountain paths, constricting them for the most part to two abreast on horseback, and the fact Don Carlos had set Woodville in charge of the rearguard, while Rodrigo's band was in the van, meant Harry had managed to avoid the knight so far, although last night he'd caught him watching from beyond the circle of his campfire, blue eyes unwavering in the flicker of flames. While the other men had bedded down under a star-dusted sky, knights and squires using their horse-blankets for comfort, infantry resting less contentedly on the dry earth, Harry had stayed awake, listening to the murmured conversation of those on watch and the snap of logs bursting in the fires, ears pricked not for the advance of any foreign enemy, but one closer to home.

Since the knight had confronted him, Harry had conjured in his mind various excuses as to his whereabouts last summer, when Tudor and his army had sailed for Milford Haven, the red dragon banner raised for war. But Woodville seemed to suspect something particular and, without knowing exactly what that was, Harry couldn't know which lie to best use to get the knight off the scent. He felt agitated, keenly aware that the man's presence was distracting him from his mission here. That Woodville was a clear favourite of Ferdinand's – an obstacle that prevented him from getting closer to the king – didn't help matters. Had Henry known the knight was here? Why hadn't he warned him?

They had reached the eastern edge of the fields, where corn gave way to grass and scrubby bushes that sloped up into boulder-strewn fields, becoming barer and greyer the higher up they went, into foothills, then scarred mountains. The sky was gilded, the sun beginning to rise beyond the far eastern ridges, casting everything in a crimson hue. The sea of wheat shivered in a hot breeze that had sprung up.

At Rodrigo's call, the fifty foot soldiers with them fanned out and began touching their brands to the corn at the edges of the field, moving backwards as the stalks smouldered. Harry kept Nieve's reins tight, the mare's ears twitching at the smoke rising on the air and the crackle of flames. The corn was dry and caught quickly, the plump heads popping with the heat. Harry wondered why no one had harvested these fields, given the risk of losing the crop. It seemed more than ready for the reaping. Looking north to the mill and buildings, he saw smoke starting to billow from two of the structures, where Don Carlos's knights had set their brands. There were no screams, no sounds of alarm. The whole place seemed deserted.

Harry scanned the rocky fields beyond, all bathed in red, shadows still pooled around the boulders and among the tangles of bushes and stunted trees. Catching a dart of movement in the periphery of his vision, he looked in its direction, hand reaching for his sword. There was nothing but rocks. An animal, perhaps, fleeing from the fires? Rodrigo and el Barbero had moved some distance away, ordering the infantry to spread out more, able to see with the advantage of height where the flames hadn't yet taken hold. Smoke was rising, tainting the air.

As his nose filled with its sharpness, Harry was struck by memory: the rush of heat flushing his face as he set the burning log to the broken splinters of the table. Wynter was on the floor, trussed like a hog, but his fierce cries and threats hardly registered above the hammering of blood in Harry's ears; his whole being caught somewhere between horror and excitement at the sight of his hated half-brother lying there helpless, at the mercy of the fire. Harry had denied the sin, telling himself it was the flames that would do it – bright little soldiers doing his bidding. That he wouldn't have his brother's death weighed against his soul. But those flames had failed him. Wynter had lived.

Up behind him came a fast pulse of hooves. Turning, Harry started as Edward Woodville rode up alongside him and reached out, grasping hold of Nieve's reins with a gauntleted fist. The steel plates rasped together as they closed.

'I want to talk.' The knight had his sword in his free hand, the great blade notched with scars.

Harry looked around quickly. He could hear Rodrigo still barking orders at the foot soldiers, but the air between them was hazy with smoke and the hidalgo had disappeared in its shifting clouds.

'Forget your Spanish friend.'

'Sir Edward, I . . .'

'When I saw my sister at Henry's coronation, she told me King Richard had come to her sanctuary in Westminster Abbey, told her the plot she devised with Lady Margaret Beaufort had ended in tragedy. That her sons, my nephews, had perished in the attempt, drowned in the Thames in the wagon that was supposed to have taken them to safety. That is contrary to the rumours, confirmed by Henry, that Richard himself murdered them.'

Harry inched his hand closer to his sword, but he knew Woodville could strike long before he freed it from its scabbard. Would the man actually harm him? He would surely put himself in serious trouble with King Ferdinand if he did. Not to mention Tudor. But the steel in the knight's eyes told him all he needed to know. If there was vengeance to be had here, Woodville would take it, and damn the consequences. 'King Richard could have been lying to your sister, to save himself the stain of his own crime. I heard it said his men found the boys that night – brought them back to the Tower, where he killed them. But who of us can know for sure? You were in Brittany with Henry and I was with the men of Kent in Buckingham's rising.'

'Your brother – the one involved in their rescue. He would know.'

'My brother is dead.' Whether true or not, the statement came easily to Harry, who had fervently wished it so.

'Dead? Well, that is strange, because I also heard a rumour that Henry was looking for a man named Wynter. That he was sore keen to find him. That is your brother's name, is it not? James Wynter?'

There it was – the scent Woodville had picked up. Harry had no idea how the knight had learned Tudor was looking for Wynter, but that was of little concern right now.

'Why would Henry be looking for a ghost?' Woodville demanded. 'And what would he want with Wynter, unless the man knows something? Something – perhaps – about my nephews? About the truth of their fate?' Woodville gripped Nieve's reins harder, staring into Harry's eyes. 'Talk to me, Vaughan, God damn you! I can tell you know something. Guilt colours your face. Where were you last summer? What were you doing for Henry when we were sailing to war? Tudor was quick to announce my nephews' deaths at the hands of his mortal enemy. Was he seeking to deflect blame?'

As Harry opened his mouth to answer, a scream tore through the air, taking the place of his words. He and Edward twisted in their saddles to see a foot soldier staggering through the corn towards them. He had dropped his torch and was grasping wildly for something at his back. He staggered a few more paces, then stopped. For a moment, he just stood there, staring at them, silhouetted by the glow of the rising fires, then he convulsed, blood bursting from his mouth. As he fell forward to disappear in the corn, Harry saw the crossbow bolt protruding from his back.

More bolts came shooting through the flames, slamming into the backs and skulls of the infantry. These men, many of whom had only padded gambesons to protect them, were utterly vulnerable to the lethal quarrels, which punched through stuffing, flesh and bone. Harry saw one man picked off his feet by the force of the bolt that lanced through his throat. Others were yelling, dropping their torches and beginning to run. Some had drawn knives or pulled maces or spiked clubs from belts, but the enemy was invisible, somewhere back behind the smoke and bright wisps of fire. And the bolts kept on coming.

'Where are they?' Harry shouted, drawing his sword.

Woodville had released his grip on Nieve's reins to keep control of his own mount, which was stamping and rearing. 'There!' answered the knight, thrusting his blade towards the rocky fields beyond.

The smoke had shifted, gusted apart by the hot breeze. Harry glimpsed figures moving among the trees and boulders, their white turbans and pale clothes making them almost one with the rocks. Had they been there all this time? The answer came with the sounds of agonised screams and panicked cries now echoing from every corner of the wheat fields. This perfect golden crop, ripe for the picking, had been left by the enemy for another harvest entirely.

Rodrigo's roars rose over the cries as he urged the infantry to move. One man went down, a bolt through the back, the barbed tip punching out of his stomach. One of Rodrigo's squires was struck in the shoulder, the impact shoving him from his saddle. As he fell, tangled in the stirrups, his horse bolted, dragging him away through the corn. Another horse, hit in the rump, careened into the fires in blind panic. Sparks burst up, the rider shouting in terror as he and the horse disappeared in the veil of smoke.

Harry wheeled Nieve around, trying to reach Rodrigo and the others, but the quarrels were shooting down all around. There was nothing to do but flee and find cover. *Wolfbane.* He thought of the ashen-faced men, dying from wounds that might have been treated and healed, if they hadn't been laced with poison. He didn't want to die that way.

'Go!' Woodville was shouting, but Harry was already off, kicking furiously at Nieve's sides.

He had only gone a few yards when the mare bucked violently, flinging him forward. Harry lunged for the saddle pommel with his free hand. He missed. One moment he was in the saddle. The next, the world was spinning wildly. Blue sky. Black smoke. Orange flames. Golden corn. Then, he slammed into it, the breath knocked from his lungs. His head cracked on something hard and pain exploded through him, delivering him to darkness.

18

Jack lost Pico at the Porto Fiesolana. The clang of the curfew bell had greeted him as he was approaching the city walls, the man just in sight ahead, the bag swinging on his back. The great gates rolled open, allowing entry to the streams of people and animals already thronging the roads and Jack had found himself trapped behind two carts, the guards halting the drivers to inspect their cargo. By the time he was through, Pico had vanished.

After trying several alleyways, where washing hung suspended like parts of people, and ducking into a nearby inn that had just opened, Jack stood in the street feeling nettled and foolish. All he had to show for his efforts were dusty boots and road-sore feet, which throbbed even more with the prospect of the return journey – all up hill. He tried to tell himself the pursuit had been a futile exercise anyway. Would Pico, if challenged, have admitted where he was going and why he'd feigned illness to excuse himself from the feast? He couldn't have forced the man to talk, except perhaps to threaten to tell Lorenzo? But tell him what, exactly? That Pico had taken an early morning walk into the city? It was hardly a crime. But – still – it felt significant; Pico hiding from Lorenzo's guards, the fact he'd gone by foot, not horse.

Speculation was pointless now though. Lorenzo would rise in a few hours. He needed to return, even if only to be formally dismissed. Jack turned towards the gates, then paused, his gaze going to the red dome of the cathedral, looming over the rooftops. It was still early. The palazzo would be quiet, especially with so many of its occupants at the villa. Lorenzo, Marsilio, Black Martin – they were all gone.

The streets of Florence were frenetic with the early morning rush to work or church; boys herding pigs down to the butchers on the Ponte Vecchio, booksellers and leather-workers opening the shutters of their shops with a bang and a rattle, drunks in doorways struggling to their feet, a finely dressed woman moving gracefully against the tide, skin whitened with lead, lips rouged for attention – the daughter of a wealthy house, or perhaps a courtesan.

The first of those hopeful for an audience with il Magnifico, or at least one of his officials, were already gathering at the benches by the entrance to the palazzo when Jack arrived. Two guards, one of whom he knew by name, were standing in the arched doorway, steadfastedly ignoring the expectant gazes of the waiting men.

As he stepped up to the archway, the gazes of the two guards alighted on him. 'Rigo,' he greeted with a nod.

'Sir James?' said the guard, surprised. 'I thought you were at Fiesole?'

'I was – I *am*. I just need to collect something of mine.'

'Of course, sir.' Rigo stood aside, motioning him to enter.

As the waiting men – many of them high-ranking officials or wealthy citizens – followed him with jealous eyes, Jack felt a bubble of satisfaction rise in him. He was starting to get used to the power this pretence gave him. It would be hard to give it up.

The palazzo was hushed even for the early hour, many of the staff having travelled with the Medici family. Jack hastened up to his room on the top floor, where he stuffed two shirts and a pair of hose into his old leather bag to furnish his lie to Rigo.

Meeting only a few servants, who passed him with deferential nods, he made his way back down to the first floor, around which Lorenzo's private suites were arranged. It was, as hoped, the quietest area of all. The shutters were closed over the street-facing windows. Blades of light sliced through the gaps illuminating the passage that led to the *Sala Grande*, before tapering into gloom. Jack headed down it, his heart picking up pace. What if he were caught? But his feet walked him forward, against the danger. Amaury's intercepted letter, the Muslim prayer behind the wall, Pico's assertion that Lorenzo was hiding something: all seemed to point towards Lorenzo's sanctum. If he was going to find anything out for himself, beyond the man's promise of answers – a promise he doubted more and more with everything he learned about the signore – he needed to get a look behind that door.

He was approaching the point where the corridor diverted – ahead, the grand staircase that wound down and, to the right, the passage that continued past the *Sala Grande*, then on in a circle around the *piano nobile* – when he heard the quiet thud of a door, followed by soft footsteps. Peering around the passage, Jack saw a figure in black robes striding down the corridor, away from the *Sala Grande*. He caught a pale fuzz of hair in the gloom. Marsilio? The priest must have returned early from Fiesole. He swore beneath his breath, listening to the footsteps receding, thinking he should return to the villa, wait for that invitation from Marco Valori and hope it would lead him to his answers. But he was here. Now. The door taunted him with its closeness.

Jack entered the grand hall, the muscled colossus of Hercules glaring at him, mid-battle, as he approached the door at the far end. It was unlocked. His eyes darted across the shadowy expanse of the bedchamber beyond. Seeing no movement among the array of furnishings – the curtained bed, the desks and leather-covered chairs, the daybed strewn with furs – he stepped inside. Scanning the mezzanine level above – Papi's domain – crowded with hanging clothes and stacked chests, Jack approached the door to Lorenzo's study. Locked.

He felt a rush of disappointment, even though he'd expected this. He bent to look through the keyhole, but the chamber beyond was a blur of darkness. Could he force it somehow? Try to work the lock?

Jack had tossed his bag on a chair and was scouring the bedchamber for some suitable implement, when he heard footfalls in the grand hall. He threw himself down, rolling under the bed, narrowly avoiding crashing into a bed-warming pan as the door opened. He watched a pair of feet pass by, boots thudding on the boards, then muffled over a rug. Sweat broke out on his skin as he thought of his old bag lying out in the open, a shabby incongruity in this chamber of riches.

The figure had reached the study door. Jack inched towards the edge of the bed, enough to see the back of Bertoldo, Lorenzo's chief steward. The man was carrying a tray, on which were a jug and plates of fruits and bread. He set it down on a table, then, lifting a key that hung from a chain on his belt, unlocked the door. Picking up the tray, Bertoldo entered the study.

Jack lay there, dust in his throat, listening to the sound of the soft scrape of what he took to be a curtain being drawn, a bolt snapped back. Was that murmured voices he heard? There was a thud, the rattle of a bolt again. Time passed. He was beginning to wonder whether he might be stuck under here for hours, when the door opened and Bertoldo's booted feet appeared again. The man headed from the bedchamber, clutching a sheaf of papers, leaving the study door ajar.

Jack crawled out from under the bed, bashing his spine on the carved base. He was at the open door in moments. The study beyond wasn't as expansive as the bedroom, but what it lacked in space it made up for in ornamentation. Two large desks faced one another across the room, one cluttered with papers, the other neat and ordered. There was a long, twisted horn that looked like it had come from some impossibly large beast displayed on one wall by a banner of the Medici arms, yet more gilt-framed paintings and bronze statues, a thick gold curtain and tapestries; each the value of a small town. But what caught his eye most were the cupboards, some with open shelves, others behind glass, each one heaving with a dazzling surfeit of treasures. Items of gold and silver, ivory and diamonds, rubies, emeralds, sapphires, coral – so much sparkle it seemed the room was filled with stars.

Jack didn't have time for more than a breath's worth of awe, before he was heading for the cluttered desk, picking swiftly through the papers on it. Accounts. Bank rolls. Lists of names, some crossed out. A few letters, one with the great seal of the Vatican attached. But nothing of any significance or value to him. What had he expected, though? A grand plan; all the Academy's schemes and designs sketched out for him to see and, at last, understand – some great map that would give sense to his mother's death and his father's life? Bring meaning to his own?

Then, he realised – there was no tray.

Not on either desk, nor the chairs, nor the floor: the only spaces in the chamber free of glittering ornaments. Bertoldo hadn't left with it, so where had it gone? That sound he'd heard? The scrape of a curtain being drawn? He crossed to the heavy gold swag that hung over part of the wall, pulled it back. Beyond was a door.

It was thick and looked newer than other doors in the palace, the grain not aged by time or use. A large bolt was pulled across it, meaning it could only be opened from this side and a steel flap was set in it at head height. Jack lifted the flap, his mind flashing with the memory of that dingy chamber in the Tower of London, Prince Edward's pale face peering back at him while he fumbled with the keys.

Beyond, behind a metal grate, he was surprised to see not a bare prison cell, but a cosy, well-appointed room. There was a large bed with embroidered cushions and covers, a few paintings on the walls, chairs, hooks for clothes, a shelf of books, a brazier glowing dully, and a table. On the table was the tray Bertoldo had carried in, beside a chessboard with a game in progress. At it, sat a man.

The man, whom he reckoned to be around his own age, was sucking thoughtfully at a segment of orange, while reading a book. He was evidently well-built beneath his silk robe, with long, muscled limbs. His shoulder-length dark hair was slicked back as if recently washed and a neat moustache and beard framed a strong jaw. Even in the dim light of the chamber, which seemed to have no window of its own, Jack saw his skin had a ruddy cast. The hue of his skin, the angles of his cheeks, the set of his eyes: all suggested a foreignness. The otherworldly call of the infidels' prayer whispered in Jack's mind.

The man glanced up. 'I am not yet done, Bertoldo.'

As he lifted the orange segment in evidence, Jack saw a knotted scar snaking from his palm down his arm. The man had spoken Tuscan, but his accent was of another place entirely. His tone was weary, lifeless.

When Jack didn't respond, the man's expression changed. He dropped the fruit and rose. There was a rattle of something as he did so. 'I do not know you.' He came forward as he spoke, the rattling louder.

Jack realised there was a chain attached to his ankle. The man was almost at the door when it halted him, snapping taut from its base, somewhere on the other side of the room. He found his voice. 'Who are you?'

The man's expression shifted, those dark eyes now flooding with hope. 'Free me!'

Hearing someone approaching, Jack whipped round. One last look at the chained man, then he let fall the steel flap, yanked the curtain across and sprinted from the room. This time he snatched his bag from the chair before throwing himself under the bed. He lay there, heart hammering, as Bertoldo returned, heading for the study.

Amelot slipped across the roof, the rising sun blazing in her eyes. Already, she felt its warmth in the tiles beneath her hands. She had mapped the city by its rooftops: the best surfaces to traverse and those to avoid, the plunging drops to steer clear of and the jumps she could make – the run and the lift, for one thrilling moment suspended in flight over the heads of people far below. The buildings were more closely packed than those in Paris, giving her plenty of routes around the city's four quarters.

It had been another fruitless night of searching, out among the domes and towers. Another night without sign of the man she had seen at Carnival, or her master. She knew these hunts were shots in the dark; no target to aim for, no mark to set her sights on. But it was better than lying awake in the palazzo listening to Jack moan and thrash in his sleep, or else trapped in the hot eaves of the Fig, Ned's snores rumbling through the room. If any of them had noticed her absence they hadn't said anything.

It seemed they had all but forgotten Amaury. A few weeks back she'd heard Valentine bluntly suggest to Jack that the priest was most likely dead by now. But she could not – would not – countenance that. Amaury had brought her in from the streets when everything had been stripped from her by the men – *monsters* – years ago. The men who had taken her family. Her body. Her voice. He had given her protection and purpose. She had to find him. To save him. As he had saved her.

Not far from the market, the streets busy with life, Amelot shinned down from the heights and moved through the throng. She was approaching the Fig, past cloth traders setting out bolts of silks, satins and velvets, when she found her route blocked by a small crowd.

Heading closer, Amelot saw a dozen armed men in tunics emblazoned with a viper. They were surrounding the open door of a house, out of which an object was being carried. A cart was nearby, harnessed to horses, more men beside it, some of them shouting for the knot of onlookers to move back. Weaving through, she got a brief look at what they were carrying. It was a body on a litter, partly covered with a sheet.

The corpse was a man. His bare feet poked from the bottom of the sheet, which was rusty with blood, along with one muscular arm that dangled from the litter. The skin of his knuckles was black with bruising. He'd gone down fighting, she thought.

One of the onlookers, a woman, crossed herself as the dead man was conveyed to the cart. As the woman turned to her neighbour, Amelot caught a few words she recognised, among them *plague*. The young man she'd addressed shook his head. Amelot stared up at him as he replied, certain the young man had said something about a demon.

There was a shout, followed by a shocked gasp that rippled through the onlookers. Looking back, Amelot saw the sheet had snagged as the men were hoisting the litter on to the cart. One of the guards hastily tugged it back in place, but not before Amelot caught a glimpse of the dead man's face. The skin looked wrong – raw and glistening. No, not skin, she realised, but the bloody tissue beneath. The man's face had been peeled.

Amelot felt the breath catch in her throat. She pushed out through the knot of people, away from the litter and the corpse. A man bellowing his wares from a shop front made her jump in fright, into the path of a horse and rider, who yelled at her, the horse gnashing at its bit as its head was jerked back. She darted into an alley, shaded and quiet. Stopping halfway down, she leaned against a wall, flicking her hands to shake away the trembling. All across her back, she could feel them come alive: the old scars. It was as though someone was trailing a fingernail across her flesh, tracing each line of pain. Images and sensations flashed through her. Fire and screams. Blood and crying. Hands dragging her into darkness. Brutal laughter. She squeezed her eyes shut.

Amaury's voice murmured in her mind, his gnarled hand on her shoulder, smell of pumice and ink, sunlight slanting through a window, fractured by old beams. *It is now, my child. Not then.*

Now. Not then.

After a moment, her breaths evened out. Beyond the alley's mouth, the rising sun had spilled its gold across the street. Straightening, Amelot headed out, back into the light.

19

The man beside him was dying. Harry could feel him shivering against him, even through the heat of the days. A rot-sweet smell came off him in waves. He guessed the man had been wounded – perhaps by one of the enemy's poisoned bolts – and the infection had seeped into his blood, although in the dimness of the cave it was hard to be sure of much.

Harry, shifting awkwardly against the ropes that bound his wrists and ankles, had managed to slide his fingers across the ground far enough to steal the man's unfinished scraps of food, doled out each morning, which he'd squirrelled behind him for consumption when neither his captors, patrolling the cave at intervals, nor his fellow captives who crowded the shadows could see. Even with the extra rations, he was half starved, his hose sagging at his waist and a band of hunger tightening in his stomach.

The man moaned. One of the turbaned men walking the cave snarled at him to be quiet. Most of them knew Castilian well enough, but they conversed among themselves in their own language. Some were tall, muscular men with brown-black skin, who exuded an aura of fierce power. Others were less dark, although swarthier than the Spaniards, turbans wrapped around their heads. A few wore armour, mostly of stiff leather. Other than their weapons, there was barely a scrap of steel among them.

Harry leaned against the stone, shifting his head to avoid the wound on the back of his skull, mostly healed now, but still sore. He wasn't sure what had caused the injury; only remembered falling from his saddle and coming to in a thicket of crushed corn stalks with a searing pain in his head, his palm coming back red with blood. He had struggled up, his vision blurred, to find a wall of billowing flames before him and, behind, in the distance, the last of the Spanish fleeing into the narrow defile that had led them to the plain. Leaving him behind.

Choking on the smoke, he had staggered after them, yelling hoarsely. He'd not gone far before his feet tripped on something buried in the corn. Going down, sprawled among the stalks, he found himself face to face with the body of one of the infantry, eyes wide to the sky, chest spattered with blood from the bolt that had punctured his throat. There were other bodies hidden in the gold. Horses too. A few more paces brought him to Nieve, struggling feebly in a flattened circle of corn the fire had yet to reach, blood seeping across her white flanks from the quarrel that had crippled her. One brown eye watched him, snorts of pain shuddering through her body as he searched the ground around her, hunting for his sword. That was when he heard them – their voices raised above the crackle of flames.

The Moors had come cautiously, but purposefully, picking their way through the field. He tried to run, but a warning bolt slamming down feet ahead halted him in his tracks. Armed with only his jewelled dagger, stolen from Henry's gifts to the monarchs, he'd stood no chance. He had been disarmed roughly, one of his captors exclaiming in triumph as he found the valuable dagger, then marched from the smouldering fields, along with fifteen others taken alive from the corn.

In the foothills, more of the enemy had been waiting with horses. It was here that Harry had first seen the tall, black-skinned men. One, who wore a studded brigandine and a belt decorated with gold fastenings that criss-crossed his broad chest, had inspected the captives. The man's face and arms were patterned with scars and one of his ears was missing. Harry had privately dubbed him the Smiler, on account that this seemed to be the man's only expression. He smiled when the captives and plunder were deposited before him, smiled as he walked their line, teeth startlingly white against his skin. That smile broadened when one of the men brought him the jewelled dagger, pointing at Harry as he did so. He said something, his voice rich and deep, before chuckling and stowing the dagger in his belt. The most discomforting thing about that permanent smile, Harry had learned then, was the contrast with his eyes – two black pools filled with humourless cruelty.

Stripped of his armour and even his boots, down to his shirt and hose, Harry had been forced to mount one of the Moors' horses, his hands bound to the pommel. The other captives were treated in similar fashion, those too wounded to sit straight in the saddle hauled over rumps, hands and feet lashed to the girth strap. There followed an excruciating two-day trek, south and east through rocky wilderness, Harry bounced painfully along, the wound in his scalp throbbing hotly, flies buzzing ceaselessly at his face until he was too exhausted to shake them off. Three men had died before they reached the cave, which opened like a dark maw in the side of a mountain.

That had been – what? Three weeks ago? More? Harry had lost count in the chilly twilight of the cave, which they were only permitted to leave twice daily to relieve themselves, the Moors herding them out in groups of four, roped together and forced to squat side by side. It was impossible to know where he was; how far from Loja. The area outside the cave was a wide outcrop, slabbed with sand-coloured stone, which fell away into a ravine, before rising steeply up the other side, blocking any view of the landscape beyond. The outcrop was scattered with campfires, the amber glow bruising the outer walls of the cave at night. For the first few days, Harry hoped those lights might prove his salvation – that they would draw the Spanish to this place – but as the days crawled on, his hope of rescue had withered.

One of the Moors patrolling the cave passed close by. Harry caught his gaze, but dropped his eyes quickly. The man gave a derisive chuckle and moved on. He had learned not to look at them, or speak to them or his fellow captives – learned it on his first day in the cave when he had addressed them, first in English, then Latin and broken Castilian, telling them he was England's ambassador to Spain; a high-ranking official – a knight indeed – with a right to be treated with respect. When he refused to quiet, he'd been hauled up in the centre of the cave, into which had stridden the Smiler.

Harry, faced with that unnerving white grin, his own dagger glinting tauntingly on the man's belt, tried again to explain himself. But either the man did not understand or didn't care. Still smiling, he gestured to two of his comrades who pinned Harry between them, holding him upright, while the Smiler proceeded to punch him repeatedly in the gut, stepping back for a grinning pause between each ball-fisted strike, until Harry was left curled on the cave floor like a baby, sucking desperately for air. He hadn't spoken since.

It was getting darker, the copper blush of the fires growing brighter in the cave mouth. The first few captives were kicked to their feet to relieve themselves before nightfall. Three of them were new, brought in two days ago, bruises still fresh. An unlucky scouting party perhaps. It was clear the Moors were gathering them up, collecting them for something, but the cave was almost full and he guessed whatever their intentions were he would find out soon. A sick feeling in the pit of his empty stomach told him he already knew the answer. Rodrigo had told him as much.

Those they do not kill they take as slaves.

Christian boys were taken for the Moors' own ranks; boys still young enough to be indoctrinated, turned to their cause and their God. Trained in the palace at Granada, brought up loyal to the emir alone, they were known as Mamluks, slave warriors. The Spanish called them *renegados* and would slay them if they caught them, even though they'd once been their own sons, but Harry knew he was far too old to be taken for this purpose. The men, Rodrigo had said, usually disappeared across the Straits of Gibraltar. The rolling darkness of a slave galley? The suffocating depths of a silver mine? Who knew what fate awaited him.

The captives shuffled back in from outside and now it was Harry's turn. He clambered to his feet with the others he was bound to, but was halted by the prone man beside him, who moaned but didn't move. The Moor shouted, then kicked at his bare foot. The man lolled against the stone. After a pause, the Moor took a dagger from his belt. Crouching, he slashed at the ropes that tethered Harry to the dying man. Calling to one of his comrades, he gestured impatiently for Harry and the other two to head out.

The Moors were settling down for the evening. Smells of spiced meat drifted from cooking pots suspended over the fires, making Harry's stomach groan. He and the other two made their way awkwardly across the uneven outcrop under the watchful eye of two guards, to where they did their business – a trough cut through the stone that served as a natural latrine. The place reeked. Tugging clumsily at his hose with his bound hands, Harry realised that where the Moor had severed the rope, the strands were fraying, twirling loose. As he pushed against the bonds, he felt less resistance, his wrists moving slightly apart. Hope flared inside him, bright and fierce.

A commotion drew his attention. The man he'd been sitting next to was being dragged out of the cave, bare feet scuffing the stone. He was taken to the Smiler, who'd just sat down to his meal. The tall man rose to inspect the wounded man, flipping up an eyelid and peering at him. He shook his head and motioned to the ravine. The man struggled feebly as he was hauled to the edge, the last of the life stirring inside him. The two Spaniards beside Harry had stopped unlacing their hose and were staring, transfixed by the horror of what was about to happen. The Smiler watched, teeth gleaming, as the man was flung over the edge. His scream was followed a few seconds later by a faint, sickening thud. One of the two men who threw him was laughing at something the other said, when the arrow struck him.

The Moor collapsed to his knees with a surprised grunt, hands clutching at the shaft that had entered his stomach. While the other was staring, bewildered, at his companion, more arrows pitched out of the shadows. Harry felt the whistling rush of one pass close to his head, before it punched into the shoulder of one of the two guards by the latrine, pitching him off his feet. Harry threw himself to the ground as more barbs followed, the two Spaniards falling down with him, one cracking his head on the rock. Harry realised the arrows were coming from across the ravine, in the shadows of the opposite hillside.

The camp was alive with shouts, the Smiler's voice booming above all others. The Moors scrabbled to snatch up crossbows, but the light of their fires made them easy targets as well as blinding them to sight of the enemy. A few, seeing this, were struggling to kick the fires out, cooking pots overturning, contents spewing into the flames, but the arrows were lancing in thick and fast, more and more men succumbing to them.

Harry, tangled up with the two Spaniards, one of whom hadn't moved since they fell, was struggling against his bonds. The severed end of the rope was unravelling as he worked his hands back and forth, the rough hemp chafing his skin. Hearing a gurgling close by, he twisted to see the second guard had gone down, an arrow protruding from his throat. The arrow was distinctly fletched with three brown duck feathers. Harry recognised it at once. It was one of the arrows used by Edward Woodville's Welsh bowmen.

Hope lent new strength to his muscles. Straining with all his might, he was able to wrench one hand free. Reaching towards the dying guard, shouting at the remaining Spaniard now struggling with his own tethers to help him – *Ayuda! Rápido!* – he got hold of the dying guard's dagger.

Those who hadn't been picked off in the first few moments were hunkered behind rocks or had fled into the cave, where shouts of alarm and confusion echoed. Some of the Moors were shooting at the opposite hillside, the harsh click of their crossbows followed, here and there, by screams. Plumes of dust tracked the paths of men tumbling down the slope into the ravine. The Smiler, crouched against a rock, a spiked mace in his fist, was still roaring orders. Keeping low, some of his men were heading towards the path that wound away from the cave. One, caught in the thigh by an arrow, went wheeling over the edge with a shriek.

Harry had tugged the dagger free from the guard's belt and, having slashed away the last strands of rope from his wrist, was sawing frantically at those around his ankles. The Spaniard was watching him wide-eyed, nodding in encouragement, wrists out for his turn. Then, as quickly as they'd come, the arrows ceased. Moments later, a horn sounded, followed by wild cries. A horde of men came charging around the side of the hill on to the outcrop, fighting the Moors as they came; clubs swinging into heads with bursts of blood, blades clashing. Overwhelming the first few lines, they stormed into the camp.

The Moors turned their crossbows on the incoming men, but although the first bolts picked off a few, the rest were on them in moments. They rose to meet them, using the bows as weapons, smashing them into faces, breaking jaws. Harry saw several knights in Woodville's colours among the leather brigandines of the Spanish. There, too, was el Barbero. The soldier, having broken a Moor's nose with a vicious back-thrust of his sword pommel, kicked the man to his knees. He swung his blade in a mighty arc, carving clean through the Moor's neck. The man's head flopped on to his shoulder, throat severed almost all the way through, blood spurting up in gouts, bathing the Barber in a red rain.

At last, Harry cut himself free. He staggered to his feet, clutching the dagger, ignoring the pleas of the tethered Spaniard. The Moors were retreating, but fighting as they came, edging back towards him.

There was a wall of them between him and the Spanish. The Smiler was among them in the fray, swinging his spiked club with devastating force. Turning with a shout, the brute set off at a loping run, some of his men closing the gap behind him and continuing to fight, others going with him.

Harry had backed away, leaving the Spaniard, who yelled in terror as the Moors came, raising his bound hands for mercy. The Smiler cuffed him brutally aside with a swing of the club, barely breaking his stride. Harry looked desperately around him – the ravine to one side, sheer rock face to the other, and, behind, an animal track which clearly the Moors intended to flee by. He could run, but knew in his weakened state they would be on him in moments. He gripped the dagger, holding its ridiculous shortness before him.

Lord, help me!

There were screams from the last line of the enemy as Woodville's knights carved through them. A flurry of motion and they were on the fleeing Moors. The Smiler was launching back his club to take a swipe at Harry, when he was caught, mid-swing, the tip of a blade punching through his throat. Blood spewed from his mouth as the blade was withdrawn with a twist. The club fell from his fingers. He followed it a moment later, knees impacting the stone. Behind him, blade slick with blood, stood Edward Woodville. The knight was bleeding from a cut on his forehead, his face wet and red in the scattered light of the fires. He kicked at the Moor, who toppled sideways.

At the sight of his captor lying there, rage surged through Harry, bursting up through his relief. Tossing aside the knife he held, he ran to the dying Moor, now choking on his own blood. Straddling the man, he wrenched his jewelled dagger free from the man's belt and began stabbing the blade into any bit of flesh he could find, yelling as he did so, all the fear and humiliation he'd felt these past weeks powering every strike. Then, his wrist was caught.

'It is done.'

Harry sat back, gasping for air, the metal taste of blood in his mouth. The Moor's face and neck were a pulpy mess of ruined flesh. One eye was gone and most of his lips. The man would smile no more. Legs shaking, Harry rose. The sounds of fighting had ended. The prisoners were being released from the cave, stumbling out, exclaiming as they saw their countrymen. Embers of fires glowed across the outcrop, like candles around the strewn dead.

Harry turned to Edward Woodville. 'Thank you.' His voice came out as a whisper. As he looked around at the camp's disarray, seeking water for his parched throat, Woodville caught his arm.

The knight's grim expression was unchanged. His sword was still in his other hand, blood dripping from the blade. 'You owe me. To repay that debt you'll give me what I want. You understand?'

As Woodville's grip tightened in question, something passed through Harry: a hot streak of defiance. The last man who'd threatened him was dead on the ground behind him. He looked the knight full in the eye. 'I told you the day these bastards took me – told you everything I know. I believe Richard killed your nephews. What more can I say?'

Woodville paused at his tone, but his eyes narrowed again. 'Your brother then. He knows something. Why else would Henry be hunting the bastard son of a dead knight?'

'As I said—'

Woodville let go of his arm and jabbed a finger towards him. 'I don't believe what you said. I think James Wynter is still alive. And you're going to tell me where I can find him.'

'Sir!'

Woodville glanced round as one of his knights hailed him. Giving Harry a last look, he moved off.

'Sir Harry?'

Harry turned to see Rodrigo. The hidalgo was covered in blood. Little of it looked to be his own. He wore a strange expression. 'What was that about?'

'Nothing.' Harry shook his head, trying to move off, but Rodrigo stepped in front of him.

'Who were you speaking of?'

'My brother – *half*-brother. Sir Edward has an issue with him. It is nothing of consequence.' Harry guessed his face told another story, for Rodrigo's questioning – almost hostile – expression didn't change. 'How did you find me?'

The furrows in Rodrigo's brow remained, but he answered. 'We captured one of the Moors from the field, took him back to our camp when we realised some of our men had been seized. Eventually, he told us about this place. These men were survivors of a garrison our forces overran last year. It seems they've been out here collecting Christians to sell as slaves in North Africa.'

Harry swallowed weakly.

'Come,' the hidalgo said after a pause. 'We need to move out. Before we left, the king declared he was ready to mount a full assault on Loja.'

As Harry, bare feet sliding in the spilled blood of his captors, walked with Rodrigo to where Don Carlos was ordering the troops to help the wounded on to horses, he caught sight of Edward Woodville mounting up with his men. The knight met his gaze, his blue eyes full of threat.

20

The change of season came violently to Florence, storm clouds towering over the mountains in the humid heat of late September. Thunder rolled down from the hills, splitting the air and trembling through the church bells. A whip of lightning struck the dome of Santa Maria de Fiore, another blasted through the roof of a bookseller's in Santa Croce, setting the place ablaze and bringing out the men of the district in lines, hauling water from the river to stop the fire spreading.

The rains followed, downpours that turned the dust and dung-covered streets into channels of viscous slime that sucked at shoes, trapped cartwheels and stank. The Arno swelled to roar between the bridges, its waters full of broken branches, splintered timbers and bloated bodies of cattle swept down from upriver. People were more generous with their offerings and more fervent in their prayers, wondering if – along with the earthquakes and the plague – the storms were a portent of God's displeasure with the republic. In San Marco one Sunday in early October, Fra Savonarola preached a formidable sermon against luxury that was talked about for days afterwards.

Jack, back in the palazzo after Lorenzo's banquet, watched the change in the weather and waited. Each morning as he opened the shutters of his room to see the terrace dashed with rain and the clouds hanging low over the towers, he hoped for word from Marco Valori. Each evening he asked Rigo or one of the other guards if any message had come and his disappointment would rise with the shakes of their heads.

In these empty days, rain hammering on the roof and into the inner courtyards, trickling down the faces of statues, he found little to occupy himself and his thoughts turned often to the man chained in the room three floors below, his presence like a tune he couldn't get out of his head. Jack was certain the man was the source of the prayer he'd heard, convinced, too, that this was the secret Pico thought Lorenzo and Marsilio were hiding: a Muslim – clearly no slave – locked in the heart of the palace. But who he was and why he was being held in Lorenzo's sanctum remained a mystery he could not hope to solve without giving away his trespass. He had wondered about confiding in Ned and David, but worried a confession Lorenzo was keeping an enemy of Christendom in state in his private chambers would only add to his companions' growing frustrations at his continuing charade, with no sign yet of any reward.

Whatever sense he thought he had of the Academy and their intentions seemed more obscure than ever. Every thread he picked at just seemed to tighten the knots. Unable to shake the fear that he was slipping further away from what he'd come to this city in search of, Jack had determined to speak to Lorenzo, but when the signore returned from Fiesole he was all but unreachable, shut away in meetings or out in the city on business. Since word spread of Maddalena's engagement, the palace was inundated with more notaries, secretaries and sycophants than ever. Messages buzzed between Florence and Rome as arrangements were made for a spectacular betrothal feast to be held at the palazzo in several months' time, after Christmas and Carnival. Lorenzo, not missing an opportunity to make some political capital, sent heralds throughout the republic to announce it. In the brief audience Jack had been granted, Lorenzo had told him, in no uncertain terms, that until he made some advance into the Court of Wolves there was nothing for them to talk about.

As the weeks passed, Jack started to feel as though he were back in Seville, guarding the map. The endless wait for his father to come, to keep his word: *I will explain everything*. The deepening fear he never would. Part of him wanted to stuff his few belongings into his bag and walk out of the palazzo, let this maze he was trapped in collapse around him. He would learn to forget the past few years of his life, go to Spain with his men, or anywhere, abandon the hope of what Lorenzo had promised. But he knew he wasn't ready to give it up. Not yet.

Then, late in October, the city preparing for the feasts of All Hallows and All Souls, the message had come. Two days later, the first in weeks without rain, Jack had set out from the palazzo into the dazzle of a bright, windy afternoon, following its instructions.

He held the letter crumpled in his fist as he made towards the Porta al Prato, the air throbbing with the pulse of drums. Up ahead, a parade of men on horseback was funnelling out through the gate, the drummers marching behind them. The riders' tunics were emblazoned with the coats of arms of two of the city's quarters: a golden sun for Santa Maria Novella, the Medici quarter, and a white dove for Santo Spirito across the river. Great standards hoisted above them bore the same symbols, while smaller banners showed off the arms of the four *gonfaloni* each district was split into – a gaudy mix of vipers, dragons, unicorns and lions.

The crowds grew denser as Jack neared the gate; a jostle of sweaty bodies and raucous laughter. The sound was deafening, but more overwhelming was the feel of it: a wild excitement like a storm charge. Jack felt it in himself – a fizzing in his chest and stomach that made him want to shout or laugh.

He had heard people speak of *calcio* – the kick-game, as Fra Vito translated for him – but other than the fact it sounded like the games of football he'd seen played in Sussex, he didn't know what to expect, only that half the city seemed to want to be a part of it. There were flags draped from many of the balconies he passed beneath, men, even a few women, leaning out to cheer or boo whichever team they supported.

Ahead, beyond the gates, in a wide open field, wooden stalls with tiers of benches built into them had been erected around a large rectangle of sand. Jack, filing in with the rowdy mob beneath flags dancing in the wind, past rows of traders selling ale and roast pork, was reminded of Diego's arena in Seville. He saw himself punching Estevan Carrillo, the rough roar of the men of Triana ringing in his ears as the arrogant nobleman went down in the dust. Seeing the setting – the sand raked and ready – brought back that old thrill. He realised he'd missed it. His weekly duels with Ned on the riverbank were no substitute for the violent release of a real fight, the feeling – dancing along the blade of death – of being truly alive.

Once inside he paused, men flowing around him as he opened the letter, creased and warm from his hand, the wax seal with its imprint of a wolf's head cracking.

The stalls by the standard of Santa Maria Novella.

The horsemen who had led the parade had split into two companies, one taking the standard with the golden sun to the far end of the field, the other moving to the end closest to him, bearing the white dove. At each of these opposite ends a net was positioned, attached to poles thrust into the sand. The drummers had fanned out and were pounding away over the din of those filling the stalls. Making his way down the field, sand caking his boots, Jack realised what a disparate mix of men were gathered here. The mob he'd been moving in had mostly been made up of rough-faced workers – wool-washers, carders, tanners – but around the arena he now saw the garish mantles, doublets and hats of the elite. One such group had taken up most of the front rows of benches behind the far net, beneath the golden sun. Among them, Marco Valori.

As Jack approached, Marco saw him and beckoned him in. Jack threaded his way along the benches to meet him, men rising to let him pass. 'Signor Marco.'

Marco stood and grasped his hand, a smile creasing his face. 'Sir James.' He edged up, allowing him to sit beside him. 'I'm glad you could come.'

'I was glad to get the invitation!' Jack had to yell to make himself heard. Back in the summer, when Marco hinted at a meeting with his brethren, this wasn't what he'd envisaged. How was he supposed to find out anything useful – make any headway into the company – in this storm of noise? 'Are your brothers here?'

Marco chuckled. 'Look around!'

Following his gaze, Jack realised that the men crowding the benches around and behind him, although a variety of ages, with some more sumptuously dressed than others, had one thing in common: a silver wolf's head badge pinned to their doublets or cloaks. There were dozens – no, scores of them. He was surrounded by the Court of Wolves.

'Signor Franco Martelli.' Marco was motioning to a man seated behind Jack – muscular, in his middle years, with a mane of greying hair flowing from beneath a jewelled cap. 'Signor Luigi Donati.' A younger man with olive skin and a lean, rather sly face. 'Signor Stefano di Parri. Signor Pacino Nardi.'

Some of those closest to Jack shook his hand as they were introduced, others merely nodded before turning back to conversations.

He tried to hold their names in his head, but as Marco continued to reel them off amid the clamour, he gave up. His eyes caught again on the badges. A glittering pack of wolves. Had one or more of these men been involved in Amaury's abduction? He wished he'd brought Amelot with him to see if she recognised any of them, but he'd been uncertain what he was walking into and hadn't wanted the girl's unpredictability to distract him. He would have to secure himself an invitation to another such gathering, find a way to bring her and Ned along.

'Is this your first meeting?' Jack asked Marco, once the introductions were done. 'Since your return to the city?'

'We've had a few forums.' Marco leaned forward to hail one of the men further down the row. 'Drinks, Lando! Before we die of thirst!' As a few of the others hooted in agreement, Marco sat back, his dark blue eyes fixing on Jack. 'I take it you have never been to a game of *calcio* before?' When Jack shook his head, the young man grinned and spread his hand to the sands. 'Welcome, then, to the theatre of blood.'

Some of those close by, catching this, laughed appreciatively.

'We'll crush those doves today!' roared Luigi, which set off a fresh round of cheers and thunderous foot stamping across the benches.

'Here they come!' shouted someone.

The crowds in the stalls rose in a wave of sound as two lines of men came jogging on to the sands. All were bare-chested and bare-footed, just a pair of hose to cover their modesty – one set red, the other white. Some were huge, mountains of muscled flesh. Others were lean, sinewy, loping in easy strides down the field. Jack counted twenty-seven in each company as they split away, heading for the centre of the field. The drums beat a tattoo as they faced one another. Two men, gold braid belting their hose, strode up and down the two lines, gesturing as they addressed the men.

'The captains,' Marco shouted in Jack's ear. 'They'll move into the nets when the game begins. Direct their men from there.'

'Direct them to do what?'

'Get the ball into the net of the opposite team of course.' Marco grinned. 'By any means necessary. Whichever side scores the most wins the game.'

'You all support the same company?' Jack looked back at the rows of men behind him.

'Well, Signor Stefano has worrying tendencies towards Santa Croce.' Valori chuckled as Stefano, in earshot, shot him a glare. 'But, yes. We support Santa Maria Novella.'

'You're all from the quarter then?'

'Our patrons are.'

'Patrons?' This was the first Jack had heard of any hierarchy in the company. 'Your founders?'

'Ah, here comes Lando.'

More applause rose as Lando returned, followed by boys bearing fistfuls of flagons, ale slopping over the rims. As the drinks were passed down the rows, Jack took one gratefully. It was a chilly day, but packed in with these men he felt hot. He lifted his flagon to Marco. 'Your health.'

'And yours.'

Jack drank deep, his mind working. It might not be the best environment, but after all this time waiting he was damned if he'd leave here today without something he could use to his advantage. David's quiet words to him last night in the Fig came back to him. *Make this work, Jack.* He needed, at least, to secure a second invite: create an opportunity for Amelot – and, perhaps, for himself. Lorenzo might hold tight to his secrets, but no doubt his adversaries would be freer with the truth.

He decided to continue in the vein he'd opened when he'd met Marco on the riverbank; prove himself a useful source of information. 'Did you hear the signore has arranged the betrothal of his daughter to the pope's son?'

'I think Signor Lorenzo has made sure all of Italy has heard this.'

'And his son, Giovanni?' Jack knew this fact was less well-known, the negotiations yet to be finalised. 'He may become a cardinal? It seems the signore has grand plans for his empire.'

Marco's eyes flicked to him. For a moment, Jack thought he'd caught his interest, but the young man simply smiled. 'There are not many rules in this arena, Sir James. But one is that we do not discuss business here. Today is for merrymaking. Enjoy yourself. This is a chance for us to get to know you. Not what you know.' Loud jeers broke his attention.

Jack sat back, frustrated, but knew he couldn't push. If he appeared too eager, too insistent, he risked having this door closed in his face again. Following Marco's gaze, he saw the captain of the Santo Spiritos hastening towards the net in front of their benches. He was clearly the focus of the jeers, but kept his head high, ignoring the taunts, some of which involved his mother. On the opposite end of the field, the captain of the Santa Maria Novellas was heading for the other net. The drummers were filing out, followed by the horsemen, all except one, who galloped into the centre between the two companies, holding aloft a leather ball.

The crowd fell into a hush, all eyes on the rider who dropped the ball in the sand, then urged his mount away, trapper flying, hooves scuffing up sand. The two companies faced one another, shoulders bunching, hands curling into fists, eyes narrowing. Jack found himself sitting forward, feeling the tension rising. The silence was shattered by the blast of a trumpet. Then, all was chaos.

The men on the field lunged at one another, fists swinging, and the crowds in the stalls leapt to their feet, bellowing. The ball was still in the sand, but the two companies were ignoring it, in favour of beating the life out of one another. A colossus of a man in the red hose of the Santa Maria Novellas had barrelled into one of the whites, tossing him over his shoulder. Seizing another by the hair, he rammed his knee into the man's face. The burst of blood from his nose and mouth drove the crowd into a frenzy. Two whites set upon the colossus in retaliation, one kicking his leg out from under him, causing him to buckle to one knee, while the other punched him repeatedly in the face. All around the sand, men were smacking and jabbing, cuffing and shoving. The crowd's excitement was infectious; the wild passion of the mob. Jack felt as though he'd been swept into a battle – but all thrill, no terror.

Suddenly, one of the reds – a beefy man, hairy as a bear – broke out of the fray and snatched up the ball. He ran down the field with it, several of his comrades running with him in a protective circle and five of the whites in pursuit. One of the whites punched out one of those defending him, got through the line, leapt to catch him, and missed. He landed hard, skidding across the ground on his stomach in a wave of sand. The captain was in the net yelling orders for his men to defend it, but to no avail. The beefy man approached him at a sprint, feinted right at the last moment, then, with a sweeping curl of his arm, tossed the ball into the net, which billowed back with the impact. The crowds beneath the standard of the golden sun went wild.

Jack, who had risen with Marco and the others, found himself cheering along with them, a fierce grin on his face – all thoughts of what he'd come here to do swept away on a tide of exhilaration.

'*Alesso! Alesso!*' the men were shouting.

Jack guessed that was the name of the man who had scored, for he turned to them in triumph, punching his fist into the air. The spectators down the other end of the field had gone quiet, bruised with defeat. But they were soon on their feet again, roaring insults and threats at the jubilant Santa Maria Novella supporters as the ball was slung back into the sand.

'Are you enjoying our city, Sir James?'

Jack turned at the shout to see Luigi Donati's lean face at his shoulder. 'More so now!'

God, but it was true. He hadn't felt like this in months, years even, not since the arena in Seville, or when he was a page in his father's command. No questions, no riddles, no confusion about where he belonged. Part of a company, moving with the same purpose.

Luigi laughed appreciatively, then thrust his finger towards the field. 'Alesso has the ball again!'

As Jack chanted the man's name along with those around him Marco caught his eye and grinned. Alesso made it almost to the net, but was tackled at the last moment by one of the whites. They both went flying, a tumbling tangle of limbs. One of the reds grabbed the fallen ball, but was rocked off his feet by a vicious head-butt from another opponent.

More goals were scored by each team and more men went down. Lando was sent to fetch more drinks. Jack found himself gulping down the ale, throat stinging from all the yelling. He was on his fourth flagon when one of the players was crushed beneath two opponents and came up screaming, leg twisted at an improbable angle. There was a brief lull while he was carried off, spectators taking the opportunity to relieve themselves in a trench behind the stalls, the men on the field catching their breath, wiping sweat and blood from their faces.

The wind was picking up, sending sand spinning across the arena. Jack went to speak to Marco, but the man was turned from him, talking with someone else. As he sat back, he felt a hand fall on his shoulder. Looking round, he saw the well-built man in his middle years with the mane of grey hair. Marco had introduced him earlier, but in all the excitement Jack had forgotten his name.

'Signor Marco tells me you're a guest of Signor Lorenzo's? From London?'

'That's right.'

The man had a rugged face and dark eyes that were hard to read. 'I should like to hear more about your family's business there.'

Jack glanced sideways at Marco, mindful of the man's insistence that this place was for pleasure not business. Out on the field, the players were getting ready to begin the game again.

The man followed his gaze. 'Not here. Come to my palace. We can drink and talk at ease.' A faint smile curled his lip, but went no further.

After a moment, his name came back to Jack. Martelli. Signor Franco Martelli. At the same time, he realised the man seemed familiar.

'I will send for you. I think we could be of help to one another, Sir James.'

The trumpet blared and the crowds roared in anticipation. Franco Martelli sat back, fixing his hard gaze on the field. All at once, Jack remembered where he'd seen him before. The party in the summer in the gardens of the palazzo, back when he'd first met Pico and Marco Valori. Martelli was the drunk man he'd seen arguing with Lorenzo de' Medici.

As the ball was tossed across the sands and the two companies hurtled towards one another, Jack wondered what sort of help Martelli thought he could be.

21

The guns were the harbingers, announcing the assault in a ruinous blast, which shook the valley. Loja's walls, scarred from months of bombardment, shuddered under the fresh onslaught. Now and then, the enemy's guns would answer, their shot smashing into the hillside close to the Spanish artillery in bursts of mud and earth, or striking the screens that protected the cannons and the men working them. Most were deflected by the barriers, but one crashed through, knocking apart one of the platforms and crushing two gunners beneath the barrel of a fallen bombard.

Whatever jubilation the Moors might have felt was short-lived, for soon after a wide top section of Loja's walls finally yielded to the assault and collapsed in a rumbling roar, chunks of masonry plummeting into the river. It wasn't a low enough breach to allow the Spanish to enter, but it served to sow panic among the Moors, their white turbans glimpsed along the walkways as they raced to defend the rupture. While they were distracted, King Ferdinand, watching the assault with his royal troops, not far from one of the town's gates, ordered the *bastidas* into position.

The four wooden towers rolled slowly to life like drunken giants advancing in shuddering, swaying steps across the flat ground by the river, towards Loja's walls. The skies, black with threat of rain since dawn, opened and rain came sweeping through the valley in blinding sheets. The men manning the *bastidas* panted, heaving on the ropes as the ground grew boggy, dragging at the towers' wheels. Rain hammered off helmets and soaked through gambesons and brigandines.

The closer the towers came to the walls, the more treacherous the ground became, littered with blocks of masonry and spent shot, bolts that stuck up from the mud like splinters and the skewed bodies of defenders plucked from the walls, left to bloat and fester in clouds of flies. Edward Woodville's archers moved in formation, shooting volleys of arrows up over the walls to provide cover. Harsh screams rose beyond, dim beneath the pummelling rain and the shouts of the Spanish commanders.

Harry, trapped inside his helm, his breaths echoing loudly, gripped his shield, holding it braced before him as he struggled on in the wake of the lurching towers, the earth churned by their passing. The rain had got inside his armour, soaking his gambeson which hung heavy on his body. The air was humid, even with the downpour, rivulets of sweat trickling down his cheeks. His feet caught in rubble and the rotting parts of men, discernible by the wisps of clothing that still clung to them like tattered flags. The slits of his visor had narrowed his vision to the mid-sections of the rolling towers and the pitted façade of the walls looming ahead, so he saw little of the things that separated beneath his boots.

All around him, a mass of men moved: infantry with halberds thrust before them in a moving wall of spikes, caballeros in their armour trudging through the mire, *homicianos* and peasants in leather tunics, daggers and clubs in their fists, some terrified, muttering prayers, others grinning savagely, eager to spill enemy blood – perhaps earn the favour of the king. Among them – though Harry had lost sight of them in the mob – were Rodrigo, Don Carlos and Don Luys with their men, battle-ready since dawn. Supported by the mass of infantry, Ferdinand had chosen some of his most experienced fighters to be the first over the walls. All of them, for the moment, were being covered by the skill of Woodville's archers, but from here on they would be in range, exposed to enemy fire.

Harry's narrowed vision picked out Woodville, not far ahead, bellowing orders, his surcoat, emblazoned with his coat of arms, clinging to his armour. The knight hadn't yet donned his helm and his straw-blond hair was plastered to his scalp, rainwater spraying as he turned his head to yell for one company of archers to let fly another lethal storm as the first of the towers neared the walls. Harry's heart thumped as he imagined a stray bolt pitching down from the walls to slam into the knight's upturned face. Each step he took, the image grew clearer, stronger, until he realised he was murmuring out loud.

'*Strike him down. Strike him down!*'

After he'd returned to the royal camp, liberated from the cave, everyone's attention had been focused on preparations for the king's major assault. But even in the midst of the planning, Edward Woodville had not forgotten him. Just last night, the eve of battle, the knight reminded him of his debt. When Loja fell he expected to be paid, not just in the blood of the infidel, but in the answers Harry owed him.

Since he'd left the Port of London, everything had conspired against Harry. From the storm-tossed seas and his own stupid mouth in the queen's presence, offering up his sword for her war, to the weeks lost, fearing for his life, in that stinking cave. And Woodville: trailing him with his cold blue eyes, needling him with questions, pressing him with menaces. It had been months since Harry's arrival in Spain and he couldn't be further from achieving King Henry's order to ingratiate himself with the king and queen, and prevent Columbus from getting those funds. He'd thought he would have a chance, here in the royal camp, to advance his purpose, but for Woodville, Ferdinand's English champion, always in the way, thwarting him, threatening him.

When might King Henry tire of his ineffectiveness? When might he send another man to do this job, remove him of his position here and any chance at one in England?

I can unmake you.

The first *bastida* was at the walls, men clustering at its base, ready to ascend as those manning it buttressed the wheels with fallen blocks of stone. Woodville's archers continued their onslaught, but the defenders were rallying. The breach had caused a distraction, but now bells were clanging, alerting men to the danger. Torches flared along the battlements, gusting in the wet as men came running to help their comrades. Crossbow quarrels lanced through arrow slits, punching into the mass of men below. Some of the bolts stuck in raised shields or thumped into the mud, but shrieks and cries rose, ragged above the tumult of rain and shouts, as barbs slammed into shoulders and heads. Harry, panting harder as he approached the killing zone, kept willing one to strike his nemesis.

Woodville's archers were shooting valiantly, turning the sky black with arcs of arrows, but more were falling now, picked off their feet by the enemy's bolts. Holding his shield above his head, teeth gritted for impact, Harry almost tripped on the body of one archer who'd gone down in front of him. Recovering his balance, he went to step over the corpse, then halted, eyes catching on the bolt. Ahead, not far, Woodville was roaring his orders as the first men streamed into the opening at the bottom of the *bastida* and began to climb the ladder within.

Fast and feverish, Harry had an idea. All around was havoc and noise. He crouched, armour flexing, reached out with his free hand and grasped the shaft of the quarrel.

Wolfbane.

Fist tightening around the shaft, he tugged the bolt from the archer's twitching body. All Woodville's focus was on the walls, eyes on the threat before him, no thoughts for his back. Harry fixed on the flesh of his neck, pale and vulnerable between the dripping strands of his hair. His mind panicked, baulked. A voice, strangely detached, asked if he was really going to do this? But he was rising now, the poisoned quarrel in his hand. It was unlikely he'd kill the man, not without precision and a huge amount of strength behind a blow, but perhaps a nick was all that was needed.

It infects any part of the body it pierces.

There was a seething sea of men moving between him and Woodville. Harry started forward, stepping over the corpse. The air was rent with sudden screams. Halting, jerking in the direction of the piercing sounds, Harry saw men tumbling out from the *bastida*. They were covered in some black substance. It took him a moment to realise it was boiling oil. The Moors had leapt on to the top of the tower and opened the hatch before the first fighters could emerge. Down inside it, they had poured a great cauldron of the steaming stuff. One of the Moors, picked off by one of Woodville's archers, went spinning from the tower-top with a shriek, his body thumping to the ground, but it was too late for the men who had been inside the *bastida*, now rolling and flailing, clawing desperately at their skin, eyes wild whites in the black burning soup of their faces.

Harry was knocked and buffeted as men surged past him. He could hear Don Carlos's voice booming somewhere close by. The other three towers had been heaved into position, men ducking inside to begin the climb. Woodville, directing his archers to continue their assault, was struggling towards one of them, hampered by the tide of men. It was now or never. Harry, weighed down by his armour, began to run. Before him, the world was narrowed to a slit of chaos, men screaming and dying, reeling from the battlements, men charging forward roaring battle-cries, swarming at the scarred walls.

Barrelling through anyone who got in his way, grunting with exertion, the shaft gripped in his fist, Harry came upon Woodville from behind. He raised the quarrel, meaning to jam the barb into the man's neck, then keep on running – disguised by his helmet – and vanish in the anonymity of the mob. Woodville was before him. He could see the veins in the man's temple, his mouth stretching for another roared command, a spray of blood painting his scarred cheek. At the last moment, Harry's foot caught on something – another body, a lump of masonry? He staggered forward, his hand flinging wide in a vain attempt at balance. He careened into Woodville, their breastplates clashing.

The knight was knocked off his feet by the impact. As he went down, Harry fell with him. His head struck something, the concussion ringing through his helm, the visor of which snapped free from one of its rivets. At the same time, he sensed something rush past him – part of his brain twitching at the danger – the thump of something punching into the mud beside him. As he turned, trying to right himself, he saw it was a crossbow bolt. A moment earlier and it would have buried itself in Woodville's skull.

The knight, struggling to untangle himself, saw it too. His eyes widened on the quarrel, then flicked in surprise to Harry, lying half on top of him, his face exposed by the broken visor swinging uselessly from his helm. Harry rolled away. He still had the bolt in his hand, but it was too late. He dropped it.

Woodville scrabbled to his feet under a renewed volley by his archers, which sent the Moors beyond the battlements ducking for cover. His surcoat was soaked with mud. Tearing his gaze from Harry, the knight turned and ran for one of the *bastidas*. Harry crawled to his feet. He stared dumbly after Woodville, who disappeared inside the tower's maw slinging his shield over his shoulder. Pushed and jostled by all those now following the knight, Harry found himself briefly face to face with Rodrigo, but the hidalgo, wild-eyed, battle-drunk, hardly seemed to recognise him. Tilting his head back, his visor swinging from his face like a metal flap of skin, Harry saw the hatch of the *bastida* burst open high above him.

Woodville emerged on the top, his blade flashing from its scabbard. He tackled the first man who leapt from the wall at him, sword scything the air. A brutal thrust of his blade and the Moor was felled, dropping from the tower like a stone. Woodville didn't even bother to stab the second man who came at him, merely grabbed the man's tunic, head-butted him in the face, then tossed him from the battlements. Then he was up and disappearing over the walls, followed by a host of Spanish fighters, erupting from the *bastida* like furious ants pouring from a nest. Beyond the walls, screams rose, punctuated by the clash of swords.

'*Para España!*' Men were howling, surging forward. '*Para el rey!*'

The bells were still clanging their warning, but to no avail.

Loja's doom was at hand.

Christopher Columbus turned his spoon in the stew he'd been served, steam rising from the bowl laced with smells of pepper and ginger. The dish had been heavily spiced, he knew, to cover the taste of the meat, which spoiled quickly in the Spanish heat. He took a few mouthfuls, swallowing down hot chunks of flesh and fat. The long day on the dockside – two new consignments to offload and process – had given him a righteous hunger.

As he ate the tavern filled up around him, merchants and captains, customs officials and dockworkers heading in at the end of their shifts, the autumn sky flaming through the windows, gilding the masts of the great galleys that were moored there. He caught a few glances from some of them, the odd smirk. He knew what most of these men thought of him: the oversized, white-haired, red-faced madman from Genoa, with his foolish notions about the world. He still could not fathom, though, why they didn't share his passion, even if they believed his plan improbable. With the Turks holding Constantinople, the transport of many of the luxuries enjoyed by their fathers – certain spices and silks, perfumes and medicines – had been stalled, curtailed or halted completely. Even with the Venetians quick to strike trade deals with the infidel, consignments from the east were far slower and subject to high tariffs.

But men, in his experience, could be short-sighted and lazy. Give a man a warm meal, a place to bed down, some ale to ease his mind and a woman to hold him, and most would be content. Like damn cattle, he thought as he chewed. Rising from the womb to breathe and eat and shit and fornicate, then falling down into the earth. Uncelebrated. Forgotten. They could smirk and whisper all they wanted, but he would not be like them. Not as long as he had dreams in his head and horizons to cross.

'I hear it was a good day, my friend.'

Columbus was distracted from his brooding by the familiar voice.

Gianotto Berardi smiled broadly as he slid on to the bench beside him, removing his cap and reaching eagerly for the jug on the table. His dark green cloak, trimmed with silver braid, was dusty from the road. 'Do you mind? I am parched.'

'How was Córdoba?' Columbus asked, watching his business partner gulp gratefully at the wine. Berardi, a trader from a well-known Florentine slaver family, couldn't be more opposite than him in looks: short and slender, with olive skin and a full head of wavy black hair that was stuck to his scalp with sweat. He had left a week ago, conveying a new batch of slaves to the market there.

'Good, good,' replied Beradi, nodding. 'Better still, I met with Queen Isabella.' He shook his head as Columbus sat forward eagerly. 'No, I'm afraid she had nothing new to say on your proposal. But she is keen to work with us. Loja has fallen to King Ferdinand's forces. A mighty victory. The queen is heading to the front line, to oversee the next stage of the war. She believes she may soon have need of our services to help traffic any captives. She has offered us a generous commission.' Berardi set down the wine, his tanned brow pinching. 'You are not pleased?'

'She said nothing? Nothing at all?' Columbus pushed away his congealing stew. 'She promised to speak to others in her court. Experts, she said, in navigation and astronomy. Promised to discuss the viability of my plan. It has been months since I saw her.'

'I am certain she will turn her attention to your proposal, as soon the Moors are vanquished.' Berardi smiled, his dark eyes catching the setting sun's fire. 'And, think, if we are called to the front line you will have plenty of opportunities to encourage her interest. Come, let us get more wine. It is a day for celebration, not gloom. Two boatloads processed, another set sold, and the promise of much more cargo to come. More days like this and we will make our own fortune, my friend, enough to sail wherever you wish.'

After a pause, Columbus nodded, but his eyes went to the windows, where the galleys shifted slowly against the harbour wall. How long must he wait for his dream to be realised? How long for a ship, all his own, that would carry him across that wide green sea?

And, just how long could he leave it, until someone else found those islands before him?

22

Franco Martelli's palazzo was in the Santa Maria Novella quarter, one street back from the river, near the Ponte Santa Trinita, a more sedate bridge than the frenetic Ponte Vecchio, with a hospital for monks at one end and a sundial at the other. Its arches were mirrored in the waters below, glowing jade in the sunlight. People were already talking about the Christmas celebrations, but for the past few days summer seemed to have returned.

Martelli's property was smaller than the Palazzo Medici, but nonetheless imposing: a bruising block of stone that seemed to elbow its neighbours out of the way. The shutters were closed along the lower level, as were the double doors, on which the black paint was peeling. Jack halted on the step, rapped his knuckles on the wood. He stood there for some time and was beginning to wonder if he'd got the right house from Martelli's message, when he heard bolts snapping back. One of the doors opened to reveal a gaunt, elderly man.

'Good day, I am here to see Signor Franco.'

'Sir James Wynter?' The man, a steward Jack supposed, opened the door at his nod.

Beyond was a large hallway, several doors leading off and a marble staircase sweeping to a gallery above. It was a grand space, the floor decorated with patterned tiles, but it was virtually empty – none of the statues, urns or ornamentation that dignified the Medici palace. There were three paintings in gilt frames: one of a man in dark, burnished armour, another of a colonnaded marketplace populated by stern-faced men in togas and one of the Virgin holding the infant Christ. Although large, they seemed too spaced out, dwarfed by the expanse of plaster and then, as the elderly steward motioned him to follow, Jack noticed faint marks on the walls, squares and rectangles, where many other paintings had clearly once hung.

The steward led him into one of the rooms leading off the hall, another airy space, mostly empty but for a long table that dominated the chamber. With the shutters closed the room was dim, oppressive despite its size.

'Please wait.'

As the steward disappeared through a smaller set of doors, Jack studied the table, counting seven places set with cutlery, plates, napkins and goblets. Each piece was highly polished and perfectly arranged, but seemed somehow demeaned by the vastness of the table, which was otherwise bare of decoration. He wondered, tensely, who the other guests might be.

Since Franco Martelli suggested they talk, Jack had been running through the questions he might ask without giving himself away. The best way to know a man, his father once said, is to ask not only his friends about his character, but his enemies. One argument wasn't enough to determine if Martelli was, indeed, an enemy of Lorenzo's, but it was clear the man had something to say. He just needed to turn the opportunity into something of use to himself. His men wouldn't wait for much longer. Adam had grown increasingly vocal in his frustrations and even Ned and David were becoming irritated by the lack of progress. Jack had asked them to help Amelot search for the man she had seen, but the fruitless trailing around the city was wearing their patience as thin as their soles.

The doors opened and Franco Martelli strode in. Close up and standing he was even more impressive than Jack had first realised, with a frame like a fighter's and that swept-back mane of grey hair giving him an extra burst of height. His eyes were bloodshot and red veins spidered his cheeks, but his grip was firm as he shook Jack's hand. 'Sir James, welcome to my home.'

'Thank you, signore. It is an honour.'

The man's eyes narrowed slightly, searching his face as if for a lie, then he was turning, gesturing to the steward who had slipped in behind him. 'Wine, Naldo. Sit,' he said to Jack, motioning to the table.

Martelli sat at the head and Jack in the place closest to him. The other five spaces were so spread out they would have to raise their voices to talk to one another. Could the places be set for members of the Court of Wolves? Might this engagement even be something to do with the test Marco had alluded to as they parted company following the game, Jack pressing him as to when they would meet again?

Be patient, Sir James. These things must happen in a certain way. Your pedigree is not in question. But suitability, commitment? These must be tested.

'How did you enjoy the contest?'

'It was exhilarating, signore,' Jack answered truthfully. He'd fed off the excitement of it for the past few days, replaying the match in his mind, part of him imagining himself in that arena, adored by the crowd.

As the steward leaned in to pour wine, the doors opened again and a woman entered, followed by three girls. As Martelli stood, Jack rose with him, smiling in greeting to hide his disappointment. So, the invitation was most likely relating to him and his business then? More probing about his father's fictitious wool company. Still, that didn't mean he couldn't ask his own questions.

'My wife, Signora Donna Santa.'

Jack inclined his head to the woman. She was slight of build and more than half Martelli's age, pretty in a thin, pale way, with sharp eyes that studied him with cool intensity, making him think of a small bird of prey.

'And my daughters, Agata, Fea and Piera.'

One, in early adolescence, was the image of her mother. The other two were still in childhood, but their pale features and twig-like bodies suggested they would turn out much the same.

'Ah, and my eldest.'

Jack looked round as another figure entered. A jolt of sharp surprise went through him. Martelli was saying her name, but Jack already knew it.

Laora.

If she was shocked to see him, she didn't show it, dutifully dipping her head in greeting as she took the chair opposite him.

Martelli's eyes pinched in on Jack's expression, but then he nodded. 'But, of course, you would have seen her at the palazzo, yes?'

Something whispered across Jack's mind, but before he could seize on it, Laora was speaking to him.

'Good day, Sir James.'

'Yes, indeed,' he said, trying to cover his fluster. 'Good day, signora.'

As the women sat and Martelli followed suit, Jack took his place, glancing at Laora, whom he'd only seen once since the dinner at

Fiesole, outside Maddalena's room with Clarice de' Medici. He guessed, after the girl's betrothal, he would see her less and less. Laora didn't meet his gaze, but sat stiffly in her chair, eyes on her plate. She was wearing the silver bird pendant, fiddling the chain between thumb and forefinger as Naldo poured her some wine. A smell of orange blossom wafted to him and Jack wondered now if the bird was the source of the scent.

'Must you wear that to dinner?' Donna Santa stared down the table at Laora. 'You know how queasy the smell makes me.' She wrinkled her nose to prove the point.

'Yes, Mother,' Laora murmured.

Jack frowned. Hadn't she said her mother was dead? A quick glance back at Donna Santa solved the mystery. Laora – with her dark hair and sharp features, chiselled rather than pinched, the smatter of freckles on her nose and cheeks, fading with the approach of winter – looked nothing like the woman or the other girls. Donna Santa must be Martelli's second wife.

As Laora lifted the chain and dropped the pendant down the neck of her gown, hiding it from view, the thought that had whispered across his mind on first seeing her returned. It was a memory: the candlelit garden, Martelli's voice rising in anger, all the guests turning to the drama. All except Laora. That flush in her face when he'd questioned her in the market.

I was going to Maddalena's room.

Martelli was speaking about the game again, holding out his goblet, already drained, as Naldo finished pouring wine for the women. 'That son of a bitch, Alesso. I put money on him to get at least three in the net!'

Jack joined in his talk politely where he could, swallowing back the wine, which seemed sour now his palate was accustomed to the smooth vintages from the Medici cellars. A servant in a stained apron entered, bearing a steaming pot of something that he placed in the centre of the table. This place, for its size, should be bustling with staff, but Jack had an impression of echoes and emptiness, stretching away beyond the reception hall. The palace seemed more mausoleum than home. Hadn't Laora said her father had worked with Lorenzo for years? If so, he didn't appear to have come out of it well. He wondered what his story was and how he might get Martelli to divulge it, but the man hadn't yet paused for breath.

'Have you heard of this monster stalking our city, Sir James?' Martelli ladled stew on to his plate.

'You mean the murders?' Last week the palace had been buzzing with news of another killing in the Santa Maria Novella quarter, similar to one the month before and one late in the summer. Only this time, the victim, a man known to Lorenzo, hadn't just been peeled of skin, but his insides scooped out and arranged beside him. Jack had heard Rigo say the *gonfalon* of the district was adamant, despite the rumours, that it wasn't the work of a beast or a demon, but a man. 'Thank you,' Jack murmured, as Martelli deposited a large portion of fat-marbled meat in front of him.

'I dare not even visit the market any more,' said Donna Santa, sipping at her wine, eyes on Jack.

'Signor Lorenzo is taking these crimes very seriously, signora,' Jack assured her. 'He has ordered the *gonfaloni* to put on extra patrols.'

Martelli scoffed at this. It was a bitter sound. 'Our great protector.'

Jack seized his chance. 'I believe you worked for a time with the signore?'

'Partners,' Martelli retorted quickly. 'The signore and I were partners.' The bite in his tone was all anger and stung pride. He drew in a breath, sat back. 'Do you know how I first made my fortune, Sir James?' He lifted his goblet. 'Wine. My father's business and his father's before him. It was a good business. We made a great deal of money, but our friends in the wool trade were making more. More than kings.' He drained the wine and Naldo was there to refill it. 'Twenty years ago, I inherited my family's company. I took all the money we made in wine and invested it in wool. Within five years I doubled it.' He swept the goblet through the air as he spoke. 'I owned some of the largest drying barns in Santa Croce. My workshops were among the busiest in the quarter. I'd swear some seasons half the girls in the city were working their spindles for me. I rose through the ranks of the Arte della Lana, was appointed one of the heads of the guild.'

Jack could almost see the memories in Martelli's face as he talked: the bustle of workers, the rough talk of men, hands red raw as they washed the fleeces in the vats, the acrid smells of detergents and dyes, the chatter of quick-fingered girls, working the yarn into threads in their homes. After almost year in this city, whose wealth had been built on the trade, it all felt oddly familiar. But he reminded himself he was no expert. He had to be careful here or risk exposing the fraud he was.

As Martelli continued, Jack took a mouthful of stew. It wasn't well spiced and what flavour there was couldn't disguise the pungent taint to the meat, past its best. Donna Santa was picking at her food, skewering tiny morsels for her mouth. Her daughters were whispering among themselves, occasionally glancing at Jack and sometimes at Laora, who was staring at her untouched plate.

Martelli, who had almost finished, talking through every mouthful, pausing only to wash it down with more wine, fixed on Jack. 'Signor Marco told us your father is on good terms with King Henry?'

'That's right.' So, Marco had been speaking about him to the company? A good sign? Jack steeled himself for the questions he guessed were coming.

Martelli didn't disappoint. 'And he has secured a preferential rate for his exports? Might be able to sell his wool abroad for a fairer price?'

'He was still in negotiations when I left. But, yes, and I know he hopes to work closely with Signor Lorenzo.'

Martelli sat forward at this, his brow furrowed. 'I said I thought we could be of help to one another, Sir James. What I am willing to tell you may be of value to you. I presume you would consent to return the favour, if I ever ask?'

Jack saw Laora's eyes dart to him. There was something in them. A warning? But he ignored it. At last, someone willing to speak openly. 'Of course, signore.'

Martelli's smile was more a twisted grimace. He sat back, goblet clenched in his fist. 'Lorenzo de' Medici came to me twelve years ago. I knew his father, a shrewd businessman.' He shook his head. 'I never understood why Cosimo favoured his grandson over his son. Lorenzo was a wild youth. Irrepressible. More wed to the pursuit of women than money, more interested in poetry, philosophy, horse racing. Unsuited to business, I thought then, and say freely now. But you know yourself his power. When he came to me, told me he wanted to open three new wool workshops in the city – using my expertise and his influence, joint investors – it was a deal I could not refuse.' He drank, eyes narrowed. 'What a fool I was.'

'Father,' Laora murmured.

'Don't interrupt,' Donna Santa said sharply.

Laora's cheek twitched. Wiping her mouth with her napkin, despite having hardly touched her food, she glanced at Martelli. 'May I be excused?' Her tone was flat, lifeless. Jack thought how different she looked, the spark gone out in her eyes.

'You may not,' Donna Santa answered.

As Laora's face flamed, Agata and the other two girls giggled together. Jack, looking at their pale, thin faces, had an image of rats in a corner, eyeing something injured.

'Quiet!' Martelli snapped, banging a fist on the table, making the cutlery and all the girls jump.

He continued for a time, waxing lyrical on the early years of the business, the great successes – all down to him – Lorenzo uninterested in the daily running of the workshops, more concerned with his *damn Academy*. Jack tried to slip in on the subject of the Academy, but Martelli ignored him. He was starting to repeat himself, his voice thick, those red veins on his cheeks spreading into hectic blotches.

'Two years ago, he came and told me he wanted out of our partnership.' Martelli snapped his fingers. 'Just like that. Out of nowhere. I knew he had financial troubles – hell, the whole republic knew that. After his imprisonment in Naples he had to beg and borrow, even steal from his own family to keep his position here. But I never thought he would turn on me.' He laughed bitterly. 'I offered to buy him out over time, but he demanded the money immediately. It took almost all my capital to honour the debt. Four months later, one of our wool consignments was lost at sea. Turks, pirates – I still don't know.' Martelli leaned forward, his bloodshot eyes fixing with some difficulty on Jack. 'It is astonishing how precarious are the foundations on which we build our lives. How one piece of bad luck can bring the whole damn edifice crashing down. When you are up in this city, Sir James, you are on the roof of the world.' He thrust a finger to the ceiling. 'When you are down you are in the dirt.' He brought his finger stabbing down on the table. 'A beggar. A *miserabile*. That's what he made of me!'

The change in the room was palpable. Donna Santa had paused in her eating, the girls had gone quiet and Laora's eyes were fixed, wide and wary, on her father. All the crags and angles of Martelli's face had drawn down into a taut façade of rage. In the hush, only Naldo's footsteps could be heard as he came to refill his master's goblet.

Jack, however, wasn't thinking of Martelli's increasingly drunken furore – he was thinking of Marco Valori speaking of Lorenzo's brutal erasure of the Pazzi line and of Lorenzino wondering how Amerigo Vespucci could sit at the signore's table after everything he'd done to his family, whatever that might mean. Thinking of the man, chained in the sanctum. For all Lorenzo de' Medici was lauded and honoured for his place as father of the republic, first among equals – il Magnifico – he was coming to see another side entirely to his governorship: one based in ruthlessness, duplicity and deception. Traits that made him think not of a republic, but of an empire, ruled by an iron fist. Had his father known this man he'd served? Been a willing supporter of all his dark endeavours?

He glanced at Laora, wondering at her closeness with Maddalena and Lucrezia. Why would Martelli continue to allow his daughter to frequent the home of a man who had betrayed him in this way – a man he unequivocally hated? Revenge, perhaps? He thought of the *Sala Grande*, the scent of her perfume lingering. Thought of Amaury's letter, intercepted, and Amelot's drawing of a wolf's head, inked in the dimness of the priest's ransacked room.

He felt cold, even though the shuttered chamber was stuffy. Was he sitting with the spies Lorenzo feared in his household? Was Martelli – Laora even – somehow involved in Amaury's abduction? He wondered if Lorenzo knew Martelli was a member of the Court of Wolves. The only time he'd seen the man wearing the company's badge was at the game.

Martelli, not noticing his distraction, was still talking about his losses. He was becoming more irate, wine splashing over the rim of his goblet as he gestured, speaking of the workshops shutting down, the creditors banging on the door, the men of the Arte della Lana turning on him, friends abandoning him, the threat of imprisonment in the Stinche, the debtors' prison.

'Do you know what they do to a bankrupt in this city?' Martelli stabbed a finger in Jack's direction. 'They whip him. Publicly! I had to give up almost everything. The wealth I inherited from my father, furniture, my wife's jewels and gowns, my daughters' dowries. My reputation was ruined. Only the brethren saved me. Brought me into their company, gave me aid and succour.' He curled his fist, his lips peeling back. 'Oh, he will pay. Mark my words, he will pay!'

'Franco,' murmured Donna Santa warningly.

Martelli didn't seem to hear her. 'The bastard came to me, Sir James, do you understand? He came to me, then walked away with all the profit and no loss. You have seen his palace. His wealth!' Spit flew from between Martelli's lips. 'Do you not think he could have afforded to let me pay him back in time?' He went to drink, then glared into the goblet. 'Naldo!'

Jack saw Laora lock gazes with the thin-faced steward, saw her shake her head. It was a tiny movement, but one that didn't – despite his condition – go unnoticed by Martelli.

'You would presume to answer for me, girl?'

Laora sat back in her chair, pinned by her father's wrath, all now directed at her. Donna Santa and the other girls were silent, watching. 'Father, I am sorry. I just thought . . .'

'You thought what? That I'd *had enough*?' The mimicry in his voice suggested it was a familiar conversation. 'I'll decide when I've had enough! Do you hear me?' He rose suddenly in his chair, which screeched on the tiles. 'I said, do you hear me?'

'Yes, Father!' Laora's eyes were large.

'What worries do you have? What responsibilities? Sitting pretty doing nothing here each damn day!'

'Signor Franco, I—'

Martelli ignored Jack's attempt to interrupt his outburst. 'I've had enough, have I?'

'No, Father, I meant only to—'

Martelli flung the goblet with all his might. It struck the wall by a painting, with a clang. Before Jack could say anything, the man was striding to Laora's chair, pulling it back with the girl still in it. He grabbed her by the arm, hauling her to her feet. She shrank back, but he had her. Jack remembered the bruise on her shoulder, imprints of fingers on skin. He stood and was about to intervene, try to calm the man down, when Martelli backhanded Laora across the face, sending her flying.

'*I'll decide when I've had enough!*'

Donna Santa had clutched her daughters to her, leaving Laora alone, dazed and sprawled on the floor. Her gown had ridden up, exposing long pale legs, a yellow bruise clouding one thigh, a kink in one knee.

'*Do you hear me, you ungrateful bitch?*' Snatching hold of her, Martelli dragged Laora to her feet. She cried out as he swept back his hand.

Jack was moving before he could think what he was doing. He seized Martelli's raised arm by the wrist, halting the blow. Franco turned on him, wild-eyed. Jack saw his mistake at once. He had been in Florence long enough to know how sacred a father's honour was. In the household his word was law, his authority absolute. To challenge that authority was a grave insult. He relinquished his grip, too late.

Martelli's eyes had narrowed to slits. He let go of Laora, who darted from the room, to turn his anger on Jack. For a moment, Jack thought the man was going to flatten him. Then Martelli spoke, the words hissing out through clenched teeth. '*Get out.*'

'Signor, I—'

'Naldo!'

The elderly steward was at Jack's shoulder in a moment. 'Sir.'

Jack stared at Martelli, his hunched shoulders, the red of his eyes. There would be no placating the man, not now. Inclining his head, he left the room. As Naldo closed the door, Jack heard the sound of things breaking beyond it.

A quick step across the hall and he was out in the sunshine, the doors closing behind him, leaving the hulking stone building to glare down on him. He cursed, running his hands through his hair. Should he attempt to go back in, at least try to calm the man down? What else might he do in such a temper?

'Sir James.'

He turned to see a smaller door had opened, further down the building. Laora was in the opening, flush-faced. He felt relief, seeing her unharmed.

'Quick,' she called, beckoning.

Without thinking, he hastened to her and stepped inside. She shut the door, plunging them into darkness. Jack had a sense of a narrow space, walls pressing in, a corridor stretching away, then Laora's hand was on his arm.

'Come.'

The sun warmed her face as she stood on the terrace, eyes tracing the now familiar skyline of disorderly tenements, immense palazzi and crenellated towers. The dome of the cathedral was the colour of dried blood in the afternoon light. Feeling a shadow pass across her, Amelot turned, gaze on the door that led into the room she shared with Jack.

It remained closed and, seeing no further movement, she guessed the shadow had been a bird. But as she returned her attention to the city she felt a prickle at her back.

Again, last night, she had heard someone moving around the top floor. She'd been aware of movement out there before at odd times, usually deep in the dark before dawn when everyone was asleep – the click of a door, the creak of a stair, a faint odour of unfamiliar sweat tainting the air. She thought at first it must be servants or Lorenzo's bodyguards on patrol, but that seemed odd when it was only their room, a library, a couple of storerooms and an armoury on the upper floor. Twice now, she had crept out to investigate, but had seen no one.

Jack didn't seem to have noticed these intrusions, his mind elsewhere. At least now he appeared to be focused on the hunt for Amaury again, since he'd gone to meet the men of the Court of Wolves, asking the others to help her in her search and telling her he hoped there would soon be an opportunity for her to get a look at the company – see if she could spot the man she'd glimpsed at Carnival.

Amelot set off across the terrace to the adjoining building. Jumping up, she grabbed the overhang of the roof and pulled herself on to it. The tiles were sun-warm under her bare feet as she crossed the expansive roof of the palace of Lorenzo's cousins, then scrambled across the next one, launching a flock of birds into the sky.

Beads of sweat broke out on her brow as she moved, eyes alert, scanning rotting balconies and expansive loggias where washing waved like flags, peering through attic windows curtained with webs and between the gaps of shutters. It was too early to venture inside any of the buildings. That she would only risk at night. In this way she had seen many of the city's secrets.

She had seen wonders. A shadowed workshop filled with masks, rows of painted heads, horned devils and gilded dragons lined up like an audience. Men tipping cauldrons of dye into the Arno that had turned the river pink. A marble giant chiselled to life in a cellar. And she had seen horrors. A girl dragged into an alley by three men, her screams stopped by a brutal hand. A tonsured friar rutting like a dog with a dead-eyed boy with painted lips in a brothel. A woman smothering her crying baby. A slave's brown back lashed to bloody ribbons by her master's whip.

She had seen arguments and kisses, slow currents of bodies moving beneath silk sheets, deals brokered and confidences whispered, pockets picked and filled. She had seen Lorenzo de' Medici in his many dealings, a spider in the centre of a web. She'd seen Giovanni Pico della Mirandola slipping from Angelo Poliziano's bedchamber and Marsilio Ficino stalking the passageways, his black habit making him one with the shadows. She had seen Adam and Valentine, buying weapons in the market, meeting alone to talk furtively. But the one person she had seen no sign of, depite her hunting, was Amaury.

Near the wide piazza outside Santa Croce, she paused for a rest, perched on the edge of a tall building with a view over the square and down into a rubbish-strewn alley. Her eyes tracked across the piazza, busy with people: Franciscans in grey heading into the church, workers entering the barns where dyed wool was hung out to dry on racks, people ducking into inns for refreshments. Outside a tavern, a man in bright clothes was juggling knives. A small crowd had gathered to watch, clapping as he threw one blade high and caught it between his teeth, while continuing to spin the others.

Amelot's mind filled with an image of her father, his sun-brown face, taut with concentration, burnished by the sputtering flames of the five torches he tossed deftly in his large hands. He grinned as she stepped up to him, but didn't take his eyes off the flaming wands. Round and round they went, a glowing circle, lighting up the tents around them. Beyond – campfires and laughter. 'Want to try, little angel?'

'No, Papa!'

'Soon, then. I have so many tricks to teach you.'

Amelot turned away, squeezing out the memory.

Her body felt sluggish today and a gnawing discomfort in her stomach made her fearful the blood might be returning. It was four months since it first appeared, trickling between her legs to soak her hose. At first she thought she'd cut herself, but her fingers, coming back red and sticky, had touched without pain. It had lasted several days, during which time the hated buds she bound so tight to her chest had become unbearably tender. She had become certain she was dying until, just days after it started, it stopped. When it came again, last month, she'd stolen one of Jack's old shirts, torn into strips stuffed into her hose to soak up the blood. She had kept the strips, washed out in the river, in case it returned. But again? So soon? She had never heard the men speak of such things or seen any sign they dealt with this. Was it another curse of womanhood? How she hated her sex. So tender, such easy prey. Why had God made her a sparrow when he could have made her a hawk?

Down in the alley, movement caught her eye. A door cracked open and a man appeared, dressed in a thick woollen cloak, the hood pulled up. Even from here she could see he was enormous; a giant of a man, his shoulders hunched and broad.

She was rising, meaning to move on, head deeper into the quarter, when a shutter was pushed open beneath her. The man's head tipped back at the bang. Terror flooded Amelot; a black, icy wave. The giant only had half a face. The rest was covered by a white mask.

23

Jack looked around the chamber as Laora pushed the door to behind him. The walls were lined with wooden panels. The room was expansive, but sparsely furnished: a bed drawn up against one wall, table and stool by tall, shuttered windows, a few chests dwarfed in a corner, dresses hanging like a row of limp bodies from hooks.

From what he'd glimpsed, hastening at her behest through shadowy passageways and up servants' staircases, past doorways that opened into space and silence, the rest of the palace was much the same. An echoing tomb for a once grand life. He wondered why Martelli hadn't simply sold the place, found a smaller home to better fit what he'd been left with after Lorenzo had been done with him. Pride, he guessed. Pride and an unwillingness to reveal to the city what had become of him. At least the palazzo's hulking walls retained the façade of power.

'They were my mother's.'

At Laora's voice, Jack turned his gaze from the row of hanging gowns. Even in the dim light he could see her cheek had already bloomed red where her father had cuffed her.

'They're all I have left of her. And this.' Reaching inside her dress, Laora pulled out the bird pendant. She went to the bed and sat on the edge, twisting the chain between her fingers. After a moment, she lifted the bird to her face and breathed in, closing her eyes.

Jack watched her, wondering why she had brought him here. Wondering, too, why he had come. Martelli was already furious. Why risk inciting more of the man's wrath? He crossed the room to stand before her. 'I should go, signora. I don't want to cause you more trouble.'

She met his gaze. 'What more trouble could I have?'

He thought of the bruises he'd glimpsed, faded tracks of violence. How often did this happen?

Laora seemed to read his mind. 'He has always been this way. Long before he and the signore parted company.' She let the pendant fall to her chest. 'It started with my mother, when I was very young. Some nights I would wake to hear shouts. Screams. I would go downstairs to see the servants huddled outside the room – watching, doing nothing – while he beat her.' Her brow pinched. 'I tried to stop him sometimes, but my mother would tell me to leave. Once, when I refused to go, she struck me herself.' Her voice cracked into a whisper. 'One night she fell when he hit her, split her head on the edge of the hearth. He left. A tavern? A gambling den?' Laora shook her head, hands clenched in her lap. 'I sat with my mother, tried to staunch the bleeding. She was talking strangely. Not herself. She slipped into sleep while I was sitting with her. I fell asleep too.

'When I woke her hand was still in mine, but it was – so *cold*.' She shivered. 'So stiff I had to pull her fingers open. I shook her, tried to wake her. But she was gone. He killed her.' Laora inhaled and pressed her fingers to her lips as if trying to put the words back in. 'I've never told anyone.' Tears rolled freely down her cheeks, but she made no sound. 'He doesn't touch Donna Santa or my step-sisters. Why her?' She shook her head, her face scrunching in self-disgust. 'Why *me*?'

Jack knew that shameful, secret question: pain and humiliation, the impotence, victim to another's fists. The taunts and kicks, punching him down into the dirt. Something in his blood, some scent that drew his tormentors. Seeing her sprawled on the floor at her father's mercy, hands raised to ward off his blows – wasn't it recognition that made him stay Martelli's hand? After a moment, he sat beside her, the bed creaking beneath his weight. 'Can you leave?'

She let out a choked laugh. 'Where would I go? Into a whorehouse? On to the street? You have seen what happens to women in this city when they have nothing. No family. No husband. No money. *Miserabiles*.'

'A convent then?'

'A prison for women without dowries,' she said, standing. 'How could you understand, *Sir* James? You, who have the freedom to go wherever you please? Do whatever you wish?' She began to pace, the skirts of her gown whispering. 'Besides, he would never release me.

He wants me here. Here to do his bidding.' She put her hands, trembling, to her brow. 'Dear God, but he has made me a thief and a liar.'

Jack thought of her slipping away at the party. Thought of her father's quarrel with Lorenzo – a distraction? 'What has he made you steal, signora?'

She looked at him suddenly. 'Nothing. I didn't mean that. I meant—' She shook her head, turned fearfully towards the door. 'You should leave. I don't know what I was thinking, inviting you here. He would—'

Jack rose, caught her gently by the shoulders. 'You can trust me, signora. I understand your pain.'

'How could you?' She met his eyes, defiant, but hope cracked her voice.

'My mother was murdered. My half-brother was, in a way, responsible. I know what it is to despise your own blood.' She had gone still beneath his hands. 'Talk to me. Let me help you. What does your father make you do for him?'

Her eyes darted away, emotions warring across her face. After a moment, she looked back, something set in her expression. Jack thought she was going to speak, confide in him, but instead she rose on to her toes and kissed his mouth.

He moved his head back in surprise, but her hands came up to slide over his, still gripping her shoulders. She kissed him again. He could feel the heat coming off her bruised cheek. Her lips were soft. He tasted wine and tears. Desire flamed in him, a lit fuse. He forgot his questions. Releasing his hands from hers, he moved them around her back, down to her waist, pulling her to him. He felt her chest pressing against his, the curve of her spine beneath his hands, sliding lower now, gripping fistfuls of silk. He kissed her deeply, felt her lips parting, her mouth opening to receive him. Orange blossom filled his senses; sweet, intoxicating.

There was a noise outside the door. A girl's laughter, sharp and high. Laora pulled from him as if burned. '*My sisters!*' She grabbed his sleeve and tugged him towards the far wall, where he realised one of the wooden panels that lined the room was a door. 'You have to go,' she breathed. 'Take the first door you see at the bottom of the stairs. A servants' passage will lead you to the street.'

Jack halted, half dazed, at the door. 'Can I see you again?' The question came fast, urgent, twin needs now burning in him: for answers and for more of this, of her.

'Laora?' A girl's voice, sing-song and mocking outside the door. 'My mother wants you to clean up the mess downstairs.'

She looked back at him. 'Please!'

Jack stood his ground, waiting.

'Yes.' Laora clutched at his arm as he slipped through the door. 'Sir James, beware of my father. He will not forget a slight.'

It had seemed an easy assignment: overseeing the men appointed with collecting anything valuable from Loja's houses, workshops and mosques; making sure the items found their way into the treasury of the crown, rather than the grubbing hands of soldiers. It was a preferable task to managing the lines of men, women and children being escorted from the town and certainly more preferable to supervising the clean-up, the dust-laced air down near the walls still thick with the stink of putrefying corpses trapped under rubble. But, after over a fortnight picking through the lives of strangers, Harry was bored.

Pushing open a set of carved doors, he entered a bedchamber. Patterned tiles decorated the floor, the bed was heaped with cushions and the domed ceiling was painted with stars. A brocaded cloak lay beside the bed. On a table by the windows, which offered a view across the river towards the mountains, was an assortment of personal items: an ivory comb, a jewel-handled razor, a glazed bowl. As Harry walked around the bed, his foot knocked something on the floor. Crouching, he picked up a hunting horn. It was beautiful; polished bone decorated with filigreed silver. Glancing furtively at the doors, he was about to tuck the horn on his belt, hide it beneath his cloak, when he saw them – two sets of eyes blinking at him from the shadows beneath the bed.

The jolt of fear passed as he realised it was just children. A boy and a girl. The two of them were huddled together, dark eyes fixed on him. He saw scraps of food and guessed they'd been hiding here since the town's surrender. The boy was staring at the hunting horn. Harry saw the conflict in his face – terror warring with fury. Was it his? His father's? He put his finger to his lips.

'Sir Harry Vaughan?'

He rose swiftly, the horn still in his hand, to see a royal guard enter the chamber. 'Yes?' he said curtly, cheeks colouring at the nearness of being caught stealing the king's plunder. Gathering his composure, he tempered his tone. 'What is it?'

The guard knew enough English to answer, although his accent clung to the words. 'My lord Ferdinand wishes to speak to you. He is in the physicians' tent. With Sir Edward Woodville.'

'Woodville?' Harry swallowed dryly. 'He's—' He stopped himself saying *alive*. 'Awake?'

'Yes, sir. And asking for you.'

Nodding tightly, Harry headed across the chamber. One of Rodrigo's squires, sent with him to supervise the search of the buildings in this quarter, met him on the landing, half a dozen soldiers following him, tramping dust on the stairs. Reluctantly, Harry handed the horn to the squire. 'There are items of value in there. And two children. Under the bed.'

He wasn't sure if the man had understood, until he was halfway down the stairs and the screaming started.

Outside, the streets were busy, men sweating as they shifted piles of rubble, digging out the dead and clearing the streets so repairs could begin on the broken walls, the town set to be garrisoned by the king's men. Loja was a Christian town now, another piece taken from the Moors in this long game of war. Carts rumbled past, loaded with clothing, coffers, chests and weapons. Many of the walls of the houses were pocked with gunshot and sprayed with vicious arcs of blood, dried to rust.

Harry breathed through his mouth as he walked with the royal guard down the steep, winding street to the gates. The reek of death turned his stomach, although it wasn't as overwhelming as it had been a week ago, when the dead were still piled high in clouds of flies, awaiting burial.

It was in these streets that he'd first found himself after the treacherous climb over the walls. The battle existed in his memory as a series of disparate images – brief, violent bursts – that continued to flash in his mind. The chaos. The concussive reports of guns. The savage crack of a sword against his helm. A man snarling in his face, before the side of his head exploded in a burst of red. A man on his knees trying to stuff his insides back through the gash in his stomach, entrails slipping through his frantic hands. El Barbero on the ground, Rodrigo grasping his shoulders, the soldier clutching one eye, blood oozing black between his fingers.

The relief Harry felt leaving the stinking city curdled at the sight of the white pavilions, rising ahead on the edges of the king's camp. It wasn't until two days after Loja's fall that he'd heard Edward Woodville had been found, bleeding and unconscious under the sprawled bodies of the enemy. He had asked Rodrigo to check on the knight's condition, nodding sombrely at the shakes of the hidalgo's head and his grim expression, while privately rejoicing. Since it seemed Woodville had spent the past weeks lingering at death's door it was a shock now to hear the son of a bitch had crawled his way back to the living.

With the surprise came fear. Had the knight recalled something from that moment outside the walls? Had he – or someone else – seen the bolt raised in his fist? Had he told the king? As they neared the pavilions, Harry's gaze flicked towards the tracks leading up into the mountains. But where would he run to in this wilderness?

The area around the physicians' tents was quiet, much calmer now than in the first days after the assault, the air rent with screams and whimpers as physicians, surgeons and servants worked to tug bolts and barbs from flesh with pincers, cauterise stumps of arms, hack off mangled legs, sew hanging flaps of skin and stuff wounds with lint soaked in wine.

Outside the entrance to the largest pavilion, two royal guards stood sentry, wearing the livery of Queen Isabella. The queen had arrived yesterday at the head of a train of knights and ladies-in-waiting, her velvet mantle a sweeping trail of scarlet, auburn tresses flaming in the sun. She had come like a beacon, shining light across the battered Christian forces, cheered by victory, but exhausted from the long siege. Her presence had given new life to their triumph and fired their blood for the next phase. The Marquis of Cádiz, Don Carlos and others had already travelled onward to prepare the ground for an assault on Íllora, another settlement to the east. Beyond that, and other smaller towns, lay the huge coastal city of Málaga; jewel in the emirate's crown and the last major obstacle to Granada itself.

To Harry, the queen's coming had both kindled his hope and renewed his sense of purpose. With Woodville out of action, possibly for good, and this new turn in the war, which had served to make Ferdinand a good deal more welcoming, he might, at last, be able to work his way in with the queen and the king, earn their trust and fulfil the task he had come here for: stop Columbus securing those funds he needed for a voyage, giving King Henry time to prepare his own expedition west.

This need had burned all the fiercer in him when, last night, Rodrigo had told him the queen had commissioned a council of experts to look further into Christopher Columbus's proposal. Harry had attempted to find out more about this council and whether the sailor might now secure Isabella's support, but the hidalgo, dismissive of the whole affair, hadn't been forthcoming.

Inside, the pavilion smelled of vinegar and turpentine, urine and sweat. Servants and a few priests moved between wooden stretchers set out on the ground. Many of the wounded, lying in various states of consciousness, had been provided with fresh blankets, gifts from the queen. The royal guard led the way past the bodies to an area at the far end, screened off from the rest of the tent. Two more guards were stationed outside. One, seeing Harry approach, ducked his head through the curtain of cloth, said something, then swept aside the screen for Harry to enter.

King Ferdinand was seated on a stool by a makeshift bed. Like most of his men, he was grey-skinned and drawn from the siege, but there was resolve in his face and a clear focus in those dark eyes. He looked like a man about to tilt at a target. Harry, heart thumping, glanced at the figure in the bed.

Edward Woodville, propped up on pillows embroidered with the queen's arms, was barely recognisable. His face was a lumpy mass of purples and yellows, lips puffy and cracked, one eye swollen shut. One side of his head had been shaved, his scalp knitted with stitches across a wide black gash. His body was hidden under a blanket, but Harry had the impression the rest of him would look just as broken. How on earth had the bastard survived? It was a damn miracle. Thinking of this as God's work gave Harry a chill as he considered the graveness of the crime – the mortal sin – he'd almost committed. As soon as he was back in the anonymity of a city he would find a priest to absolve him.

Removing his cap, he bowed low, trying to avoid the one perfect blue eye now staring at him out of the ruins of Woodville's face. 'Your highness.' He cleared his throat. 'You asked to see me?'

The king rose, reached out and, to Harry's bewilderment, grasped him by the shoulders and kissed both his cheeks. 'Sir Harry, I am in debt.'

Harry caught a whiff of leather, sweat and sandalwood as the king stepped back. 'My lord?' he stammered, wondering – since he knew the king's knowledge of English was scant – what the man might mean.

'You save Sir Edward. And he save Loja. I write to King Henry. Tell him your brave acts.' Ferdinand looked between him and Edward, lying silent in the bed. 'God's blessings upon you.' He called to one of the guards outside, switching into Castilian.

Harry looked round as one of them entered, holding a war sword in a decorated scabbard. It was an exquisite weapon, with a gold disc pommel engraved with a sun, rays carving outwards. The guard handed it to the king, who held it out to Harry.

'I gift to you.'

As Harry went to take it, cheeks warm with surprise, an image of Wynter brandishing their father's sword ghosted across his mind.

I know, brother, what it is to bear his blade.

The image vanished as Harry took the weapon. 'Thank you, my lord.'

'With this, you spill more blood. Infidel –' Ferdinand swept his hand in a slash through the air.

Harry faltered at the prospect. It was just such an offer that had led him into this hell and away from his purpose. But he could hardly refuse. He bowed mutely, the sword heavy in his grip. At a mumble from the bed, he glanced round to see Woodville was speaking. The words were hard to understand, since the knight had lost most of his front teeth.

Ferdinand placed a hand on Woodville's shoulder, then nodded to Harry.

As the king ducked out through the screen, leaving them alone, Edward Woodville gestured weakly to a goblet on the floor by the bed. Stooping to pick it up, Harry handed it to him reluctantly. The knight slurped awkwardly at it, wine spilling down his cheeks like red tears. When he was done, he passed it back to Harry.

'I wanted to thank you.'

The words, although thick, were now clear enough for Harry to hear. They took him aback completely.

'It is strange, Harry, the clarity that comes when you are near death.' Woodville wiped his wet cheek with a shaky hand. 'Lying here with only pain and prayer for company, I have had time to see my errors.'

Harry sat on the stool, warmed by the king. 'Errors?'

'I came here on crusade to honour my brother. But when you arrived, I allowed the doubts I'd been harbouring to turn me from my cause.'

Not just you, *you bastard*, thought Harry. 'It is understandable, Sir Edward.' Oh, how easy it was to play the saint when the sinner was concealed. 'You wanted the truth of your nephews' fate.' Harry shook his head, sighed expansively. 'But I'm afraid the one man who could give you that is gone. And may the devil take Richard,' he added. 'For that whoreson killed your brother and my father.'

Woodville nodded after a long pause. 'By saving me from the infidel's bolt, you put me back on the path. Allowed me to complete my mission. Further this holy cause.'

Harry let out a breath, this one not for show. Woodville hadn't seen him rushing up behind him, quarrel in his fist. 'Then, you believe me? When I tell you I know nothing of what happened to the princes?'

'I do.'

Harry tensed, seeing there was something else.

'But I still wish to speak to your brother, James Wynter. King Richard may be gone, but I feel certain Wynter – if he is alive – must know something.'

'I believe he is most likely dead, as I told you. But if not, I know nothing of his whereabouts.'

'If you hear anything of him, anything at all, you will send me word?'

'I will.'

Woodville sank back on the pillows, closed his one good eye. 'I must rest. I need my strength for the journey.'

'You are leaving?'

'I have done what I came for. Done what was needed.' Woodville's eye flickered open. 'You must take my place, Harry. Continue the fight. Acquit yourself well. For England. For your father.'

'I shall.'

This time, when the knight's eye closed, it didn't open again.

After a moment, Harry rose and slipped out. He strode from the tent, past prone and broken bodies, relief opening like a fan in his chest, the king's sword gripped in his fist.

Rodrigo de Torres watched Harry leave, the screen that separated Edward Woodville from the common soldiers left drifting in the breeze flowing through the tent. The young man hadn't even noticed him there, just strode straight past, eyes on the exit.

That name again. He had not misheard that night at the cave, the blood of the enemy smeared down his blade, Harry in front of him, eyes widening as Edward Woodville greeted him – not in gratitude or relief, but fear.

James Wynter.

In his mind Rodrigo saw that day, over three years ago now. The sun-scorched earth, the sweet tang of the olive groves, the river glittering blue. The dark-haired Englishman with the angry eyes and the sword, ready, in his hand. They had intended to teach him a lesson, bloody his face and wound his pride. Show him his place. Rodrigo hadn't imagined that day would end with Estevan Carrillo, his friend since boyhood, bleeding out in the dust.

He still bore the scar in his side, slashed open by the stranger who had come to find the Englishman, interrupting their duel. But the deeper hurt had come later, having to tell Estevan's father, returning from a campaign against the infidel, that his son had been murdered and, worse, his killer had escaped justice. This had been made all the more bitter by the fact that the man had word of a death for him too – that of his father, struck down in the ambush by the forces of Muhammad al-Zagal.

It had been a time of unspeakable grief for them both and the years since had brought them close, each seeking the comfort the other could bring for the absence in their lives. Rodrigo had become like another son and promised he would find the young man's killer, but although he'd questioned various officials during his visit to England for the king's coronation, no one he met had heard of the man he'd known as Jack, or, as the stranger had called him that day, James Wynter. He hadn't thought to ask Harry Vaughan. What a miracle God had worked for him, bringing them together.

'You look as though you've seen a ghost, Captain.'

El Barbero had shifted on his pallet to stare up at him with his one good eye. The other, ruined in the battle by the brutal thrust of a Moorish dagger, was hidden behind a leather patch. The soldier's scarred face was pale and oily, but the man was as strong as an ox and Rodrigo had no doubt he would recover from his injuries. 'I need to go to Íllora, my friend. I will return as soon as I can.'

'Íllora? I did not think the king had ordered you there?'

'He hasn't.'

The soldier's brow puckered. 'What is wrong, Captain?'

'Don Luys Carrillo is there. I need to speak to him.' Rodrigo's gaze flicked to the cloth screen covering Woodville's sickbed, then back to the tent opening Harry had disappeared through. 'I'm going to find the man who killed his son.'

24

Dawn was breaking, thin fingers of light pushing through the gaps in the shutters. Jack scanned the gloom, eyes moving over the hulking shapes of four catapults that stood along the far wall of the armoury. The wheels were propped beside the frames with the axles and boards of disassembled carts. On the floor were rolled field tents and thick coils of rope.

All around the expansive chamber, which, along with the Medici Library, spanned most of the top floor of the palazzo, shields were banked up, decorated with the Medici arms. There were lines of spears and halberds, arquebuses and crossbows, swords and breast-plates, helms and heaps of mail, glimmering in the half-light. It was enough to equip a small army, but all of it mottled grey with dust. There was no movement, no sign of life.

Heading out, Jack's gaze passed over the fresco that decorated one wall, depicting a battle, mounds of hills needled with cypress trees descending to a tangle of men, horses and swords. It was faded by time, the plaster cracking, but he could just pick out the faces, contorted in fury. He wondered if it was some ancient conflict of the Medici, back in the days when they fought their wars with weapons, rather than the cut and thrust of politics. A time when their struggles were perhaps simpler to understand, settled with the swift strike of a blade in the open. Not like now, in whispers behind closed doors. Even in the fight between York and Lancaster – family against family – Jack had known what side he was on, who he risked his life for and the God-blessed rightness of that cause. It was a long time since he'd felt such certainty.

Moving down the passage, retracing his steps past the locked library and the couple of storerooms he'd already checked, he paused to listen. But the hush descended as soon as he stopped. Other than faint noises drifting up from the kitchens below, the top floor was silent. He reasoned it must have been something outside, or elsewhere in the palazzo that had woken him in the darkness; that what he'd imagined were footsteps and the creak of a door was his mind playing tricks.

Returning to his room, he saw, now his eyes were accustomed to the gloom, that the door to the store cupboard where Amelot slept was ajar. Inside, her blanket lay in a heap and her grey cloak was gone from its nail. Often, she would slip out while he was sleeping, despite his warnings she shouldn't go alone into the city after curfew. He had guessed from her narrow-eyed glares at his admonishments that she was still searching for Amaury. But for the past few weeks she had been disappearing more frequently, for longer. He wondered now if it might have been her he had heard in the passage. She knew not to go wandering about the palazzo, but she'd been acting strangely, more skittish than usual. Cursing, he abandoned the fading warmth of his bed in favour of the chilly silk of a doublet and his boots, and headed out to check for her.

On the floor below he was surprised to find a flurry of activity around the kitchens, unusual for the early hour. Smells of food and the shimmer of lanterns seeped down the passage, shadows of servants hastening in and out of the pantries.

'Sir James?'

He turned to see Bertoldo approaching, trailed by two boys hauling a basket of logs between them.

The chief steward's eyes were red-rimmed, his face pillow-creased. 'I am sorry if we woke you. The signora returned from Prato late last night.'

'With Mistress Maddalena?' Jack berated himself as the words jumped, quick and keen, from his mouth.

Bertoldo, however, didn't seem to notice the odd impertinence of his question. 'Yes, a little earlier than expected. Caught us unawares. I can have food sent to your room, once they have broken their fast?' Taking Jack's silence for agreement, Bertoldo dipped his head and hurried on to the kitchens, pressing the boys to keep up.

Jack turned for the stairs, the last vestiges of sleep slipping from him as he descended to the grand passages that connected the family's quarters, passing servants hastening with armfuls of linen to dress the dining salon. He had been waiting for Maddalena to return, ever since the fateful dinner at Franco Martelli's.

That afternoon, after sneaking from Laora's room, he had paced the streets, his mind in turmoil, troubled he might have found the enemy Lorenzo feared within his household – and all he could think of was the enemy's lips on his.

The lie he sensed Laora had told him the day of the quake; the fact her father – a member of the Court of Wolves and a man with clear reason to go against Lorenzo – had been arguing with the signore at the party, attracting everyone's attention while she disappeared upstairs; her confession in the hush of her chamber – *he has made me a thief and a liar* – his questioning of this interrupted by her kiss? As Maddalena's friend, Laora had easy entry to the private quarters of the Medici. There was access and there was motive.

It was enough, Jack knew, to take to Lorenzo. Enough to bring him, after all these interminable months, closer to understanding what his father had been striving for and what his mother had died for. Enough to secure that promised gold for him and his men and to think on the path that might lie beyond. Ned, at least, would be a willing travelling companion. With his knowledge of the map and enough coin might they seek for themselves the lost land described by Plato and glimpsed by sailors on the *Trinity* that Lorenzo and his brethren were so keen to locate? Find the rewards – unimaginable – that might come with such discovery? Such thoughts, set flickering in him by Amerigo's words at the feast, had been burning brighter, catching easily in his restless mind.

But Laora had trusted him, confided in him. And, with that kiss, she had awoken something else in him. Something he wanted more of.

In the end, shadows sliding up the buildings, whores stepping from darkened doorways, Jack decided that before he either took his suspicions to Lorenzo or confronted Laora again he would go to the one person who would know for certain if the girl had lied about where she was going that night. But when he returned to the palazzo, he had found Maddalena de' Medici gone, left for Prato with her mother, to see a famous tailor who was to make the gowns for the girl's wedding trousseau.

In the wait for their return, the household preparing for Christmas – the season's festivities enlivened by Maddalena's betrothal and Giovanni's anticipated entry into the College of Cardinals – Jack had found himself haunted by Laora. His days were spent mulling over their few conversations, trawling his memory for evidence to suggest she could be innocent, even if her father was not, or thinking of ways to accuse Martelli without implicating her. At night, his thoughts drifted to that moment in her room, her cool hands sliding over his, her lips rising to meet his, her mouth parting. The catch in her breath as he'd gripped her, pressing her against him. With each recollection the moment became more vivid, memory slipping into fantasy, wicking him with desire, leaving him sleepless and tense.

His only relief in these restive days was the arrival of an invitation to a gathering of the Court of Wolves, which meant that at least his disagreement with Martelli hadn't damaged his tentative standing with Marco and the company. From the message, stamped with the wolf's head, Jack guessed it was what he'd been waiting for: an assembly to be held at the palazzo of one of the members across the river in Santo Spirito, at which his suitability for their company would be settled. Determined Amelot would survey it – wondering if he need involve Laora at all if the girl spotted Amaury's abductor – he had told Ned to scout out a position from which she would be able to spy on the gathering. He just hoped, given her recent behaviour, she would be ready when the time came.

Having seen no sign of Amelot in the palazzo's corridors, Jack guessed she must be out on one of her nightly ventures. There would be time, later, to chide her. Now, he had more pressing concerns.

The passage where Maddalena's room was situated was quieter, a single torch flushing a marble bust of Cosimo de' Medici – all hook nose and stern mouth – that glared at him as he approached. Despite the hush, Jack felt his tension rise, both at the prospect of being caught at the girl's bedchamber and of the answer he was, on the one hand, impatient for and, on the other, wasn't sure he wanted. After checking to see if he could hear any voices within, he knocked.

The door opened a few moments later and Maddalena peered out, her honey hair sleep-tousled. She started, surprised to see him standing there. 'Sir James?'

'Signora. I beg your pardon for the intrusion and the hour of it. But I need to speak to you.'

'To me?'

'It's about Laora.' He meant it to sound nonchalant – a passing question, light conversation. But now he was here at the girl's room, off-bounds, need sharpening his tone, he realised it sounded anything but.

Her eyes widened in concern. 'Wait here,' she told him, pushing the door to.

He lingered in the passage, glancing up and down it, until the door opened and Maddalena ushered him in, a fur-trimmed cloak covering her nightgown.

Jack had caught glimpses into the grand suites belonging to Piero and Giovanni when the servants were cleaning them, but had not seen into those of Lorenzo's daughters. Maddalena's chamber was much smaller than her brothers', but nonetheless well-appointed, dominated by a four-poster bed, its satin curtains still partly closed. Several travelling chests stood in the centre of the room, clothes spilling from them.

'What is it? Is Laora all right?'

'Yes,' he said quickly, turning to her. 'She is fine.'

Maddalena put a hand to her heart. 'You scared me.'

'I am sorry, signora. It really is a trifling matter.'

Maddalena eyed him, unconvinced. She had changed these past few months since the banquet at Fiesole, where her betrothal had been announced to the republic's elite. She wasn't the weepy, frightened girl he'd seen being comforted by Laora. Her cheeks were still plump with girlhood, but there was a new bearing in her body and maturity in her tone; a sense she was trying to fill the role fashioned for her by adults. She moved to a cushioned chest at the foot of the bed and sat, looking up at him. 'What is this matter?'

He opted for an easy question to begin with. 'When did you last see her?'

'Oh, weeks ago. Before Mother took me to Prato.' Maddalena sighed. 'It feels like an age since we spoke. I have so much to tell her! I cannot imagine what it will be like when I am married.' The smile slipped slightly.

Jack nodded sympathetically. 'Laora speaks so highly of you, signora. I am sure she will miss you too.' He thought of the sorrow he'd glimpsed when Laora had spoken of Maddalena's betrothal. Her sadness at the prospect of being parted from the Medici household and the girls she'd grown up with was all the more understandable now he'd seen into the dark, empty chambers of her own family. He had wondered if this – not an interest in his family's business – had inspired Martelli to invite him to dinner? If he had been using Laora to spy on Lorenzo, then her position here would soon vanish. The question was had Martelli been working with the knowledge and consent of the Court of Wolves, or was it personal, spurred by his hatred of the man who had ruined him?

'I see how much of a friend she's been to you,' Jack continued. 'How she has stood at your side.' He was wondering how to steer her towards the night of the party, when Maddalena cut in.

'Sir James, why are you here? What is your interest in Laora?' As soon as she uttered this her eyes widened again and he thought she'd somehow seen through his charade. Then she smiled, her hand rising to cover her mouth.

'Signora . . .?'

She was grinning conspiratorially now, sitting forward. 'My cousins, Lorenzino and Giovanni are holding a party, a masked ball, for Epiphany. My father and mother don't know, but I am planning to go. Laora said she would come. My sister, Lucrezia too. Will I see if I can secure you an invitation?'

At once, he realised – the girl thought he was asking about Laora because he liked her. Those lips, a soft surprise on his. Her perfume filling his senses. What better opportunity would there be to catch her alone? In all the ways he now wanted to. 'You would be doing me a great kindness, signora.'

Maddalena sat back, smoothing out the folds of her cloak. 'I really will miss her. Perhaps she could be my maid? When I am married?'

'I think she would like that,' he answered distractedly, poised to ask her the question he had come for. 'Do you recall the party in June, signora?'

Maddalena was frowning now. 'Of course.' She shook her head. 'Her father was so *angry*. Did you see? He made a terrible fuss.' Her voice lowered. 'I thought he was going to strike my father!'

Jack stared at her. 'You saw the argument?'

'Everyone saw it!' Maddalena paused. 'Well, not Laora. She left early. Her head was paining her. I am glad she wasn't here to witness it. Everyone staring, whispering as Signor Franco was led away by my father's guards. She would have been mortified.'

'Indeed,' murmured Jack, his heart beating so hard he felt sure Maddalena must hear it. At the sound of brisk footsteps passing in the passage, he looked round. 'I should leave you to be about your day, signora. But thank you, for entertaining my enquiries.'

Maddalena rose, smiling shrewdly. 'I shall get word to you about the ball, Sir James. You will have to find yourself a mask.'

In this city? How many there were to choose from.

Several hours later, Jack was up in his room, his breakfast untouched congealing on the plate, mind loaded with the proof of Laora's lie and thinking on what he should do next, when there was a knock at the door.

A servant was outside. 'Signor, one of your clerks is here to see you.'

Descending to the inner courtyard, where the marble was bone white in the early morning sunlight, Jack was surprised to see David Foxley. The soldier had come in his disguise, blue woollen robes and a pair of spectacles balanced on his nose. His fringe was combed over the brand on his brow, but his grey hair was thinning and the felony mark was getting harder to hide. As David turned from studying the statue of his namesake, Jack saw at once from his expression that something was wrong.

'Sir,' greeted the soldier, playing his role. 'You're needed at the Fig.'

Out in the street, away from the earshot of Rigo and the other guards who nodded as he left, Jack turned to David. 'What is it?'

'My brother and Valentine – they're planning to leave.'

'Leave?' Jack took this in, not with surprise, but the heavy settling of something he had feared was coming. All their complaints these past months, their threats to walk away. 'When?'

'Soon. They've been saving some of the money Signor Lorenzo provides for provisions, bought weapons and armour.'

'They're going to Spain?' Jack was surprised they'd managed to set aside enough for that journey, let alone the equipment, given how much all of them liked their drink.

'Not Spain. They met a trader in arms two months back. He introduced them to a *condottiero* who captains a company in Venice.'

'Mercenaries,' murmured Jack. It made sense. The wars that had wreaked havoc across the Italian states might have paused, but there were always masters with a need for armed men, willing to get their hands bloody for a price. He searched David's face. 'Why are you telling me? Do they expect me to leave with them?'

'No. But they've asked Ned and me to go.'

Jack felt a stab of something. Resentment? Loss?

'I said we should give it longer, at least until you've met the company, but I don't think they're willing.'

Jack thought of the invitation in his room, the wolf's head seal cracked open. If his companions weren't here, how could he be certain Amelot would keep to her post and watch for Amaury's abductor? Anger rose in him. Why now? When he might be about to enter the company? When he might have found, in Martelli, Lorenzo's enemy? But his anger was hot bluster, no real substance. How could he blame them, when he'd walked them halfway across the west on a promise that had led to no more than a dingy tavern room?

The thought of them going curdled in him. Once this charade of his ended, what then? Even if he got what he came here for he'd have no friends to share it with, or join him on any onward journey. No one to watch his back, keep him company around the campfire nights, save for a wild mute girl and a head full of ghosts. His companions were gruff, hot-headed and hot-tempered, but they were still the closest thing he had left to family.

'You should come with us, Jack,' David prompted in his silence.

'I can't.' Laora's face in his mind, the mark of her father's hand on her cheek. 'Not yet.'

'Then give us reason to stay.'

On entering the lodgings in the tavern's eaves, the drab room an uncomfortable reminder of the disparity of their living situations, his companions were surprised to see him.

'Jack?' questioned Ned, rising from the table where he was sharing a meagre breakfast with Adam and Valentine. He glanced from him to David. 'We weren't expecting you.'

'So I see,' Jack said, ignoring Titan barking happily at his feet, eyes on the sacks in the corner, from which poked sword hilts and the gleaming edges of armour. He saw, with a prickle of anger, his father's sword among them, propped against the wall in its old scabbard.

'You told him?' Adam demanded of David, tossing the crust of bread he'd been chewing on the table.

'He had a right to know, brother. We've come this far together.'

Jack gave David a nod, grateful he had come to him – that he had one ally here. But he would have thought it would have been Ned. At least the large man had the decency to look guilty as he met his gaze.

'We were going to tell you. We want you to join us,' Ned added earnestly, although Valentine only grunted and Adam hadn't yet taken his eyes off his brother.

'Why now?' Jack demanded. 'When the Court of Wolves has invited me in?' He had shared the news of this only a week ago, sitting here with a cup of ale, part of their circle. It all felt very different now.

'We're to be in Venice by the Christ Mass,' Valentine answered. 'If we is to join this company. You in, boy?'

'Not until I've done what I came here for.'

'Then it's us, lads,' said Valentine, scanning the others. 'Time to look to our own fortunes. We was agreed.'

Adam nodded curtly, while Ned stuck his thumbs in his belt, shifted awkwardly. Jack looked between them, feeling desperate. 'Ned,' he began, wishing he'd confided in the man more. In all of them. If he had trusted them – shared his growing doubts about Lorenzo, his discovery of the Muslim in the hidden room and Martelli's vendetta, Amerigo's words about the sailor and his own emerging thoughts of a journey west – might they have stayed? Or would they have gone months ago? He caught David's meaningful stare. *Give us reason to stay.* 'What about the money Lorenzo promised us? Surely that's worth waiting for? Just a while longer?'

'For how long, Jack?' Adam challenged. 'Months? Years?' He flung a hand at the chamber. 'Us stuck in this fleapit, waiting on you to bring us some scrap of news from that palace you seem so settled in? And why not?' His stool clattered back as he stood to face him. 'A feather bed and fine clothes? Wine and meat for your table, and servants at your call? I would not blame you, but for the fact that in living this lie you've left us here to rot!'

'I couldn't have entered the company any sooner. Could not make Marco accept me. But now I might!' Jack looked to Ned for support. 'You said you'd keep watch with Amelot.'

'Then what?' Valentine demanded before Ned could respond. 'You think if you point out one man Lorenzo will give up the prize? He's not kept you in luxury for one poxy victory, boy. You agreed to enter their company, see if he has anything to fear. This goes beyond what happened to the priest. Once you is in, he'll want you stay.'

'He promised to—'

'And what are his promises worth?' Adam cut across him.

'They were worth something to my father – to the man you all followed and swore your oaths to. Worth enough for him to risk his life.' Jack ignored the little voice in his head that reminded him he still did not know if this allegiance was good or bad. 'That should mean something.'

'Our master's been in the ground near four years,' Adam responded. 'It's time to take off the black. You've mourned him long enough.'

Jack, seeing he would not win with Adam or Valentine, turned again to Ned. 'I've been thinking about what you said, the day of the quake – about us following the map? Amerigo Vespucci, the clerk to the signore's cousins, spoke to me of a sailor in Spain, who is seeking funds for a westward voyage. Maybe, with enough gold, we might look to do the same?'

Ned's face filled with interest at this, but Adam spoke before he could answer.

'No! No more of your claims!'

Adam was over a foot shorter than Ned, but the spark of anger that lit his blue eyes gave him an air of menace. Jack realised he'd underestimated the depth of the man's frustrations.

'We came to you in honour of your father, stood beside you, fought for you, followed you into exile. Hugh Pyke lost his life. We lost our kingdom. We'll lose no more, by God!'

Jack saw that another part of his life, perhaps the last part that meant anything, was about to be stripped from him. What would be left when his companions were gone but the lie he was now living? A lie that at some point – whether he failed or succeeded in his task here – would simply dissolve. 'I think I know who's been spying on Lorenzo,' he said, as Adam turned away. 'The one who intercepted Amaury's letter. Maybe even ordered Amaury's abduction.'

'What?' Adam demanded, turning back. 'Who?'

'Franco Martelli. The man I went to meet.' Jack hadn't told them what had transpired at the palazzo, just that Martelli had been interested in his business. 'What I don't know is whether he's been working with the knowledge of the Court of Wolves, or acting alone.'

'Why didn't you tell us sooner?' Ned asked, surprised, wounded.

'It's complicated. A meeting I just had gave me more understanding, but I still don't–'

'Have you told the signore?' David wanted to know.

'No.'

Adam let out a frustrated sound. 'Why the hell not?'

'I wanted to wait for the gathering. I thought I might be able to shed more light upon my suspicions if Amelot saw the man she recognised.'

Ned stepped forward. 'Jack, what more light do you need? If you have cause to believe Martelli is the traitor then tell the signore. It could be the best chance we have to get our reward. Then we can leave here together. All of us. Go to Venice. Or Spain?' he added, glancing at the others.

'I think Martelli involved his daughter. Against her will.' Jack met his friend's gaze meaningfully.

'Laora?' said Ned, frowning. 'This woman you've taken a fancy to?'

Jack flushed, annoyed Ned hadn't taken the meaning to be implicit. He had confessed his attraction in private last week, after one too many cups of ale. 'If I tell the signore and he moves on Martelli, she could be in danger.'

'Blood and thunder!' Adam spat. 'I'll be damned if your cock will be our compass here!' He stepped forward, thrust a finger at Jack, shrugging away David's hand as his brother tried to calm him. 'You'll go to your signore now.' Adam's voice was low, but his tone was implacable. 'You'll tell him you have what he wants – that you'll give him the name of his enemy when he hands us what he promised. You owe us, Jack. On your father's grave, we'll not give that up for some God damn whore.'

25

Jack caught Papi on the stairs as the old man was huffing his way up, rolls of paper bundled in his hands. 'Is the signore in his chambers?'

'He's meeting with Fra Marsilio.' The servant's tone was wary. 'Why, sir?'

'I need to speak to him. It's important.'

'Very well. I will ask if he will see you.'

Papi led the way up the stairs, but before they reached the top their path was barred by Clarice de' Medici, appearing above them like a colourful bird, her voluminous dress puffed out around her, head-dress decorated with a cluster of feathers.

'There you are, Papi.'

As she glanced at Jack her face tightened. She rarely acknowledged his presence here, treating him like another of the many servants, slaves and secretaries who thronged these halls, although clearly he was an oddity that fitted none of their roles. He had wondered what Lorenzo had told her about him.

'You have the accounts?'

'Yes, signora.' Papi lifted the papers he was clutching in evidence. As he did so, one slipped through his fingers.

Jack tried to grab it, but the roll went bouncing down the stairs.

Clarice tutted irritably. 'Gather yourself, Papi, I will meet you in the salon.' With that she swept down the stairs, her skirts gliding obediently after her.

The old man looked uncertainly from her retreating form to Jack, who nodded. 'I know my way.' Before Papi could respond, Jack was hastening up the steps, heading for the *Sala Grande*.

When no one answered his knock, Jack entered the bedchamber. At the far end of the room, the study door was slightly ajar. Making his way towards it, feet soft on the rugs, he heard voices within. As he moved closer, they separated into Lorenzo's nasal tones and Marsilio's rasp. Jack's feet slowed. Didn't this provide the perfect excuse – the signore too busy to see him? But he dismissed the fleeting thought. The pretext wouldn't hold for long before his companions demanded their answer.

Frustration gripped him as he thought of Adam's ultimatum. Ned, following him into the street as he'd fumed out of the tavern, had vowed to keep the others in the city, while Jack took his suspicions to Lorenzo and pressed the man for their price. But that was only part of the problem. He felt torn, pulled in two directions. He knew his men were right in their demand – was desperate for what Lorenzo had promised himself – but he also knew the moment he revealed his belief that Martelli was the spy, Lorenzo's suspicion would fall upon Laora too. Could her friendship with Maddalena protect her? No, he guessed, with all he knew of the signore.

An image flitted through his mind: he and his companions leaving the city, carts laden with their promised fortune, Laora behind him on a horse, saved from that tomb of a palace and the brute inside it, her thankful arms around his waist. The thought settled into decision as he reached the study door. When he was done here, he would go to her and warn her.

Marsilio's voice came through the door. 'Then hide him in Careggi, signore. Or Fiesole? Cafaggiolo would have been perfect, of course.'

Jack faltered, fist poised to knock.

'No. I want to keep him close.'

Him? The prisoner?

'Until after the betrothal feast, then. The risk is too great.'

Jack stepped back from the door, eyes roving to the mezzanine level where Papi slept. Moving swiftly, he climbed the steep steps, wincing at every creak. Up in the rafters, hidden from view, he peered down at the door, but now he could only hear the men's conversation as a series of mumbles. He looked to the far end of the mezzanine, where the wall adjoined the study. Slipping around stacks of chests and items of furniture, passing the pallet where Papi slept, blanket and pillow smoothed neat, he found his way barred by rows of cloaks and gowns hanging from perches. Crouching, he crawled through them, furs brushing across his back, his nose filling with musty smells of cloth and leather.

The wall loomed ahead, a grey cliff of plaster. Jack could hear Lorenzo and Marsilio through it, but muted, as though they were talking underwater. He got in closer, pressed his ear to it. As he did so, his knee dislodged something which fell back against him. At the same time, a pinpoint of light appeared. Looking down, he saw a panel of wood – it looked like part of an old floorboard – had been resting against the wall. Where it had fallen he could see a hole. Carefully placing the panel on the floor, he slid on to his stomach, put his eye to it.

There was a moment's dizziness as he found himself looking down over the dusty tops of shelves, into Lorenzo's study. The signore was facing him, leaning against one of the two desks, dressed in a high-necked scarlet robe. Marsilio was standing before him in his black habit, the tonsured circle of his scalp surrounded by a white fuzz of hair. Withdrawing, Jack inspected the hole. Too high up for a mouse, it was clearly man-made. His first thought was Papi, but surely the old man had no need for a spy hole when he was one of the only men permitted in the signore's inner sanctum?

Lorenzo was speaking. 'Cybo will only come to the palazzo for the feast.'

Franceschetto Cybo. The pope's bastard and, soon to be, Lorenzo's son-in-law.

'I will lodge him in the city. Somewhere he can enjoy his vices. He'll spend his time distracted by drink and dice. I tell you, Marsilio, there is no danger of this fool discovering anything.'

Jack's eyes followed Lorenzo's hand as he gestured to the thick gold curtain. He thought of the bolted door behind it, the man chained beyond. Those dark eyes widening. *Free me!*

Marsilio stepped forward, drawing Lorenzo's attention. 'I say again, signore, if His Holiness discovers you are the one who has taken his prize it will not only be your dream of securing your son's place in the Vatican that will suffer. It is not so long ago that you were in conflict with the Holy See. Florence cannot afford another war with Rome.' Marsilio raised his hands imploringly. 'And what of these murders? A fifth now?'

'The captains of the watch have doubled the guard. They assure me they will hunt the killer down.'

'But what if there is a connection? The last victim was the brother of one of those you sent to take him. What if the pope's men have trailed him here?'

'Pope Innocent is not Sixtus,' Lorenzo retorted. 'For all his flaws, can you imagine him employing such a monster?'

'The Turks then. We know they have men hunting him. The Knights of St John had to move him to France for fear of the sultan's assassins.'

'I have planned too long and risked too much to quail now.' Lorenzo's voice lowered, Jack straining to hear him. 'I have lost a great deal these past years. My brother to the blades of my enemies. My influence in the world with the collapse of our banks and changes of regime in England, France and Bruges. You more than most, Marsilio, understand the weight of the legacy upon my shoulders. I will be damned if I fail my grandfather. My family.' His gaze went again to the curtain. 'That man is the key to our future. To securing our power in this world. The key to everything the Academy was founded upon. I will not let him out of my sight. Not until I am certain the alliance will stand.'

Jack flinched at the knock that jolted through the wall as someone rapped on the study door below him.

Lorenzo's eyes narrowed. 'Yes?'

'Signore?' came Bertoldo's voice. The door opened. 'The priors have arrived for the meeting.'

'Tell them I will be with them shortly.' Lorenzo fixed on Marsilio, his broad face adamant. 'We are done here.'

Back in the safety of his room, Jack closed the door and leaned against it. Memories crowded his mind: his father handing him the map and ordering him to take it to Seville; Carlo di Fante in that alley begging him not to give it to the Academy; Prince Edward's words outside the hunting lodge; Amaury's talk of lost lands and paths to darkness; his mother held in the flames by a monster in a mask; his father's last testament. Meaning everything. Meaning nothing.

I pray you have found the answers I could not give you.
That the Needle has pointed the way.

Each thread had led him deeper into the labyrinth. He had believed, on his journey to this city, that whatever he found here would bring him peace, a way forward, out of the grief and the uncertainty. But now he felt only danger, waiting in the heart of the maze.

Who was the prisoner – this enemy of Christendom? A prize for the pope? Hunted by assassins? Key to Lorenzo's power? Jack felt as though he'd been looking for a hole and had stumbled over the edge of an abyss. What if there was something worse than no answers? What if those answers could destroy him?

Goro stared down at the naked form before him: pale arms and legs splayed like a butterfly's wings, ropes twisting ankles and wrists to the table. Blood continued its steady drip, drip on to the floor. The youth's eyes, clear as glass, were open. So, too his stomach, from sternum to groin; split like fruit to show the seeds and tissues, all the secrets within. All those inner workings. A map of life.

Carlo had once shown him the inside of a clock: an intricate series of teeth and barrels, wheels grinding round. But although his master had been able to tell him how the device worked, he'd never been able to explain – beyond that it was the will of God – how a living man worked and moved.

The youth's bound hands had clenched into such tight fists in the final stages of the cutting that his nails had entered his palms. Goro had prised them open to find livid, crescent-shaped wounds. Soon, his skin would tighten, turn hard like cooling wax, as the warmth of life faded and the rigor set in.

He had found the boy late last night, in the alleys of Oltrarno. It was a good place for victims, the young and the desperate, waiting in shadows for the rich in their silks and velvets to come satisfy their appetites; the thrust of a coin in a hot hand, the clink of a belt buckle. He touched the tips of the youth's fingers, one by one, noting the blue tinge in the sickly glow of the lantern. Carlo would have abhorred this place. Would have called it a Babylon. A wretched, stinking whore of a city.

Hearing the clang of the cathedral bell, four tolls for the hour, Goro shuffled to the window, careful to avoid the creeping slick of blood that was following the slope of the floor. Its metal tang filled the room with the acerbic odour of bile: a meaty perfume. Outside, beyond the rooftops, the sky was tinged grey. He had dallied too long. The monsignore would be furious if he found him gone when he woke for prayers. He had no excuse for being out alone in the city at night. No good one, at least.

Goro looked back at the body, pale and red and shining. Of all the lives he'd taken since they left the castle of the Knights of St John, this was now the third that was for him alone. He had been able to take longer with them, to relish each incredible moment of the uncovering, no need to keep removing the gag to ask the questions Battista di Salvi wanted answers to, no need to wait until the victim regained consciousness for the demands and torture to begin again.

He knew it was dangerous. Beyond foolish. Their hunt had brought them, on the wings of the confession in the cell of the Knights of St John, closer to the object of their quest. Close enough, from the final agonised moments of their last victim, to know with near certainty that Lorenzo de' Medici had what His Holiness wanted. The monsignore was now considering how they could pinpoint the man's location and make their move. Goro had been ordered to lie low, the presence of watchmen greatly increased across the city. But he'd not been able to bear it, trapped in their lodgings day and night, the very air poisoned by Battista's contempt. These moments, out in the city alone, were the only thing that gave him release.

Goro looked at the dagger in his hand. Gore slimed the blade and spattered the mother-of-pearl crosses on the hilt. He remembered the swell of pride he'd felt when Carlo handed him the princely gift. He had done such bloody works as this for his beloved master too, but they had always been executed with purpose – a higher purpose. What were these deeds he did now, alone and unbidden? *Works of the devil*, came the reply as he glanced from the blade to the body.

Works of the devil in that long-ago dungeon, where rats nipped at torn flesh and men and women prayed and screamed; a wretched choir singing a song of pain for the young man with hell in his eyes. The man who had made monsters of them all: Galeazzo Sforza, the Duke of Milan, whose very name meant force.

Son of a famous *condottiero*, who, in alliance with Cosimo de' Medici, had taken control of the dukedom, Galeazzo had inherited all his father's bloodlust, but had channelled it not towards enemies on fields of war, but towards his own people in the dungeons beneath his castle. Not for punishment, but for sport.

Goro had been a labourer on the castle. Big and strong, he had worked hard and lived a humble but decent life. One day, he spilled some mortar that had ruined the passing duke's silk shoe. Moments later, the duke spitting venom at his incompetence, Goro found himself seized by guards and taken down into that place from which it was rumoured no one returned. He didn't know how long he had spent down there. All he remembered was the savage, searing pain and the duke's smile as he carved and sliced.

It was Carlo who saved him, on the day Galeazzo Sforza was stabbed to death by local noblemen, who conspired to end his tyranny. Carlo di Fante. His light. His world.

Goro's fist tightened around the stiletto's bloody hilt as he thought of the man – *James Wynter* – who had taken his saviour from him in that foetid Southwark alley. All those months searching London for the wretch had come to nothing and Goro's hope of vengeance had wilted.

In the end he had returned to Rome, aimless and destitute, to find Sixtus dead and a new pope on the throne of St Peter. Innocent had taken him in, treated him like a man, fed him warm meat and good wine while Goro spoke of the map and their mission to find it for his predecessor, lest the Academy use it to unleash their evil upon the world. Under Innocent, he had found purpose, but his new master, the monsignore, had been cruel and, more often than not these days, he found himself caught in that old hell Carlo once saved him from. A hell, he now knew, had never left him, but had become part of him.

Hearing laughter from the street, Goro turned back to the window. In the dirty glass he saw himself, a man with half a face. He raised his hand, ran his fingers over the cracked leather of the mask that hid the peeled horror beneath. The metal plate was showing; splinters of steel, like stars trapped in his skin.

Turning, he moved away. Pausing to wipe the blade on the dead boy's discarded tunic, he left the miserable room alone, his shadow following him down the wall of the passage, hunched and huge. A monster, always at his side.

26

Ned Draper peered over the lip of the roof. The world spun precipitously away, plunging to the street far below. He clutched the chimney tighter, holding himself against the angle of the roof they'd positioned themselves on, speckled grey with bird droppings.

He glanced at Amelot, perched on the edge, her short hair tousled by the wind that rippled through her thin tunic. It looked as though a gust could snatch her off at any moment; send her small body wheeling, smashing to the ground. At a fresh wave of dizziness, Ned concentrated his gaze forward, across the closely packed rooftops around Santo Spirito, over which hung a dirty smear of wood-smoke. The sky in the west above the hills was a dull burnt red, but darkness was coming quickly from the east, shadows pooling in the alleys as watch-fires flickered to life along the city walls.

The street they were overlooking was one of the widest in Oltrarno, otherwise a chaos of muddy alleys, tight market squares and frenetic inns. Winding alongside the river, which flowed at their back, it was flanked by tall tenements and cramped workshops, interspersed with churches and the odd palazzo, one of the grandest of which stood opposite. There was a sense of space beyond the imposing building, tips of trees pointing to the sky. Gardens, Ned guessed.

The street, which earlier had been busy with workers returning home from their day's labour, was quietening down. Ned saw two men in the colours of the quarter's watch moving along it, lighting lanterns. 'It's getting dark. Will you still see them from up here?' Looking back to where Amelot was perched, Ned realised she had vanished. Half rising, clutching at the chimney, he scanned the roof. The girl had moved without his notice to the other side. She was staring out across the river, where the Ponte Vecchio spanned its murky waters. 'Amelot!' He frowned as she turned. 'You'll not see anyone from there.'

After a pause, she slipped back to her position, surefooted as a goat along the blade-thin edge of the building.

She seemed distracted, more silent than he would have thought a mute girl could be. What was on her mind was anyone's guess, but this was the best hope they'd had for her to spot the man she had seen all those months ago and Ned wasn't about to let her ruin the chance. 'You want to find your master, don't you?'

Her tawny eyes flicked to him. After a moment, she settled, fixing once again on the entrance to the palazzo.

The clop of hooves announced the arrival of four more guests. Guards and servants emerged from the arched doors to meet the men, taking the reins of their horses, which they tethered alongside the others to iron rings attached to the wall of the palazzo. Ned forced his hand from the solidity of the chimney, crawled a few paces on sweaty palms. 'What about them?' he murmured, eyes on the men as they accepted goblets from the servants, voices and laughter drifting up on the wind's cold currents. 'Isn't that Marco Valori?'

Amelot nodded.

'And the others?' At the shake of her head, he sighed. 'That's over two score now.' He studied her pinched features, her furtive, darting eyes. Had she really seen one of the men who had taken the priest that day at Carnival? They had all wondered it in the months since. But the wolf badge – she had been right about that. 'Maybe we should go down. Pretend we're beggars? Sit near the doors for when they leave?' But even as he suggested it he knew it was risky. Valori, at least, might recognise them.

As the men disappeared inside, Ned inched his way back to the chimney. The red in the western sky had dimmed to black and there was a mist of rain in the air. The cathedral bells rang out, joined by others, a clanging conversation. Ned found his gaze drifting past the city walls, to where the hills marched steeply towards the battlements of mountains.

The question of what lay beyond had itched in him since they first arrived. It was the same itch he'd had as a boy, standing on the banks of the stream outside the hovel he'd been born in, watching the currents carry away the sticks he tossed in, and, later, as a man, plucking shells from the mud of the Thames, its great grey waters crowded with ships that came and went to places he knew only as names, strange and exotic on his tongue, overheard in taverns on the docksides along with snatches of stories that suggested something more, something *better* might lie beyond the flowing tide.

He had thought this itch – his need to be off – would be relieved in part by their move to Venice. But when Jack had spoken of the sailor in Spain, Ned's imaginings had once again shifted west, his memory caught in the moment he had stood in the Ferryman's Arms with Jack and Hugh Pyke looking down on that map, islands and coastlines spidering away; new worlds falling off the margins.

It was why he had fought Jack's corner in the days since the young man had admitted his suspicions about Martelli, Ned convincing the others to stay in the city until Jack managed to report to Lorenzo and press the man for their reward. He had told the others what Jack had told him – that he'd requested an audience with the signore, but Lorenzo had been too busy to see him. Even as he relayed this news to Adam and the others, Ned had wondered at the truth of it. He had known Jack since the young man was a boy; felt he knew a lie when he saw one. But he had kept this suspicion to himself, comforting his unease with the memory of that map and Jack's intimation that he might now be willing to search for what it showed.

Amelot whipped round, eyes fixing on something behind him.

Ned jolted round to see a figure clambering over the edge of the roof behind them. 'Christ!' he hissed, as David slid his way across the tiles, face sheened with sweat from the climb. 'Don't start a man! Not this high!'

'Has Adam been up here?'

Ned frowned at his troubled expression. 'No. Why?'

'He left over two hours ago to get food.'

'Maybe he's off drinking?' Ned had pulled Adam out of many a tavern these past months, his mouth and fists all too ready for a fight. It was another reason they needed to move on. Men of war should not sit idle. Thomas Vaughan had told him that. *For a soldier in idleness, Ned, there is only fat for the body and demons for the soul.*

David shook his head. Reaching for his belt, he held up a worn leather pouch, hanging beside his own. Ned recognised it as Adam's.

'I found this in the alley outside the Fig. Something's happened to my brother.'

A sharp rapping on the tiles turned their focus to Amelot, who was pointing into the street. This time, Ned saw only one figure, approaching from the east. It was Jack.

Light rain veiled the air as Jack followed the guard through a maze of hedges towards a large round structure in the grounds beyond the palazzo. Torches, staked in the earth, formed a snaking path of gusting lights. A brittle crust of leaves crunched beneath his boots. He gripped the goblet of wine a servant had handed to him back in the marble entrance hall, where wreaths of ivy and a candlelit model of the Nativity signalled the approach of Christmas, less than a week away.

As he neared the structure, Jack heard the hum of voices. Through a wide set of doors he saw figures, silhouetted in the fitful glow of torchlight. The anticipation he'd been feeling through the day pulled taut inside him like stretched wire.

Entering at the guard's gesture, he found himself in a circular space, sand covering the ground. The place had a warm, animal odour to it. Seeing whips and bridles hanging from hooks Jack guessed it was a horse-training paddock. It reminded him of a smaller version of the bullring in Seville. The place was filled with men, sixty or so, standing at the edges, talking and drinking. Most wore sumptuous cloaks and mantles trimmed with sable and ermine, each with a silver badge pinned to his garments. A Court of Wolves. At his entrance many eyes swivelled to him, voices dying to a hush.

Jack felt the tension twist in his gut. These weren't the courteous, curious or even mildly dismissive looks that had greeted him at the game of *calcio*. This was something else. He scanned them, seeking a friendly face, and when Marco Valori emerged from the crowd he felt a wash of relief. 'Signore?'

Marco nodded in greeting, but the young man had no easy smile for him today. There was a coolness to his manner, steel in his eyes.

A voice sounded in Jack's mind. *They've found you out! They know who you are!* 'What is this?'

'As I told you when we last met, Sir James, your suitability would need to be tested. It is something we require all prospective members to face. An initiation, if you will, to gauge your commitment before we consider accepting you into our company.'

Jack looked over Marco's shoulder to the space the men had left, the circle of sand ruddy in the torch glow. 'A fight?'

'We are a duelling company,' Marco reminded him.

'I don't have my sword.'

'We have what you need.' Marco studied him. 'You missed your friends, you told me. Your comrades-in-arms. You wanted to find men you could trust here? Allies to watch your back? You can have that, Sir James, within our circle. If you are willing to prove yourself.'

Jack nodded slowly. His heart was pounding, but now he knew what was coming a heavy calm was settling over him. The duels with Ned by the river, those months in Diego's arena, the fields of war under his father's command: he'd spent half his life in training for this. 'Who will be my opponent?' he asked, eyeing the silent gathering.

Turning, Valori gestured. The crowd parted and Jack saw a figure being led out by two guards. He was hooded, hands bound behind his back, head twisting this way and that as he was hauled into the centre. His hands were freed with a slash of a dagger. The blind was ripped off and there, blinking in the light, his grey hair wild from the hood, stood Adam Foxley.

Jack's poise shattered. 'What is the meaning of this?' He turned on Marco. 'Why do you have my guard?'

'I think it's clear he's more than just a guard. That brand on his forehead. He is a criminal, yes?'

'It doesn't matter what he is.' Jack met Adam's gaze. The soldier was breathing hard, eyes fixed on him. 'I'll not fight my own man. Choose another.'

'The test isn't just about skill. It is about loyalty. Loyalty to us over any other.'

Jack guessed, by the way Marco said this, that he meant Lorenzo. They wanted him to prove that his interest in their company and his misgivings about the signore were genuine. That he would do anything they asked.

'I can assure you, Sir James,' Marco continued in his silence, 'every man here has faced a similar trial.'

Jack caught something in Marco's tone, some suggestion of doubt, falsehood even. As the man's gaze flicked towards the crowd, Jack followed it to see Franco Martelli standing there. In the torchlight, his craggy face was unusually animated. Jack knew then, whatever other men had faced to enter this company, this test had been designed specifically for him; a punishment for his interference at Martelli's palazzo. Laora's warning, her hand on his arm. *He will not forget a slight*. He knew, too, that if he didn't go through with it, this opportunity would be gone for good.

For days after the conversation he'd overheard between Lorenzo and Marsilio, he had thought again about abandoning this tortuous quest – of leaving with his men for Venice. But the questions, strong enough a year ago to draw him all the miles to this city, were now so bound around him, so much a part of him, that he could not simply shrug them away. He had followed his father's footsteps into darkness and was lost in the maze. Only the truth could guide him out – even if that truth was abhorrent, even if it meant his worst fears about his father were confirmed. He had to see this through. He had to believe, despite his concerns, that Lorenzo would keep his word if he succeeded here.

Jack met Adam's gaze across the sand. The older man's confusion had settled into grim acceptance, his fists flexing at his sides. Jack tried to communicate with his eyes what he intended – that Adam should play along, work with him until this was done – but he couldn't tell from Adam's rigid expression whether his friend understood. A fresh bruise on his cheek suggested he'd come here fighting.

As Jack shrugged off his cloak and handed it to Marco, a ripple of excitement passed through the watching men. The lean-faced Luigi Donati, one of those he remembered from the game of *calcio*, approached with another man, bearing between them a sword, a shield and a leather brigandine, studded with silver-tipped nails. Jack removed his doublet and slid his arms into the brigandine, which Marco helped him buckle, the steel plates pressing against his torso. Adam was being similarly clad.

The shields that were handed to each of them were bucklers, small and oval, with a boss protruding from the centre and a hook at the top for snagging and deflecting. Jack pushed his fingers through the strap on the back and curled them tight, the shield becoming an extension of his fist. The sword was shorter than the war blades he was used to, with a sturdy hilt, the grip bound with leather. The edges weren't blunted. A misjudged blow could maim. Kill even. As he swung the weapon, checking its balance, the blade catching the torch-fire, he thought of Estevan Carrillo in the olive grove.

'To first blood?' he asked, glancing at Marco, then at Adam.

'No.' It was Martelli who answered. 'Until we say.'

Moving into position, Jack noticed a few of the men exchanging coins with eager murmurs, eyes flicking between him and Adam. He moved towards his friend slowly, swinging the sword back and forth to loosen his muscles. He was used to fighting Ned, but this was different. This wasn't about disarming an opponent and scoring points. These men wanted blood for their sport here tonight. Blood and proof. How far would they make them go for that?

His mind filled with memories as he circled the older man. A younger Adam, black still threading his hair, seated beside him at a campfire showing him how to whet a blade. Later, crouched beside him, reaching out to gently reposition the crossbow he held, both their eyes on the deer through the trees. Adam, soaked in sweat, in the foggy dawn of that field at Barnet, the crossbow in his own hands, standing side by side with David, the two of them shooting in unison, one click and hiss after another, as the cannons thundered and Warwick's men hurtled towards them. In the aftermath, himself bent over, vomiting into the mud, dagger slick in his fist, christened with the blood of his first kill, the stink of death and bile and sulphur in his mouth and nose, Adam's hand on his back.

Nodding to his friend, Jack stepped forward. His blade flicked out in a teasing stroke, which Adam batted aside easily. Adam parried, a neat slice towards his side, which Jack cuffed away with his shield, the sound echoing like a bell around the circular space. A few more soft lunges, wide blows and comfortable side-steps the watching men allowed, but soon they became impatient. Martelli's was the first jeer to sting their ears, quickly followed by others.

Adam glanced at them, then back at Jack, his blue eyes narrowing. Now, he struck out, hard and fast, a jab that could have pierced Jack's brigandine had he not moved swiftly, catching Adam's sword with his own and turning it away. The men's jeers turned to shouts of approval. Jack, expecting another lull, was surprised when Adam came at him again, a bold series of strikes that had him stepping backwards with each defence, sparks spitting off their blades. What was he doing?

'The guard has guts!' shouted Luigi. 'My money's on him!'

The cheers reminded Jack of the kick-game, where their allegiances had shifted from one player to another depending on his performance. His face grew hot, not just from the rise in effort. In their eyes he was a knight – a knight being bested by his own man. Cursing Adam for forcing the issue, he lunged. Ducking a cunning swipe at his head, he thrust at Adam's thigh while his defences were open. Adam dodged away, but the blade just caught him, slicing a line through his hose that quickly bloomed red. Now, the men were shouting all at once, hands digging into jewelled pouches for fistfuls of coins. The fight had just become real.

Jack circled his opponent, heart thrumming. Adam had looked surprised at the strike, but it didn't deter him. Coming in again, he jabbed at Jack's stomach. As Jack was smacking away his blade, Adam struck out with his shield. Jack threw his head to the side, but the shield cuffed him, making his ear ring. Dazed, he stumbled backwards. His cheek throbbed and at the trickle down his face he guessed the hook on Adam's shield had cut him.

Martelli's voice rang out. 'Sir James, has your man been guarding your back, or eyeing it?'

Laughter echoed. It stung Jack's ears, sent him barrelling forward to batter at Adam, no longer pulling the blows. The clash of steel resounded. The two of them stamped across the circle, swords wheeling, arcing, smashing. Sparks flew; red-hot slivers of metal that died in the sands. The watching men were hushed, transfixed. Adam, blood now soaking his hose, fought Jack fiercely, but his skill was with the crossbow, not the sword. With every lunge he was weakening and Jack was getting his measure, seeing which way the man tended to feint, his favoured moves.

Jack hadn't fought like this in an age. He felt alive, his body humming, each concussive impact sending a rush of pain through his arm. That pain was fuel, pushing him faster, harder. He was forgetting himself. Forgetting what he'd come here for. His vision was narrowing, focusing in on the win.

Adam lurched away from a series of brutal attacks, his sword flung wide with the last, mighty stroke. Jack drove into the opening to punch him in the face with his shield. The man's head rocked back and he fell into the sand, sword skittering from his grip.

Jack went down on top of him, arm shoved up against Adam's throat, holding him there. He bent forward, so close he could smell the drink, sour on his friend's breath. He thought of David, some nights, sliding the tankard away from his brother, seeing that look that sometimes clouded Adam's eyes when he'd had too much. He saw the same look there now. '*Stay down!*' he hissed in his ear.

After a moment, Jack felt Adam go limp. He pushed himself up, swiping away the sweat that was burning his eyes. He was looking to

Marco, about to tell him they were done here, when he heard a scattering of applause. The men's expressions were changing from resigned agreement to anticipation. Turning, Jack saw Adam had risen. As he watched, his friend spat blood into the sand and bent to pick up his sword.

'He has the balls of an ox!' Luigi Donati shouted, grinning.

Franco Martelli joined in the rising applause, face savage with glee. 'Perhaps we have picked the wrong candidate, Signor Marco?'

Jack looked to Adam. What the hell was he thinking? Then, seeing the taut lines his friend's face had drawn into, the tight hunch of his shoulders, his white-knuckled grip on the sword, he knew Adam didn't care any more about why they were here in this arena – about his role or Jack's. The soldier was raging. Jack wondered, heart thudding as he faced him, how much of the fury he saw in the man's eyes was caused by the humiliation he'd just inflicted and how much had been there all along, growing and festering these past months.

Blood was oozing from Adam's nose and mouth. Sweat dripped from his chin and strands of grey hair were stuck to his face. He came at Jack head-on. Switching away at the last moment, Adam spun to deliver a vicious kick to the back of Jack's leg, buckling him to one knee. Jack hefted his sword, just in time. It caught and crossed with Adam's. Adam had the stronger position, bearing down on him, lips peeled back, blood spitting between his teeth. Forced to yield, Jack rolled away, his blade sliding with a screech out from Adam's, causing the other man to stumble forward.

Up on his feet, sand gritty in his mouth, Jack charged him. This time, as Adam drove his sword towards him, Jack dodged and swung his shield down on the blade, snagging it with the hook. A fierce twist of his wrist and the sword was pulled from Adam's grasp. The blade went skidding across the sand, disappearing among the feet of the men.

'Well done!' Marco shouted, clapping approvingly.

'It's not over,' Martelli cut across the younger man. He took up Marco's clap, but his was slow, like a drum or a heartbeat. Others joined in, the sound reverberating around the space.

Adam's sword was gone. Jack, breathing hard, tossed aside his own, eliciting surprised murmurs from some of the watching men. Now, he would end this. Flexing his hand around the shield's strap, tightening his grip, he stormed towards the older man, meaning to put him down. But Adam came just as strongly to meet him. They boxed and cuffed, smacked and ducked. Jack raised his arm to block one blow, missed another and caught the concussive impact in his temple. Two more blows landed on him in quick succession, one catching him square in the midriff, winding him even through the brigandine.

The men's slow clapping stung his ears, filling his brain like a maddening chant. He felt rage, pulsing through him. He rushed at Adam, snarling as he pummelled him with his free fist, catching him on the cheek, then backhanding him with the shield. Adam launched himself at him in retaliation, but he was tiring and the move was clumsy. Jack batted Adam's arms aside and head-butted him in the face. The painful crack of bone against his own forehead was satisfying.

As Adam went down, Jack fell on him. This time, he wasn't going to let him up. He was done here. Done with all of this. Men using him. Pulling his strings. Goading him. Tearing off the shield, Jack threw it aside to tackle Adam with his bare fists. With every punch, the beast inside him roared its approval. With every wet thud that split the skin of his knuckles, he felt the satisfaction of its release.

Adam wasn't Adam any longer. He was the boys in Lewes holding him down while they kicked him, called him a bastard and his mother a whore. He was Harry Vaughan setting those flames around him and the man in the mask, who'd murdered his mother. He was his father's broken word and Lorenzo's endless promises. Blood spattered him. He felt the impacts of skull and jaw, the soft yield of nose and lip. Somewhere, someone was shouting. He felt his arm caught mid-strike, held fast.

'Enough!'

Jack's vision cleared. It was Marco who had caught him. He hung there panting, sweat pouring off him. Beneath him, skewed in the sand, lay Adam. All at once Jack's rage vanished, the beast slipping away now it had had its fill, leaving him wretched at the damage his own hands had wrought. Adam's face was a dark mess. As he turned his head weakly, spitting blood, sand crusted his torn skin.

'We will see to him,' Marco said, reaching in. 'Luigi! Have your steward fetch a physician!'

'No!' Jack pushed him aside. 'I will do it.' Grasping Adam's hands, he hauled the dazed man to his feet, slinging his friend's arm over his shoulder and holding him around the waist. He turned to Marco. 'Was that enough sport for you?'

Marco said nothing, but he nodded.

The ring of men was silent, watching as Jack helped Adam towards the doors.

Before they reached them, Franco Martelli stepped in front of them, face split in a tight rictus of a smile. 'Impressive, Sir James.' The smile vanished. 'Now, stay away from my daughter.'

They made it out of the palazzo and on to the street before Adam collapsed.

Jack, exhausted, his muscles trembling, couldn't hold him up any longer. He bent to help him, rain soaking them both. 'Adam, please, we can't stay here.'

'Get away from me, you son of a bitch,' Adam groaned, pushing feebly at him.

'God damn it! Why did you fight me?' Jack turned, hearing running footsteps, to see Ned and David emerging from the shadows of an alley. He rose at the sight of them, but his relief died as soon as they saw Adam's crumpled form at his feet. A fresh wave of shame flooded him.

'Christ alive!' Ned shouted as they reached them. 'What happened?'

David crouched beside his injured brother, checking him with his hands, talking quickly and quietly to him.

Ned caught Jack by the shoulder as he staggered. 'Where did you find Adam?'

'You did this?' exclaimed David, looking up suddenly from where he was bent over his brother. He went to rise, then stopped as Adam groaned thickly again.

Ned looked between them in confusion. His eyes took in the unfamiliar brigandine and Jack's ripped knuckles. 'Jack?'

'Where's Amelot?' Jack looked past him, scanning the street. 'Did she recognise any of them?' His voice, a dry croak, sounded as desperate as he felt. Dear God, let this at least have been worth it. 'Did she see the man?'

'I don't know.' Ned was shaking his head. 'She didn't see them all.'

'Why not?'

'One moment she was with us. The next she wasn't.'

'What do you mean?'

'She left us, Jack. Amelot's gone.'

27

All through the city they moved, masked and hooded; an army of revellers, adorned with bells and feathered wings, gem-dazzled headdresses and horned helms. Women teetered on heeled shoes, arms interlinked, ignoring the whistles and calls from the bands of young men questing through the mist-wreathed darkness in search of merriment and wine-soaked adventures in dingy taverns and stifling gambling dens, gilded palazzi and squalid whorehouses. The glacial air was filled with rough shouts and laughter, bawdy songs and the clatter of clogs. The flames of oil lanterns outside inns fluttered in glass; trapped butterflies of light.

Earlier, the feast of Epiphany had been celebrated in solemn dignity, Lorenzo de' Medici leading the heads of the elite families, the lords of the Signoria and members of the Company of the Magi to the Christmas Cradle in San Marco, where a host of friars dressed as angels were waiting to say the prayers and pass around the statue of Christ to be adored. But now the hymns and rituals were done, and Twelfth Night had been taken by the young.

Leaving the Palazzo Medici, Jack stepped into the street. A group of youths charged past him, whooping. The cracks and bangs he'd been hearing all evening echoed sharply off the buildings as men shot burning tubes filled with black powder into the sky. Heading along the Via Larga, he made his way to the adjacent palace of Lorenzino and Giovanni di' Pierfrancesco, where the balconies were garlanded with black and white ribbons and firelight shimmered like a promise in the windows.

The entrance to the palazzo was thronged with people, friends greeting one another, guests waving invitations at the guards, beggars trying to persuade a coin or two from the affluent gathering. Jack held out the stiff roll of paper, slipped under his door last week. One of the sentries inspected its gilded writing, then gestured him through. Beyond was an inner courtyard, a mirror of the Palazzo Medici, only less ostentatious in decoration; a stately younger brother, prince to a king. Torches were set around the walls, the plumes of flame illuminating the painted faces of men and women gliding through the space, hailing people and plucking goblets from the trays carried by servants who moved like shades among them. A spirited tune, all drums and clapping, sounded from an arched opening leading off, through which Jack saw a whirl of limbs and cloaks. Through another doorway were gardens, where fountains sparkled among trees festooned with lights.

All the guests wore masks. Some had antlers or horns protruding, were crested with feathers or covered with fur, fashioned in the slant-eyed images of birds, foxes and wolves. Some were held in place by silk ribbons, others by a bit clasped between the teeth. The women seemed to favour half-masks of plain black velvet, which covered only their eyes, leaving tantalisingly rouged cheeks and lips on show. Gowns plunged and bare throats were ornamented with pearls and diamonds. Jack guessed most of the gathering was made up of the sons and daughters of Florence's elite. Medici and Donati, Strozzi and Bardi.

He pulled down the mask he'd bought in the *mercato*. Made of papier mâché and painted black with slitted holes for his eyes, it was fastened around his head with a leather strap. Epiphany. He could hardly believe he'd been in this city for a year. Time, the great trickster, had both crawled and flown.

Moving through the crowd, he searched for sign of Laora: dark hair piled up, narrow waist, chiselled cheeks. Now this night had finally come, the need to see her burned in him, forcing him through the hot jostle of raucous, faceless celebrants. She was all he had been able to think about this past fortnight – the one hope he had left of recovering anything of what he'd come to this city seeking.

Following the music, Jack headed through the arched opening into a magnificent chamber, lit by many-branched candelabras and strung with mirrors. Their surfaces, dazzled with candlelight, were alive with movement, men and women dancing across them as they twirled down the room to the pulse of drums. As he scanned the chaos, he caught sight of himself in one of the mirrors; black velvet cloak swinging from his shoulders, the mask staring back at him, its blank expression hiding all. Beneath it was another mask and maybe another behind that. So many he hardly knew who he was any more.

Jack saw a figure in a red half-mask appear behind him, felt the hand as it reached out and grasped his shoulder.

'Sir James?'

Turning, he saw Marco Valori, his neat dark beard framing his angular jaw.

The cleft in the young man's cheek appeared with his smile. 'I was told you might be here tonight.'

Jack's surprise faded quickly. He should have expected Marco and maybe others from the Court of Wolves would be in attendance; sons of some of the city's richest families. The sight of the young man struck something in him that sent a low note of anger humming through his blood. He'd not seen him since the night of the fight.

The day after, Rigo had knocked on his door, eyes on the bruises that clouded Jack's face as he handed him a parcel that had been left for him. Inside, Jack had found his cloak, forgotten in the furore, and a brief note from Marco, telling him he would be in contact. That had been two weeks ago and his knuckles were still scabbed and raw.

'Come. We have things to discuss.'

Jack hesitated, fearful of missing Laora. But he wanted to know what Marco had to say.

The young man led him towards the gardens, taking two goblets from a servant as he pressed his way through the crowds. Outside, the air was flint-sharp, the lights in the trees pale phantoms in the mist. As Marco leaned against the stone lip of a fountain and handed him one of the goblets, Jack recalled the night he'd first met him, seven months ago, in a garden like this one, just beyond the high wall, trailed dark with ivy, which separated the two palazzi.

Marco raised his goblet. 'Blessings of the season.' When Jack didn't follow suit, Marco lowered the glass, his expression sobering. 'How is your man?'

'He'll heal,' Jack replied tightly. It was over a week now since he'd seen Adam, but the sight of his friend had stayed with him: Adam's face swollen beyond recognition, one eye bloody, the other crusted shut, two teeth missing, a lump swelling one side of his head, four fingers broken where he'd held up his hands to stop the blows.

Jack had tried to do what he could – told Adam he would ask Lorenzo if his personal physician would see him, bought healing salves from an apothecary and wine for the pain – but Adam rejected his offers of help. David wouldn't even speak to him. Ned, quiet, subdued, had taken him aside, suggested he leave them be for a while. Their planned journey to Venice had been delayed, Adam in no state to travel. In the reprieve, Jack had privately vowed to do whatever he could to get them their reward. Make amends. It was why he'd come tonight, hoping Laora would help him.

Marco was studying him. 'I imagine you feel resentment, for what we asked of you? But I assure you all members of our company were tested martially before they were permitted to join our circle.'

Jack took a drink. The wine was warm and spiced. 'But it was Franco Martelli who devised that test for me?'

'Yes. He said you had gone to his home to talk business? Something happened, I presume. He wouldn't say what.'

Jack thought of Laora, sprawled on the floor, hands held up. He pushed the mask on to his head, the cold air stinging his cheeks. As Marco's eyes skimmed his face, he guessed the man was taking in the cuts and bruises that still mottled his skin. 'We didn't see eye to eye.'

'Signor Franco isn't the most genial of men,' Marco agreed. 'But he is popular, with some.'

'How long has he been a member?'

'Around two years.'

Jack recalled Martelli's tirade at the dinner table. Two years? When his rift with Lorenzo had begun? If he joined at that time did it mean Martelli saw the company as natural enemies of the man who had ruined him? Had he known something Lorenzo didn't?

'I want you to know, Sir James, I vouched for you. But it was felt, given your allegiance, that a true assessment of your potential commitment was needed.'

'Allegiance? To the signore?'

Marco sipped from his goblet. 'In Florence a man may have many loyalties – to father and household, guild and fraternity. Such is the spirit of a republic. But there will always be one that steers his heart. One he will fight and strive for above all others.'

'And yours is the company?'

They glanced towards the doors as three men spilled into the gardens, laughing. One wore a white mask fashioned like a skull. Jack's eyes caught on it, his gut coiling.

'I have something for you.' Setting his goblet on the edge of the fountain, Marco reached into a black velvet pouch at his belt. He reached out, placed something small and cold in Jack's palm. It was a silver wolf's head. 'Welcome to the Court of Wolves, Sir James.'

Jack stared at the badge, slant-eyed and winking at him in the lantern light. He had waited months for this, but the victory felt hollow. When he'd first gone to Lorenzo after Carnival, offered to infiltrate the company, he hadn't expected it might come at the sacrifice of his friendships. Back then, he had thought only of gain, not of loss. Still, this was what the signore had wanted. If Laora couldn't – or wouldn't – help him, he now had this to bargain with. He closed his fist over the badge, ignoring Valentine's words in the Fig. *Once you is in, he'll want you to stay*. 'What happens now?'

'You will be invited to our meetings. Get to know our members.' Marco spoke lightly, but there was something beneath his smile: evasiveness, or guardedness. 'Find new opportunities for business. Friendships.'

'Is that all?' Jack knew he was walking an edge here, but he was wearying of all these façades; false faces and half-truths, secrets behind locked doors. 'I am not so naïve that I haven't noticed your interest in my closeness with the signore. In what I might be able to discover for you about his affairs.'

Marco's dark blue eyes glinted at him through the mask. 'That is a road that travels both ways, is it not? Let us say, we are as interested in the signore's affairs as he is in ours. There are some within our ranks concerned that your enthusiasm for joining us is a ruse – that he is looking to gain access to us through you. Those doubts were assuaged by your performance the other week, but it will take time for true confidence to be built.' Marco looked as though he was going to say something more, but a voice called out.

'Signor Marco?'

A figure in a splendid gold and turquoise doublet had appeared in the archway, jewelled goblet in hand. A gold mask covered half his face, exposing a full, sensuous mouth. 'My brother is looking for you.' The man's eyes flicked to Jack. He seemed to hesitate, then returned his gaze to Marco. 'There are some people he wants you to meet.'

'Then I will not keep him waiting.'

As the figure turned on his heel, Jack recognised the cinnamon curls pinned beneath the mask strap. It was Lorenzo's cousin, Giovanni di' Pierfrancesco.

Marco rose and inclined his head. 'We will talk again soon, Sir James.'

When he had gone, Jack turned the badge in his fingers. He thought of Amelot's crude drawing, wondered if he was a step closer to those who had taken her master. The girl had been missing since the fight. Jack had no idea where she was or what had made her vanish that night, but he knew she was still alive for her cloak and blanket had disappeared from his room a few days afterwards and, since then, he'd noticed scraps of food gone from his meal trays before the servants cleared them and, once, a set of small muddy footprints leading away across the terrace.

Stowing the badge in his pouch, Jack returned to the frenetic heat inside, hunting for Laora. It was even more crowded now and he kept his mask perched on his head as he moved through the crush, hoping she might spot him.

'Sir James!'

A figure emerged through the press in front of him – a young woman with a blue mask on a stick strung with bells. She slipped it aside with a silvery jingle to show her smiling face. It was Maddalena de' Medici.

'Signora,' he greeted keenly, raising his voice over the clamour.

'Now, where has my sister gone?' Rising on her toes, Maddalena peered around her. 'Lucrezia!'

Her dark-eyed sister appeared at her side after a few moments. Her stomach, swollen with child, bulged from the folds of her fur-trimmed mantle. Jack noticed that the young woman appraised him coolly.

'Where is Laora?' Maddalena craned her neck. 'She was just with you.'

'She needed some air.' Lucrezia said this a little too quickly, her tone forced.

Jack frowned. Glancing over the young woman's shoulder, he glimpsed a figure in a gold gown threading swiftly through the crowd towards the doors. He recognised that dress. Laora had worn it to the banquet at Fiesole.

'She doesn't want to see you, Sir James,' warned Lucrezia, as he moved to go after her.

'Sister?' questioned Maddalena, clearly confused.

But Jack was gone, hastening through the crowd in Laora's wake. Knocking into a thickset man with a bald head wearing a wolf mask, he pushed on through, ignoring the man's call at his back.

Out in the street, surrounded by a knot of masked revellers, he turned in a circle, searching. There – a flash of gold, burnished by a lantern's glow. As Laora disappeared down an alley, he followed. She wasn't far ahead, a ghostly figure slipping through the darkness, slippered feet pattering over the cobbles.

'Laora!'

At her name, she faltered, footsteps slowing. She turned on him as he caught up with her, her face just visible in the ochre gleam of firelight seeping through a window above. A black velvet mask followed the prominent contours of her cheeks. Her dark hair was pinned at the sides, but left loose at the back to tumble around her shoulders, lustrous with oil. 'What do you want from me?'

Jack was surprised by the force in her voice. Of all the scenarios he'd imagined for their meeting, this had not been one. He had come tonight to confront her, meaning to tell her he knew she had lied about going to Maddalena the night of the party. Had intended to persuade her to tell him the truth about her father and what she did for him; get a confession he could take to the signore in return for that reward for his men – more pressing now than ever. But this was not the only reason he had wanted to see her. Now that kiss, which had both warmed him and burned in him these past miserable weeks, felt as though it had never even happened at all. 'Why did you run?'

'Maddalena said she had a surprise for me tonight. I did not know it would be you.' Laora's eyes were dark pools, glimmering from the depths of the mask. 'When she told me you had come to her, asking questions of me, I knew.' She shook her head, her shoulders slumping. 'Did the signore send you? Does he know I am the one who took it?'

'Took it?'

'The chalice.' She pulled off the mask and stared up at him. 'Is that not why you came to my father's house? Why you were asking Maddalena about me?'

Jack hid his confusion. 'I just want the truth, signora.'

She was still staring at him, but her expression had changed slightly. 'You're hurt?' She reached out as if to touch his face, but stayed her hand. 'When you questioned me in the market, before the tremor – said you'd seen me that night, going upstairs – I thought you must have suspected me. But then you were so kind, I convinced myself that maybe I was wrong. That you didn't know what I had done.' She looked down at the mask in her hands. 'I didn't want to take it. But my father insisted. Said its value was beyond the telling. Ten thousand florins or more.'

Jack was stunned by the sum, more than even the most well paid men in Florence – lawyers and professors – would make in twenty years.

'But it is worth more than gold to the signore,' Laora continued, her voice smaller now. 'I used to play with Maddalena and Lucrezia in his study. We knew where Papi kept a key. We spent hours in there with his treasures, trying on diadems, playing at kings and queens. But the chalice – that we never touched. Lucrezia told me Signor Lorenzo's grandfather had given it to him. That it was important to him and his Academy.'

A memory crept into Jack's mind: Lorenzo in the chaos of the move to Fiesole. *Look again, Bertoldo. I will want it for the meeting.* 'Your father acted as a distraction that night? Allowed you to go unnoticed to Lorenzo's study?'

She nodded. 'Papi kept the key in the same place he always had. Under his pillow.'

Jack thought of the hush in the hall, the scent of blossom lingering.

'Why did you invite me to your room? If you were worried I knew?'

'I wanted to be certain. But then . . .' She put a hand to her lips, averted her eyes.

He thought of those lips on his. Had the kiss been just another distraction? Had he been a fool to think it sincere? To fantasise about another – and more? 'Has your father asked you to do anything else? To spy on the signore? Read his letters?'

'No.' She sounded startled, despite her admission of guilt. 'Of course not.'

'You've not heard of a man named Amaury de la Croix? A priest, from Paris?'

Her brow furrowed with what appeared to be genuine thought, an uncertain shake of her head. 'I don't think so.'

'The antechamber off Lorenzo's study? Did you ever see inside when you played there?'

She was looking confused now, anxious. 'The storage room? With all the chests?'

So, the Muslim was a recent occupant? 'What about the Court of Wolves. You know your father is a member?' At her nod, he pressed on. 'Do they know about this? About what you took?'

'No! No one does. If the signore found out . . .' Laora wrapped her arms around her. 'Does he know, Sir James? I beg you, just tell me that.'

'No. Or, at least, I haven't told him.'

She stared at him, searching his face. Seeing she was shivering, he unpinned his cloak and wrapped it around her shoulders. She tensed at first, then settled, nestling into his warmth, trapped in the garment. She exhaled, nodding tightly. 'Then I have time to leave.'

'Leave?'

'If the family knew I had stolen from them? I couldn't bear it.' Her eyes were bright in the dark. 'I did it because I was frightened of what my father would do if I disobeyed him, but I did it for me too. I hoped it might change him, if some of what he lost – his fortune – could be returned?' She sagged against the alley wall. 'But he is worse than ever.'

'Where will you go?' He had wondered this himself, meaning to help her if he could.

She laughed helplessly. 'I have no idea.' A loud bang made her start upright. Sparks glittered red in the slice of sky above the alley. Hoots of laughter echoed.

Jack thought. 'Does your father still have the chalice?'

She nodded. 'I think he is biding his time until he can sell it without suspicion falling on him.'

'What if I was to return it to the signore's study, without his knowledge? He would just think he had misplaced it. No one need ever know.'

'You would do that?' Hope burned in her eyes. 'But how would we return it?'

'You could take it from your father's—'

She was shaking her head wildly before he'd finished. 'No. *No!* I will not take it from him!' All her poise, the façade of strength she hid behind, was gone. She was just a terrified girl, tears in her eyes. 'You saw what he is like! I told you – what he did to my mother!'

He reached out to take her shoulders, trying to calm her. 'There are other ways. You do not have to do it.'

After a pause, she leaned in against him, resting her head on his chest. He smelled her perfume, so familiar now it was comforting.

'Please, help me. Tell me what I should do.'

The plea was faint, more breath than words, but he heard it clearly. More than that – he felt it – an urge to protect her rose in him, despite the voice that warned him. Sliding his arms around her, he drew her closer, but even as he felt her relax against him, his mind filled with questions. If everything Laora had told him was the truth, then it pointed towards Martelli as simply an agent of vengeance – a man using his daughter's closeness to the Medici to regain some of his lost fortune. But if that was Martelli's sole aim, then someone else must be the traitor? Someone else, who had read Amaury's letter and hunted the priest to Paris? Made that hole through which to spy on Lorenzo?

Jack thought of the badge in his purse, the eyes of the wolf slit with cunning. Felt his hope for that reward – answers to his past and gold for his men, and the future he'd begun to dream of, shimmering on a distant horizon – slipping away from him, back into darkness, until only Laora remained, solid and warm in his arms.

Moonlight slanted through the arcade, the shadows of pillars marching down the flagstoned floor like a ladder. In the shelter of the passage, a man was waiting, seated on one of the stone benches that looked out over the lawns, cast in ghost-blue light. His black robes were drawn tight about him and his breaths misted the air, still sour with sulphur from Twelfth Night's revelry. Beside him was a bag, the leather warm beneath his grip. Hearing footsteps, the man rose to see a figure approaching, the hood of his fur-trimmed robe pulled low.

The two men embraced as they met.

'I came as soon as I received your message,' murmured the figure in the cloak, pushing back his hood. 'You have news?' His tone was taut with anticipation.

In answer, the man reached into the bag. He pulled out a book.

'What is this?' asked the figure, taking it from him. The book was newly bound, the boards stiff, the leather as yet uncreased.

'I believe it could turn your fortune.' The man paused as the bell in the tower above them clanged the hour, shattering the hush. Even after it had silenced, its echo seemed to hang in the air around them, a low hum. 'I think you may be able to use it to contest the signore's new alliance with Rome. Curtail his growing power. Once his son is in the Vatican, your chance to challenge him will fade.'

The man opened the first page, squinting to read the text. There was a name inscribed there.

Giovanni Pico della Mirandola

28

'If you please, Your Holiness.'

At the gentle touch of Rinaldo's callused fingertips on his chin, Giovanni Battista Cybo – who, on his election to the Holy See, had taken the name Innocent VIII – leaned back his head. As his scalp sank into cloud-like softness, he realised the barber's attendant must have slipped in while his eyes were closed to place a cushion behind his head. He caught the scent of rose petals seeping from its feathered innards. The perfume mingled with the incense that burned in censers around the palatial chamber and the sweetness of the myriad concoctions on Rinaldo's table: scented waters in glass bottles, perfumed balls of soap in tall, cylindrical jars, ointments and powders in ceramic pots.

Innocent usually enjoyed the weekly ritual, the old barber's skilful hands soothing him into drowsy reveries, the scrape of the razor across his skin, the cool sting of perfumed oils. Afterwards, his face clean-shaven, nostrils plucked, skin pumiced and teeth cleaned with cuttlebones and dragon's blood, he always felt like a man reborn, cleansed and pure. Today, however, he was finding it hard to settle, his thoughts lingering on the unexpected visitor who had come yesterday afternoon.

His eyes opened, fixing on the intricate bosses that encrusted the chamber's ceiling, every inch of which, like all the private apartments in the Apostolic Palace, was painted and gilded, cherubim dancing, plump and pink, across it. His impatience rose as he wondered what was taking Franceschetto so long. He had expected his son to have arrived hours ago.

As Rinaldo massaged the soap into his jowls, filling his nose with smells of olive oil, honey and lavender, Innocent's eyes swivelled to the marble table by the window. The book lay on its surface. Such a small, innocuous object it looked. Yet, perhaps, it offered so much more than the sum of its pages. Most of last night, ensconced in the curtained privacy of his bed, he had lain awake reading it, turning it over in his hands while he pondered how best to use it to his advantage. After Mass that morning he had come to a decision. Now, he was impatient to set his plan in motion.

His attention flicked across the chamber as one of his attendants opened the embellished gold doors, but he was disappointed to see it was just a slave, bearing the wine he had asked for. The slim, dark-skinned youth – one of almost two score *moros* sent to him by the monarchs of Spain after the fall of Ronda – crossed the chamber to place the tray on a table near the grand, canopied bed. After filling the gem-crusted goblet, the youth approached, eyes downcast.

As Innocent took it, a stray drop of wine dripped from the base to bloom red on his voluminous white robes. 'You have to wipe it,' he admonished the youth. 'How many times must I tell you? Rinaldo . . .'

The barber was there in an instant, taking the goblet and giving it a swipe with one of his towels before returning it to his grasp. At a dismissive flick of Innocent's hand, the slave hastened for the doors.

'They are not much of a gift, are they?' Innocent remarked. 'When you have to train them to do the slightest thing?'

'No, Your Holiness,' agreed Rinaldo, letting him take a sip of wine before continuing to gently knead the soap into the folds of flesh at his chin. 'More a burden than a gift I should say?'

'Indeed,' sighed Innocent, tempered by the barber's sympathy.

One of the first proclamations he had made on attaining the papal crown was to call for a new holy war – his great ambition to be the pope who wrested Jerusalem from the infidel and delivered it back to the righteous. But the papal coffers, diminished by his recent predecessors in their pursuit of the lavish restoration of the Eternal City, would not go far to fund such a dream and even though, in the two and a half years since that proclamation, he'd acquired some wealth by selling church benefices to certain rich individuals, it was still nowhere near enough for such a massive undertaking as a crusade and he'd been left to watch while Isabella and Ferdinand won the praise and gratitude of Christendom for their battle against the great evil of Islam.

A solution – a way to both flood his barren coffers and raise the spectre of war in the face of the mighty and arrogant Ottomans who had had a hand squeezed around the throat of Christendom for the past thirty-four years – had presented itself two years ago, but his plan had faltered with the failure of the Knights of St John to deliver what they promised. The scant news that had trickled to him in the time since from his agents, sent to search for his missing prize, had been a source of increasing frustration. But perhaps, he mused, eyes straying to the book, Fortune's wheel had finally begun to spin in his favour?

It wasn't until Rinaldo had finished shaving him and was patting him dry with herb-scented towels, that there was another knock on the door and one of the papal attendants opened it to his son.

'Your Holiness,' greeted Franceschetto, going down on one knee before him and taking his proffered hand, ornamented with rings, to kiss.

Innocent had sired the boy when he was only seventeen, but knew his fifty-five years hung heavier on him than his son's thirty-eight summers. His hair, carved into a neat tonsure by Rinaldo, was ashy grey and his body had ballooned these past few years with his rich and expansive diet, making him look, to his chagrin, like a pregnant woman, while his chins had sagged, leaving his only well-defined feature his beak-like nose. Franceschetto, with his strong face, coal-black eyes and sun-dark leanness, had taken after his mother, a rare beauty from the court in Naples, daughter of a friend of his father, the viceroy. It was, Innocent had discovered, a discomforting thing to be jealous of one's offspring. This was one of the reasons he'd distanced himself from the youth in his early years. But with all that free rein the young man had virtually strangled himself.

The marriage into the House of Medici offered an opportunity for Franceschetto to take on a more valuable role that Innocent anticipated would benefit him as much as his son – bonded with one of Christendom's most powerful and affluent families – but clearly he would need a firmer hand to guide him. Not only was his son half a day late in answering his summons, he was clearly still suffering the effects of yet another debauched night, his eyes bloodshot and unfocused, breath poisoned with drink.

'I sent for you hours ago, *nephew*,' he said, pronouncing that title, as he always did, loudly, deliberately – and let any man dare say otherwise. Removing his hand from Franceschetto's clammy grip, Innocent eased his corpulent body upright in the chair. Rinaldo and his assistant were busy packing away their tools. 'Where have you been?' The young man had risen and was standing uncertainly before him, clutching his hat. Innocent could see his drink-addled mind working behind those clouded eyes. 'The card tables in Trastevere again? How much did you lose this time?' When Franceschetto avoided his gaze, he exhaled sharply. 'Never mind.'

Innocent rose and crossed to the marble table. Setting down his goblet, he picked up the book. The leather was creased along the spine where he had read and re-read it last night. 'I had a visitor yesterday, who brought me this.' As he held it out, Franceschetto came forward to take it. The young man opened it.

'As you can see, it was penned by Giovanni Pico della Mirandola.'

'The philosopher?'

'And close friend and confidant of your new father-in-law.' Innocent watched his son turn the pages. 'It is highly unorthodox, bound in the tenets of humanism, but so far beyond the doctrine of Christ's teachings as to be – though I want my cardinals to read it before I make such a proclamation publicly – heretical.'

'You plan to have him arrested?' Franceschetto placed the book quickly back on the marble table as if it contained some contagion.

Of all the traits he had failed to instil in the young man, true faith at least wasn't one. 'Yes. But—'

'Shall I seize him when I travel to Florence next month? Bring him back for interrogation?'

His son looked at once awake, eager even. Perhaps the approach of his new role and responsibilities were starting to shape him? Lord, that it were so.

'If I can arrange it thus, you will not be going to Florence. Not yet at least.' When Franceschetto shook his head, confused, Innocent continued. 'In my questioning of the man who brought it to me, I discovered something else – something my agents in the city have suspected, but have not yet been able to prove. I am now certain Lorenzo de' Medici has the Turk and is keeping him in his palace.'

The last vestiges of stupor had fallen from Franceschetto's eyes. 'If that is so, then send me to Florence for the betrothal as planned. I can get closer, far closer, to the signore, than Battista di Salvi and that beast. Let me bring the heretic and the Turk back with me.'

Innocent smiled to see his enthusiasm, felt a rare surge of fatherly pride. He was about to answer when there was a crash of glass. He turned to see Rinaldo's assistant had dropped two of the scent bottles he had been packing away, filling the chamber with a sickly breath of rose water. With bows and apologies to Innocent, Rinaldo hastened to the young man, whom he berated in whispers as the two of them bent to clean up the scattered splinters of glass. Several attendants moved in to help them.

'No. I have another plan,' said Innocent, turning his attention back to his son. He stabbed a finger at the book. 'And this is going to help us.'

Franceschetto nodded slowly. 'The man who brought it to you, who was he? What were his motives?'

'He represents men who seek to overthrow the signore. They hoped, by bringing this to me, that I would aid them in this – that proof of heresy among his inner circle would ruin my alliance with the House of Medici and spur me to take action against its head. They offered, of course, to step into the breach of power that would be left by Signor Lorenzo's downfall.'

'Overthrow him?'

'Do not fear, nephew. No matter this sacrilege and no matter Signor Lorenzo's treachery in taking what was mine, I have no intention of undermining him – not when you are about to enter his household. No. Far better to feed the lion than enrage it. His Holiness, Sixtus, felt the power of the signore's bite when he tried and failed to destroy him. We will come with meat, a friendly countenance and a soothing hand. He will not even know it when we have him caged.' Innocent smiled. 'Your future will be secured in one of Christendom's most powerful dynasties.' His eyes went to the book. 'And I will have my crusade.'

Dark was descending, the wind picking up, as the young man ran alongside the fortified walkway of the Passetto di Borgo towards the Tiber. Above him, torch flames gusted, catching the curved blades of the guards' halberds. Behind him, St Peter's Basilica towered like a pale god against the sky, its sweeping archways spread like wings beneath a domed head. Ahead, loomed the Castel Sant'Angelo.

Passing beneath the circular walls of Hadrian's tomb, he hurried on to the Ponte Sant' Angelo, following the route pilgrims took to the

Eternal City. Its wide girth was busy with people heading home from work or evening prayers, cloaks and mantles flapping in the wind whipping up the surface of the river. There were a few fishing boats out on the inky waters, lanterns bobbing like fireflies. In his haste to cross, the young man knocked into two gentlemen, one of whom shouted at his back that he smelled like a whore. He didn't look back, but a sniff of his hands told him he was still covered in rose water from the broken scent bottles. Rinaldo, the miserly bastard, was docking his pay for the next month for that. Still, it was worth it to have kept himself in the chamber long enough to hear everything he needed to. And, if he was paid what he'd been promised for this information, he wouldn't miss those wages.

Once over the Tiber, he entered the gateway beneath the lion banners of Borgo. The wind was less fierce here, away from the river. Passing neat market gardens in the shadows of ancient, pillared ruins, grand mansions, the cladding of which was still clean and new, a large stone pyramid and several bathhouses, he entered a poorer area, where the houses sat close and cramped and the street was strewn with mouldering rubbish where pigs rooted.

At a peeling blue door beside a carpenter's workshop, he paused to catch his breath, then knocked. After a few moments, the door opened a crack. The young man caught a glimpse of a dark, wiry beard and a black eye, rimmed yellow.

'Yes?' came a murmured voice, thick with accent.

'Tell Orhan I have it. Tell him, I know where the man he's been hunting for is.'

Lorenzo strode down the passageway. Rage simmered in him, a fever burning through his body. That morning he had woken with the hot tenderness in his foot that usually heralded an excruciating attack of the gout that had crippled his grandfather and killed his father – the Medici curse. Now, though, he couldn't feel a thing. Anger had blasted the pain right out of his body.

He hadn't felt this furious in years, not since the day he buried his brother and unleashed his wrath upon his killers. Servants and secretaries, busy about their errands in the hallways of the palazzo, parted before him in haste. Behind him marched Black Martin and Crooked Andrea, swords swinging from their hips, his bodyguards' countenance as black as his mood.

Reaching the door, he hammered on it with his fist. Not waiting for a response, he pushed it open. Angelo Poliziano stood like a statue in the centre of the chamber, transfixed by his violent entrance. 'Signore . . .?'

'Where is he?' Lorenzo's baleful gaze swept the chamber, moving over the clothes strewn haphazardly over the back of a chair, the crumpled bedcovers. For a moment he wondered if Rigo had been mistaken – that Pico wasn't here after all – then he saw the two goblets, one empty, one half-full, on the table by the bed.

He had suspected some time ago that the two men had grown closer than friends. But even though he'd guessed this had been going on under his nose for months, perhaps longer, it was still a shock to see the casual intimacy in those goblets; to imagine the murmured conversations over the lips of them, heads bowed in the dark, laughter and secrets shared.

Was Poliziano in on this? Did he know what his lover had done? He wanted to shout the question at Poliziano, standing there like a damn mute, but just then Pico emerged through the narrow door that led to the water closet, looking as dishevelled as the bedcovers. At least Poliziano had the grace to hang his head in shame. Pico, on the other hand, bare-chested, tousle-haired, cocky as a *calcio* champion, kept his head up, meeting his gaze.

For Lorenzo, this struck a match to the powder of his rage. 'You betrayed me, you son of a bitch!' He thrust out his hand, in which was gripped the message that had come, the vellum crumpled by his fist, the heavy seal dangling from it. 'You set down our secrets in ink! Displayed them to the world when I forbade it!'

Pico was shaking his head. 'Signore, I—'

'The thesis, damn it! You wrote it! *Printed it* for Christ's sake!'

Pico's grey eyes were flicking from the parchment to Lorenzo, trying to piece the puzzle together. 'It is true, signore,' he said, glancing at Poliziano, who made a shocked noise at this. 'But I haven't distributed it. Not widely. Indeed, hardly at all!'

'When? When did you do this?'

'You must understand, signore, I was angry – *humiliated* – when you took my papers, berated me in front of our brethren at Fiesole. I returned to my room in a fury, rewrote it all. I took it to the printing press at San Jacopo di Ripoli, the morning after your feast. I was planning to talk to you about it when it was printed. I wanted you to read it. Understand my view.'

'I understand your view very well,' retorted Lorenzo, brandishing the message. 'And, now, so does His Holiness.' He derived some small satisfaction from Pico's shock. 'Your text found its way to Rome. Into St Peter's itself!'

'That isn't possible.' But the truth was there, in Lorenzo's hand, and Pico's poise was dropping, slipping from him like a whore's silks. 'I only gave it to a few men!'

'Why would you do this, Pico?'

Hearing the stunned disbelief in Poliziano's tone, Lorenzo felt a surge of hope. Had the man been kept in the same dark as he had? He had imagined a conspiracy. The two of them laughing behind his back. More traitors in his household.

The question seemed to galvanise Pico. He stood straighter. 'I had to do something. As I said at our last gathering, the Academy is losing its way, in danger of falling into obscurity. All our grand plans? Lost. Forgotten. Until we are just a herd of fattened old men, chewing cud like cows out to pasture. No meaning to our lives, our words. No fire to our ambitions!'

'You have no idea of my plans.'

'Because you refuse to tell us! You will not share your secrets. You do not trust us!'

As Pico's voice strengthened, Lorenzo felt Black Martin shift at his back. 'And with good reason!' He tossed the crumpled parchment at Pico's feet, the papal seal striking the tiles. 'Heresy, the pope has declared your writings. He wants you brought to him for questioning.'

Pico took a step back at this, but some of the vigour returned to his tone. 'We need to challenge the faith, the corrupt power of the Church. Innocent has sired two bastards. Sixtus sanctioned your murder! We have all heard how the cardinals frolic around the Eternal City with their mistresses and whores, others taking boys – *mere babes* – to their beds. They hold us to a standard all of them fall far short of. The *Corpus Hermeticum* has taught us another way to reach for God. To stretch out our hands towards the stars. To rebuild the world and usher in a new age. A new dawn. One of peace, prosperity. A brotherhood of men, stretching across the globe, just as the angels surround the heavens, free of strife and sin. As above, so below.'

Lorenzo felt some of the rage seeping from him at this. However furious he was with the betrayal – both kinds, he thought, looking between Pico and Poliziano – the young man's words held only the clear ring of truth. His passion reminded him of his grandfather, some of the old man's wisdom echoing back to him, as though a bell struck. Still, he shook his head, forcing this away. However right his intentions, Pico's actions had wronged him – badly. 'His Holiness is demanding that the betrothal feast for Maddalena and Franceschetto is now held in Rome. He does not feel that with this accusation of heresy hanging over my household that he can countenance such an occasion taking place here in Florence.'

'Signore,' murmured Poliziano, his tone reflecting the gravity of this revelation. 'Can you attempt to change the pontiff's mind?'

'If I do not accept, he tells me he will have no choice but to withdraw his offer of Giovanni's entry into the college.'

Even Pico saw it now, Lorenzo was satisfied to see; the depth of his mistake. 'All the time and money I have spent planning this celebration is nothing compared to the loss of face I shall suffer in the republic. I wanted to show my citizens that I was right – the implacable stance I took after my brother's murder, my time in Naples – that it was worth the sacrifices. The betrothal, here in Florence, was supposed to be the cementing of our accord with Rome. The end of our long and bitter struggle. Now, I must take my daughter, my whole household, to Rome, under a cloud of suspicion. Make myself weak in the face of the Church and my republic. All because you could not trust me.'

Now, the shame coloured Pico's cheeks. 'Signore, let me go to Rome. Let me beg forgiveness from His Holiness. I will distance myself. Tell him you have no part in my dealings.'

'No. You know too much.'

Poliziano and Pico shared a look – a flicker of fear in both their eyes at the threat; the prospect of interrogation, the spectre of a heretic's pyre.

'What should I do, signore? Tell me. Let me make amends.'

'You will leave Florence, Giovanni,' Lorenzo told him, using the young man's formal name for the first time in years. They had been friends for a long time, the three of them. Wine on sun-warmed terraces, he and Poliziano sitting close, laughing at some ribald poem Pico had plucked from the air; winter darkness and hearth fires, passing around the chalice his grandfather had passed down to him, eyes bright as they shared their vision for a new world. In the chamber he felt it – a sense of something tearing, never to be mended. 'Leave the republic. Never return.' He didn't use the word, but they all knew what he meant.

Banishment.

The flames in Pico's cheeks had died, leaving him pale. Poliziano had turned away, but not before Lorenzo saw the anguish in his eyes. While Lorenzo knew Pico had room in his heart for many loves, Poliziano – it was now clear – had given the young man his, wholly and completely. Pico had burned like a fire between them, leaving nothing but ash.

Turning, Lorenzo left the chamber, leaving Black Martin and Crooked Andrea to wait while the young man gathered his clothes and belongings, ready to escort him from the palazzo.

Lorenzo was approaching the *Sala Grande*, feeling utterly spent, when Bertoldo emerged to greet him.

'Signore, there is a man here to see you.'

'Not now, Bertoldo. I need to be alone.'

'I beg your pardon, signore, but I brought him to the salon. He said it was a matter of urgency. Regarding Sir James Wynter?'

Beyond his steward, through the open doors of the grand hall, Lorenzo caught sight of a middle-aged man, staring up at the paintings of Hercules, his grey hair pulled back in a tail, his face marked with wounds, faded green and yellow. He recognised him as one of Jack's men. His name came to him after a moment.

Adam.

29

After Loja, Íllora fell to the Christians, its walls pounded into dust by Spanish guns, the inhabitants fled or captured, its ramparts rebuilt for the defence of the new Castilian garrison. Moclín, known for its strength and strategic position as the Shield of Granada, followed, then Colomera and, last, Montfrío.

Queen Isabella, with her train of royal guards, hidalgos and bishops, followed in the wake of her husband's forces, seated on a magnificently caparisoned palfrey, the banner of Castile unfurled above her. Under her command, Christian prisoners were released from the bowels of Moorish dungeons, mosques were consecrated to Christ and the dead, found bloated and putrefied among the ruins, were buried.

King Ferdinand moved on with the bulk of his army, laying waste to the Vega of Granada, sacking settlements and scorching the earth until most of the western half of the emirate lay in ashes or was subsumed under the Spanish crown. There was little succour for the ordinary men and women of these towns, villages and fortresses, trapped in the fast-closing jaws of the enemy, their leaders too busy warring among themselves, the factions of Boabdil and Muhammad al-Zagal still in conflict for the dominion of the beleaguered kingdom; a conflict the Spanish monarchs were only too happy to encourage, offering the errant Boabdil their support if he defeated his implacable uncle.

Harry, bearing the king's sword gifted to him at Loja, had been chosen, after the city's fall, to accompany the queen in her host. He had been elated. At last, he was inside the royal circle, honoured and welcomed – could turn his mind to his true purpose here. But, before he'd even left the camp at Loja, where winter rains had swelled the river and turned the earth to stinking bog, he caught a fever that swept him, on a burning, delirious tide, as close as he'd ever come to the doors of death.

He'd barely been conscious – incapable of protesting – when Peter secured his place in a heavily guarded caravan bearing the crown's plunder through the bald mountains of the Kingdom of Granada to the fertile valley of the Guadalquivir. The journey had existed for him as a series of disjointed, tormented moments: the endless jolting of the wagon, sweat pouring off his shuddering, aching body, Peter and Hervey attending to him, mopping his brow and forcing foul concoctions down his throat, which spewed and spattered from him as quickly as they entered.

In Rodrigo's house in Seville, he spent weeks in bed, dreaming and waking, no longer certain of the boundaries between. In the feverish gloom, he was rarely alone. Sometimes, Peter was with him. Other times, a stranger in dark robes who smelled of turpentine and rose water as he peered into his eyes and prodded his body, sniffed at his bloody defecations and poked his veins with needles. Henry Tudor was there, too. Occasionally, Harry would jolt round, tangled in sweat-soaked sheets, to find the king seated on a throne at the foot of his bed. Sometimes, he was standing, sword in hand. Harry would be kneeling before him, expecting to receive the kiss of knighthood, and would scream himself awake as Henry raised his blade – not to touch his shoulders in accolade – but to strike off his head.

By the time the fever subsided and he regained his faculties, the year had turned and Christmas had come and gone. He was stunned by the sight of his wasted body in mirrors, the skin shrivelled on his sunken stomach, his eyes dark and hollow, but as his appetite returned and his bowels strengthened, the flesh built on his bones and the pallor faded. He saved himself from boredom by applying himself to his study of Castilian under Peter's tutelage, surprising himself by how much of the language he'd already absorbed. After a few more weeks, he was up and moving about, keen to know if Peter had heard anything from the queen and king, or Rodrigo. While no news had come of the hidalgo – vanished without word after Loja's fall – he learned that Isabella and Ferdinand had retreated to Córdoba for the winter, laden with bounty, and were preparing an assault on Málaga, the last major obstacle to the city of Granada. There was other news too, in the form of two letters, bearing the seal of King Henry.

Peter, who'd been keeping them until he regained his strength, handed them to Harry one morning with a jug of wine out in the courtyard, where the surviving hound that was supposed to have been gifted to the king and queen dozed in a sunny corner, much fattened by Rodrigo's servants. Harry, his throat drying at the sight of the letters – an image of the king from his dreams ghosting in his mind – had opened the first with trembling hands. The neat script of the royal clerk had filled the page with keen words, Henry pleased to receive Harry's message that he'd been accepted by the Spanish monarchs as ambassador and was joining them on campaign, the better to secure their trust and confidence. It ended with a note that Henry's reign had been strengthened and blessed by the birth of a son and heir, and he was now eager to further his plans for expansion. Harry, thinking of the map spread across the king's lap in the Painted Chamber, had known without doubt what he meant. He sensed, too, the impatience in the lines – a sense that was more than borne out by the second letter.

This one had come recently, since he'd been in Seville. It was shorter, but no less impactful for that; ominous in its curtness and loaded with meaning, as clear to Harry as if the king had been standing there speaking the words, his glacial eyes upon him. It was implied that Edward Woodville had returned to England a hero, but his report included the fact that Queen Isabella had opened an inquiry into Columbus's proposal; a fact the king surmised, correctly, meant Harry was no further forward in fulfilling his mission to prevent the sailor from gaining support for a voyage, leaving Henry Tudor free – when ready – to launch his own without fear of competition. The letter ended bluntly, with request for an immediate response and a warning that should he make no better progress, someone would be sent to replace him.

So shaken was he that Harry retreated to his bed, leaving Peter fearing the sickness had returned. But there was no blood-letting or bitter potion the physician who'd attended to him in his delirium could offer that could ease him this time and Harry had stayed under the blankets, the shutters drawn, his appetite gone, for several days. Alone, he had circled endlessly in his mind, from the seeming impossibility of his task to all he would lose if he didn't execute it to the king's satisfaction, plagued by memories of the day his inheritance had been stripped from him by the Act of Attainder, anguished by the knowledge that he would truly be left with nothing – no land, no title, no money, no hope – if Henry made good on his threat. He wouldn't even be able to stay in Spain, keep what little comforts he'd enjoyed here; would be sent home, disgraced, dishonoured. By the third morning, lying there listening to the tolls of the cathedral bell, he had come to a feverish decision.

The next day, ignoring Peter's protestations, Harry had headed to Seville's docks. He had eased himself with the thought that he would simply enquire about where the sailor was lodging – a first step – but on the walk to the dockside, the air over the city perfumed by orange blossom, he found himself fingering the jewelled hilt of the dagger on his belt. The blade, stolen from Henry's gifts to the monarchs and wrested from the Smiler in the bloody skirmish at the cave, now felt as though it had always been his. But in that short journey it had taken on new weight and importance. Henry had been clear in his message: he must halt the sailor's plan by any means, or lose everything.

By attempting to end Edward Woodville's life, he – Harry – had inadvertently brought about the victory at Loja. How else might a murderous hand achieve great good? If he killed Columbus, might he accomplish something magnificent, not just for his own future, but his king and country's? If Columbus died and Henry was left free to undertake his own voyage west, what glory and riches might God bestow upon England? It had thus been with a growing sense of certainty that he had approached the glittering Guadalquivir, the smell of brine and smoke in his nostrils.

But, on the dockside, Harry had found his notion thwarted by the words of sailors, happy to talk in exchange for a coin, who told him Columbus and his business partner, Gianotto Berardi, were now in the north, conscripted to transport the Moorish captives taken after the fall of Loja to the markets of Toledo and Madrid for the queen.

Still, Harry had a plan – one that quickly settled and solidified in him – and, as royal commissioners sent heralds throughout the city calling men to arms for the assault on Málaga, he wrote to Isabella at Córdoba with news of his good health and a request that he be allowed to return to her side, guessing his best chance to get close to the itinerant sailor would be from within the royal court.

As the call to war went out around the kingdom, news filtered in from merchants and spies, telling of how the Ottoman Sultan, Bayezid II, son of Mehmet, the conqueror of Constantinople, had been roused to action at the threat to the Muslim kingdom in Spain. The sultan, it was rumoured, had forged an alliance with his former rival, the Mamluk Sultan of Egypt, and they were now preparing to send an armada of ships to defend the emirate. To counter this peril, King Ferdinand sent a fleet of galleys to blockade the coast. But rather than shrivelling the hearts and minds of the Spanish, this ominous news served to fire them. Memories of the ravishment of Constantinople by the Ottoman Turks were still potent in the minds of many and this new threat – combined with Ferdinand's triumph at Loja and the other border towns – lit a fierce flame in many Castilians. Dukes and hidalgos, warrior priests and peasants answered the king and queen's call, bringing sword and fire for the final clash against the infidel in defence of the ramparts of Christendom itself.

East into Granada this army marched, a massive column of mules, engines and men – it was said more than seventy thousand – snaking in lines through the rising mountains, rejoining garrisons and companies who had guarded the frontier through the winter; King Ferdinand's plan was to circle around and attack Málaga from the east. The journey was arduous, recent rains swelling the streams and rivers, breaking up roads and washing away passes through the peaks. Men battled through mud and rocks, mules stumbling, gun carts lurching and dragging.

Harry, in the vanguard, was one of the first to ride down out of the grey heights, having left the safety of Seville far behind, his letter to Henry, swearing he would not fail him, winging its way across the sea to England. In Córdoba, he'd been welcomed back into the king's company, Ferdinand insisting that he – the saviour of Edward Woodville, champion of Loja – bring his sword to the campaign. Harry had attempted to stay with the queen, but every able-bodied man bar her personal guards was heading east and he'd not been able to turn down the honour of Ferdinand's request. But his plan remained alive, pulsing within him, for he knew now that Columbus and Berardi had been called to the front lines in their commission for the queen, collecting the captives that had been taken and sold for the crown. And, when Málaga fell, their services would be called upon again.

Harry fixed on the verdant valley that stretched before him, cradled by the mountains, patchworked with fields of grain and flower-speckled meadows, olive groves and vineyards and, beyond, the blue shimmer of the sea. Around him, men sighed with relief and praised God for their safe arrival, but they soon sobered as they focused their attention on the object of their coming: a vast and sprawling city, surrounded by walls punctuated all around with formidable towers. Málaga.

Down near the city's harbour, where the sand-coloured walls rose sheer from the azure Mediterranean, a tiered fortress, the size and strength of which Harry had never seen, marched up and around a spine of rock. The outer walls of this bastion, which the king referred to as the Alcazabar – the citadel – encircled the lower slopes, protecting grand domed buildings and hanging gardens of cedars, palms and pomegranates, while, beyond, a covered corridor of stone ascended to the gods, where another, no less indomitable ring of crenellated stone, spiked with towers and battlements, crowned the peak itself. It was known as the Gibralfaro, the rock of the lighthouse.

The sight made Harry quail. The Spaniards had been so convinced they would triumph, that God Himself had blessed this campaign, that he had journeyed here with them feeling as though victory had already been won – his mind on another target entirely. Now, faced with the city's might, his confidence died inside him.

King Ferdinand ordered camp to be made in the foothills some distance from the walls, in the shadows of the mountains. As tents were erected and scouts sent to watch for any approach of the enemy, animals paddocked, latrines dug and grain piled up, the Spanish vanguard waited for the remainder of the army and the artillery to labour through the rocky wilderness to their position.

Leaving Peter and his servants to set his camp, Harry walked through the growing city of tents and men, searching for Rodrigo de Torres, who he'd learned had spent the winter garrisoned in the Vega of Granada. Harry was keen to see him. Rodrigo was the closest thing he had to a friend here and, faced with the might of the infidels' stronghold and the coming battle, he felt he needed one. Rodrigo had been in the emirate since Loja's fall; would perhaps have words of comfort or encouragement for him. But it wasn't until the second night that he found the hidalgo. Or rather – the hidalgo found him.

Harry, crouched in his tent over a bowl of soapy dregs, razor in hand, heard the swish of canvas at his back. A rush of night air guttered the candles. 'Finally,' he muttered as he turned, expecting to see Hervey, who'd gone to fetch fresh water so he could finish his shave. 'Rodrigo!' Harry rose, smiling at the sight of him. The hidalgo looked rangier and darker, with a new scar on his neck, red and sore-looking beneath the black curtain of his hair. Harry's smile faded as a muscular, middle-aged man ducked into the tent behind Rodrigo, a black cloak, lined with white leather, swinging from his shoulders. Don Luys Carrillo.

'Hervey told me where to find you,' Rodrigo explained, his coal-black eyes following Harry, who bent to pick up a cloth. 'My lord Ferdinand said you had taken ill at Loja? That you returned to Seville?'

Harry nodded as he wiped the soap from his jaw. 'I came as close to God as a man can without meeting Him.' He glanced at Don Luys, then back at Rodrigo. 'I heard you stayed on the frontier. How did you fare?'

When Rodrigo looked at Don Luys instead of answering, Harry felt uneasiness rise. This wasn't the greeting he'd expected from his friend and what was Don Luys Carrillo – who'd always manifestly ignored him – doing here? 'Is something wrong?'

Don Luys, not taking his eyes off Harry, addressed Rodrigo in Castilian. 'Ask the English son of a bitch where his brother is.'

'My brother?' Harry felt as though the world had dropped away from under him.

'You've been learning our tongue?' said Rodrigo, taken aback.

Harry didn't speak, still reeling from what Don Luys had said.

Was this a jest? A bad dream? Why in Christ's name would Don Luys Carrillo be asking about *Wynter*? Had Edward Woodville said something to them? Would the knight continue to torment him with questions even in his absence? A memory came to him: Rodrigo's strange, almost hostile expression outside the cave that night, after Woodville had confronted him. So much else had happened since he'd forgotten that. 'What do you want with my brother?' he demanded, looking between the two men. 'He is no one!'

'To you, perhaps, señor,' said Don Luys, his voice low. 'To me he is everything. Your brother murdered my son.'

Harry recalled Rodrigo explaining the reason for the man's antipathy towards Englishmen, but he couldn't grasp how on earth Wynter would have met Don Luys's son.

'Your brother was in Seville four years ago,' Rodrigo prompted in his silence. 'You did not know?'

'No,' murmured Harry.

Rodrigo exchanged a look with Don Luys. 'I recognised the name the moment I heard Sir Edward utter it, that night at the cave.'

The hidalgo continued, speaking of a duel between Don Luys's son and Wynter – then calling himself Jack – but Harry was only half listening. His brother had been in Seville? Had that been something to do with the map? Or another mission his father had entrusted to that bastard over him? Everywhere he went Wynter seemed to haunt him.

Harry felt a creeping certainty that there was more – much more – to his brother's life with their father than he'd ever suspected. There was that old rage, boiling in the pit of his stomach. After all those years fearing Thomas Vaughan would grant his inheritance to Wynter, he had been so triumphant, so *gleeful*, when he finally received it for himself. But what if there was something more, beyond the dilapidated mansion on the Strand and the houses scattered across Sussex? A legacy he hadn't even known existed? A legacy of secrets his father had left to James Wynter alone?

Harry glanced at Rodrigo, realising the man had asked him a question.

The hidalgo repeated it. 'I asked what issue Sir Edward had with your brother? Why he was so keen to find him?'

'It was a matter with Woodville's family. Nothing of consequence.' Harry spoke briskly, not wanting to be drawn into details when he had no idea what these men wanted of him. 'I couldn't help him. In truth, I never even knew I had a brother – not until some years ago.' That warm evening, following his father along the skirts of the Downs, the little house in the woods, the woman who had run to embrace his father, the youth – an older reflection of himself – appearing in the doorway. 'The last time I saw him we fought.' Harry met Don Luys's eyes. 'There is no love lost between us, of that I can assure you.'

'You have no idea where Wynter is now?' There was a twitch in Don Luys's face when he said the name; a tic of hatred.

'As far as I know he left England after King Henry was crowned. I cannot say where he went. Or even if he is alive.' As Rodrigo and Don Luys shared another look, Harry knew they were sensing his reserve. Could he bluster his way through it? No. The last thing he wanted, after Henry's threat, was to be distracted from his mission again. He couldn't afford another man hounding him over his brother's whereabouts. He had to nip this in the bud. 'Wynter was declared an outlaw by the king. My brother, señor,' he added, addressing Don Luys, 'made a great many enemies.'

Rodrigo cut in. 'King Henry? But when I was in England I asked several of his officials if they knew of a James Wynter. They swore ignorance.'

'Most of those who knew my brother would have been of the House of York, many of whom were dead or gone by the time you came to the court. The king entrusted me to hunt him down and bring him in, but I found no trace of him.' Harry hoped fervently that they wouldn't press him on this. He couldn't divulge much more without exposing his master's secrets.

Don Luys, however, didn't seem interested in whatever wrong Wynter had committed against the king. To him, the only crime that mattered was that against his son. At Harry's admission, he looked all at once like a man crushed. His head hung low and his broad shoulders slumped, making him appear diminished, more tired old man than veteran warrior. 'I never truly believed I would see justice for my son, or take my revenge against his murderer, but when Rodrigo came to me at Íllora, told me he might have found trace of that wretch – through you . . .?' Don Luys's eyes smouldered in the tent's gloom. 'Now, it is as though he has been taken from me all over again.'

'Señor,' murmured Rodrigo, clasping the man's shoulder. When Don Luys said nothing, but shook his head, the hidalgo glanced up at Harry. 'You know of no one who could find him? No friends or family he left behind?'

Harry opened his mouth to confirm this, but the words didn't come. His eyes remained on the defeated visage of Don Luys. The man was one of Queen Isabella's trusted advisers and a distinguished veteran in King Ferdinand's company. He had access to privileged information and authority within the court. Might he be able to use that to his advantage? Might Don Luys be able to get him close to his target – close enough to do what he planned? Harry, realising his fingers had drifted to the hilt of his dagger, took his hand from his belt. 'No. He left no family. But . . .'

Don Luys raised his head, his expression changing. 'But . . . what?'

'There is a chance King Henry could track him down.'

'How?' questioned Rodrigo, shooting him a warning look, suggesting he shouldn't give the man false hope. 'If he sent you to do this and you failed?'

'The king – when you met him – had just stepped from the field of war to his crowning. It was a chaotic time. Now, things are different. His reign is established, as are his allies at home and abroad. He has resources he didn't possess at the time. I could, at the very least, request it?'

'You would do this?'

'Yes, señor,' Harry answered Don Luys. He paused. 'I would request the hunting down of my own brother. In return for a small favour.'

'Name it.'

Harry spoke slowly, giving his thoughts chance to catch up. 'Over the winter, I received word from my king, wanting to know how the Lady Isabella and Lord Ferdinand fared in their holy crusade. He also asked about Christopher Columbus,' he added, glancing at Rodrigo, who first told Henry of the sailor. 'He is intrigued by this notion of a westward voyage.'

'A fool's dream,' said Don Luys sharply. 'You should tell your king not to waste his time.'

'Of course, but I would like the opportunity to ascertain that myself. Perhaps an audience with—'

'With Cristóbal Colón el Loco?' Don Luys didn't wait for his reply. 'If it will get him away from the queen you may have as much time with him as you wish. My Lady Isabella has many brilliant attributes. Unfortunately, her generosity and curiosity work against her when it comes to that madman.'

Harry held out his hand to Don Luys. 'Then, señor, I shall write to my king. If Wynter can be found, you will have your justice.'

Jack watched Laora sleep. Her palm and cheek rested on his chest, rising and falling with the rhythm of his breathing. Her eyelashes fluttered, stirred by dreams. Her hair, which had tumbled in a black mass over his arm, tickled him, but he didn't want to disturb her. He hadn't slept himself yet, even though dawn could not now be far away. But this peace, here in the silence, lying on her narrow bed in the halo of light from a single candle, felt like a sleep in and of itself; as if the world beyond didn't exist.

When, earlier that evening, escaping the Palazzo Medici – hectic with the move to Rome for the betrothal, rumours flying about Pico being banished from the republic – Jack had met Laora at the side entrance, following her up servants' passageways and back stairs to her room, he hadn't intended to stay longer than to talk through the tentative plan to take back the chalice, which she believed was most likely locked in her father's study. But their talk, whispered in candle-light, had gone beyond their plot, following paths into one another's lives: she speaking of her mother, eyes now bright with happier memories, he speaking of his boyhood in Lewes, shrugging off the role he'd been playing all these months, like a jacket grown stiff and uncomfortable. He hadn't told her the full truth about himself, but he had walked close to it, as she laid her head on him and listened, her face bathed in restless light.

As he traced the skin of her fingers, the creases in her knuckles, the olive-hued smoothness of her hand, he wondered at the ease with which they seemed to fit together. It didn't matter that she didn't know who he really was; it felt as though they knew one another beyond words, something in their fates, past and present, binding them, something he couldn't articulate, only feel. He sensed the danger; that this was an alliance that could hurt them both. But, for tonight, he had pushed his cares aside.

He would do as he had promised her – take the chalice from her father and return it to Lorenzo's study while the signore was in Rome. He had considered using the priceless object to bargain for what he wanted, but knew he could ill afford the signore's suspicion falling on him and, without implicating Laora, he couldn't tell Lorenzo the truth. This left him with only one option: to continue his charade within the Court of Wolves and find whoever had taken Amaury de la Croix. But his frustration hearing Laora's confession in the alley – knowing he was back where he had started – was lessened now, soothed by the solace he felt lying here beside her. After months of uncertainty, it was the first time he'd felt he was where he was supposed to be.

Lulled by Laora's breaths, Jack was drifting towards sleep when a loud banging woke him.

Laora started upright, eyes wide. 'What was that?' she breathed, gaze darting to the door of her room.

The banging sounded again, shattering the hush. It was coming from outside. Jack slipped off the bed and crossed to the window. Laora followed, the candle fluttering, throwing their shadows up the panelled walls. Jack peered through the shutters. Down in the street were six black-cloaked men. Two held torches, which smoked and sputtered. Another harsh hammering told him a seventh was pounding on the palazzo's doors. Across the street, a dog was barking. A shutter clattered open and a man shouted at the group, but they ignored him. As the one who'd been knocking stepped back, evidently talking to someone who had opened the doors, his face was illuminated by torchlight. It was Black Martin, Lorenzo's personal guard. The guard reached towards his hip as if for his sword, then stepped forward. The others followed him into the palazzo.

Jack turned to Laora, hovering anxiously at his shoulder. 'It's Signor Lorenzo's bodyguards.'

'What are they doing here?'

'I don't know,' he murmured, but a voice in his mind told him he did. Why else would the signore's guards have come, armed, to beat down Franco Martelli's door in the middle of the night? Lorenzo knew. Somehow he knew Martelli had been working against him. 'Do you have somewhere you can go? A friend?'

Laora was shaking her head. 'Why? You don't think . . .? Do they *know*?' She fixed on him, her hazel eyes hardening. 'Did you tell him?'

'No. I swear.' Jack heard faint shouts downstairs. He took her arm. 'Laora, we don't have much time. It will not go well for either of us to be found here together.'

This seemed to focus her. 'Pia,' she said. 'The cloth-seller, from the *mercato*. She lives close by.'

'Let's go.'

'Wait.' She pulled from his grip to snatch the silver bird pendant from the table by the bed.

Laora drew the chain over her head as he opened the door, hidden in the panels. Heading down the narrow stairs, hands feeling along the walls in the pitch black, they made it to the first floor, where shouts and the thud of opening doors were punctuated by a child's high-pitched wails. When they reached the mouth of the passage, which they would have to cross to reach the stairs down, they saw a group of figures at the far end, lit by the torches of Lorenzo's guards.

Black Martin was among them and, in the centre, Franco Martelli, dressed in a crumpled nightshirt, his mane of hair wild from sleep. He was shouting, gesturing angrily at Black Martin, who stood his ground while, beyond, other guards thrust open doors, ignoring the small knot of servants looking on fearfully. Close by stood Donna Santa, her daughters clustered around her, Fea crying loudly. When one of the guards went to move her away from the door she was blocking, Martelli stepped towards him enraged, but as Black Martin drew his sword and gestured for two guards to seize him, the man was powerless to stop them compelling his wife to move aside.

'My father's study,' whispered Laora, as one of the guards snatched a set of keys from Martelli's elderly, gaunt-faced steward.

Seeing the group was occupied, all eyes on the guard now unlocking the door, Martelli's protests drowning out his daughter's sobs, Jack urged Laora across the passage and down the stairs. Her father's desperate shouts followed them all the way to the street.

Pia, who lived two streets away in a tiny cottage wedged between a shoemaker and a hatter, opened the shutters and peered warily down at Jack's insistent knocking. 'Signora?' she exclaimed, her voice rising with surprise as she saw Laora's face upturned beneath her.

Once the door was opened, the young cloth-seller ushered Laora inside, her voice soft with questions and concern.

As Laora glanced over her shoulder at Jack, he forced what he hoped would be a reassuring smile. 'Stay here. I'll return as soon as I've found out what's happening. I promise,' he added, but the fear didn't leave her eyes.

The sky was lightening to a pale, washed-out blue by the time Jack reached the palazzo, his breaths fogging in the chilly air. Most of the city was still dark; frail glow of nightlights behind shutters, a tang of smoke from dying fires, but the Palazzo Medici was lit up like a church on Easter morning, shutters open, lanterns blazing. He could see Rigo and several other guards clustered around the arched entrance. Along the street stood six of the wagons that would convey the Medici household to Rome for Maddalena's betrothal. Porters, shoulders hunched against the cold, waited with them, rubbing their hands and talking in low voices. As Jack approached the steps, one of the guards spotted him. The man said something to Rigo, who spun round.

'Sir James!'

Jack halted at the shout, seeing the others all turning to him. Rigo's smile of greeting was tight, not reaching his eyes. He faltered, sensing the threat, but before he could move, Rigo gestured to two of his comrades who circled in behind him.

'The signore has been looking for you, Sir James,' Rigo said, hand on the pommel of his sword.

Goro had been at the inn's window for hours, only pausing from his watch to relieve himself in the bucket under the bed.

He had seen the wagons arrive at the palazzo and the first chests being loaded, watching the servants and porters filing from the arched entranceway and the officials who followed. He counted the guards as the monsignore had ordered, wanting an accurate observation of the palazzo's security, ready for the arrival of the men His Holiness was sending to aid them. In and out, swiftly and silently, no sign they were ever there. That was their task.

All this time and the man they were searching for had been right under their noses. They had suspected as much after their last interrogation, but it grated on Goro that his powers of persuasion hadn't been enough to identify the precise location. Battista di Salvi had been swift to point this out, furious that someone else had now taken the credit for informing His Holiness exactly where his prize was hidden. The monsignore had vowed that when they returned to Rome, Goro would take responsibility for their failings before Pope Innocent. Of that he would make sure.

Often in these hours of watching, Goro's eyes flicked to the stone shield above the palazzo's entrance, decorated with the seven red balls: arms of the family who had once allied with Galeazzo Sforza, allowed that monster to thrive and grow, caring nothing for his tyranny since it suited them. Feeling his mind wandering down into darkness, he would pull himself back by pacing the room, but he kept finding his gaze dragged back to that shield, his thoughts blackening, hands twitching into fists.

Settling on the window seat, which creaked under his weight, Goro contemplated his options. Should he leave? The monsignore had what he needed to complete the mission now: allies willing to help them enter the palazzo in secret when Lorenzo de' Medici was out of the way, as the pope had arranged. Battista was right. What use was he any more? Why return with him to Rome only to be further chastised? But he rubbed his palms together nervously at the thought. What would become of him, adrift in this world?

Across the street, a shout caught his attention. The wagons were still there, the porters clustered around them. There, too, the guards, illuminated by the torches that pushed back the dawn shadows. A man had appeared in the street, not far from the steps. As Goro watched, one of the guards gestured, sending two others to surround the man, who was marched up the steps and into the blaze of torchlight. The breath left Goro's body at the punch of recognition.

The man was James Wynter.

30

She hadn't believed it could be him. Not at first.

When she had stumbled back from that roof edge, the alley and the masked face below her disappearing, Amelot had run until her legs had given way three rooftops later. There she had crouched, until the shaking in her body had passed and she had forced herself to return, breaths catching in her throat as she peered over the building to look down into the alley, empty of anything except a slinking cat and scraps of rubbish eddying on the wind.

By that evening she had convinced herself that her mind had deceived her. She had lived with nightmares for years before the masked man had tortured her in that room in the shadow of St Paul's. She knew how they lingered: ghosts in the corners of her vision, a half-recognised face that would freeze her in a crowd, a brutal dream that would stun her awake, a voice at her back whispering someone was behind her.

She had not slept easy after that though. Unable to settle, she found herself watching for a new face in Florence's crowded thoroughfares, alert to the rumours of a monster stalking the city, her mind on that corpse she had seen being carried away on a litter, the dead man's skin peeled from his face. Could the monster be the man – Goro – who had sat before her and removed that mask to expose her to the horror beneath? A lump of gristle where an ear should be, a shrivelled socket that once held an eye, stubs of rotten teeth in the puckered gap where his lips had been. A face ravaged and raw.

Then, on the night Jack set her and Ned to watch the men gathering for the Court of Wolves, she had seen him again. He had been stalking along the bank of the Arno, his hunched figure unmistakable, swaddled in a grey cloak, the white mask like a glint of frost in the dark of his hood.

This time, she hadn't let him go. Despite her fear, she had forced herself to follow him, over the river and into the city, winding north and east under the great dome of the cathedral, slipping behind a cart to avoid being seen, all the way to a hostelry close to the Ospedale degli Innocenti; the foundling hospital, where unwanted infants were left on a wheel of cradles outside.

All this time since, she had trailed him, following his movements from the hostelry, where he shared a room with a man she heard him call monsignore, and out around Florence, threading after him like a confused spider, haphazardly spinning a puzzle around the city, returning to the palazzo only to collect her cloak and pinch food Jack had left lying around. Goro, whose name she knew from her ordeal in London, had been part of the pope's company searching for the map in England. He and the others had killed Amaury's men and seized her for it. With his presence here in the city, Amelot had become convinced he must have something to do with her master's abduction from Paris.

The more she followed him, her terror began to diminish. The monster who had hunted her through dreams became a shambling object of pity. She saw how cursed he was by his deformity; how people hastened to avoid him on the street, how others gawped and pointed. Youths pulled faces at his back, screeched with horrified laughter if he turned. The man he shared his lodgings with – the monsignore – was no less disdainful of his presence, every word and look holding the bite of contempt. But although Amelot rarely let Goro out of her sight, sleeping most nights on the roof of the hostelry, warmed by the heat of a chimney, he had not yet led her to her master.

The two men had a purpose for being here though, that much was clear. It was a purpose that had evidently become more pressing in recent days; messengers arriving at the hostelry, the monsignore scouring papers and ordering Goro out on errands. Amelot understood enough to ascertain that their plans had something to do with Lorenzo de' Medici.

That morning, after a fitful night on the roof, she slept longer than intended and woke to find Goro gone. Waiting through the day, she watched people come and go through the hostelry doors. By the time the sun was going down, setting fire to all the glass in the city, she was starting to worry. She forced herself to stay awake through the long dark, pacing the tiles, but it wasn't until the gleam of dawn that her fraying patience was rewarded.

Amelot's eyes picked him out in the street, the only figure that had moved there for hours. She knew it was him, his form now as familiar as her own shadow. Goro was moving with haste, head down and purposeful. She crept across the roof as he entered the hostelry, the thud of the door intrusive on the quiet. Just along from the room he shared with his companion a dilapidated balcony sagged from the adjacent building. A scrawny black cat would sometimes lie there, stretched out in the sun. Amelot, slipping down there one afternoon to stroke its warm belly, had discovered that by climbing over the edge of the balcony, one hand holding the rotting rail, the other gripping a protruding beam, she could peer in through a gap in the faded drapes of the window.

Inside, the room was a dance of shadows, a lantern burning on the table and a nightlight flickering by the bed where the monsignore slept. Goro's sleeping place was a pallet, too small for his large frame, close to the door. The monsignore was up, sitting in the circle of light at the table, which was strewn with papers, some attached with seals. His black hair, salted white, hung in his eyes as he pored over them. He was in his nightshirt, rather than the neat scarlet and black robes he wore during the day, but his ornate cross was, as ever, around his neck, the green jewels glowing in the lantern light.

He looked up suddenly, his face sharp in profile. Amelot followed his gaze to the door, which opened. Goro entered, pushing back his hood. The monsignore rose, his voice, coming muted through the glass, abrupt with question. Goro spoke, his own tone stiff with suppressed emotion, which, after watching him stalk about the room, fingering his mask, Amelot realised was rage.

The monsignore cut across him, his voice a blade, laced with scorn.

'*Carlo!*' she heard Goro bellow in return, followed by an incoherent tirade. He raised his clenched hands, which he then opened in an imploring gesture. 'Monsignore!'

The two men were both shouting now, throwing their words at one another, so loud surely those in the rooms around them would soon awaken. In the torrent, Amelot caught a name that almost made her lose her grip.

James Wynter.

It was Goro who roared it, his hands balling into fists again. He shouted something about the Palazzo Medici, then something about guards. An arrest?

Amelot tightened her hold on the beam as the monsignore shook his head, unmoved by Goro's angst. The man was turning back to the papers on the table, muttering to himself, when Goro lunged, swinging a balled fist into his side.

The monsignore staggered away, his face a mask of surprise and pain, but before he had time to react, Goro was punching out again, this time connecting with his jaw. The man's head snapped back, but rather than let him fall, Goro grabbed him by his hair and, with a howl of pure rage, slammed his head down on the desk. He continued to roar as he did this again, and again.

The skin of the monsignore's forehead split open. His nose broke. Then, his front teeth, crunching loose as his face struck the wood again, spattering the papers with blood and spit. He had screamed at the first strike. Now, he was just making a high, keening noise. Still, Goro continued to smash his head down, until the monsignore's face was a shattered vase of skin and blood and bone.

Weak with horror, Amelot pulled herself back on to the balcony and dropped over the rail, crouching against the wall as the sickening thuds continued. She felt each one resonate through her, shooting her back to another time and place, as the monsters who had come out of the darkness around her family's camp set upon her father and the other men of the troupe. The shrieks and cries. The screams of the women that had continued long after the men were silenced. Screams that, for her, had gone on longer still, until there was no more screaming to be done. As the thuds went on, joined by shutters banging open, voices calling in alarm, Amelot squeezed her eyes shut and pressed her hands over her ears.

Jack tried the door again, even though he knew it wouldn't open. Finally, he kicked it and turned away. He paced the few steps to the back of the storeroom, which was lined with shelves. He'd scoured them when Rigo first locked him in here, but had found only folded napkins and towels, bed covers and lambswool blankets; nothing he could use to try to prise open the door or fiddle the lock.

The only light came from under the door. Earlier, as it had grown stronger, illuminating the shelves, the passage outside had filled with noise: the chatter of servants, the stomp of boots, the squeak of wheels and the rumble of things passing; chests, he guessed, being taken to the wagons. He had shouted and banged on the door, but no one had let him out. After a time, the noises had faded, until the only sounds were his own breaths. Eventually, the light had begun to dim as evening came on. Now, it was almost pitch black, just a feeble shimmer that told him a candle was burning somewhere down the hall.

Jack knew that, along with the betrothal festivities in Rome, Clarice de' Medici planned to visit her family estates near the city, which meant he could be held here for weeks. Would they even think to feed him? He had shouted at Rigo and the other guards that he was a knight – that they could not do this to him – but whatever anyone else thought of his treatment, Lorenzo knew the truth. Knew it meant nothing to lock up some ignoble bastard in a cupboard for as long as he pleased.

His mind tormented him with the story he'd once heard Piero tell Giovanni, of the servant who'd been shut in here and forgotten, and visions of the dark-skinned man held in chains all these months at Lorenzo's pleasure. But mostly, he was haunted by two questions: who had told Lorenzo of Franco Martelli's treachery and, presumably, his own knowledge of it? And what would become of Laora, now waiting for him to return? The first had provoked an uneasy answer, for the only people he'd told about his suspicions of Martelli were his own men and, the more he thought on it, the more he felt certain he'd been betrayed.

His breaths quickened with his rising agitation. He couldn't be shut up in here much longer. For weeks? He'd go mad. He lunged at the door, hammering his fists on it. 'God damn it, Rigo! *Let me out!*' Jack kept on pounding, assaulting the quiet. He'd wake the whole damn palace staff – what was left of it.

After a time, his voice hoarse, fists bruised, he saw a disturbance in the amber gleam coming through the door, the shadow of feet blocking the light. Jack heard the metal jitter of keys in the lock. He stepped back, but kept his hands balled into fists. He'd fight his way out if he had to. There were more rattles in the lock, as if the person were trying different keys. Finally, a resolute clunk. The door opened and he sprang out. A wide-eyed, whip-thin figure in a ratty tunic staggered back from his fists.

'Amelot!'

In one hand the girl gripped a ring of keys. In the other, a crumpled roll of paper.

'Where did you get those? How did you know I was here?'

She nodded to the door.

Jack, touching his sore fist, shook his head. Of all the people he'd thought he'd summon by his din? 'Where have you been?' This was a pointless question right now. 'Never mind. Are the guards nearby? Did they see you enter? Good,' Jack murmured, at the shake of her head.

She thrust the roll of paper towards him. In the shadows, she looked as feral as when he'd found her in Paris, her face streaked with dirt, brown hair hanging in her eyes; two large, troubled orbs. Where the hell had she been all these weeks?

'Come, we must go.' The palazzo was silent, but Jack feared his banging would have surely disturbed others.

Amelot stood her ground, still holding out the paper. Murmuring a curse, Jack took it. Unfurling it, he saw it was a drawing – a large square, with many smaller boxes and tracks of lines within it. There was some dark substance spattered across the paper. Ink? Several of the boxes had writing in them, but only a few of the letters were visible through the stains. He held it close, struggling to see in the shadows.

Madd . . .

. . . anni.

Pi . . . o

. . . enzo

Names, he realised, as he followed the boxes that marched around the square. *Maddalena. Giovanni. Piero. Lorenzo.* He was looking at a plan of the first floor of the Palazzo Medici. There were the children's rooms, the dining room and Lorenzo's private suites: grand hall, bedchamber, study. And there, mostly clear of spatters, the hidden room, with a cross marked upon it. 'Where did you get this?'

In answer she raised her hand, placed it over one half of her face.

Jack shook his head, not understanding. He went to question her, then stiffened, hearing the creak of the stairs that led up to the upper storeys. The sound surprised him. There shouldn't be anyone on the floors above, not with most of Lorenzo's household gone. A patrolling guard perhaps? If he knew the direction the footsteps were taking, he could decide which way they might slip out unnoticed. Holding his hand up to halt Amelot, Jack stole down the passage and peered around the corner.

There, away down the corridor, five – no six – men, were descending the stairs. Their voices were hushed, but in the grave-deep silence of the palace, Jack could just make them out. The men were speaking a different dialect to Tuscan, but many of the words were familiar enough for him to understand. In the dark folds of their cloaks, he caught the gleam of weapons.

'Which way?'

'We should have waited for Battista. He had the map!'

'We waited long enough. We'll split up, try each room until . . .'

Jack didn't catch the last words, but he didn't need to. It was clear what they had come for; Lorenzo summoned to Rome, the palazzo emptied, the plan in his hands, the hidden room marked. He sensed the connections, but there was scant time for thought. Slipping back to where Amelot was waiting, Jack grabbed her hand and pulled the startled girl down the passage towards the *Sala Grande*. As they passed the candle, guttering in a sconce on the wall, he saw the spatters across the map of the palace were not ink, but blood.

They ran the length of the grand hall, Amelot light as a feather on her feet, his own footsteps echoing painfully. The bedchamber was locked, but one of the keys on the ring opened it. Frail moonlight bled through the shutters, casting the chamber in grey twilight, blocky shapes of furniture and the unsettling figures of statues looming all around. Jack reached the study door. The keys jingled in his fumbling fingers. None of them worked. Laora's voice echoed in his mind.

Papi kept the key in the same place he always had. Under his pillow.

Thrusting the keys and map at Amelot, Jack darted for the steps of the mezzanine. He bit back a grunt of pain as he cracked his hip on the daybed and hastened up the steep stairs. Feeling around in the dark, bumping into chests, fur-lined cloaks wisping across his face, Jack found Papi's bed more by memory than sight. He shoved a hand under the pillow, slid it around; breathed a prayer for the old man as his fingers found metal.

As the key turned in the study's lock, the door groaned open into black. Not pausing to allow his eyes to become accustomed to the new depth of gloom, Jack entered, hands out before him. Sliding around the first desk, he headed for the wall where he knew the curtain was. As his fingers grasped hold of the thick silk, he tugged it back. He felt for the bolts, snapped them across. The door, heavy, reinforced, opened inwards.

The chamber beyond was lit by a candle burning on the table, illuminating a pile of books and the remains of a meal. Jack wondered who Lorenzo had left in charge of the prisoner's care. Bertoldo? The light gilded the room, bright to his eyes. He fixed on the large bed, where a figure lay swaddled in blankets. He approached cautiously, heading round to wake the sleeper. He was moving in, bending over the prone form, when a hand shot up and grabbed him by the throat.

'Release me,' came a hiss of Tuscan. 'Or I'll snap your neck!'

Jack, choking at the tightness of the man's grip, dug his fingers into the prisoner's wrist, where he'd glimpsed that knotted scar. The man cried out in pain and relinquished his hold, enough for Jack to pull himself free. 'Men are coming for you. Wait for them, or come with me.'

There was a brief pause as the man weighed his options. He sat up, swinging his legs over the bed. His dark eyes smouldered like coals in the candlelight. 'My bonds,' he said, picking up the chain, attached to a manacle around his ankle.

'The key?'

The prisoner shook his head.

'*Damn it!*' Jack had forgotten about the chain. He followed it to the wall, where it joined a thick ring on an iron plate. He pulled at it.

'I have tried many times,' said the man, behind him. 'It will not yield.'

'With two of us it might.' Jack sat on the floor, wedging his feet against the wall, either side of the iron ring. He took the chain in both hands.

The prisoner stood behind him, taking up the slack. Together, they heaved. Jack wrenched on it until his muscles were screaming. But the ring and the plate remained fixed. He glanced up at the prisoner, both of them staring at one another; strangers, united in frustration.

The prisoner whipped round as a figure darted into the chamber.

'It's all right,' Jack assured him, eyes on Amelot, who was brandishing something.

Ignoring them, she ducked down at the prisoner's feet. As the object she held caught the candlelight, Jack realised it was a stiletto dagger, the blade long and thin enough to pierce mail and the gaps in plate armour. He guessed she'd found it in Lorenzo's study. Amelot inched the point into the lock on the manacle, both men watching her as she twisted it this way and that, face taut with concentration. After a few moments, there was a solid click. The manacle fell open. Beyond, in the hall, came a whisper of voices and footsteps padding closer.

'There!'

At the murmur from one of his men, Orhan looked up. His dark eyes picked out three figures moving across the roof of the building adjacent to the palazzo; ghosts in the moonlight.

Ordering two of his men to keep watch on the main entrance, Orhan gestured the other three to follow. Emerging from the alley, he led them down the deserted street. A rat scuttled across their path as they moved in silence. Orhan didn't take his eyes off the roof. As the figures disappeared over the ridge, he ducked down an alley between the buildings, drawing his blade as he went.

On the other side, he was rewarded with the sight of the three, making their way slowly down a building, using window ledges as hand- and footholds. The one descending first, sure and nimble, was a skinny youth. The next was a tall, well-built man with long dark hair, who wore only a nightshirt, his bare feet slipping and scrabbling at the stone. The last, also tall and athletic of build, with cropped dark hair, had a bag slung over his shoulder and seemed an incongruous contrast to the other two in his silk doublet and hose.

'It isn't them?' murmured one of his companions in confusion, as Orhan motioned them into the mouth of an alley close to where the figures were descending.

'No,' agreed Orhan. 'Not Innocent's men.' His eyes lingered on the one in the nightshirt, who jumped the last few feet and stood back for the third man.

Voices sounded, somewhere close. Orhan turned to see firelight on the buildings further along the street, shadows of men looming across the façades. Guards, he guessed. They had seen many patrols on their way through the city, following the pope's men to the palazzo. As he looked back, he saw the third man drop to the ground. The one in the nightshirt now turned in the direction of the approaching guards. Even in the shadows, Orhan knew his face.

'By Allah's grace,' he whispered.

'It's him!' breathed one of his companions, reaching for the crossbow that was slung across his back.

'No,' Orhan said, halting his hand and glancing at the watchmen, coming closer. 'Not here. Get the others.'

31

After talking his way past the bleary-eyed innkeeper, Jack led them up to the top floor of the Fig. As he banged on the door, there was a volley of barks beyond.

'Get gone!' came a rough shout.

'It's me, Valentine.'

The door opened and the gunner's slab of a face appeared. 'It's the devil's hour!' Valentine took in Amelot and the stranger beyond, dressed in only a nightshirt. He stood aside, allowing Jack to enter, eyes narrowing on the dark-skinned man. 'Who's this?'

Jack didn't answer. Around the gloomy chamber, lit by tallow candles sputtering on the table, the others were stirring: David and Adam sitting up on their pallet, Ned rising, clicking his tongue to hush Titan's barks.

As Valentine closed the door, Jack took his bag from his shoulder and slung it on Ned's bed. It was filled with a few items of clothing, the wolf badge and his father's Book of Hours, snatched from his room in the flight from the palazzo, following Amelot out from the terrace and across the rooftops, then a perilous climb down. 'Who told him?'

'Jack—' Ned began.

'Which of you told Lorenzo I suspected Franco Martelli?' Jack cut across him, scanning them in turn. For a moment, none of them reacted and he faltered, wondering if he was wrong. Then, a voice broke the silence.

'I did.'

All eyes turned to Adam, who stood facing Jack. His shirt and hose were crumpled and his grey hair hung lank around his face, still marked from their fight: a red scar across his forehead, a kink in his nose, two teeth gone and a third chipped in half. But despite his dishevelled appearance, his blue eyes were clear, and he met Jack's gaze without compunction.

'Brother?' David gripped Adam's shoulder when the man didn't answer. 'You did this?'

'He lied to us,' said Adam, eyes not leaving Jack's. 'You told us you tried to speak to Lorenzo, said he wouldn't see you. But you never even went to him, did you? He knew nothing of it when I spoke to him.'

'I wanted to make sure I was right in my suspicion,' Jack replied, voice low with anger. 'Wanted to be certain Martelli was the spy. And good that I waited – since I don't believe he was.' Feeling a pull on his sleeve, he saw Amelot had moved in beside him and was staring intently at him, but Adam was speaking again.

'What makes you so sure? Let me guess – his daughter told you?' Adam shook his head when Jack didn't answer. 'And you believed her?'

'Jack, what in Christ's name is going on?' Ned questioned, stepping in. His eyes went to the stranger, standing between Valentine and the door, watching the exchange in silence, Titan sniffing curiously around his bare feet. 'And who is he?'

'Why did you do it, brother?' David asked Adam before Jack could answer. 'If Lorenzo knows Jack kept his suspicions about Martelli from him, surely none of us will now see that reward?'

Adam crouched and pulled out a bag from beneath his pallet. 'We already have.'

'He paid you for your betrayal?' murmured Jack.

'Fifty florins,' Adam retorted. 'Enough to see us to Venice. More than enough, with the weapons we've bought, to join the company as we planned. I was going to tell you,' he added to Ned and Valentine, who had both turned to him.

'When?' asked Ned.

'Fifty florins?' Jack gave a rough laugh. 'I've drunk wine from goblets worth more! Enough to get to Venice? Lorenzo promised us enough for *life*! If only you'd waited. Let me finish what I started.' Jack felt Amelot tug his sleeve again, but he shrugged her off. 'Lorenzo used you. Took you for a fool!'

'As he's been using you? Or as you've been using us?' Adam's voice rose. 'You God damn near killed me, you son of a bitch!'

'I wouldn't have had to if you'd stayed down!' Jack felt anger swell, a beast awakening. 'What was it, Adam? Pride? Couldn't bear to be beaten by your master's son?'

'You mean his *bastard*.'

Rage took Jack full in its red jaws. He lunged at Adam, standing there remorseless.

He was grabbed by Ned, the larger man halting his strike. '*Damn it, Jack!*'

'No, Ned, let him come,' Adam growled, fists clenched.

Titan was barking madly, jumping in distress around Ned and Jack as they wrestled, knocking into the table, which screeched across the floor, the candles almost flickering out. David was shouting, hands planted on Adam's chest. Suddenly, a scream tore across them; a ragged, piercing sound that stopped them all in their tracks.

Jack, gripping hold of Ned, turned to see Amelot, her mouth still stretched open, but now in silence. Her eyes were wide, as if she were as surprised as the rest of them at the sound she had made. She focused, her gaze meeting Jack's. Slowly, she raised her hand, pressed her palm over half her face, just as she had done in the palazzo. Only, now, Jack felt something go through him at the gesture: a cold, creeping chill. He had seen that gesture before tonight. Amaury had made it, imitating Amelot's description of the masked man.

In his mind, Jack saw his mother's murderer, towering over him as he lay sprawled on the floor of the Ferryman's Arms, that white mask covering half his face. 'The pope's man?' he murmured, dropping his hold on Ned, all thoughts of avenging himself on Adam gone. 'The one who was after the map? He is here?'

Taking her hand from her face, Amelot raised her arm, finger pointing towards him. *You*, it said. *He's come for you.*

'Jack?' questioned Ned, eyes flicking between him and Amelot.

'The man who killed my mother. The one who attacked us in Southwark.' Jack turned again to Amelot before Ned could respond. 'Do you know where he is?' When she nodded, he reached under Ned's pallet, fingers snagging hold of the rags he'd bound his father's sword in. Jack drew it from the scabbard Grace had given him. 'Show me.'

'I'll go with you,' Ned said quickly.

'No,' answered Jack, eyes on Adam. He went to Ned, clasped his shoulder. 'I need you to guard him,' he murmured, nodding to the prisoner. 'Make sure he stays here. That no one sees him.' The stranger, who had tensed during the argument, seemed more alert now, dark eyes straying to the door where Valentine still stood. He had come willingly from his prison in the palace, but Jack doubted he would agree to stay locked in another for long. He lowered his voice further. 'There's a chance I can salvage our deal with Lorenzo. Make this right.'

Outside, the night air cooled his face. As Amelot led the way down the alley, Jack followed, gripping his father's sword. The *mercato* opened suddenly before them, its emptiness eerie. Atop the pillar in the centre, Abundance was an ashen goddess in the moon, arm thrust aloft, still broken at the wrist. Jack thought of the trembling earth and crumbling stones, Laora's hand tight in his. But as they passed out of the moon-washed square and plunged once more into darkness, all thoughts of her – of anything other than his enemy – vanished. There was room only for vengeance; a single heartbeat pounding inside him.

They heard the noise first. Then, turning a corner near the Ospedale degli Innocenti, they were confronted with scores of people milling in the street, many dressed in nightclothes. Torches had turned night to blazing day and in among the sleep-dazed citizens Jack saw the city watch, tunics decorated with symbols of the *gonfaloni*. Amelot pointed to a tall building, around which most of the watchmen were gathered. In their midst was a cart, something stretched out upon it. Stepping through the throng, Jack saw it was a body.

Ned glanced again at the man, seated on the edge of the pallet. So far he'd remained silent, except to politely decline a cup of wine. The stranger had not made any move to leave, but while pulling a tunic on over his undershirt and hose, Ned had surreptitiously slipped a dagger into his belt, now hidden in the small of his back.

Valentine was sitting on a stool by the table, brow puckered, fingers tapping on the wood. Adam and David were by the window, speaking in heated tones. David was demanding why his brother had gone behind their backs, Adam was angrily justifying himself. Ned's gaze flicked to the door. He shouldn't have let Jack go alone. He remembered well the man in the mask – still had the scar where the brute had stabbed him.

'Where you from?' Valentine spoke roughly in the silence. 'Spain?'

The stranger met his gaze, but didn't answer.

'Can't speak English, no?'

Titan, curled on Ned's pallet, lifted his head from his paws. Jumping down, the dog trotted to the door, paws clicking on the boards. He stood facing it, nose pointing forward.

'Jack not tell you who he is, Ned?'

'Valentine . . .'

'I'm just . . .' The gunner trailed off, seeing Ned fixed on Titan. A low growl was coming from the little dog, the fur on his back starting to stiffen and bristle. Valentine rose slowly.

Ned reached under his tunic, fingers brushing the cold steel of the dagger. Adam paused in his argument with David, seeing the two men rising to face the door.

'Is that him back?' Adam was striding across the room before any of them could react. 'We'll settle this now, God damn it.'

'*Adam!*'

Not heeding Ned's shout, Adam grasped the door and opened it.

For a moment, nothing happened. Darkness filled the passage beyond. Titan's growling was the only sound. Then, there was a sharp *click*, followed by a rush of disturbed air.

The crossbow bolt buried itself in Adam's chest, throwing him off his feet. He landed on one of the stools, which shattered beneath him. David roared and dived towards his brother, as Ned threw himself at the door. He crashed against it, shouldering it shut and shoving the bolt across, as another quarrel punched through the wood, the barb emerging inches from his face. '*Help me!*' he shouted, reeling away to grab hold of his pallet. Valentine, seeing what he was doing, moved to aid him.

Together, they hauled the block of wood, with its straw mattress, to wedge it against the door. It wouldn't keep anyone out for long, but it would slow them. David was on his knees by his brother, shouting into his upturned face. The bolt, protruding just above Adam's sternum, had gone in deep. Blood was blooming on his shirt. More trailed in a line from the corner of his mouth, which was opening and closing, a wet gurgling coming from his throat.

The stranger, who had leapt to his feet, was staring at the weapons and armour that had been hidden beneath the pallet, now revealed. At a shout from the passage, his head snapped up.

Ned wasn't sure what had been said. It sounded like *gem*. More shouts followed, a stream of words he didn't recognise, the language fast and harsh. The stranger, however, clearly did understand, his dark eyes narrowing in recognition. 'They've come to take you?' Ned questioned, striding to the weapons and snatching up his sword. He brandished it at the stranger.

'No. To kill me.'

'Valentine!' Ned began, turning. But the gunner was already going for his arquebus.

Snatching up the gun, Valentine upended his sack, the apostles of powder tumbling out on the floor, along with a pouch of shot, a ramrod and tufts of wadding. There was a rattle as someone tried the door, then a determined thudding as the men beyond attempted to shoulder it open.

'David! Your bow!'

But David wasn't listening, still holding his brother, shouting for him to get up.

'Let me go to them,' said the stranger to Ned. 'See to your friend.'

Ned shook his head, Jack's words in his mind. 'We stay together.' The thudding on the door was louder, the bolt rattling in its fixings. 'Down!' he yelled, racing to Adam and grasping the man's shirt in his free hand, dragging him back, as Valentine pushed over the table, bowls and candles falling. David, coming to his senses, scrabbled back, helping Ned pull his brother behind the table. As the stranger ducked down with them, Ned saw he had taken up one of their swords.

Valentine was stuffing shot and wadding into the barrel of the gun. 'Fuse, Ned!'

Snatching up a trailing length of hemp, Ned held it to one of the fallen candles, the wick still alight, fluttering in a pool of molten wax. The brutal banging of the door filled the room. As the fuse smouldered to life, Valentine opened an apostle with his teeth and shook the powder into the barrel and the priming pan, some trickling over his hand and on to the floor in his haste.

'*Titan!*'

The little dog, cowering under the remaining pallet, scrabbled out at Ned's shout to leap into his arms, then the door heaved open, the wedged pallet falling with a crash.

For a moment, the only sounds were the faint trickle of falling powder and Adam's wet breaths. Then, they heard footsteps and a heavy scrape as someone shoved aside the pallet and mattress. Valentine grasped the stock of the gun, *God's Messenger* carved into the pitted wood, the fuse gripped in his fist; no time for him to fix it in the jaws of the serpentine.

'*Jesus!*' hissed Ned, stuffing Titan, struggling, into his shirt with one hand and trying to hunch his shoulders up around his ears, as the gunner sucked in a breath and turned, aiming the barrel over the edge of the upturned table.

There was a warning shout from one of the men who had entered. Valentine set the lit fuse to the priming pan and the powder burst into life. Sparks exploded across his fingers and into the hole in the barrel, igniting the powder within, the shot launched with a flashing hiss and an ear-blasting bang. Valentine, on his knees, rocked back with a grunt, the stock jamming into his shoulder. The shot struck one of the men in the doorway full in the chest. He flew back in a burst of red, knocking one of his companions off his feet.

Valentine was already stuffing more shot into the barrel, but the men were in the room now and even with the ringing in his ears, Ned heard the rasp of swords being drawn. Then, he was pushing himself up, no time to think, roaring as he went, barrelling through the blue haze of smoke, sulphur stinging his eyes as he swung at the first comer: a short, wiry man with a dark beard and fierce black eyes. The man ducked his strike, then thrust in, hard and fast, Ned only just managing to batter the blade away. He switched back with a cutting sweep to the man's side, which was neatly blocked, the man gritting his teeth, yellow against his ruddy skin, as he lunged for another jab.

Out of the corner of his eye, Ned saw the stranger had been set upon by three of the men. He flicked expertly out with the sword, slashing one across the cheek, sending him reeling away, then clashed with another, their blades locking. The third lunged in, sword raised. Ned, smacking away another of the wiry man's vicious strikes, yelled a warning.

Something punched into the third attacker's back, sending him staggering forward, sword clattering from his fingers. David had risen behind the table, crossbow in his hands, face pale in the guttering light of the remaining candles, his fingers already slipping another quarrel into place. Valentine was with him, aiming his gun at another man who staggered in through the door, spattered with the blood of his fallen comrade. The arquebus exploded in another vicious flash, the bang resounding around the room. The man entering was spun by the impact, half his face shattered away.

Ned saw the stranger stamping and thrusting now with only one opponent, focused and skilled. The fight seemed personal, the fire of rage in both their faces. Distant shouts sounded, footsteps pounding on the floors below. People waking, alerted by the sounds, or more men come for the stranger? Titan, still stuffed in his shirt, scrabbled at his chest, claws raking his skin. It distracted Ned enough for his opponent to step in and stab him in the thigh. As he stumbled, the man caught Ned's blade with his cross-guard and twisted it out of his hand.

Ned collapsed to one knee, pain screaming through his leg, blood pulsing from the wound. Titan's barks filled his ears, the dog desperately trying to get free. The man cried out in triumph as he leapt forward. Ned reached round to his back, wrenched free the dagger stuffed in his belt and jammed it in the man's groin. He freed it with a savage twist that felled the man instantly. He went down mewling, blood spurting from the severed artery.

Ned, sagged on his knees, saw the flame of one of the fallen candles gust across the powder-speckled floor around Valentine's feet, where the man had dropped another apostle to reload. He yelled a warning. Too late. The powder flared to life at the kiss of flame and flashed into the half-full apostle, which erupted in a chest-shuddering bang, sending the table, and Valentine, flying. Ned just had time to see more sparks hissing across the floor, following the scattered lines of powder to where the other apostles lay in a heap.

'*Oh, Mother Mary*,' he breathed, as the explosion ripped the room apart.

The corpse was not that of his enemy; that much was apparent in the dimensions of his body. Jack, forcing his way through the onlookers, had glimpsed a man in a blood-soaked nightshirt lying on a litter, face smashed beyond all recognition. Amelot had pointed to the hostelry around which the crowd was clustered, telling Jack that was where she had seen the masked man, but with the city watch guarding the entrance, he'd not been able to get inside.

His enemy had been there, though, that much he'd discovered from one of the onlookers. An elderly man, shivering in his nightclothes as the guards questioned witnesses, had spoken of a monster in a mask, fleeing the building, covered in blood. The same monster, it was believed, had terrorised the city these past months. Jack had been stunned by the words. Had his mother's murderer been here all this time? Under the same sky? Breathing the same air?

With no sign of his enemy and the guards urging people inside their homes, Jack had been forced to turn back. Vengeance, unsated, was sour in him, bitter as bad wine. But, as he neared the Fig, Amelot struggling to keep up with his furious stride, all thoughts of his long-dreamed revenge were swept aside.

They saw the glow around the tavern several streets away – the livid pulse of a large fire. Jack broke into a run, Amelot at his side. Turning down the street they were greeted with the sight of flames streaking from the inn's upper storey. Part of the top floor was completely gone; a jagged hole where the wall had been, smoke billowing from it. Below, the street was littered with rubble and charred pieces of timber. Screams echoed above the snap and crackle of flames, some people dashing from the door, others running in, carrying buckets of water and sand – goaded by the innkeeper, shouting, red-faced, in the heart of the chaos. A bell was clanging an alarm. Other people spilled from nearby buildings, some to help, others to stand and gawp.

Jack entered the confusion, searching frantically for Ned and the others. Hearing a dog barking, he elbowed his way through the tumult, in the direction of the sound. There, bent double, hacking dryly as Titan barked at his feet, was Ned. The large man was in a state. Half his shirt had been blasted from his body, the rest, blackened and torn, hung in flapping rags on his torso. His hose were soaked with blood and his thatch of brown hair had been burned away on one side, his scalp and face blistered.

The man started as Jack grasped him. His dazed eyes focused. 'Jack!' His voice came out as a hoarse shout.

'What happened? Where are the others?' Even as he asked the question, Jack saw Valentine sitting on the floor, his arquebus lying beside him. The gunner was less bloody, but just as singed, wiggling a finger deep in his ear and turning to spit out a plug of black phlegm. Jack could smell the sulphur on him. Glancing up at the blasted hole in the tavern, he knew only gunpowder could have done such damage. 'Ned, what in hell . . .?' He trailed off as the crowds parted and he saw two men on the ground close by. One was on his back, the crossbow bolt sticking out of him an obscene exclamation. Adam. The other, crouched over him, face and arms scorched by fire, was David.

The younger man was weeping, clutching at his brother's clothes, trying in vain to force life from his corpse.

'They came for him.'

Jack turned at the croak, to see Ned's eyes on a figure who was watching David's anguish in silence. What was left of the prisoner's nightshirt was soaked in blood. More slimed the blade in his hand. Jack crossed to the man. 'Who were they?' he demanded, turning the prisoner to face him. 'Who came for you?'

'Assassins,' the man answered, after a pause. 'Sent by my brother.'

'Your brother? Who are you, God damn it?'

The prisoner met his gaze, his eyes full of flames. 'I am Prince Djem, son of Sultan Mehmet, whom your people called the Conqueror. Half-brother to Bayezid, the pretender. And rightful heir to the throne of the empire.'

Goro stood on the fringes of the crowd outside the burning tavern, the flush of fire warming his face. The chaos was like a dance, people weaving in and out of one another, their screams and cries the music.

He had followed James Wynter and the girl from the hostelry, where he'd been hiding, watching the guards carrying out the monsignore's broken body. While the first sighting of the man who killed Carlo di Fante had been a shock, the second had been a prayer answered. Now, at last, he would put his master's soul to rest. The stiletto dagger, gripped in his fist, would be his benediction; a gift from the man whose life Wynter had taken in that Southwark alley.

In killing the monsignore – who so callously refused his request to take Wynter for himself when they entered the palazzo – Goro had ended his tenure as the pope's interrogator. But he cared not. The death of Battista di Salvi had liberated him; those words, so many barbs in his soul, plucked free. He didn't need the pope, nor anyone else. With the realisation he had felt a soaring sense of release, as though he were being pulled anew from Sforza's dungeon. Once he killed Wynter and avenged Carlo, he knew he would truly be free.

A harsh cry jolted him from his focus on Wynter, now crouched beside a dead man. Goro realised an elderly woman was pointing at him. There was something in her face – fear, yes – but something else too. Recognition? Other eyes turned in his direction at her frantic gestures and more shouts sounded. The monsignore had been the expert in the Tuscan tongue, but Goro caught a few words he recognised. Among them, *blood.* Glancing down, he realised his cloak was open, revealing his tunic, still spattered red from Battista's broken skull.

Several watchmen, drawn to the burning tavern by the clanging of the bell, cast their attention towards him at the cries. Goro turned away, but found his path blocked by more, moving in behind him, drawing swords. All around him suddenly, people were pushing, pointing, shouting. He spun, looking for escape, but all he could see were a whirl of snarling faces. A hundred masks of hatred.

32

The Spanish advanced on Málaga, through a burned and blistered landscape. The Moors had set fire to farmsteads and villages on the outskirts of their city, so the Christians would find nothing to sustain them. The inhabitants fled, bearing what they could carry, leading children and animals inside the walls. Smoke shrouded the sky, smouldering from blackened grain fields, on the borders of which orchards of citrus were withered by flame, blossom burning like paper, scattering on the wind.

Eyes stinging, throats parched in the rising heat of the days – the sea a blue temptation to their left, speckled with the white sails of the fleet of Spanish ships blockading the coast – the army moved in bristling columns, mules struggling to haul the gun carts up punishing hills and into sudden valleys, the land near the eastern walls as crumpled as cloth, rising into craggy mountains at their backs.

Banners were raised above the king and his royal guards, the companies of dukes and counts, hidalgos and caballeros, warriors of the Holy Brotherhood, farmers and criminals; all moving as if a single host – the very body of Spain – ready to flex steel sinews and iron muscles, ready to smash the stone might of the enemy.

The Christians were the first to gain a bloody victory, the vanguard under the Marquis of Cádiz taking the ground beyond the eastern walls in a fierce skirmish against the Muslim garrison who sallied down from the heights of the Gibralfaro that soared above the city on its invincible rock. Forced back behind their defences after a day of intense fighting, the Moors watched from their towers as on this claimed ground the Christians built an enormous timber fortress – big enough to house a battery of artillery and sixteen thousand men

– augmented by defensive palisades and ditches. Protected by these barriers, the Spanish spread out around the walls, until it seemed as if all of Málaga was surrounded by a living moat of flesh.

On rocky hills the leaders of the companies set their flags and erected tents, digging more trenches and raising barriers, buttressed with packed earth for the protection of the siege engines and gun platforms the engineers and carpenters set about building. The Moors, visible in the day by their turbans and at night by their watch-fires, were not idle in this time, firing a constant barrage from the walls. Wherever defences were weak missiles found targets: stones flung from engines exploding through barricades, half-built siege towers struck ablaze by flaming arrows, men pierced with bolts sent plunging into the ditches, others ripped to red ribbons by cannon fire.

Soon, King Ferdinand ordered work to be undertaken at night and men toiled and sweated through the sultry dark, fingers fumbling with ropes, feet stumbling on ground littered with rocks and mangled limbs of fallen comrades, stinking and swarmed with flies. There was a grim sense of determination when the Christians were at last ready to answer the Moors with the roar of their own guns.

At a blast of trumpets, the first barrage was launched, the earth shuddering with the tremendous power of bombards and mortars. Smoke and flame erupted in thunder all around the trenches, as if the earth had split open and hell itself had come belching up through the fissure. Shot smashed into towers and through walkways, striking houses and the minarets of mosques. Men were dragged, screaming, from crumbling platforms, cheers resounding from the Christian camps wherever the enemy fell or a breach was made. But these walls, raised in the Moors' first conquest of Spain, had stood for eight hundred years and the Spanish guns were, to their stone might, the bites of ants to a lion.

Day after day, the bombardment continued. Every evening, the artillery falling silent under scarlet skies veiled with dust and smoke, the Muslims' prayers sang out from their towers to compete with Christian psalms. Every morning, the onslaught began again, missiles hurled at the defences, fiery barrels of pitch launched from siege engines exploding across rooftops, palms and pomegranate trees burning.

The Moors' war machines kept up their own continuous assault, catapults firing javelins into the seething masses, skewering men, arrows picking off the unwary. One morning, soon after the Christians launched their daily attack, enemy engineers managed, by luck or skill, to shoot a flaming barrel of naptha into a gunpowder cart near one of the main Spanish positions. Shouts of alarm sounded as the barrel struck and men rushed to try to remove it, but in the thunder of the guns only a few heard the warnings. The explosion ripped through the Spanish lines, blasting men into bloody mist, tearing through animals, wagons and tents, leaving behind a smoking crater of broken rock, splintered timbers and shredded bodies.

Still, the Christians continued, pounding at the walls, day after shattering day. Spring was marching on and the sun baked down. Sweat, blood, smoke and dirt turned men's skin dark; beards and hair grew long and lice festered in mud-crusted blankets and clothes, the foetid soup of latrines reeking in the heat. Men and women slipped in from nearby villages, looking to sell the enemy their wares; fruit for the eating, herbs for healing, a warm mouth to satisfy. But, when rumour spread of a plague swelling in some of these settlements, the soldiers became fearful. The desertions began, most of them peasants and townsmen with little to gain by staying, trickling away in the dark.

King Ferdinand grew troubled. The city walls, although pitted and scarred, stood fast against him. He was still tied in an uneasy peace with Boabdil in Granada, but there were reports that the emir's uncle, Muhammad al-Zagal, was raising a force to tackle him from the rear. His army was being supplied by sea, but although food was plentiful, the black powder was not and the assaults were growing shorter. When Queen Isabella, in Córdoba, heard of his perilous position she begged him to raise the siege and retreat, but, in turn, he implored her to come; let her grace breathe new life into his flagging forces. And so, on the dusty winds of early summer, Isabella came, with her train of prelates and royal guards, servants and ladies-in-waiting.

The men of the Spanish forces were so overcome by the sight of their queen, walking through their midst on the front line of battle, pausing to speak to the captains about the siege and to comfort the wounded, her red hair flaming in the sun, that when they returned to the assault – the queen, her ladies and priests clasping hands over their ears at the shuddering din of the guns – it was as if it were the first day again.

A few days into her visit, the queen, noting the danger in the dwindling supplies of powder, sent emissaries to the gates of Málaga to offer terms for surrender and a threat if these were not accepted. The Moorish garrison, led by an experienced commander and supported by soldiers from towns and fortresses that had fallen to the Spanish, refused. But, while the Christians were troubled by the enemy's defiance, the citizens of Málaga were themselves not without worry.

Some inhabitants, escaping the beleaguered city to throw themselves on the mercy of the Spanish, told of the worsening situation within the walls. What the Christians lacked in gunpowder, the Moors lacked in provisions. Rations were so low that people, forced to kill horses and dogs for food, were now eating leaves and hides cooked over fires. Flies and rats were said to be growing fat on the corpses that littered the streets, while the living starved.

As the siege ground on and the old and young and sick succumbed to ravishing hunger, more citizens began to quail, begging their captains to accept the Christians' terms. Faced with the brutal choice of slow starvation or enslavement, the inhabitants chose the latter. And so it was that Málaga, one of the biggest and brightest jewels of the Nasrid Kingdom of Granada, surrendered to the Christian king and queen.

Harry Vaughan stood in the shade of a broken archway that would have once opened on to a lush expanse of lawns. Now, the area was covered with debris, the grand buildings that overlooked the gardens turned in places to rubble, the grass burned brown, fountains choked with dust, trees charred. Scraps of clothing protruding from a pile of stones and a putrid smell told him there were bodies still buried here. He tugged the perfumed cloth tighter over his mouth and nose, eyes smarting at the grit blowing on the hot wind.

Beyond, the shattered city stretched away. Smoke still hung on the air from fires that had ravaged some quarters in the final days. The four horsemen had ridden wild through Málaga and the trail of their destruction was laid bare in every place: bodies crushed by stones and pierced by arrows, the elderly and young withered to bones in their beds, others sick or dying of disease. Isabella and Ferdinand had not yet entered their new city, waiting for the corpses to be cleared from the streets and survivors to be turfed out of homes and hiding places, and corralled for their fates. Combatants were to be executed and citizens enslaved – all fifteen thousand of them.

From his vantage, Harry could see the masts of the ships crowding the harbour in the shadow of the towering walls of the Alcazabar. He'd heard that the noise and stink down there were unbearable: children wailing, men shouting, bodies floating in the polluted water, wretched lines of emaciated citizens, stricken dumb with shock and grief, being led on to the waiting vessels. The king and queen had divided the population into three: one third to be exchanged for Christians in North African prisons and mines, another to be gifted to the leaders of the siege, the remainder to be sold in the markets of Christendom. With so much human cargo to process, a number of slavers had been brought in, but chief among them were Gianotto Berardi and Christopher Columbus.

Harry turned sharply, disturbed by a harsh cry. It was just a bird, one of the many carrion eaters that circled over the dead city. Still, though, his eyes raked the ruins, drooping fronds of palms rustling in the breeze making his neck prickle with unease. He wore a studded brigandine over his shirt, but had discarded his cumbersome helm and breastplate weeks ago. He now felt naked, vulnerable without the armour. The king's guards had declared that this quarter had been thoroughly swept of citizens, but that was before another company had been surprised down near the western walls by a knot of enemy soldiers hiding in a cellar. The desperate Moors had cut a bloody swathe through the king's men before they'd been surrounded and put down.

Harry curled his hand around the hilt of his sword, feeling the comfort in its grip. The blade, gifted to him by the king and well christened now with infidel blood, hung from his hip alongside his dagger. But it hadn't been protection he'd had in mind when he'd strapped on his belt that morning alone in his tent, the knowledge of what he intended today – planned for all these months – throbbing in him like a second heartbeat. One of these blades would taste blood today. Not the blood of the enemy, but a fellow Christian.

'Sir Harry Vaughan?'

He started round to see a figure approaching across the rubble-strewn courtyard of the abandoned building. Harry had only seen Columbus once, at his first meeting with the queen in Córdoba, almost a year ago now. But he recognised the man immediately: six feet tall and broad with it, his red face a startling contrast to his crop of white-blond hair. The sailor with the dream. The man the Spanish called el Loco.

Harry searched the courtyard behind him, but it seemed Columbus had come alone, as Harry had requested when he asked Don Luys Carrillo to set up this meeting in a place of his choosing. Don Luys had been only too happy to oblige, so long as Harry kept his word and wrote to King Henry about renewing the hunt for Wynter. It was a promise Harry had no intention of keeping, but Don Luys need never know that. He tugged down the perfumed cloth and forced a smile out of his tight lips, inclining his head to Columbus. 'Thank you for meeting me.' His voice was dry and he had to clear his throat. 'I wanted somewhere we could speak in private. I'm afraid there is not much in the way of comfort. But I can at least offer you a drink.' Harry picked up the flask of wine he'd brought, saved from his rations.

Columbus barely glanced at it, keeping his ice-blue eyes fixed on Harry. 'Señor Luys said you are England's ambassador?' His Castilian was rendered blunt by his native accent.

Harry found his frank manner unsettling. He needed time here. Time to gather himself. To prepare. He gestured through the archway to the gardens. 'Come, let us sit.' He made his way to where a stone bench stood among withered bushes, grateful that Columbus followed him.

Columbus paused at the bench, but then sat beside him, large callused hands resting on his knees, his white hair whipped by the acrid wind. 'I'm told your king may be interested in supporting my venture?'

'Perhaps,' said Harry. That wasn't exactly what he'd advised Don Luys to tell the sailor, but if the man's interest had been piqued enough to bring him here then so be it. 'Lord Henry is certainly keen to know more.'

'I am glad to hear it.' Columbus's gruff tone didn't change, despite his assertion. 'There are too few men, I have found, with minds and hearts open to the possibilities of this world. Tell me, what does King Henry of England want to know?'

Harry tugged the cork from the flask and took a swig to settle his nerves. The wine was strong and burned his throat. He passed it to Columbus, who took it with a curt nod and drank. Harry had brought it with him in the hope it would make the man drowsy and slow, but he'd forgotten how huge the sailor was. Watching him drink, he thought it would take a barrel to fell him. 'My lord king is interested to know how you hope to realise your dream?'

Columbus's ruddy face hardened at this. 'It is no dream. Nothing so flimsy. So intangible. No, Sir Harry.' He swigged at the flask again and gestured to a wooden bucket, lying on its side by a fountain. 'What I seek is as real as that.' Shrugging off his black cloak, he rose. His shirt was stained yellow with sweat under his arms and down his broad back. Leaving the flask on the bench, he strode to the bucket. 'The only question is how far it is between here and there.' He halted. 'You have heard of Toscanelli? The great scholar and astronomer of Florence?'

Harry shook his head, but he was only half listening. Sweat was threading greasy lines down his face and his mouth was dust dry. Talk was not what he'd come here for. He needed the man to sit still beside him, drink some more wine; be unsuspecting when the dagger was slipped between his ribs.

Columbus's brow furrowed at his lack of knowledge. 'Fifty years ago, the banker, Cosimo de' Medici, hosted a council in his republic to which men came from across Christendom and as far as Byzantium, Rus and Tartary. Toscanelli – by questioning these men and gauging the times and distances of their journeys, as well as hearing the stories of travellers from other lands to their own – came to the conclusion that a man sailing west would eventually reach Cathay, Cipangu and, indeed, the Spice Islands. Seventeen years ago, he wrote to the King of Portugal of his theory and, shortly before his death, he confirmed it to me in a letter.' Columbus put his foot on the bucket. 'Men say the earth is too large for such a journey – that a ship could never carry enough food and water to reach those lands. The ancient Greeks believed eleven thousand miles lie between the Pillars of Hercules in the west and the golden cities of Cathay in the east.' Columbus gave the bucket a shove with his foot.

Harry watched it roll across the withered grass towards him.

'By Toscanelli's reckoning it is five thousand.' Columbus walked to the bucket, shoved it again and followed in its wake. 'Since his letter, I have read countless books, studied maps and travelled the seas in many directions. Based on all I have discovered, I believe it is a mere three thousand miles.'

Harry followed the bucket's last clumsy roll, as Columbus returned to sit beside him.

'No dream,' the man repeated, his pale blue eyes alight.

Harry took another sip of the sour wine. His heart was thumping furiously. He had planned for this moment all these past weeks, since the city had fallen and the sailor had come. A deserted place, where they would meet alone. He would say they were attacked without warning – an enemy, overlooked in the search. He had tried to save the man, but failed, the Moor fleeing before he could catch him. He would cut himself, to make the struggle real. Not that he thought many would mourn the sailor's death. Columbus was a sailor, a slave trader. He wasn't a lord or a knight. Isabella might be interested in his plan, but most men thought him a fool.

Harry set down the flask, shifted his hand to his belt, fingers creeping to the dagger. He had seen so much blood spilled here; faces caved in, stomachs split, legs torn away. He should be inured. What was keeping him? He thought of Prince Edward, small limbs fighting against him as he bundled the boy back into that cell in the Tower. Thought of Wynter tied at his feet, thrashing and helpless as he'd set the flames around him. Thought of Edward Woodville's neck bared for the barb in his hand, the Smiler twitching beneath him, skin parting with every slash of his dagger, and all the nameless meat into which he'd thrust his steel these past weeks. But those had been moments of hate and fury, rage and need. This felt as though he were about to leap off a cliff into an icy lake.

Columbus was watching him closely. He shook his head, the creases in his sun-scorched brow deepening. 'All these men who doubt me,' he murmured. 'Few of them have even been to sea. I know what the Spaniards call me. Men said the same in the court of King John of Portugal, behind my back and to my face. But if they had seen what I had, their minds would change.'

'What you have seen?' Harry asked the question to keep the man occupied and talking, while his fingers grazed the cold hilt of the dagger, but as he did so an image of the map from the *Trinity* drifted into his mind. Had Columbus seen what those sailors had? That strange coastline trailing off the edges?

Columbus locked eyes with him, unable to contain his passion. 'One day on Porto Santo, off Madeira where I worked for my father-in-law, a Spanish ship struggled into port, its mast broken. The hold was full of bodies. Most of the crew had died of thirst and starvation. Only the captain and two others survived. They told me they had been blown off course for many days by a terrible storm. Eventually they sighted islands, far to the west. They put ashore on one, searching for food and water, only to be chased off by men and women, naked as the day they were born, wielding spears and sticks. None of the crew had ever seen these lands before, nor heard tell of them.

'Before that time, I spent months on a dogger off the coast of Thule, on seas vast as mountains, where men who'd fished those waters for generations told me stories of great cod banks where the ocean seethed with fish and giants of the deep. Some of these men, their vessels lifted on waves like peaks, had glimpsed lands of green and ice and snow to the west and north. Soon after that I was in the Port of Galway, where I learned a tiny boat had been hauled ashore by traders, who found it drifting off the coast. Inside, were a man and a woman.

'Skin like cinnamon they had, with hair black as jet. Strange round faces and dark eyes shaped like – like almonds.' Columbus made a narrow oval with thumb and forefinger. 'Everything I know tells me they were of Cathay. I have navigated the Aegean, the Mediterranean, the green Atlantic. I have sailed the coasts of Portugal and Ireland, and down the coast of Africa to El-Mina. All along these shores I have heard tell of things washed up – fruits and plants, strange objects and, sometimes, people. Can you tell me, sir, having heard my words, that you do not believe the lands of the Orient – lands of spices and silks, jewels and gold – could lie but a few thousand miles off our shores? And that a vessel, larger and better stocked than all those lost or wrecked, could not reach them?'

Harry, despite himself, felt a prickle of something – excitement, curiosity? *Do it and be done*, came an urgent voice inside him. *Do it now!* His fingers closed over the hilt. He would return home to King Henry in honour. His soul could be saved by a priest.

'Even in your own country there are stories,' Columbus continued. 'A ship out of Bristol, the *Trinity*, is said to have sighted land to the west some years ago. There was rumour of a map.'

'Oh?' Harry felt his heart skip.

'I hoped, when Don Luys told me of your wish to learn more of my plans, that you might have heard word of this yourself? Some knowledge, perhaps, that had spurred your king's interest?'

Harry thought again of Wynter – the bastard – to whom his father had chosen to entrust that map. If what Columbus said had any truth, his growing suspicion that Thomas Vaughan had left his half-brother a secret legacy was surely right. Wynter might not have inherited the mansion on London's Strand, but perhaps, instead, he had been given a key to the whole damn world. *But you can have more – much more – if you do this!* Harry rose as if to stretch his legs and drew the dagger partway out of its sheath, hiding it with his body. 'I have heard of the ship and the rumours. But I know of no map.'

'Perhaps, when I hear from the queen's council, I might speak to you about requesting an audience with your king? Maybe he would help me look into those rumours? Money, Sir Harry,' Columbus said gruffly, squinting up at him. 'That – and faith and courage – are all that stand in my way.' He rose suddenly, towering over Harry. 'I must return to the docks, attend to my business there. But I would appreciate another meeting.' He thrust out a callused hand. 'If you would accept?'

Harry stared dumbly at it. He had to let go of the loosened dagger to take the sailor's hand. After a pause, he did so. He was opening his mouth, thinking of something to say to keep the man here, but Columbus was already off. Plucking his black cloak from the stone bench, the sailor strode away across the grass.

Harry watched him go, all his fierce intent draining from him. His gut twisted. Fear had stepped him back from the brink at the moment he could have jumped, leaving him shaking on the edge. When Columbus had vanished, he turned with a hoarse shout and kicked away the bucket that was lying there, sending it flying.

It was almost dusk by the time Harry returned to the chaos of the camp beyond the city walls. His fists were bruised and stinging from where he had beaten them on the broken ground in fury at himself. Only the fact Columbus had suggested another meeting had kept him from sticking the dagger into his own weak flesh. He had failed, yes. But he would have another chance. And, this time, he would do what he must. His future depended on it.

Harry was already planning to send Peter with a message for the sailor as he ducked into his tent. He was brought up short by the sight of King Ferdinand sitting on a stool in the centre, long legs stretched out before him, passing a wrinkled orange between his hands. 'Y . . . your highness?' he stammered, eyes darting to the two royal guards who stood at the sides of the tent, the black eagle glaring from their chests.

Ferdinand rose, his dark hair brushing the vaulted canvas roof. Harry watched, his throat closing, as the king drew a dagger from his belt. He took a few steps back, but the king merely sliced the orange in half and handed one piece to him. 'My scouts found a whole orchard, untouched by fire. These are so much sweeter than those we have in Córdoba.' He smiled as Harry took the dripping wedge of fruit. 'Another reward for our long struggle.'

'Thank you, my lord,' murmured Harry, watching as the king sank his teeth into the flesh, juice trickling down his chin. He nipped politely at the orange, but hardly tasted it, his heart in his mouth.

'So, you met with the sailor?'

Harry swallowed hard, the bite of fruit sliding down with difficulty. 'I—'

'I have seen you, in conversation with Don Luys Carrillo. I am well aware of his hatred of your people and knew it must have been something important to have given rise to such an exchange. He told me of your interest in the sailor and his plans. That he had secured a meeting for you. Told me, too, that in exchange you offered to help find the man who murdered his son?'

Harry forced back his panic. 'I apologise, my lord, if you feel I have moved behind your back. I did not want to bother you with such a . . .' He fought for the Castilian words, his mind fogged with fear. 'Such an insignificant matter. It is simply that King Henry had heard of this sailor's theory and wished to know if it had any basis in fact.'

Ferdinand nodded thoughtfully, licking juice from his hand. 'And, now you have spoken to him? What do you think, Sir Harry?'

'I am not sure, my lord,' Harry replied slowly. If Ferdinand now suspected he had been delving into a Spanish interest for his own king then he was surely in serious trouble. But the king did not seem angry. He seemed – curious? 'The man was certainly fervent in his enthusiasm for an expedition.'

'Indeed,' murmured Ferdinand, 'and it seems that fervour is contagious.'

'My lord?'

'Lady Isabella has been rather captivated by his theories. My wife is a strong-willed woman, Sir Harry, with her own mind, but her curiosity and her faith sometimes cloud her eyes to the ambitions of unscrupulous men.'

'You do not believe what he says could be true?' Harry felt his heart begin to steady. The king's ire was not for him. It was for Columbus.

'That it is only three thousand miles to Cathay? That he could reach the Orient by sailing west?' Ferdinand shook his head. 'None of my advisers, nor any of the sailors I have questioned believe it can be done. Some years ago, Cristóbal Colón was in the pay of King John of Portugal, crewing ships down the African coast. John has proven keen to continue his kingdom's explorations, begun decades ago by Prince Henry of Viseu, but even with his passion for expedition and access to the knowledge gleaned by Prince Henry, he refused to support Colón's dream. That tells me he did not believe it to be possible either.

'After five years in King John's pay, the sailor came here, to Castile. My fear, Sir Harry, is that the man is a leech, sucking dry whoever will countenance his wild theories. Lady Isabella has paid him a generous stipend to keep him in Spain, has offered him and Gianotto Berardi lucrative slave contracts and has employed the efforts of her ministers in her commission to examine his proposition. Of course, men like him can be found everywhere. But I do not want such a creature draining my wife. You understand?'

Harry nodded.

'In your discussion, did Cristóbal Colón give you any sense that he is using her? That his vision is merely a ploy for money?'

Harry saw it before him – another blade, this one made of words. 'May I speak plain, my lord?'

'I would wish you to.'

'The man did gloat of his relations with the queen. In truth, I found him distastefully boastful of his position under her.' Harry noted the tightening of Ferdinand's jaw. 'I was also disappointed, given my Lord Henry's interest in his ideas, to discover his theories amount to no more than incoherent ramblings. I am no navigator, my lord, but nothing of what the man said made any sense. I fear his nickname may be well earned. I do not think him dangerous,' Harry went on hastily, 'and perhaps not even ill-intentioned, but maybe, as you say, an ambitious man, who has had a little too much sun.'

Ferdinand studied him for a long moment, then let out a satisfied grunt. 'My agents say he is the son of a cloth weaver. Tell me, Sir Harry, can you imagine a man of such low pedigree holding the key to the richest lands on earth?' The king took another bite of fruit. 'No. The way to the wealth of the Orient lies through the Turks in Constantinople. Once the infidel stain is wiped from our own lands, perhaps my wife and I will lead Christendom in another holy crusade east.'

Harry stepped back as the king went to move past him.

Ferdinand paused in the opening. 'What will you tell Lord Henry?'

'That he should put his faith in alliances he can trust, my lord.'

The king smiled. 'Indeed. Do send him my regards when you next write to him and let him know that I and the Lady Isabella were delighted to hear of the birth of his son. You may tell him our daughter, Princess Katherine, is also in good health.' With that, he ducked out, his guards following.

Harry waited until he'd gone, then turned away, tossing the orange on the ground and pushing his hands through his hair.

'The ship is almost full. We can fit ten more at most. Juan is checking to see if there are any more viable girls. The younger ones do well in the Italian markets.'

Columbus nodded at Gianotto Berardi's words. The two of them were standing on the dockside, close to where a four-hundred-ton caravel was still being loaded with the slaves Berardi and his men had corralled and inspected that day. The sun was sinking in the west, gilding the waves. A breeze had sprung up, clearing some of the putrid air that hung over the vanquished city. 'You are still planning on sailing tomorrow?'

'Yes.' Berardi paused, catching his gaze. 'You've been quiet ever since you spoke with the Englishman. Is something wrong?'

Columbus's eyes narrowed as he stared beyond the masts of the boats that crowded the harbour to the open sea. 'Perhaps, after I have sold my share for the Lady Isabella, I should arrange a meeting with his king? Travel to England?' His face tightened. 'I cannot wait any more.'

'But, as you said yourself, the queen may be more willing to advance your proposition, now Málaga is tamed and her coffers replenished?'

'If I delay much longer, I fear another man may chance this course. Then, all these years will have been for nothing.'

'I doubt it, my friend.' Berardi clasped his shoulder. 'As they say, you are the only one mad enough to try.' He grew serious when Columbus didn't lighten. 'Stay in Spain. Wait for the queen's verdict.

As I said, there may be men in Florence interested in our venture. There are rich patrons to be found there and I will seek them out once my business in the markets is done. Besides, there is no one else I trust more to run my company while I am gone.'

Columbus didn't answer, but he nodded, eyes on the gold-capped waves.

33

Jack walked through the grand hall, Black Martin and Crooked Andrea close behind, their booted feet heavy at his back. They had searched him for weapons, but he had come unarmed.

He thought of the first time he'd been escorted into this palace, marched in by these men, his beard as long as a vagrant's, shoes worn to parchment by the miles from Paris. He had come with a bargain then, too. Only, now, he wouldn't make the same mistake. Now, Lorenzo de' Medici would pay in full before Jack gave him what he wanted.

The signore was waiting for him in his study, seated behind his desk, framed by his glittering wealth. Jack had learned of his return from Rome a week ago, when heralds had ridden through Florence announcing the glorious betrothal of Maddalena de' Medici and Franceschetto Cybo, and the republic's new accord with the Holy City, to be sealed, in time, with Giovanni's entry into the College of Cardinals.

Lorenzo was dressed in scarlet robes, the high collar buttoned to his neck, hiding the scar. His dark eyes regarded Jack as he entered. Under that steel gaze, Jack almost felt himself falter. He'd forgotten the intensity of the aura of power that emanated from the man. But he forced himself forward to meet him, knowing Lorenzo would exploit any weakness he showed. He noticed the gold curtain was drawn across the door to the hidden room, even though its occupant was no longer inside.

'Signor Lorenzo.'

'James.'

The lack of title was telling, but not unexpected. It had always been a false cloak, Jack reasoned. It would have disappeared at some time.

Lorenzo nodded to his bodyguards. 'Leave us.'

Jack heard the door close at his back.

Lorenzo sat back, arms on the carved rests of his chair. 'Prince Djem is in your custody?'

'Yes, signore.'

'And, in your message, you said you wish to exchange him?'

Jack nodded. 'For what I was promised when I first came to you – answers and money. I believe I have earned both. I infiltrated the Court of Wolves and I saved Prince Djem. Lost one of my men in doing so.' *Two*, Jack thought, his mind on David: a ghost since the death of Adam, more often to be found lingering by his brother's grave than in their dingy new lodgings in Oltrarno.

'You believe you have earned this?' Lorenzo echoed. 'Yet, you did not tell me you had discovered Franco Martelli was a member of the Court of Wolves?'

'I didn't know you were unaware of his allegiance.' Jack knew it was a poor excuse, Lorenzo clear from the start that he wasn't aware of the exact nature of the membership.

'Nor did you tell me of your suspicions that he was working against me, with the help of his daughter – a traitor in my own household? A serpent among my children?' The first sign of emotion hardened Lorenzo's voice. 'It was left to your man, Adam, to inform me of this.'

'I wanted to be certain before I came to you that my suspicions were right.'

'Your man said your affection for Laora Martelli had clouded your judgement. That you were merely protecting her.'

Jack felt a rush of anger, but it vanished immediately. His feelings of betrayal paled into insignificance with his guilt and sadness over what had happened to the man he'd known since he was a boy, had lived and fought alongside. The memory of his fists striking Adam's face and the fury in the man's eyes on that night of fire and death refused to leave him. 'That wasn't what stopped me from informing you.' He paused, aware he would keep the door to suspicion open if he admitted what he believed. But to close it would seal both Martelli and his daughter in guilt, and he would not do that. Not while there was still a chance Laora's name could be cleared, at least from crimes she'd not committed. 'I am certain Martelli is not the enemy you fear.' He thought of the hole, high up in the wall behind him. 'The one who may have spied upon you and been involved in Amaury's abduction.'

'And yet,' said Lorenzo, rising and crossing to one of the shelves that lined the walls, this one enclosed behind a set of doors, criss-crossed with iron. 'When my guards searched his palace, they found this.' Lifting a key from his belt, Lorenzo twisted it in the lock on the cupboard door and opened it. He withdrew an object.

It was a gold chalice of extraordinary craftsmanship, two serpents twisting around its stem, rising to the cup which was cradled with wings – a caduceus, the staff of Hermes. Its rim was crusted with precious gems. At least ten thousand florins, Laora had said it was worth. Jack could see that value in every flash and glitter as Lorenzo turned it carefully in his hands. After a moment, he returned it to its place, locked the doors.

'The theft is, I believe, the only crime Martelli committed against you,' Jack said, when Lorenzo sat back down.

'It was Laora who took it, wasn't it? She knew where it was kept.'

Jack wanted to deny this, but knew it was futile. 'She did so under duress. You must know her father's temper. She was frightened for her life, signore. She intended to help me return it to you.'

'Where is she now? After Martelli's arrest, he and her stepmother claimed to know nothing of her whereabouts.'

'I haven't seen her since you left for Rome.' Jack held Lorenzo's needling stare. 'My guess is she left the city.'

'Well, God willing, I will find out soon enough in what ways Martelli was against me. He is in the Stinche. No one in there remains quiet for long.'

'The Stinche?' Jack knew of the notorious prison in the centre of the city, where debtors, traitors and murderers would await execution. He wondered what Laora would feel.

Lorenzo steepled his hands. 'Explain to me, James, why you took the prince from my custody. How did you know he was in there?'

'I didn't know if I could trust you. I needed answers and felt I was getting no closer to them. I knew there was something you were hiding here, from what I overheard between Pico and Poliziano. I gained entry while you were at Fiesole.' Jack felt Lorenzo's eyes boring into him. He could see anger in those dark depths, but the man's thoughts remained inscrutable.

'You say you saved Djem? That men came for him that night? Yet I left Bertoldo and a dozen guards here when I went to Rome, none of whom reported seeing any intruders, only that my study had been broken into and you were missing.'

Jack described the events of that night: how Amelot had let him out and had given him the blood-covered plan of the palazzo, the six men he'd seen descending the stairs and those who had come for the prince at the Fig, killed in the fight with his men. 'The city watch will verify what happened at the tavern,' he added.

'Two different companies?'

Jack nodded. 'The men I saw here were speaking an Italian dialect. The others – Prince Djem said they were assassins, sent by his brother, Sultan Bayezid.'

'The plan of the palace? Where did the girl find it?'

Lorenzo listened closely as Jack spoke of the man in the mask. He didn't have all the facts, since Amelot had not been able to give them, but he'd been able to glean enough to put some of the pieces together. 'Amelot took it from his lodgings,' Jack finished. 'In the hostelry where he was staying. The watch found the body of another man there.'

'And this masked man is the same one you spoke of when you first arrived – the one you say was in England searching for the map on Pope Sixtus's orders? The man who killed your mother?'

Jack fought to hide his emotions. All this time, since he'd followed Amelot across the city, his father's sword in his hand, he had been hunting for his enemy. But the only place he'd found him was the flame-wreathed landscape of his dreams. His frustration – being so close yet denied the chance to face his mother's killer – burned in him; a flame that wouldn't go out. He nodded tightly, realising he hadn't answered.

Lorenzo was watching him intently. 'What I cannot fathom is how these men you say you saw simply entered my palace then vanished, leaving no trace?'

'I can only think by the same way we left – the roof.' Jack heard the doubt in his own tone, just as he saw it in Lorenzo's face. It had been difficult enough to make the tricky descent with Amelot's surefooted guidance; he couldn't imagine six armed men being able to accomplish it in the dark, not without being seen or heard. But it was the only explanation he had. 'Bayezid's assassins must have then followed us from here to the Fig.' Jack could tell Lorenzo was wrestling with whether or not to believe him, but he could see other thoughts forming behind the man's eyes, his gaze narrowing on the gold curtain that covered the door. 'You have a sense, signore? Of who these men were?'

'If what you say is true, then my guess is they were sent by Pope Innocent.'

Jack had wondered this himself; thinking back over the conversation he'd overheard between Lorenzo and Marsilio, talking about the prince – a prize for the pope – the signore's unexpected departure for Rome that had left the palazzo deserted, and the appearance of the masked killer who'd been in the pay of Sixtus. But it was still a surprise to hear the suspicion spoken out loud. He nodded, waiting for Lorenzo to continue.

Lorenzo pressed his fingertips together. 'Sir Anthony Woodville is recruited by your father into the Academy. He betrays us, revealing our plans to Sixtus, who sends agents to London to seek the map from the *Trinity*. You tell me their leader died there, but one, this masked man, returns to Rome? Perhaps he tells Innocent what he knows? Innocent later recruits him, and others, to retrieve the prince. They must have discovered Djem was in my custody by hunting down those I paid to take him from his prison in France. That would perhaps explain the murders here. Fra Marsilio was right,' he muttered. 'I should have seen the connection. Been more wary.'

'What took you to Rome, signore? I heard a rumour it was something to do with Pico? That he was banished for it?'

Lorenzo's jaw tightened. 'A book he wrote found its way into the hands of the pontiff. Innocent found it – objectionable. Enough to demand the change in location for our children's betrothal. He would not say how he obtained it. I thought at the time Pico had just been careless in its publication. But I presume, now, that this was part of a larger plan, to remove me from the palace that the prince might be taken.'

'If His Holiness is somehow against you, why would he have agreed to the betrothal? Surely there would have been other ways to summon you to Rome?'

'Innocent plays a long game, as do I. Both of us stand to gain, through our sons, access to the influence and power of the other. He would not want to relinquish that. Not even for Prince Djem.'

'What would the Holy Father want with the Turk?'

'A new crusade. Around two years ago, Innocent entered into negotiations with the Knights of St John to take the prince into papal custody. Djem has intimate knowledge of his brother, Sultan Bayezid, and his armies, of the Turks' strongholds and terrain. If he could be turned to the side of Christendom, he would be the perfect weapon in a war against the Ottoman Empire. He is also a useful tool for bribery. The Knights of St John forced Bayezid to pay a substantial annual ransom to keep Djem incarcerated. You see, then, why the sultan would want his brother dead. His assassins have tried in the past. My guess is Bayezid had spies in the papal court. They could have discovered Innocent was making his move. Followed his men here.'

Jack was nodding. This all made sense from the little Djem, himself, had been persuaded to tell him. 'And why do you want him, signore? Not a crusade? Or money, surely?'

'Where is the prince, James?'

The change of tack caught Jack off guard, but he recovered quickly. 'I will tell you, signore, when you give me what I came for. I want to know – all of it. The Academy? Its aims and purpose? The map I guarded for my father? Amaury de la Croix said you believed it showed Atlantis. The land you call New Eden? Amaury, my father, me – we risked so much to secure it for you. Amelot was tortured for it. My mother *died* because of it. Yet when I told you the map was in King Henry's possession you seemed to lose interest in it?' The questions, pent up inside him all this time, were tumbling out of him. 'Things my father said, about Muslims not being the true enemy? Amaury spoke of corruption in the Church, yet it seems two popes now have moved against you. So much of what the priest told me in Paris sounded like heresy. I do not know who I should trust. My past, my birthright – my *faith*, signore. All of it is shaken, uncertain. My father told me to come here, that I would find my answers in you. That you would point the way. And so, I ask you, who was my father? Was he a good man? Or was he not? I need to know the truth.'

Lorenzo held his gaze for a long moment. 'Truth? You think it a fixed point? A target you can aim at? Surely you see by now, James, that truth is fluid, changeable? That it means different things to different men, at different times?'

'Then what is your truth? Now?'

Lorenzo sat back, arms resting on the chair. 'When he was a young man, my grandfather, Cosimo de' Medici, was sent by his father to a council at Constance in the company of Pope John, one of three rival claimants to the papal throne in the schism that followed the Avignon papacy: the council's intent to heal this split in the heart of Christendom and choose one successor to take the throne of St Peter. It was a period of adversity, of poverty and war in the west, but my family had worked hard and, by then, were the bankers for Pope John.

'During his time at the council my grandfather saw, first-hand, the rifts in the Church and the sins of the men who served it. John, whose past was mired by piracy and violence, was a notorious drunk with a weakness for women. My grandfather told me he found himself, having been filled with pride at the task his father set him, disillusioned with the world and questioning his own faith. There, in Constance, he met a man who, like himself, had studied humanism. Sharing a passion for the philosophies of the Greeks and Romans, and the poetry of Petrarch, who sought to reinvigorate those ancient worlds, they became friends.

'Before they parted ways, this man gave my grandfather a copy of a text called the *Emerald Tablet*. It was through this that my grandfather first discovered Hermes Trismegistus – Hermes the Thrice Great – who was said to have written it. The *Emerald Tablet* taught my grandfather that earth and heaven are not separate, but so ineffably linked that what occurs in one affects the other. As above, so below. It is one of the primary tenets of Hermeticism, the teachings of Hermes himself, which my grandfather set out to discover and explore, spurred by a sense that by divining the past he might come to better understand the present. That, perhaps, there were other ways of seeing the world and our place within it, beyond the impaired walls of the Church.'

Jack was reluctant to interrupt when Lorenzo was speaking so openly, but neither did he want to be left in the dark again at the end of this. 'I understood Hermes to be a Greek god, the patron of thieves. But Amaury spoke of him as a messenger. As . . .' He fought to recall the priest's words. 'As a bridge between this world and the next?'

'He wears many guises. Mage and prophet, sorcerer and priest. We, in the Academy, see him as the first philosopher; keeper of the arcane knowledge of the world. My grandfather founded the Academy to hunt down, translate and interpret that knowledge that we, too, might learn the secrets of the ancients: secrets of long life and health, death and rebirth, the stars and the tides, the worldly and the divine.

The more texts he and his hunters found, the more they came to see that Plato's belief in a World Soul – a soul that connects us all – was right. That a single, perfect theology exists with roots in every belief and that, through it, all mankind could once again be united under God, as once we were.'

'You believe that? Even after what the infidel . . .?' Jack paused. The reflex of that word no longer felt right after being in the company of Prince Djem; the man's dignity and quiet authority, his honour, paid in respect to them all, but especially David after Adam's death in his defence. Jack had been surprised when the prince, whom he expected to have to chain up until Lorenzo's return, had not only consented to remain in his custody, but maintained his calm even when Jack admitted he was planning to return him to his gaoler. Following the attempt on his life by his brother's assassins, Djem seemed to have become resigned to his fate. Jack had wondered whether he'd become inured to captivity – at ease, even, with the safety of four walls and his escape into the books they brought him, which had been his only demand. 'After what the Turks have done to us?'

'There was a Greek scholar, who, shortly after the fall of Constantinople, in the horrors of which he himself lost family, declared that were a man to unite Christians and Muslims in faith, his praises would be sung by all of earth and heaven. It was a thought shared by my grandfather. War, he believed, narrows and limits man's potential. Rather, he saw the future in the expansion of shared understanding and commerce. Trade, he always said, brings mankind together and casts glory upon those who venture into it.' Lorenzo gave a half-smile as if in memory and took a sip of wine. 'Hundreds of years of hatred, however, will not be erased overnight. Both sides are ignorant, intolerant, unable to see the invisible cords that bind us, unwilling to admit we are all brothers, sprung from the same womb.'

'My father knew all this? Believed this?' Jack shook his head. 'But it is heresy.'

'Heresy to a tradition which has itself become corrupt. Me, your father, Marsilio, Pico, Amaury; we are all Christians in faith, James. But we see the limitations of a singular doctrine.'

'The God we all worship, no matter the language of our prayers or the traditions of our ancestors is one and the same? Amaury said that,' Jack explained to Lorenzo's surprise.

'When he was set in charge of King Edward's son, I asked your father to teach the boy our values and ideas. We planted others in the courts of the west that we might advance our aims from within the fabric of each nation.'

'What are your aims though? I still don't fully understand.'

Lorenzo arched a sardonic eyebrow, lifted his hand towards the gilded ceiling. 'Perhaps, if you spent the years my grandfather and I have reading the thousands of manuscripts in our library . . .' He sighed. 'In its simplest form? Faith without war. Trade without boundaries.'

'And Prince Djem? If Pope Innocent wants to use him for a crusade, why do you want him?'

'He has not said?'

'He will speak little of his life.'

'Well, he is a proud man and his story one of humiliation. When their father, Sultan Mehmet, died six years ago, without naming a successor, Djem and his half-brother, Bayezid, vied for the sultanate. Bayezid believed that as the elder of the two he was rightful heir to the caliphate, but Djem claimed his right as the son who was born *after* his father had ascended the throne. Allegiances were split and war broke out. Djem won an early victory, but that was overturned by Bayezid and the prince was forced to flee to Cairo, where the Mamluk Sultan supplied him with men and arms. The following year, buoyed up by support from Egypt and allies in Anatolia, Djem made another attempt on the throne. Once again, he failed to break his brother's hold on the caliphate and, separated from his army and surrounded by enemies, he fled in the only direction still open to him – the sea.

'In disguise, he took a boat to Rhodes, where he asked the Knights of St John for protection. There, he made the knights a promise – a permanent peace, between Christendom and the Ottoman Empire, between Christianity and Islam – if they would help him claim the throne. The knights told him they would consider, but instead they informed Bayezid that they had his brother in their custody and offered to keep him there in return for a ransom. Bayezid agreed, Djem was retained as a prisoner and the knights were paid, handsomely.

'Later, Bayezid sent assassins to Rhodes in an attempt to remove the threat posed by his brother and end his payments to the knights. They failed and Djem was moved to France. That was when I first learned of his incarceration and of his offer of peace to the knights, who by then were in negotiations with Innocent for his transfer to Rome. I paid mercenaries to extract Djem and bring him here to me. I have spent the time since trying to gain his trust – not easily won after the knights' deception. Nor,' Lorenzo added ruefully, 'my own incarceration of him. Necessary though I felt it was, given his importance and those who were hunting him. I hoped, in time, he would prove a valuable ally. That, one day, I would help him take his place on the throne.'

'Constantinople,' murmured Jack, the knots all unravelling before him. Now, he understood why Lorenzo had called Djem the key to the future of his empire. With an ally on the Ottoman throne, he could secure the old roads to Cathay and the Spice Islands. The roads to the wealth of the world, closed to the west for over thirty years. 'You wanted access to the trade routes?'

'As I said – faith without war, trade without boundaries. A man cannot change the world, James, without first having some control over it.'

'And New Eden?'

'Through years of conflict, from petty skirmishes to ravaging wars, my grandfather dreamed of finding a safe haven where the men of the Academy – humanists like him – might kindle a new world from the embers of the old. After Sixtus authorised the attempt on my life, I knew I had to follow that dream, or risk losing everything my family had built over generations. When the astronomer Toscanelli told me he believed the crew of the *Trinity* had seen Atlantis we knew we had found it. What better place to build a new world than the land Plato himself had prophesied would return? The map may be lost to us, but now we know for certain there is land out there the dream need not be dead. If I make a deal with Djem – if I secure peace and trade with the east – I will be able to fund a fleet of ships to find it.'

'Why did you banish Pico? Was he working against this plan?'

Lorenzo ran a finger around the rim of his goblet. 'On the contrary, Pico was one of the most ardent supporters of our aims. His issue was I wasn't moving fast enough. That is why he wrote that book. He wanted the world to know what was possible.' His eyes hardened. 'He did not know about Djem. Did not understand why I wanted us to lie low until my plans had come to fruition. Marsilio advised me to wait, to keep the prince a secret until we knew what was possible. That was perhaps my greatest mistake,' Lorenzo said quietly. 'Not trusting them. If I had, Pico would not have gone against my orders and Poliziano would still . . .' He trailed off. 'I have given you your answers, James. You know everything your father knew. Now, it is your turn.'

Jack felt suddenly exhausted. He had made it to the heart of the maze and uncovered his father's secrets. There was relief in that. But what had changed? His father was still gone and his mother's death remained a splinter in his heart. Ned had been right. He really had been chasing ghosts. But there was something else now, he reminded himself. A new plan. A new hope. He just needed one thing to see it realised. 'My money, signore?'

Lorenzo tapped a thoughtful finger on the table. 'I am curious. When you have been compensated, what then?'

'My men and I will leave. Start new lives.' Jack's heart thumped. He would not tell Lorenzo the truth here – that these new lives might be sought in the very place he himself was searching for. *New Eden.* He and Ned, and, later, Valentine, had talked through the possibility for weeks, until it had formed into a plan. None of them wanted to remain in this city. Not after what had happened at the Fig. When Lorenzo paid them, they would head west to Spain, seek out the sailor Amerigo Vespucci had spoken of. They had seen the map with their own eyes. There was value in their knowledge. The sense of direction, of purpose, had kindled a fire in Jack.

'What if I had another task for you?'

'Another task? After all—' Jack stopped himself saying, *I've done.*

'You saved my asset and have proven your honour by admitting your actions these past months. I see no reason in us not continuing to work together. I have two problems, both of which I believe you – perhaps you alone – can help me solve. First, Prince Djem must be held in a new location. I cannot keep him in the palace, not after what you've told me, and I'm unwilling to widen the circle of those who know of him. You and your men could guard him for me, somewhere secure. Somewhere I can continue to cement my alliance with him. You would be paid, of course. Second, much time and effort has been spent embedding you within the Court of Wolves. Why waste that now you are in their company?'

Jack heard Valentine's words. *Once you is in, he'll want you to stay.* But there was no more power in Lorenzo's terms. The man had given him what he needed and his heart was set on another path. 'I will bring Djem to wherever you want, once you have paid me, signore. The Court of Wolves – well, you have Martelli.'

'You said yourself you do not believe him to be the one who has been working against me here? If that is so, stay, help me find the traitor. Someone gave Pico's book to the pope to be used against me. Drew the plan of my palace and handed it to my enemies. Someone took Amaury.'

'No. I—'

'Franco Martelli isn't the only prisoner I have locked in the Stinche, James.'

Jack prickled at the man's hard tone. 'What do you mean?'

'The masked man. The one who killed your mother? Committed the murders in my city?' Lorenzo nodded at Jack's expression. 'The watch took him into custody.'

All at once, Jack knew Lorenzo had him. He thought he'd been the clever one – getting the signore to give up what he wanted. But he had shown his hand when Lorenzo questioned him about his mother's killer; shown him what he wanted most, the grief and rage surely etched across his face.

'Stay,' repeated Lorenzo. 'Finish what you've started here and I will give you your mother's murderer. To do with as you wish.'

The sun was descending, gilding the domes and towers, by the time Jack reached Santa Croce. The air in the quarter was humid, thick with flies and sour odours of the river. In his mind he had left this city months ago. On his way to a new life. A new world. Now, pulled back by the hand of fate, tethered here again, it felt more stifling than ever.

Groups of people passed him, voices lifting on the wings of the day, the clatter of clogs echoing along the streets as they made their way home from the drying barns and washing sheds, freed from their labours. All this time, these men and women had been little more than background noise. Now, Jack found himself looking at them as they passed, some hurrying, others slow, bantering with one another. He envied them: the simplicity of their lives, daily routines bound around duties and families, work and home. If he'd never found out Thomas Vaughan was his father, might such a life have been his?

He slipped down an alley scattered with rubbish, the stones of the buildings sprouting weeds. Halting by a door, its paint peeling, he opened his hand and looked down at the band of gold, warmed by his fist since he'd left the Palazzo Medici.

His father's ring.

It was a token from Lorenzo; part pledge of faith, part burden of trust. The signore had forbidden him from wearing it, but it was his to keep. Jack stared at the snakes binding the staff, those wings outstretched above. He took a breath, then knocked: two raps, a pause, then two more. After a moment, there was a sound of a bolt sliding back. The door cracked open.

Laora let out a breath of relief as she saw him, opening the door wider for him to enter. She closed it quickly behind him, snapping the bolt back in place. Jack entered the dim chamber, where the only source of natural light came through a grated window, high up in the wall that overlooked the alley. Laora had made the place her own, as much as she could; sweeping clean the dusty floors and shelves, nesting the wide bed with blankets he bought her from the market, around which she hung faded lengths of cloth she'd found in a chest. The soft glow of tallow candles gave the tented space a warm, womb-like feeling.

They had worried at first that someone might find her here, but Marco Valori had assured them the workshop, which backed on to one of the warehouses owned by his family's company, had not been used for over a year and she would be safe. Jack had come to rely, more and more, on the young man, who had proven himself a worthy friend. Now, at Lorenzo's orders, he would have to turn against the only company in which he'd found safety and succour these past months.

'Jack?'

He turned. The name still sounded strange in her mouth. Laora had only started using it recently, after he told her who he was. Not a knight, but the son of one. Not here to represent his family, but to seek answers to his past. Given all the upheaval: her father imprisoned, her home and possessions confiscated – just the gown she'd been wearing and her beloved bird pendant left to her – Laora had taken his admission surprisingly lightly. But, he'd supposed, she had little choice. After everything had been swept away, he was the only solid thing that remained for her to hold on to. But in her need, he, too, had felt himself held. Each keeping the other afloat.

Laora's hazel eyes were wide with question. 'Did the signore give you what you wanted?'

He sank heavily on to the edge of the bed, utterly spent.

She crossed to him and crouched before him, her hands on his knees. A breath of blossom surrounded him. It was a smell of home, of comfort. Her face, pale from lack of sun, the freckles still winter shy, tightened with worry. 'Jack, what happened? Tell me. Are we leaving?'

'Not yet,' he murmured, sliding his hands over hers, lacing her fingers in his. 'Not yet.'

Giovanni Pico della Mirandola opened the shutters, wincing as the glare blinded him, the sun bathing his nakedness in a rush of warmth. As he peered through sleep-crusted eyes, the world solidified into a dark maze of rooftops and spires, dominated by the towers of Notre-Dame. People were moving in the street below, the clop of hooves and rumble of carts telling him morning was wearing on.

Pico's head swam and he felt a bubble of nausea float up from his stomach. How much wine had they drunk last night? He glanced at the clothes strewn over the floor, the three jugs, one on its side, on a table. Poliziano would never have let him drink so much. The thought came with a pang of sorrow, but Pico forced it back. To hell with Poliziano and temperance. The man hadn't even fought for him to stay. Initially, such thoughts had been kept at bay by the knowledge he had brought this banishment upon himself by betraying Lorenzo and the Academy, but these months in Paris had faded the guilt, leaving anger to shine through, bright and hard.

'Dear God, what havoc we made!'

Pico turned to see his companion sitting up in bed, staring in amused disbelief at the mess of the chamber. He had met Philippe, a young nobleman from the south, who was studying at the Sorbonne, several weeks ago. Normally, his trysts didn't last so long, but Philippe had enamoured him; his compelling eyes and sensual lips, and poetry that set his skin on fire. He grinned through his queasiness. 'I'll wager we can make more before Our Lady's bells sing for noon.'

Philippe went to throw back the covers in readiness, but was distracted by a banging on the chamber door. Frowning, he jumped from the bed and snatched his robe from the floor. He waited for Pico to slip out of sight behind the latrine screen, then opened the door.

Pico heard the urgent tones of Philippe's servant.

'Monsieur, a company has come, from Rome.'

'Rome?'

'Yes, monsieur, they bear the seal of the pope!'

Fear rushed through Pico, a cold, sickening wave. They had found him. He had not run far enough. Nor been careful enough. Who had informed on him? Spies at the Sorbonne? In the royal court? God only knew who he'd spoken to in drunken, reckless evenings with courtiers and tutors, whores and servants. He grabbed a robe and struggled into it, before rushing to the window. His mind flashed with foetid chambers and rough questions, black-clad officials, machines of torture and the chains of the pyre.

'Pico . . .?' Philippe questioned, bewildered, at his back.

Pico leaned out, over the drop to the cobbles. Too far. He could hear booted feet pounding up the stairs. There was nowhere to run.

34

The summer was passing, the year turning, but, for Jack, time had stopped, trapping him in a season of restless frustration. Every day, no matter his tasks or the directions he took, the maze of the city always somehow led him back to the high, blank walls and guard towers of the Stinche Prison, which squatted, like a stone tomb, in the middle of a confusion of streets near the Church of Santa Croce.

He'd been told the austere structure had once been a palace, but now its walls housed criminals and those who guarded them. Many of the prisoners were bankrupt cloth merchants and guildsmen accused of fraud, but there were others incarcerated there too, charged with murder and robbery. Now and then, one of these men or women would be hauled out, blinking in the daylight like an animal poked from a burrow, to be whipped through the city amid the jeers, only to be marched back to the prison walls, outside which they were hanged before a crowd.

Only one small door, reinforced and guarded, allowed access. Above it was an inscription, carved in stone:

We Should Be Merciful

Every time he read those words, Jack would feel an itch of rage. There would be no mercy. Not for the monster within those walls. Not for the man who'd left his mother's body to burn, after whatever he'd done to her. When Lorenzo finally gave him his reward – not in gold now, but blood – he would be as pitiless as St Michael, avenging with his blade.

Each time he came before Lorenzo to report on who he'd met at the last gathering of the Court of Wolves, what they'd said and what business they were involved in, Jack would beg him to be allowed into the prison, if only to find answers to the questions that burned him. How did his mother die? Was it quick, or did she suffer? Had she said anything at the end; some parting declaration perhaps, of love or wisdom, that he had been denied? But Lorenzo remained firm in his offer – uncover the intentions of the Court of Wolves, whether they were working against him to some design, and who among their number Amelot had seen in Paris – and he would get what he wanted. Jack's frustration simmered all the hotter with the knowledge that by offering to infiltrate the company in the first place he was the one who'd fashioned the cage into which he had walked, Lorenzo now standing outside, dangling the key just out of reach.

Even the hope that Franco Martelli, another soul trapped in the prison's stone hulk, might give up any secrets the Court of Wolves was keeping, had dwindled. The man had apparently resisted all methods of interrogation and would speak to no one. So, while Lorenzo continued the endless dance of Florentine politics, the deals and bribes, the threats and alliances, moving his pieces around the board – the plans for Maddalena and Franceschetto's marriage continuing apace, Prince Djem hidden away, Giovanni being readied for his entry into the Vatican by the tutelage of Poliziano, a lonely figure these days, glimpsed in the halls of the palazzo, an air of sadness clinging to him like rain – the task was left to Jack.

And so he did as he was bid, attending the gatherings of the company, more infrequent now it was summer and many of their number had left the stew of the city for the Tuscan hills; donning his wolf badge and his lies, accepted now among their number. But in all this time he'd discovered nothing that indicated these men had any sinister plan. They were, it seemed, merely what they appeared: a fraternity of ambitious young blades and old generals, looking forward or harking back, all sharing a passion for sport and politics, enterprise and endeavour.

It was true, they remained interested in the signore and his dealings, Marco Valori often asking him questions, but to Jack that seemed no different to factions he'd observed in the royal court in England: men, drawn to the power of the throne, seeking to understand their king and how they might benefit from his largesse, or avoid his wrath, some hoping to court his favour, others to manipulate it.

Sometimes, though, he wondered, thinking back to his first encounters with Marco – the man's interest in where Lorenzo might be weak and his own usefulness in exposing that. Had they become wary after the arrest of Martelli? One of their own? Jack had confided in Marco about the stolen chalice, desperate to find Laora a place to hide out of Lorenzo's sight, but even the fact he was now harbouring a thief from the signore hadn't made the young man any more forthcoming with him. Nor had he been able to persuade Marco to speak more of the enigmatic patrons he sometimes caught mention of, but never by name.

Occasionally, Jack thought something else might have caught their eye, turned their focus from him. Other times he worried if the rare moments of distraction he had in their company – cheering on the players of Santa Maria Novella at *calcio* games, betting on horse races and jousts, dining in splendour at their palazzi – had blinded him to their intentions. But none of these thoughts brought him any closer to answers and, when the thrills and laughter, wine and camaraderie faded, his mind would circle right back to those high prison walls and the monster within.

In those times, only Laora eased his discomfort, arms around him in the candle-flamed dusk of the old workshop, curtained by the faded lengths of cloth stirring in the warm air, separating them from the world. There in the dark they escaped into one another, with quiet breaths and slow releases, in whispered promises and restless dreams; each stalked by their nightmares chained in the same prison, only streets away.

Jack's plan to head west had not dimmed, his desire to take that road only increasing in the months trapped here. Early on, Ned had tried to convince him to leave; give up his chance at vengeance, be done with this city. But Jack could not. Not while the masked man still lived; his mother's blood on his hands. Only once he'd given Lorenzo what he wanted and had taken his payment would they go. He and Laora, Ned, Valentine and Amelot. Not David Foxley though. He had gone already, slipping away without a goodbye, soon after Jack had given him his and Adam's share of the money Lorenzo had paid; first instalment of a promised larger sum.

Jack had glimpsed David once after that, stooped and unsmiling in the warm summer rain down near the docks, where the barges brought goods from the Port of Pisa. Gone before he could reach him. He'd not seen him since. Jack, anguished by Adam's death and his part in it, accidental though it was, couldn't help but feel some measure of relief, his guilt less painful without the constant reminder in the eyes of his brother. He prayed, fervently, that David would find the comfort they could no longer offer. But he knew well how the demons of grief and loss could cling to the soul.

Ned and Valentine's impatience to be off had been tempered somewhat by their well-remunerated task of guarding Prince Djem in the nondescript little building Lorenzo had bought for the purpose, nestled among a row of tatty shops north of San Marco. For his part, the Turk seemed to have accepted his new life, watched but no longer chained, with an enclosed courtyard where he could sit and read, feel the sun on his face.

Valentine remained suspicious. But Ned, despite initial reservations, fell into an oddly natural friendship with the man, chatting while they played chess, asking about his homeland and listening, rapt, to Djem's talk of snow-crowned mountains rising from great plains, skies of stars beyond measure and markets perfumed with spices. Ned, who'd lost his precious shells in the destruction at the Fig, seemed to have found himself a new collection in these stories, hoarding them like treasures.

Jack, too, had come to feel a connection with Djem, not only through the man's poised presence, but by the fact he knew what it was to have a brother – a man of his own blood – who had wounded him more deeply than any stranger. So it was, he found himself, one morning in early September, heat simmering off the stones of the courtyard, flies droning around a plate of fruit, confiding in the prince.

Valentine was sitting on a stool in the shade, arquebus propped beside him, head resting against the wall, mouth open, snoring. From the shadows of the house, Ned was telling Titan to quiet. Jack, sitting opposite Djem, felt the back of his neck burning as he waited for the Turk to make a move. Again, he was struck by the oddness of this scene: him sitting here with a prince – a would-be *emperor* – drinking wine, while Djem, dressed in his silks and turban, sipped at warm milk sweetened with honey, the two of them like old friends. He clicked his tongue irritably as Djem took his rook, knowing he should have seen the move coming.

The prince sat back, eyes on him. 'You aren't playing as you usually do.'

'I'm just tired.' Jack hadn't slept last night, assailed by dreams.

'You are thinking of your mother's killer again?'

Jack's eyes flicked up to meet Djem's. Over these months, sitting here in this courtyard, he'd found himself talking about his life; his past and his time in the city, his frustrations with Lorenzo and his task here. To him, they had been mere drops of information, sporadic, unconnected, but Djem had surprised him by collecting them into a pool, into which he often dipped without warning. Jack, glancing at the goblet of wine near his hand, guessed the man, with nothing more potent than his sweet milk, always had him at a disadvantage. He nodded, but said nothing.

'Vengeance is a powerful force. We must be careful its fire does not burn through us. It can hollow a man out from the inside, leave nothing but a shell.'

Jack paused, thumb and forefinger hovering over a pawn. The board, its pieces made of jade and jasper, had been a gift to the prince from Lorenzo. 'Has it diminished for you?'

Djem considered, then answered carefully. 'Yes, I will seek retribution for my brother's actions against me. And, yes, if I have the chance I will take the throne from him. But I no longer allow my hatred of him to have mastery over me. Now, a more powerful force compels me. Love – for my family, my home. The desire to return to them.'

'It isn't only your brother who has kept you from them all this time,' murmured Jack, pinching the pawn and moving it towards Djem's bishop.

Djem gave him a sage smile. 'You do not need me to justify your own anger towards the signore.'

Jack rubbed at his sun-sore neck. 'I don't understand why you aren't furious at him? Keeping you imprisoned? Just as the knights did?'

'I was, of course. But since my brother's men came for me?' Djem let out a breath. 'Now I see that my only way back lies through the signore. The knights kept me for money. Your pope wants me for a crusade against my own people. No matter my thoughts on his methods, I know Lorenzo does not view me as merely a tool, but a potential partner. He has offered me the chance to go home, with his help. To build something new. Something that, perhaps, will benefit both our peoples.'

'You really believe we can have peace?'

'We are sitting here now, are we not? If there are leaders with the will for it? Then, yes. In time. I laud his notion of peace and trade between our worlds.'

Jack watched him pluck his jade bishop out of harm's way. 'Lorenzo will get what he wants, too, of course.'

'All men want something. Signor Lorenzo knows that more than most. It is what he plays to his advantage. He knows what I want. But now I know what he wants. So, we are, as you say, in a draw.' Djem took up his cup and drank. 'I played this game with him many times during my incarceration in his palace. I came to know him as much through his moves on this board as by his words.' He set the drink down, turning the cup thoughtfully on its base. 'Signor Lorenzo needs to be the one with the power, or at least believe that he is. He has had it all his life – was born to it. Because of that the loss of it is what he fears most.'

Jack thought of the attempt on Lorenzo's life by Pope Sixtus, those months in the custody of the King of Naples when he'd been forced to squander much of his family's fortune, his concerns about the Court of Wolves and what they might be plotting in the shadows, Pico's betrayal, Martelli's theft. It was no wonder he was so guarded.

'With a man like that,' continued Djem, 'the only way for you to gain power is to make him believe he has not lost any.'

Jack played his own bishop towards Djem's knight. 'How?'

Djem gestured away with one hand. 'You focus him here. While you move there.' He chuckled when Jack looked back at the board and saw his mistake. 'Checkmate.' He sat back, eyes on Jack. 'You know what he wants.'

'Answers I cannot give him.'

'But you believe the man in prison, your woman's father – might have those answers?'

Jack reached for his goblet, then decided against it. Clearly, he'd been far too indiscreet. 'Perhaps. At least about the company. Yes.'

'And the man who killed your mother is in the same place.'

'Yes, but—'

'Then give the signore what he most wants,' ventured Djem, holding one hand out, palm cupped, 'while at the same time taking what *you* want.' He held out his other hand, as if they were scales.

Jack exhaled. 'It is a prison, not a tavern. I can't just walk in. I have no authority. Besides, even if I could enter, Martelli has refused to speak. I tell you, if he's not been compelled to answer his gaolers, there is no chance he'll talk to me.'

'Sometimes, in order to survive,' murmured Djem, reaching over the table to pick up Jack's queen, 'you have to risk your most powerful piece.' He placed the queen on the board, showing him the move he could have made to avoid checkmate.

Jack stared at it, the realisation of what Djem meant dawning on him. 'No,' he said, shaking his head. But the prince wasn't the first to think it. The same thought had crossed his own mind.

There was one person Franco Martelli might speak to.

Gianotto Berardi sat on the bench outside the tavern in the September sunshine, nursing a cup of spiced wine and watching the crowds surge past, on their way to or from the *mercato*. He had forgotten how close and crowded the city of his birth was. He missed the palm-fronded fringes of the Guadalquivir, on which he could always smell the sea.

His gaze caught a stately matron, a train of plain-dressed women following in her wake, baskets on their arms. Their features and the variations in their skin tones told him they were slaves. The younger ones walked at the back, hurrying steps and downcast eyes. An older one, however – a Tartar he guessed by her face – walked almost at her mistress's side, the two of them chattering away, both equally outraged at the price a butcher had set the day's meat at. He wondered if any of his girls from Málaga, sold for a princely sum in the markets of Genoa and Pisa, had trickled their way down here yet.

'Good day, signore.'

Berardi looked round to see the man he'd come to meet approaching. He rose with a smile. 'Good day.'

Amerigo Vespucci removed his cap, his bald head gleaming in the sunlight. Glancing at the spiced wine in Berardi's hand, he nodded appreciatively and gestured to a man inside the tavern. 'It is never too early for Vincenzo's medicine.' As he sat, the bench creaked under his thickset frame.

Berardi, who'd never had time for pleasantries or idle conversation, came straight to the matter. 'You spoke to your masters?'

'I did.'

'And they are interested?'

'Most interested. As I said when we were first introduced, they have been seeking to expand their business interests and the markets in Spain, increasingly lucrative so we hear, have long been a draw. Slaves, grain, alum, olive oil – they would be keen investors in all such trades. They are willing to meet with you to discuss a possible deal. Ah,' Amerigo declared appreciatively, as the innkeeper ducked out to hand him a goblet.

Berardi watched him take a deep draught. 'That is good news.' He paused. 'I also told you I'm involved in another venture, beyond the realm of trade? With my new business partner?'

'Yes, indeed. Exploration, you said?'

Berardi saw the shift in the man's face, the keen interest in his eyes. He smiled inwardly, knowing his first impressions of Amerigo Vespucci had been correct. He had seen the same fire in the eyes of Christopher Columbus. 'Yes. We are looking for investors for a voyage. A voyage, we believe, that could change the world.'

35

Ahead, at the end of the street, the high walls of the prison reared up, blocking out the sky.

Jack turned before they reached it. 'You don't have to do this.'

Laora halted with him. 'You have said that,' she murmured. 'But I want to. Besides' – she gave a tight smile, plucking at her hair, shortened to her ears – 'this butchery will have been for nothing.'

He still couldn't believe the transformation. From the young woman he'd woken beside that morning had sprung an elfin lad, with hazel eyes and chiselled cheeks, dressed in a black tunic and hose, a heavy cloak draped around her slim shoulders and a cap perched on her cropped hair. That afternoon she had sat, stock-still, eyes closed, while he – gentle, reluctant – had cut away those lustrous black waves, Amelot cross-legged on the workshop's bed, watching him work. Afterwards, he had left the chamber, leaving the girl to bind Laora's breasts with bands of linen. Despite their intimacy, it had felt indecorous to remain and watch.

'Losing your hair is one thing. I don't know what we might find within those walls, or the repercussions if we're caught. I can go in alone.'

'My father will not speak to you. It is why you came to me, Jack.'

Jack exhaled sharply. He had regretted it almost the moment he'd broached the subject, shortly after his talk with Prince Djem over the game of chess. Expecting her to reject the idea, he'd been shocked when Laora had keenly agreed to it. 'I can do what I need to, then we can leave the city. Forget my pledge to Lorenzo. We have gold enough to get to Spain.'

Her brow furrowed as she pointed to the roll of parchment he held. 'It was me who asked Maddalena for this. She agreed because I told her I thought it might help her father. That, through it, I might make amends. Perhaps even win the signore's forgiveness?' Her eyes flashed with defiance. 'I will not be made a liar by you, Jack!'

He nodded, sorry for the suggestion. Laora had wept, bitterly, when Maddalena de' Medici had entered the old workshop, summoned in secret by him. She cried even harder when, after telling her girlhood friend everything – the crime her father had compelled her to commit, her shame and sadness for the theft – Maddalena had taken her hands and promised to help in any way she could.

It had been a risk, bringing Lorenzo's daughter – more and more a composed young woman these days – into the plan, but one that had paid dividends. A week later, Maddalena had returned, bearing a blank sheet of parchment, with the seal of her father attached.

'This isn't about what you want.' Laora's voice had softened, but her face remained set. 'This is my chance to make up for what I did. I have to see him. I want answers too. You know that.'

He thought of warning her that not all those answers might be satisfactory; or fill the hole in her heart, but she was adamant. 'Stay close to me,' he told her. 'I'll do the talking.'

Jack knocked, his eyes drifting to the inscription carved in the stone above the door. As he read the words, he felt the cold solidity of the dagger pressing against his calf, hidden by his boot.

A wooden hatch at head height in the door lifted and a man's face – square jaw stubble-rough – appeared. His eyes creased in question. 'Yes?'

'We've come to see a prisoner.' Jack passed the scroll to the man, who took it and snapped the hatch shut.

The moments passed, Laora staring fixedly at the door, Jack tapping his foot as he thought of the guard reading words he'd written on the parchment. Would the man know it hadn't come from the signore? Would they be caught in the deception before they'd had a chance to execute the plan?

There was a clatter of bolts and keys. The door opened.

With the guard stood another man, portly and grey, but better dressed and groomed, with a large ring of keys attached to his belt. The warden, perhaps.

'Signor . . .?'

'James. Signor James.' There was little point in giving the man a false name, since any description of him – not least his accent – would be enough for Lorenzo to know who had been here. Jack's only hope, if it came to light that he'd entered by this forgery, was that he would have, in his defence, the answers Lorenzo wanted.

The portly man studied him closely. 'I haven't seen you before?'

'The signore has new information regarding the prisoner.' Jack nodded to the parchment. 'He has sent me to question him.'

'I see. And who is this?' He peered over Jack's shoulder.

'My assistant.'

The portly man breathed in through his nostrils, then took a last glance at the parchment and the instructions upon it, ratified by Lorenzo's seal. 'Very well.' He gestured inside. 'Bartolo will take you to him.'

Jack ducked in through the door, Laora following close behind. He felt, as much as heard, the thud of it shutting behind them, the man sliding the locks and bolts back in place.

'Will you need access to the interrogation chamber today, signore?'

Jack turned at the question.

'I can send men to help administer the apparatus?' offered the portly man.

Jack felt Laora stiffen at his side. 'No. I only need to talk to him.'

'As you wish,' said the warden, looking unconvinced.

The guard, Bartolo, led them down a dim passage, a few chambers – guardrooms, Jack guessed – opening either side. There was another reinforced door, which the guard paused to unlock, before ushering them through. A passage stretched off to the left, while, ahead, an archway emerged on an inner courtyard.

The last of the sun lit up one corner of the yard, a tiny pool of light in an otherwise barren enclosure. Doors lined the walls, windowed with grated openings. Beyond the iron bars, murky stone chambers, bare of anything except narrow wooden benches, were populated with ragged clumps of human beings. Most were motionless, cramped up on the benches or stooped against the walls, but some stalked the cells, eyes wild under matted thickets of hair.

Bartolo led them through a door at the end, then up a set of stairs. A tight passage lined with more doors stretched away. A single brand was burning on the wall. Taking it from its bracket, Bartolo guided them along, the torch sputtering. The grilles were smaller here, cells filled with shadows and incoherent murmurings, the air acrid with urine and other odours. Someone shrieked and flung themselves at the bars, making Jack start and Laora jump back. A flash of bared teeth in the torchlight, then they were moving on.

'We've kept him isolated from the other prisoners,' Bartolo said, as they approached one of the last doors. 'As the signore requested.' He paused, unhooked a key from his belt. 'He's chained, but keep near the door,' warned the guard, a growl in his tone. 'Some of these bastards are shit-flingers.'

Unlocked, the door groaned open. Torchlight spilled across a small space, a bench on one side, a bucket on the other. There was a figure hunched in one corner, wearing only a dirty tunic, his face smothered by a tangle of grey hair and beard. Laora sucked in a breath as the figure looked up, blinking painfully at the light.

The change in Franco Martelli was astonishing. Gone was the towering, proud and angry man. In his place was a gaunt wretch with red, seeping eyes, filthy skin and an anxious, unfocused gaze. Jack had kept back, out of the pool of light, not wanting the man to see his face and react in some way that might alert the guard, but it didn't seem to matter – Martelli hardly seemed to recognise his own gaoler. Lorenzo had stripped the man of his wealth and power. Now, he'd taken whatever was left. Jack found himself struck again by the Medici capacity for ruthlessness. The Father of the Fatherland could be a cruel and vengeful master.

Forcing his gaze away, Jack turned to Bartolo. 'You have another prisoner here. The murderer – the one in the mask?'

'Him?' said Bartolo, looking taken aback.

'The signore wanted me to inspect him while I was here.'

'Inspect him?'

'Yes,' said Jack, his tone firm. From inside Martelli's cell came the clunk of a chain. 'He has a personal interest in the case. He knows one of the men killed by him.'

'You'll get nothing of use. He's . . .' The guard shook his head, almost shuddered.

'Still, I have my orders. Orders,' Jack added carefully, 'from Signor Lorenzo himself.'

At the mild threat, Bartolo capitulated with a curt nod. 'As you wish.'

'My assistant can get started on the interrogation here. Can't you?' prompted Jack, seeing Laora was still staring, transfixed by her father.

She flinched when he tapped her shoulder. 'Yes. Of course.'

Bartolo looked a little surprised at the pitch of this young man's voice, but he motioned Jack on, tight-lipped. 'I'll take you down.' Passing Laora the torch, reminding her to stay in the doorway and not to venture into the cell, the guard led Jack back the way they had come. 'We're holding him below the north tower. It's where we usually keep them.'

'Them?'

'The insane.'

As they spiralled down into the dank, foul-smelling bowels of the prison, Bartolo brandishing another torch for the descent into darkness, Jack felt his whole body begin to prickle. His chest grew tight, breaths fast. He had been so preoccupied on getting into the Stinche, his thoughts hadn't strayed much beyond, into the realms of what he planned to do once he was inside. Now, his mind was full of it. Anticipation blazed in him. After all these months – *years* – he would silence the demon that stalked his dreams and set his mother's soul free. With every step that took him closer, he felt the hardness of the dagger hidden in his boot.

There was a single door at the bottom, no grate, the wood pitted. There was a noise coming from beyond: a high keening sound. Bartolo murmured something as he reached for a key on his belt. Jack thought he was talking to him, then realised the guard had muttered a prayer.

'Father?' The word came as a whisper. Laora swallowed thickly, tried again. 'Father? It's me.'

The face lifted again, the watery eyes drifting towards her where she stood, trembling, in the doorway. This time, his gaze seemed to fix on her, some quickening of awareness behind it. He shifted, the chains around his ankles dragging on the floor. 'Who are you?' His voice was tremulous.

'It's me,' she repeated, stepping forward, over the threshold of the cell door. 'Laora. Your daughter.'

He moved again, hands clawing the wall to help himself stand. 'Laora?'

She was surprised to feel tears spring in her eyes at the sight of him: his emaciated body, the sores on his legs and arms, the stains on his tattered tunic. It was as if he had aged a hundred years since she had seen him last. There was something terrible in the change; fragility and hopelessness, a life abandoned yet not relinquished. Purgatory, she thought. Not dead. Not living.

Despite the brave face she had shown to Jack, she had been so frightened of seeing him, of entering this place. The last thing she had expected to feel was pity. But, however much she'd hated and feared this man through her life, he was still her father, her blood.

The torch spat sparks across her hand, startling her back to the task at hand. She wouldn't have long. 'Father, I need you to talk to me. I need to know about the Court of Wolves. What are their plans? Are they a threat to Signor Lorenzo? To the House of Medici?'

'Laora?' he muttered again in confusion. He took a few stumbling paces towards her, the chains uncurling like heavy snakes of iron. There was a sour reek coming off him. 'My daughter? What has happened to you? Dear God!'

Her free hand strayed to her cropped hair. 'I had to. It was the only way I could see you. It will grow back,' she added anxiously.

'Help me, Laora,' he said, his voice strengthening, something of the old power grating in it. He halted close to her, brought up short by the chains. 'You must help free me!'

She nodded uncertainly. 'I will try. But, Father, you must answer my questions.'

His brow puckered, eyes narrowing under his matted fringe.

Laora had a flash of memory: lingering in the doorway of her parents' bedchamber as a young girl, watching as he stood before a mirror, carefully brushing that mane, a rich perfume filling the air from the oil he had sleeked through it, a rare smile reflected in the glass as he caught her looking.

'It's that whoreson, isn't it?' growled her father, slamming her back to the present. 'The Englishman? What has he done to you? God damn it, I'll break his neck!'

Laora stepped back. Her father's hands had bunched into fists, the knuckles torn and bruised as if he'd been punching something. All at once, something rushed up in her. 'Why did you hurt my mother? All those years, Father? How could you? *How could you take her from me?*'

At her cry, a howl echoed from one of the nearby cells.

Jack stared at the horror, chained to the wall of the cell in the sickly glare of the torch Bartolo had set to life. The figure was twisting this way and that, squirming vainly against the manacles that bound his wrists and ankles to the stone, mewling as if in pain. The years, and his mind, had turned his enemy into something enormous: a mountain of a man with massive fists and a leering death-mask face. The reality was quite different.

Yes, the man was large, but no taller than Ned and not much broader than Valentine. His mask had gone, lost or removed. What remained was a face ravaged by some terrible force. Man-made or natural, Jack couldn't tell. The man's skin had been stripped away – peeled, he thought – healing back only reluctantly in puckered ribbons of raw-looking flesh. His lips had been cut away on one side, brown stumps of teeth visible in the gap, as if his mouth were crooked in a permanent lopsided grin. His eye had been removed, a warped hollow where it had been, and his ear was a root of flesh. The mask, once so sinister – such a feature of his dreams – was all at once understandable. Who wouldn't wish to hide such hideousness?

After the shock had worn off, Jack moved closer, assaulted by the rancid stink coming off the man. He continued to whimper and fight, the manacles rattling against the wall, his one eye swivelling in its socket, never quite landing on him.

'Do you remember me?' Jack murmured.

The man's whines faded at the sound of his voice, but he didn't stop struggling. Jack glanced at the door. Bartolo had agreed to leave him alone, but he knew the guard was waiting at the top of the steps. He would have to do this quickly, quietly. He looked at the manacles, wondering if he might somehow open one when the deed was done? He could say the man got loose, tried to attack him. That he'd acted in self-defence. He doubted anyone here would be aggrieved by the loss. Bartolo had said the man had spoken no sense at all since he'd been brought in and had wounded several guards in his repeated fights to get free. The guard had confided that he didn't know why the signore had ordered him kept alive, when the end of a rope was all the fiend was good for. Jack knew, though. The monster was the snare that kept him here, under Lorenzo's control.

Bending down, eyes not leaving his enemy, Jack reached into his boot and drew the dagger from its sheath. It was a stiletto he'd bought in the *mercato*, long and razor-keen. One stab up under the ribs and it would be done. Jack felt sweat break out on his brow. His mouth was dry. He realised he felt afraid. Not of the man, but of what he'd come here to do.

He hadn't expected this. This was not the first life he'd taken. Yet this was different. This wasn't a battlefield, where everything happened in brief, brutal bursts, where to kill was a necessity to live. He thought of Estevan Carrillo, his sword punching into the man's throat as he'd come at him, thought of his brother, Harry, his hands wrapping tight around his throat. Passion, violence and impulse. No. This was very different. This was the killing of a man in cold blood: a man who couldn't fight back or defend himself. A man who was suddenly not so much vicious beast, but wounded animal caught in a trap.

All at once, he was back in Lewes, a lifetime ago. He had been out in the woods with Grace, her hand warm in his; had come home to find his mother perched on the mossy tree-stump in her garden, her hair loose around her shoulders, a hum of bees in the lavender. Approaching, he had seen she was bent forward, touching something on the ground. Turning to see him, Sarah had pressed a finger to her lips and beckoned him forward. Curled on the grass at her feet was a dog, with patchy fur and jutting ribs. A single gold feather was stuck to the corner of its trembling jaw.

'I caught him trying to take one of the hens,' she whispered, reaching out to stroke the panting dog, which opened one eye warily.

'Why didn't you kill it?' murmured Jack, astonished. His mother loved her hens, whose eggs were a bounty in the lean times.

'He is injured, look,' said Sarah, pointing to a seeping sore on the animal's hind leg. 'I cannot blame him. He was just hungry.' Her eyes flicked up to his, flashing in the sunlight. 'Fetch me some water will you, James. Some cloths. We will help him.'

And so they had and the dog had become part of their family for a few short months; flopped on his bed at night, making Sarah laugh as he pelted around the garden chasing flies, until Jack had found him one day, shot with an arrow, sly grins on the faces of the boys who tormented him.

He gripped the dagger tighter, fingers whitening around the hilt. 'You killed my mother.' His voice was ragged. 'Do you remember, you son of a bitch? I want you to tell me. How did she die? Did she suffer? Did she—'

The man was muttering. Jack took a step closer, straining to hear. It sounded like an Italian dialect. A few words he recognised sprang out here and there, fragments, he realised, of a prayer. For a moment he thought the man had seen the dagger and his intentions, but then he saw his eye was fixed on a point somewhere behind him. He turned as that eye suddenly widened as if in terror. There was nothing there but mildewed wall. Whatever he was seeing, Jack could not. There was no recognition. No sanity at all in that staring gaze.

Jack lowered the blade, staggered back. The beast of rage clawing at him all these years had slunk beneath the surface, leaving only his mother's face in his mind; her soft smile and loud laugh, her kindness and her pity. He had thought, by killing the man who had murdered her, that he would set her soul free. But now, he knew, she wasn't the one who'd been chained.

Leaving the man, whimpering and gibbering, Jack stumbled up the stairs, every step lifting him out of the darkness, into the light. Bartolo noted his pale face with a nod and not a little satisfaction, before descending to lock the cell door, then leading him back to Martelli's cell where Laora was waiting, ashen and dazed.

The light was fading by the time the two of them left the Stinche, both of them tight-lipped and silent. Laora halted outside, sucking in a long breath as the bolts and locks snapped back into place behind them. 'Jack,' she began.

As she raised her hand to her head, he saw she was shaking. Across the street, a drunk was shouting at passers-by, becoming more vociferous.

'Not here,' he said, placing a hand on her shoulder and steering her gently back towards the workshop, a few streets away.

As they entered, the rush of air setting all the candles aflutter, Amelot hopped off the bed and pushed through the curtains to meet them, her stare keen with question. Jack glanced at her as Laora removed her cap and shrugged off the cloak. He'd promised the girl he would ask the masked man about Amaury before he ended his life: demand to know if he'd been involved in the priest's abduction. He would have to let her down in a moment. First things first.

Laora had sat on the edge of the bed and was staring at the floor. As he crouched before her, she met his gaze, her eyes bright. 'What did they do to him, Jack?'

He shook his head, not knowing what to say.

Drawing a breath, she slid her palms along her thighs. 'He wants a pardon, sealed by the signore. He told me he knows things – Lorenzo's enemies and their plans – but he won't speak until he is freed.'

'Why didn't he offer this months ago?' questioned Jack doubtfully. 'He could have saved himself from that place.'

'I don't know.'

Jack, looking up at her, wondered if Martelli had seen, in his daughter, something to live for. Whatever the reason for the man's change of heart, it didn't help him. If he went to Lorenzo with this, he would have to admit his deception and Laora's part in it, putting her at risk. 'He said nothing else? Nothing about the Court of Wolves?'

'There was one thing,' Laora said, after a pause. 'He said the signore would want to hear what he had to say. That his enemies were closer than he knew – closer to home.'

'Closer? Someone in his household?' Jack shook his head. 'But this is what Lorenzo has feared. We need to know who. Are they connected to the company?'

'That is all he said. But . . .'

'But what?'

Laora frowned. 'There was just something in the way he said it. Closer to home.'

Angelo Poliziano made his way back to the palazzo, a bag of books slung over his shoulder: volumes of poetry for Giovanni. The boy had become fractious with the pressure of his intensive schooling, readying him for the College of Cardinals, and Poliziano knew he needed some light relief. Perhaps he should speak to Lorenzo about bringing in another tutor for Giovanni's lessons in theology? The Dominican friar, Savonarola, was highly regarded as a fierce orator, a skill that any prospective cardinal would do well to learn.

'Hello, my dear.'

Poliziano turned, recognition of that voice sending a rush of heat through his face. There he stood. Giovanni Pico della Mirandola. Thinner, paler, but familiar as an old song; one he knew by heart. Pico wore a black cloak, the hood drawn up to shadow his face.

Feeling himself start to smile in greeting, Poliziano forced back his joy. He glanced anxiously around the busy street as he went to him. 'Pico? Does the signore know you've returned?'

'No! And you mustn't tell him. Not yet. Not until I have spoken to him myself. Come,' Pico urged, steering him off the thoroughfare and into a gloomy side street. Once they were out of view he smiled, shook his head. 'Oh, my friend.' He reached up to touch Poliziano's cheek. 'I couldn't stay away.'

Poliziano drew back. 'You shouldn't have returned, Pico. He banished you. You betrayed him. Betrayed us all.'

'You haven't missed me? Do not lie,' Pico murmured as Poliziano shook his head. 'I see it in your face. Just as I have missed you.'

This time, as he reached up, Poliziano let the man touch his cheek. His fingers were cool.

'There is a hole in my heart, Angelo. Nothing has been the same without you. Not food. Not poetry. Not wine.'

'Not lovers?' muttered Poliziano, but he didn't pull away. 'Where were you?'

'France. Other places. It doesn't matter.'

Poliziano caught the young man's hand as his gaze darted away. 'What is it?' He stared at his friend, trying to divine the unfamiliar emotions flickering in those grey eyes. Was that fear he saw? 'What has happened, Pico? Why have you returned?'

'I told you. For you.'

Pico turned back to him, his smile now sly and keen, filled with that wild spirit that had ensnared him years ago.

'Come, my dear.' Pico threaded his arm through Poliziano's and tugged. 'A jug of wine? Just the two of us? I will tell you my adventures.' His smile broadened when Poliziano didn't resist. 'And you can tell me all that has happened in my absence.'

36

The air on the top floor was musty, as if it hadn't been disturbed in a while, shutters drawn across windows, doors closed. Jack could hear the faint clatter from the kitchens below. He ran his hands over the wall of the passage, plain of any gilding up here where no one important ever ventured, decorated only with cracks. On the other side, through layers of mortar and stone, was the palace of Lorenzino and Giovanni di' Pierfrancesco de' Medici.

Closer to home.

When Laora had said this, Jack, thinking through the possibilities of what Martelli could have been implying, had come to wonder if he'd meant it literally. Might that explain the noises he'd sometimes heard on this deserted floor and the pope's men – coming for Prince Djem – appearing as if from nowhere, unseen and unheard?

He had asked Laora whether she thought Lorenzo's cousins could be working against him, but she hadn't thought it possible. Yes, there had been disagreements in the Medici family over the years, disputes even. But Lorenzo had taken the boys in when their father died, had raised them as his own. He had given them everything they could want, even granting them his estate at Cafaggiolo. No, she was adamant, Lorenzino and Giovanni were family, bonded to the signore in blood. In Florence, a man could have no greater loyalty than to his house and his father. But Jack, thinking of Harry, knew kin could be the worst kind of enemy.

His inspection of the passage wall revealing nothing, he headed into the armoury. He was due to report on Djem – Lorenzo demanding regular accounts of the prince's cooperation in his new place of confinement. The signore was at Mass, but he wouldn't have long. The expansive chamber was shadowy, arrows of light lancing through the closed shutters. The air in here was thick with odours of iron and rust, leather and steel, making Jack think of camps and battlegrounds. Catapults and weapons haunted the shadows, forgotten, dust-filmed; wars for the Medici fought now behind the counters of their banks in the clink of coins, behind the seals that stamped trade deals to life and the doors of the Signoria, where power was cultivated and brokered. Jack turned his attention to the fresco of the battle that decorated the wall that adjoined the cousins' palace, hills and cypress trees descending to a thicket of spears and men.

Starting at the far end, stepping over chests and around piles of brigandines, he was surprised to find not plaster, but panels of wood beneath his hands, the cracks in the grain and in the gaps between the boards. Looking closer, he realised there were latches set at regular intervals along it, almost indistinguishable from the mass of colours in the sprawl of horses and men. A series of small doors, hidden in the painting.

Jack opened the first, his heart picking up pace, until he saw it was just a cupboard, filled with coils of rope. Crouching, he reached in and rapped on the far wall. The lime-washed stone was solid against his knuckles. Closing it he moved on to the next, crammed with small barrels of grease that stank of dead things as he leaned over them to knock again. In this way, he moved methodically along the wall of storage compartments, but although his body was focused on the task, his mind began to drift.

He didn't have to do this. He had faced his mother's killer in the Stinche, had felt the torch of rage he'd been holding all these years blown out at the sight of that chained and piteous thing. That night, held in Laora's arms, he had slept without dreams. When he woke the next day it was as though a tide had passed through him, leaving a beach bare and new, his feet upon the sand. He had known then that he was done; that he could take the money Lorenzo had given to him and leave this city. There was nothing else tying him here and the road west was calling.

But Laora had begged him. Amelot too, in her silent way. Both of them had things that tethered them here, ties they could not yet cut. No matter how much Martelli had hurt her, Laora was desperate to see her father released from the Stinche, even though she did not plan to stay, and Amelot would not give up her search for Amaury. Not while there was one trail left in the hunt for his abductors. So, Jack had come, in hope this might lead to the answers that would free them, these two women who had become part of his strange new family. Ned with his unwavering humour. Valentine's rough loyalty. Fey Amelot. And Laora, her softness, her light, filtered though it was through a prism of sadness, no less rich or warm for that. The way she understood him without words. The ways they fit together. *Old souls*, she said.

Ned and Valentine were packing their gear and gathering supplies in readiness. His father's ring and sword, and the silver wolf badge Marco Valori had given to him were with them for safekeeping. The road, when they took it, might not lead him to the life he had dreamed of; the shining cloak of knighthood left far behind him. It wouldn't be what the son of a nobleman should have, perhaps. But it might be more than the bastard boy of a widow and a suicide, and a band of outlaws could hope for.

Jack had opened a fifth door on some folded gambesons when he saw it – a mark in the dust that layered the cupboard floor. Looking closer he saw it was a handprint, fingers trailing from it. But it wasn't facing inwards – it was facing out, fingers pointing towards him. Removing the gambesons, he reached in and knocked. The sound echoed, hollow. As he felt along the top, he realised the whole back panel was loose. Digging in his fingers, sweating in the close air, Jack pulled it down to reveal a tunnel, no more than a crawl space, the sides and roof wedged by beams. It was short, the other side visible by a frail rectangle of light. He stared at it – until the deep toll of the cathedral's bell started him to life.

He could wait, show Lorenzo what he'd found, let the signore follow this trail and – if it led him to his enemies – appeal for Martelli's freedom in return for his indictment. But a dogged need to see for himself what was on the other side tugged at him. He still had some time; the signore always stayed chatting after Mass at San Lorenzo. Jack grabbed a dagger from one of the shelves and crawled inside. Turning awkwardly, he pulled the gambesons in after him and closed the cupboard door, easing the latch back into place. He did the same with the panel, not wanting to alert anyone on the other side to his discovery. As he made his way through, inching towards the light, dust puffed up around him, making his eyes itch. Crumbled chunks of stone and mortar jabbed at his palms, his shoulders and head bumping against the beams.

Feeling around at the other end, he found another latch. Lifting it carefully, there was a click as a catch released and the door opened. He peered cautiously into a bare room, shuttered and empty. As he squeezed through, his leg scraped on something. Wincing, he looked down to see a nail poking out of the floor. He saw a scrap of material caught on it and pulled it free, thinking it had been torn from his hose. But his hose were blue. This wisp of wool was black. He thought of the pope's men, slipping down the stairs, at one with the shadows in their cloaks.

Out in the room, he rose, brushing dust from his hands, to see a row of cupboards on this side too, only these made of plain wood. Marking in his mind the one he'd come through, he crossed to the door and, when he heard nothing beyond, opened it and stepped into a passage.

The palazzo of Lorenzino and Giovanni was smaller and less ostentatious than their cousin's. Jack, who had only entered the ground-floor reception rooms during the masked ball at Epiphany, was surprised by how plain and dingy the upper storeys were by comparison: a series of boxy storerooms, some empty, others cluttered with chests and broken furniture, and cramped chambers he took for servants' rooms. The third and second floors were much the same; the rooms here grander in scale, but furnished sparsely, and there was little in the way of the extravagant gilding and marble embellishments, paintings and statues that graced the Palazzo Medici. Jack knew Lorenzo's cousins spent most of their time at Cafaggiolo, out in the Mugello, and guessed more of their money and attention had been lavished there.

He was descending to the first floor, where some decoration was now visible – a painting of the Virgin on one wall, a small bust of a full-lipped man with curly hair perched on a plinth that he thought might be of Giovanni di' Pierfrancesco, the younger of the two brothers – when he heard footsteps. He darted behind the corner of the passage as a figure emerged from a door next to the bust. He caught sight of black robes and a pale fuzz of hair around a tonsure. For one shocked moment, he thought it was Marsilio Ficino. But, as the figure strode away down the passage, he realised it wasn't the elderly priest, but the friar from San Marco. Fra Giorgio Antonio Vespucci – Amerigo's uncle and tutor to Lorenzo's cousins.

A memory drifted across his mind. That day, when he'd followed Pico from Fiesole – the day he discovered Prince Djem – he had seen a figure in black stalking the halls of the palazzo. He had assumed at the time it was Marsilio, returned early from the villa. He thought of Lorenzino, the night of the feast, walking out with Amerigo, those words he had murmured about family. *After all he has done to yours?* Thought of Amerigo's interest in what might lie beyond the Western Ocean, his feverish talk of lost islands and the sailor – Columbus. Hadn't Lorenzo said Fra Giorgio had been a member of the Academy under his grandfather? A translator of manuscripts like Amaury?

After waiting, listening for footsteps, sweat trickling down his neck, Jack risked a look inside the room the friar had emerged from, the door of which was ajar. It was a study, not as expansive as Lorenzo's and nowhere near as jammed with wealth, but well-appointed, with a desk and cushioned chair beneath a pair of tall windows, a few paintings on the walls – scenes of Roman temples and men in togas – a large armoire, shelves of books and rows of chests.

Jack tried the doors of the armoire, almost as high as the ceiling, but it was locked. The chests too. He crossed to the desk, ears pricked for sound of approach. One of the shutters was open at his back, a hot breath of wind curling the papers on the desk. He glanced through them. They looked like accounts, but nothing that held any significance for him. He cursed beneath his breath. Time was running short. He should return to the palazzo – let the signore deal with this. But this knowledge came with a stab of frustration. All these months and now it felt as though an answer were just in front of him; one last thread that might unravel the final knot. He shook his head. This wasn't his business any more.

As Jack turned to go, his boot caught something under the desk. Glancing down, he found a coffer, inlaid with mother-of-pearl. He bent to move it back in place, then saw a key poking from the lock. He paused in the stillness, head cocked. Hearing nothing, he lifted the coffer, placed it on the desk and turned the key. Inside was a compartment filled with a score or more other keys. But there was no time left to go exploring. He was about to close the lid, when he realised the compartment only went two-thirds down inside the coffer. There was something underneath. Pinching the sides, he pulled, felt the whole thing lift free. Beneath was a smaller section. He caught a glimpse of silver pieces and thought they were coins. But, as he lifted the compartment away, he realised his mistake. They weren't coins. They were badges. Each one, the head of a wolf.

As he stood there staring down at them, the world beyond the shutters erupted with noise. Jack whipped round to see dozens of birds casting into the sky from window sills and rooftops, the air filling with the clapping of wings. He could hear dogs barking – some near, some far – as if every animal in the city had awoken at once. Moments later he felt it: a low rumbling, like a cart on cobbles or distant thunder. The wolves in the coffer were trembling. Then, he knew. He'd felt this before.

Beneath his hands the desk was rattling, the shutters at his back banging. Books tottered off the shelves. The clothes' perch jolted on its base, went crashing to the floor. Bits of masonry were crumbling from the walls, cracks snapping across the plaster in white puffs of dust. He could hear the sound of things above and below, outside and in, collapsing and falling. Screams in the distance. The wild clang of church bells in their towers. This was far more violent than the tremor he'd experienced in the market. It felt as though vast hands had seized the city and were shaking it viciously, side to side, up and down. Felt like the world was ending.

He tried to walk, drunken, lurching steps, the floor juddering and undulating beneath him, tiles rattling, floorboards flexing. The armoire was swaying. A book flew from a shelf to strike him on the shoulder, then one of the shelves broke from the wall, flinging more objects at him. He staggered away to avoid them, arm up to protect his face, a shower of plaster raining down on his head. Jack was almost at the door, when the armoire tipped forward. The great thing swung out into space, like a clumsy dancer reaching for a partner, then crashed down on top of him, slamming him into the floor.

37

Jack came to, his mouth gummed with dust and the copper tang of blood. He stirred slowly, eyes cracking open into blurred darkness. As he tried to move, pain lanced through him and he sank back with a gasp. Beneath him was something soft. His head was swimming. From somewhere close by came an odd shuffling that conjured images of animals sniffing their way towards him in the black. He tried again to sit, his body shouting with a hundred different voices of pain.

'Here,' came a papery voice. A shadow, looming over him. 'Drink!'

He felt liquid flood his parched mouth, trailing bitter down his throat. He coughed, spitting up bloody water, then seized the vessel and drank, a sudden thirst overwhelming him.

'Careful now!'

As the man tugged the cup from his hands and helped him sit, Jack realised he was speaking French. The pain in his torso was a solid band, wrapped like armour around his ribs, shooting outwards, bright and sharp as glass, as he breathed. He felt the area tenderly, winced to find every part sore and bruised. Were all his ribs broken?

He focused with difficulty in the gloom and through the pounding in his head, to see the figure stooping awkwardly to sit before him. For a moment, all he saw was an old man, so near death as to be almost skeletal; wisps of white hair floating around a skull-like face, skin grey and wrinkled, spotted with sores, one eye clouded white. Then he saw the withered stump where one of his hands should be, and felt the shock of recognition.

'Amaury?' Fear seized him. He'd long ago given up any real hope of finding the priest alive. 'Am I dead?' Christ, was this hell? It certainly smelled like it. Rot and urine. Dank despair.

The old priest chuckled toothlessly. 'Perhaps!' His mirth faded. 'But, no. I think not.'

He looked like an Old Testament hermit, come wandering out of a cave.

As his shock faded, Jack cast his gaze around the space he was in. It looked like a cellar, barrels stacked along the walls, mouldy smells of earth and wine turned to vinegar. There was a door to the left of the heap of tattered blankets he was sitting on and a faint source of light bleeding from somewhere deeper in.

How had he come to be here? His mind struggled to piece together the fragments floating in it. The secret door in the walls between the palazzi. The silver wolves in the coffer. An earthquake. He had been struck, crushed. Those memories were solid, but there were others, strange and formless: voices in a haze of dust, hands on him, a sensation of release, then pain and blackness, the agonising motion of a cart, smell of rain and pine, a tower rising above him, hooves clattering on stone. 'Where am I? How did I get here?'

'They brought you. Two days ago.' Amaury peered at him, a smile cracking his sunken face. 'I knew you would come, James Wynter. I heard them speak of you sometimes. I knew you would come.' He sucked in a wheezy breath. 'Of course, I hoped you might release me, not join me. Still, it is good to have company. Isn't it?' he called, addressing the darkness. He waved his hand apologetically when there was no response. 'Don't mind them.'

Jack stared at him, not knowing what to say. Had the old man lost his mind? He took in his surroundings again. Had the priest been down here all this time, alone in the dark?

'As to your other question, young man.' Amaury clambered upright with a pop of bones. 'We are under the ground. Come!'

As the priest limped into the shadows, using barrels and crumbling bits of wall to support himself, Jack got to his feet with effort, a hiss escaping his lips at the pain. Pausing to let the swimming in his head subside, he walked unsteadily after him, towards the faint light source, which he realised was coming from above. Things scuttled away from him, darting behind barrels. Rats, he guessed. There were chunks of masonry on the floor, scatterings of dust like ash. A few of the walls were traced with deep cracks. Jack guessed the quake must have happened here too. Where were they? Somewhere beyond the city if his fractured memories were correct.

Amaury pointed to the cellar roof. 'There!'

Jack could see slivers of bluish light like veins twisting their way across the uneven ceiling. But it wasn't just rough-hewn stone. There was something strange up there, brown and soft like moss, growing in a jagged line across a small section of the cellar roof. Jack blinked up at it, trying to work it out. There was an awful smell here. Meat spoiling.

Amaury tugged at his sleeve. 'It got bigger!' he exclaimed in hushed tones. 'When the earth shook. I told you it would, my lord!' he added, grinning sagely, his one good eye flickering somewhere over Jack's shoulder. He ambled to a nearby barrel. 'I put them up there, so they wouldn't see.' He put a gnarled finger to his lips. 'Sssshh!'

As he began to heave the barrel closer to the cracks of light, Jack moved to help him, grimacing with the effort.

Amaury made a shooing motion once they had it in place. 'Up! Up!'

Gritting his teeth, Jack climbed slowly, gingerly on to the barrel. He reached for the roof, then recoiled as his fingers touched something soft and mushy. The smell of putrefaction was overpowering. Then he realised – it wasn't moss sprouting from the cracks in the stone, but rats, scores of them, their broken bodies stuffed into the gaps through which the daylight was struggling to bleed. 'Dear God,' he choked, fighting off a wave of nausea.

'All day and night, I tempted them out. Bash! Bash!' Amaury slapped the side of the barrel.

Forcing back his disgust, Jack peered up between the bodies. He could see a slice of deep blue sky – autumn rich – heard the chatter of birds. 'Where does it go?'

'Out!' exclaimed Amaury, peering up at him. 'The world!'

'Why didn't you try to escape?'

'Too high,' said the priest, waving his stump. 'Too high.' His head jerked suddenly in the direction of the door, eyes narrowing. 'Down!' he hissed. '*Get down!*'

Jack jumped from the barrel, stifling a yell at the shock of pain. He helped Amaury shift it away, then both of them struggled back to the blankets, half-leaning on one another, as footfalls descended beyond the door.

Jack collapsed on the blankets, sweat breaking out all over his body. There was a clatter of keys and the door opened. Two men appeared, neither of whom Jack recognised, although each wore a silver wolf badge on his tunic.

One, a dark-haired man, with a jutting jaw and close-set eyes, beckoned to him. 'Out.'

Jack glanced over at Amaury, who had shrunk behind one of the barrels and was humming a tuneless melody. After a moment, Jack struggled to his feet. The second man entered, impatient at his slowness, seized his arm and marched him through. The last thing Jack saw before the door was shut was the priest, peering out from the barrel, finger to his lips.

The men escorted him up the steps through another door, then out into blazing sunlight, dazzling after the cellar dark. He caught a glimpse of a blocky tower with a red-tiled roof thrusting above a series of other imposing buildings, castle-like in design; orchards and ornamental gardens, outbuildings with forested hills rising up beyond, then he was being thrust into a barn-like structure stacked with more barrels, sacks of grain and shelves of casks and jars, the vaulted roof supported by wooden pillars.

There was a stool placed beside one of the pillars, which he was pushed roughly down on by the man with the jutting jaw, while the other snatched up a length of rope that was used to bind his hands behind the beam, every movement sending pain lancing through his broken ribs. The two men left the storeroom, leaving him sagged on the stool, sweat dripping from his nose. There were fissures in the walls here, too, and a pile of broken pots and jars, swept hastily into a corner. More evidence of the quake? Two days, Amaury said he'd been here. Jack thought of Laora, Ned and the others, prayed they were safe in the city.

The door behind him opened. He twisted painfully at the sound of footsteps and drew a breath at the sight of the approaching figure. It was Marco Valori.

The young man was dressed in black hose and a doublet trimmed with silver braid, on which was fixed his wolf badge, glinting in the sunlight streaming through the store's high windows. As he came to stand before him, Jack saw he was holding a goblet.

Marco shook his head as he studied him. 'You look as though you have been through a war, my friend. Here.' He moved towards him with the goblet. 'It is wine,' he assured, as Jack jerked his head away. 'There,' he murmured, tilting it carefully into his mouth. 'Better?'

Jack took a few sips, the wine sweet and cool in his dry mouth. He nodded.

'Good.' Marco smiled tightly, then dragged a stool from a corner to sit before him, placing the goblet on the floor between them. 'So, we find ourselves in an interesting place.'

Jack guessed he didn't mean the store. He had many questions, but he wanted to wait, see what his friend – if he could still call him that – would tell him of his own accord.

Marco let the silence drag on, then took a breath. 'I am assuming, given where Fra Giorgio found you, that you must have discovered the passage. Did you tell anyone about it? The signore?' When Jack didn't answer, Marco sighed heavily. 'I want to help you, Jack, truly I do.'

The man had started calling him by the name some months ago, after he'd heard Laora use it. Jack, more and more easy in their friendship, hadn't stopped him.

'But, before I can do that, I need some assurances. Some show of good faith.'

'No,' Jack said, after a pause. 'I didn't tell anyone. I didn't have time.'

Marco nodded. 'It is what we hoped.'

'And who is *we*? Fra Giorgio? Amerigo? Lorenzino and Giovanni di' Pierfrancesco? You? The company? Are you all in this together? Are you all working against the signore?'

If this was true, then the conspiracy reached far deeper than Lorenzo de' Medici had feared. The signore, although troubled by the Court of Wolves, had nonetheless seen them as a force beyond his immediate sphere: something he could seek to infiltrate and then control – certainly not directly connected to members of his own family. That was something the signore had always refused to countenance when Jack had reeled off lists of potential traitors in his household. It was as if Lorenzo's eyes were blind to the possibility that someone of his own blood could betray him. As if any member of the House of Medici was beyond reproach.

'How did you find the passage?' Marco pressed. 'Did Franco Martelli tell you of it?' The man nodded at Jack's surprise. 'We know you went to the Stinche. Well,' he said grimly, when Jack didn't speak. 'Martelli won't be around much longer to talk of things he shouldn't. He knows the price of betrayal.'

'How do you know I went to see him? Have you been spying on me too?'

'Yes.' Marco's tone was calm, matter-of-fact. 'As you have been spying on us. Don't look so shocked, Jack. It was clear, soon enough, that the signore was using you to get close to us. So we drew you in. Showed you what we wanted you to see. Enough to keep you – and Lorenzo – occupied. Enough to keep your focus on us and away from our masters.'

Jack's heart was pounding. Now it made sense, why Marco's early eagerness to know about Lorenzo's weaknesses had waned: they had known he was a fraud. He struggled through the fog in his mind to think back through the times he'd spent with him and the men of the company – the kick-games and the banquets, the laughter and wine. Had there been signs? Why hadn't he seen them? 'When did you know?'

'It doesn't matter. What matters is what happens now. You see, Jack, I believed from the beginning that you could be of great use to us, even after we knew your interest in our company was duplicitous. I told our patrons I thought you could be turned to our cause. I saw how frustrated you were with the signore. You tried to hide it, but those evenings in the taverns, at the arena, the drink flowing? It always surprises me how loose men allow their lips to become with this.' He nudged the goblet with his boot. 'Englishmen, in particular, seem to have a weakness for it. It is why I drink my wine watered.'

Jack closed his eyes. All those nights, Marco, flush-faced and loquacious at his side, had really been soberly taking everything in?

'Not that you didn't play your cards close to your chest,' Marco added, seeing his mortification. 'You kept up your disguise, if not your frustrations. But when you needed my help, hiding Laora? That was when we learned what you had come to this city for. What was important to you. What the signore wanted from you.'

'You've been watching us?' Jack demanded, face burning, thinking of him and Laora, limbs entwined, truths shared in the darkness. He strained against his bonds, but they held fast and he only succeeded in launching a sickening wave of pain.

'In this city even walls have ears, Jack.'

'Your patrons?' Jack gritted his teeth against his fury. 'Who are they?'

'Signori Lorenzino and Giovanni di' Pierfrancesco de' Medici.'

'They are behind the Court of Wolves?'

'Not in its initial guise. The company, when it was first established, was merely a fraternity for *condottieri*, little more than a duelling society. Seven years ago, Signor Lorenzino entered the company. Immediately, he saw its potential. He used his name and influence to build and expand it. In time, he brought Signor Giovanni in to help him lead it.'

'Saw its potential for what?'

'Support – military, economic, political. Everything he and his brother have been denied under the signore.'

'Denied? All I have seen is what Lorenzo has given them.'

Marco smiled humourlessly. 'Then you haven't been looking closely enough. I told you, when we first met, that the signore found himself in financial trouble after his incarceration in the court of King Ferrante of Naples and the collapse of several banks? That there were rumours he was forced to use money from the city's coffers to shore up his wealth? That wasn't the only theft. They might have been born to a secondary line of the Medici, but Lorenzino and Giovanni were left a vast inheritance by their father. When he took them into his custody, the signore gained access to it. More than one hundred thousand florins.'

Even through his racing thoughts, the sum stood out to Jack. It was a fortune.

'The brothers saw none of this money. As Lorenzino and Giovanni's influence grew over the Court of Wolves and as they drew more young men from the city's elite into its ranks, their authority in the republic increased. Several years ago they were able to bring that pressure to bear on the signore and secured this estate.' Marco spread his hands to take in their surroundings, proving what Jack had suspected.

'We're at Cafaggiolo?' He tried to recall how far from Florence the estate was. A few hours' ride, he'd heard Lorenzo say. He thought of the crack in the cellar roof. If he could get free, he could make it on foot to the city.

'But although this gave them a base from which they could continue, more privately, with their ambitions, they were still left far short of what they were due. Lorenzino tried to enter the Signoria, to counter his cousin in the political sphere, but Lorenzo made certain the votes were all against him. Like the twins, Romulus and Remus, the brothers found themselves removed of their inheritance, their destiny. Cast out by a member of their own family.'

'Found and nurtured by the wolf,' murmured Jack, remembering Marco's words the night they first met.

'Hence the name they gave to the company they hoped would sustain them.'

'And what then? Romulus and Remus went on to found Rome. Do the brothers seek to take control of the republic from the signore?'

Marco met his gaze, his dark blue eyes steady, but he didn't answer the question.

Jack tried another tack. 'What of Fra Giorgio and Amerigo Vespucci? What is their involvement? They both once served the signore?'

'Indeed they did, but the Vespucci family have suffered first-hand the ruthlessness of il Magnifico. Years ago, a nephew of Fra Giorgio's was married to a woman many said was the most beautiful in Florence. Lorenzo's younger brother, Giuliano, lusted after her and pursued her forcefully with Lorenzo's knowledge, his support even. The affair tore the Vespucci family apart. Later, when the signore was hunting down those connected to the Pazzi family in the wake of his brother's murder and the attempt on his own life, it transpired that another nephew of Giorgio's had harboured one of the conspirators. The young man was tortured and sentenced to life imprisonment. He died in the Stinche.

'Fra Giorgio bore these wounds upon his family with dignity, remaining loyal to the signore, whose grandfather he once served. But he helped raise Lorenzino and Giovanni as though they were his sons, and, when he saw the signore's treatment of them, he could no longer keep his faith. Neither could Amerigo, their friend since boyhood. Each of us, we all share the same view: that the signore is no longer simply first among equals, master of the republic, but a tyrant king who has abused his position and authority to further his own ends and the future of his empire.'

'You speak of abuse? What of the man you are holding prisoner? Amaury de la Croix? He is a priest for Christ's sake. You have him kept like a dog!' When Marco looked away, a tightening in his expression, Jack pressed him. 'Why did you take him? Why have you held him all this time?'

'Some time ago, Fra Giorgio found a letter from the priest, writing of a map that seemed to indicate land in the Western Ocean. New Eden he called it. Giorgio hadn't been in the Academy since the days of Cosimo, but he knew enough to know that this was something crucial – something that could greatly expand the Medici fortune and, with it, the signore's power. On learning this, Lorenzino and Giovanni determined to discover what the map showed and how they might circumvent their cousin, seizing the opportunity it presented for themselves. A way, they believed, to reclaim the inheritance that was stolen from them. Unfortunately, Amaury de la Croix has not been forthcoming. He was offered better treatment in return for information. He refused it.' Marco lifted his shoulders. 'Sometimes, when a fight is rigged in favour of one opponent, a man must use underhand tactics to gain the ground.'

Jack thought of the black-robed figure glimpsed in the halls of the palazzo, whom he'd taken for Marsilio Ficino. 'So Giorgio is the one who's been spying on the signore?'

'His closeness to the family made him the perfect candidate. If caught, he had an excuse to be in the palace. Until two years ago, it was relatively easy for him to gain access to the signore's plans and dealings. When the signore took to locking his private chambers, his observations were forced to become more subtle.'

'The spy hole?' Jack was gratified to see surprise in Marco's face at this. He thought of Pico's book; used to get Lorenzo out of the palace and the men who had entered, seeking Prince Djem. 'Are the cousins in league with the papacy?'

'The Pazzi had the blessing of Pope Sixtus to remove Signor Lorenzo from power. It was hoped Pope Innocent might prove such an ally. We tried to secure his help – showed him proof of heresy within Lorenzo's own household – but what he wanted in return was unattainable.'

Jack said nothing, thinking of Prince Djem. 'I understand, if all you've said is true, why the cousins would seek to ruin the signore and, I presume, usurp him?' He continued when Marco didn't answer. 'I see, too, why the Vespucci family would have turned against him. But why you and the others in the company? Why do you seek his downfall, Marco, if not for personal gain or revenge?'

'We believe in the republic,' Marco said simply. 'As our fathers and forefathers before us. We built it, all of us together, with sweat and toil, labour and gold. The Medici rose above us and became its masters, not because they were more worthy than the Donati or the Strozzi, the Pazzi or the Valori, but by use of cunning and deception, brute force and fortune. You must have heard it said that to deal with the Medici you cannot afford to be one-eyed? Now, their dominance is so entrenched that Signor Lorenzo believes his own family's propaganda. He is so blinded by his conviction in the greatness of the Medici – in his own magnificence – that he has become as an emperor, with an unswerving belief in his divine right to rule. They are tyrants, Jack. This is not the republic our families built together. It has become a kingdom. We want to take it back.'

It was hard to deny any of this. Jack had observed it with his own eyes. But he felt certain, too, seeing what he had of the guarded Lorenzino and the arrogant Giovanni that the poison of such power had seeped into all branches of the family. He had no doubt the men of the Court of Wolves would simply be removing one tyrant to replace him with two.

'So, you see, Jack,' said Marco, fixing him with his cool, clear gaze. 'You are now the only piece left in play. The best chance we have for the future of the republic.'

'What do you want from me?'

'You know the answer.'

'My loyalty.'

Marco nodded. 'And information. Everything you know of the signore's plans. This map Amaury de la Croix spoke of. The land it shows. New Eden?' He sat forward, his arms on his thighs, the oil in his neat-cropped beard gleaming in the sunlight. 'I believe you could be a valuable asset to us, yes – for what you know and the position you are in with the signore. But I also believe we could be of value to you. I see your struggle, Jack, your search for a place in the world, your desire to belong. We can offer you that – a place, a purpose. You must know Lorenzo is using you. You must see by now he will use you until he is done with you. He will never give you power. Never see you as an equal.'

For a moment, Jack felt the lure of Marco's words. His mind flashed with memories of his time among the Court of Wolves; the feeling of belonging, of solidarity and friendship. Many of the men were as ignoble as him by blood, but, here in Florence – cradle of endeavour, ambition and wild dreams – they had raised themselves up into nobility. Through them that shining cloak of knighthood he'd abandoned on the road might even be salvageable. But these thoughts were fleeting. He thought of Amaury, left in the cellar until his mind was as rotted as the walls. Under the cousins, he would just be another pawn in the Medici game of power. The board beneath him would be no different. Only his colour would have changed.

He shook his head slowly. 'When I went to the palace, before I found the tunnel, before the quake, I was planning to leave the republic. That is still my intention. Florence holds nothing for me any more. I will keep your secrets, Marco. I will not tell the signore. Just let me leave here with Amaury. I'll take him and Laora and disappear. You have my word.'

Marco exhaled. 'I am afraid that cannot happen, Jack. My masters want this information from you – preferably willingly, with your agreement for continued cooperation – but they will take it by force if necessary.'

'They cannot force me to work for them.'

'No?'

'No.' Jack met his gaze steadily, even though his heart had quickened at the threat in Marco's tone.

Marco rose. 'Then, I am sorry, Jack. For what must happen now.'

'What do you mean?'

Bending to pick up the goblet, Marco walked away.

'What do you mean?' Jack yelled at his back, twisting against his bonds. '*Valori?*'

Amelot sat cross-legged on the bed, watching Laora pace, worrying at a short strand of her cut hair. She knew the young woman was concerned about Jack. She was too. Inside the dusty workshop the candles glowed brighter as, outside, evening fell – the third since he had gone to the palace. The third since the earth had shaken, ringing all the bells, collapsing walls and statues, and a whole row of houses near the market.

Laora turned suddenly, her voice sharp with question. Amelot wasn't certain of all the words, but guessed the young woman was asking her what could have delayed Jack. But she didn't know the answer and, even if she did, could not say. Laora, seeming to realise this, wheeled away with a sigh, fiddling with the bird pendant around her neck.

Amelot hugged her knees to her chest. She thought the young woman blamed herself for Jack's disappearance. It was, after all, the words of her father that had sent him to the palazzo, searching for signs of those ghosts in the walls Amelot herself had sensed during their time there. Had he found something? Or had someone found him? She doubted he would have been gone this long otherwise. Amelot understood Laora's guilt. As she looked over at the bags in the corner, packed and ready, she felt it too. They shouldn't have pressed him to go. They could have left by now, all of them together.

When Jack first told her his plan to leave Florence, she had shaken her head wildly at him, making her sign for Amaury repeatedly and furiously. But even as she had fought against it, she had known the battle was lost. It had been two years now. She had traversed every inch of this city and there was no trail left to follow. Her master was gone.

Laora had turned back and was speaking again. This time, her meaning was clear. She was asking if Amelot would return to Ned and Valentine, check to see if they'd found anything out. Amelot had visited them that morning in the little house north of San Marco, where they were guarding the Turk, who always had a smile for her and a greeting in French. When Ned finally understood her gesticulations, he had promised to go to the palace and ask for Jack.

Amelot hopped off the bed, happy to do something rather than sit and wait. She picked up her cloak, swung it around her shoulders and slipped out. It was nearly October and the days were wearing on. The alley was dim. There was a clop of hooves and the rattle of cartwheels echoing from further down the street. Grabbing hold of the window ledge, Amelot pulled herself up. Florence, as Paris and London, was full of men who favoured the dark for their deeds. She rarely used the streets, let alone when night fell. Her hands grasping sills, jutting stones and beams, feet digging into cracks, she shinned her way up the side of the building and on to the roof, lungs filling with chill air and wood-smoke.

She was making her way along the edge of the roof towards the thoroughfare at the end, when she saw the riders, four of them, trotting down the street at the head of a covered wagon, drawn by two horses. As they drew to a stop in front of the alley, the horses foam-mouthed and stamping, Amelot was surprised to see Marco Valori swing down, pushing back his hood. Might he know where Jack was?

She was thinking to slip back down to the alley to try to catch his attention, when her eyes caught on one of the other men who had dismounted with him.

She halted, freezing in shock. After all this time it seemed impossible, but there he was. That prominent chin, those close-set eyes. It was him – the man she'd seen on the dais at Carnival. The man who had come with the others, forcing their way into Amaury's room to seize her master; rough voice, glint of a dagger and a flash of silver from the wolf on his tunic. She flattened herself on the roof as Marco and the man made their way down the alley towards the workshop, while the others waited with the wagon, casting glances up and down the street. She wanted to move, to warn Laora. But there was no time.

Marco rapped on the door. Two knocks, a pause, then two more. The door opened. Amelot saw him barge in, followed by his companion. A moment later, she saw Laora being hauled out, her screams muffled by Marco's hand. She was dragged down the alley, struggling all the way, then bundled into the back of the wagon. Amaury's abductor jumped in with her, while Marco and the others mounted up. A kick of heels, flick of a whip and they were off.

Amelot pushed herself up and sprinted across the tiles, leaping gaps between the buildings, hauling herself up on to higher ridges, past chimneys and over loggias, birds startling into the darkening sky as she followed the wagon, heading for the city's north-east gate.

38

Jack twisted his face away as grit and dirt rained down on him. He paused for breath, sweat pouring off him, his ribs throbbing, knuckles torn where he'd bashed them on the jagged edges of the fissure.

'Careful!' came Amaury's croak from below, the priest blinking up at the growing gap of sky. Every now and then he would shuffle to the door to listen for any sound of approach, before limping back and nodding encouragingly.

When the guards had locked him back down here, hours ago, Jack had moved quickly, Amaury following him with a string of anxious questions as he hefted the barrel in place and climbed on to to it, tugging out the dead rats, the priest flinching away from the falling bodies.

Jack had been discouraged to see that the crack, at its widest point, wasn't much more than two hands apart and several feet up to the surface – too narrow even for the emaciated priest, let alone himself. Scraping at it, though, he'd discovered that parts of it crumbled under pressure, the hard-packed earth, softened by water and riven with the roots of plants, weakened by the quake. Choosing one of the chunks of stone on the cellar floor, he had set about gouging out what he could, all the while Marco Valori's last words ringing in his mind. *I am sorry, Jack. For what must happen now.*

It was almost fully dark outside. Several hours ago, they had heard the pulse of hooves and what Jack had guessed to be the heavy rumble of a cart, but, since then, nothing. The chatter of birds had faded and only the sounds of the wind rushing in the trees in the twilit world above and Amaury's occasional mutterings accompanied the scrape of the stone.

'She was always with me.'

Jack glanced down at the priest's voice, but continued hacking. 'Who?'

'Amelot. Even when all else was gone.' Amaury tapped his head. 'She remained.' His watery eyes glinted in the shadows. 'Perhaps I sensed she was near?'

'Perhaps.'

'Thank you, James, for taking care of her. She was as a . . .' Amaury shook his head, chuckled dryly. 'Well, as much of a daughter as a tonsured old ruin could have.'

They had talked through the afternoon while Jack had laboured, Amaury listening keenly to all that had happened since they met in Paris, over two years ago. Sometimes, the priest interrupted to ask questions or to clarify something himself, other times he repeated a question Jack had answered only moments ago, his mind like a butterfly alighting briefly on a subject before floating to the next, then back again. But much of the time he just listened, expressing sorrow at the fate of Prince Edward, anger over the loss of the map to Henry Tudor, eager interest at the signore's plans and his pact for peace with Prince Djem.

He had been clearly troubled by Jack's confirmation of Lorenzino and Giovanni di' Pierfrancesco's control of the Court of Wolves, their treachery against Lorenzo and intent to bring him down – some of which he'd discovered for himself during his incarceration. But he remained silent, contemplative, through Jack's vocal frustrations at being manipulated by all these men. The signore. Marco Valori. His father.

'And for what?' Jack had demanded, pausing in his chiselling to suck blood from his knuckle and spit it out vehemently. 'To make them all richer? Give them more power? I should have stayed in Sussex, laboured in a lord's field for what little I've seen for my service.'

Out of everything he'd told the priest, however, the news that Amelot was alive and well in Florence had drawn the most emotion from Amaury, tears welling in his eyes as Jack told him she had never ceased in her search for him.

Another lump of stone and earth showered down, peppering the floor around them. Jack smelled cool night air, felt a mist of rain on his face. 'We're nearly there,' he panted. A few more chunks like that and he would be able to squeeze through, pull the priest out after him.

Jack felt it before he heard it: a murmuring in the earth beneath his fingertips. For a moment, he thought it was another tremor, but the trembling quickly separated out into the rumble of hooves and wagon wheels approaching. His heart thumped as he heard voices breaking the hush. They were too far for him to hear what they were saying, but he guessed their time was up.

'Here,' he said, tossing the stone aside, holding out his hand to Amaury. 'I think it's wide enough.' As the priest grabbed his hand, Jack strained to haul him up on to the barrel beside him, gasping with the effort. Amaury weighed little more than a bag of bones, but it was more than enough for his broken ribs to scream out.

As he grasped the priest around the waist, readying himself for the lift, Amaury clutched him in panicked confusion. 'James, you have to go first! I cannot pull you out.'

'It's still too narrow for me. But you have to go,' Jack pressed in as Amaury went to argue. 'Get to Florence. Warn the signore. Can you make it?'

Amaury nodded, but he gripped Jack harder. 'What you said earlier – about your father? That you had wasted these years following in his footsteps? That it had been for nothing?'

'Amaury . . .!'

'Do you know why I recruited your father into the Academy? What made me choose him?'

'I don't know,' Jack said, agitated. 'His position under King Edward? His access to power?'

'No, James. It was you.'

Jack, taken aback, released his grip on the priest.

'We were at a feast, years ago, with the royal court in France, Sir Thomas and me. Your father had been talking about his family. He was homesick, I suppose, all those months away as ambassador, and, of course, the wine was flowing. Sir Thomas started telling me a story of his son. How he'd set up a target for his boy to practise with the sword while he was away – a man of straw, painted black like a Saracen.'

Jack's mind flickered with images: him and Sir Thomas stuffing handfuls of straw into a pair of old hose, big hands and small working side by side, smell of fallen leaves and tang of wood-smoke. How old had he been? Seven? Eight?

'He said he'd come home after months away to find this target still hanging from its perch, barely a mark upon it, and demanded to know why his son hadn't been practising. His son declared that he had been practising, but not with this target. When Sir Thomas asked why, the boy had said because—'

'Because he's my friend,' murmured Jack, amazed by the clarity of a memory that had sunk beneath the years long ago.

Amaury nodded. 'The two of us laughed at that, but then Sir Thomas grew serious, said he had asked you how a Saracen could possibly be your friend. The enemy of Christendom? The ravagers of Constantinople? You told him you had been at a sermon where the priest had spoken of the glorious crusades against Islam, where the Christians had wrested Jerusalem from the infidel, bathing the streets in their blood. You asked your father why you should hate the Saracens when they had only been doing what had been done to them. Our conversation moved on, I cannot recall to what, but I could see that your question – naïve though it was – had resonated in him, plucking at strings I believe were already there. I assumed at the time, knowing nothing of you, that he'd been speaking of your brother, Harry.'

'No,' said Jack, his voice thick. 'It was me.'

'I guessed as much when I first met you. Of course, I was interested in Sir Thomas's authority and his access to power, but it was what he revealed of himself in that conversation that first drew me to him as a man. His willingness to open his mind and heart to a simple question from the boy he loved. His willingness to look at the world through the eyes of innocence and wonder how it might be made different.' Amaury let out a wheezing sigh. 'We are men, James. Me, your father, Signor Lorenzo. We are not without flaws, tethered as we are to this world with our feet of clay. But we believe in an ideal, beyond ourselves and our petty desires, beyond faith and country. A dream of peace, which you yourself grasped at even as a boy. You talk of finding the truth, of needing to understand your father. Was he good? Was he bad? But you have searched by looking at his actions in isolation of meaning and by asking who or what he was to other men. Who was he to you, James?' He nodded as Jack turned away, eyes stinging with grit and emotion. 'I think your answers lie here.' The priest prodded him hard in the chest. 'I think they always have.'

Jack looked back at the priest, a thousand thoughts bubbling up in him, but there were voices on the air now, coming closer, the thud of booted feet descending the cellar stairs. They were out of time. 'Go!' he urged, lifting Amaury up, blinking away the dirt as the priest scrabbled, fighting his way through the narrow space. Then he was up and out.

Amaury reached down, grasped his hand, brief and tight. 'Keep faith, James.'

Jumping down from the barrel, Jack heaved it away, as bolts rattled back and a key turned in the cellar door.

'He's in there? You are certain?'

'Yes.'

'How many guards?'

'I told you. Two men. Three at most if Wynter is with them. Now may I leave?'

'No. Not until we have him.'

Pico bit back his frustration as Mani turned to confer with his comrades in low tones. The five of them were all the same: thick-armed, gruff-voiced and humourless. Mercenaries. He had been with them since leaving Rome and wasn't any more enamoured with them than when he'd first been placed in their company, or custody as was more accurate.

Pico leaned against the wall of the building they had concealed themselves behind, the wind plucking at his hair. It was growing dark, clouds scudding low across the sky, rolling in from the mountains. The air was cooler now, the heat having broken soon after the quake. He had lived in this city for years, walked its streets with Lorenzo and Poliziano and the men of the Academy, like young gods of ancient times, drunk with power and passion, mere mortals turning to watch them, eyes filling with awe. Now, it felt like a mausoleum, a twilight world of crumbled statues and lost dreams. If only Lorenzo had trusted him more. *And if only you had trusted him*, whispered a voice in his mind.

Along the street, further down from the building they were watching, the windows of a tavern glowed with candlelit promise. He wished he could be back in the warmth of the bed he'd shared with Poliziano these past nights, not out here with these grim soldiers, the wine he'd drunk with his friend earlier that day sour in his mouth, his own breath smelling like betrayal.

It hadn't been hard to coax what he needed out of his old lover. In his absence, it seemed the signore had opened up to Poliziano, drawing him back into his trust. Knowing, now, what he was looking for, Pico had only needed to employ a few steers and prods, innocent questions between caresses. Poliziano, back in his arms – happy, unwary – had confided in him, worrying that the signore was putting too much faith in James Wynter, who had been entrusted to guard a special asset – an Ottoman prince, no less. After that, Pico, accompanied by Mani, had trailed Wynter until they discovered where the Turk was being held.

Just words, Pico had tried to tell himself: that was all he had taken from his friend. But such reasoning was a child's defence. He closed his eyes. He should have said no, back in Rome. Been bold as Socrates; drunk his hemlock like wine. Died a philosopher's death. But His Holiness had made clear his fate if he refused the task, and the prospect of the pyre, promised for his crime of heresy, had weakened him with terror.

It was for the good of the Church, Innocent had assured him. Indeed, for the good of Christendom. With Prince Djem in his custody – with all the man's valuable knowledge of his brother, Sultan Bayezid, his armies and country – he could begin preparations for a new holy war against Islam. Take back Jerusalem. Innocent had called him a hero, a champion of Christ. But Pico had other names for himself since he'd made the pact with the pontiff, names that jabbed at him in the wakeful dark, Poliziano's head on his shoulder.

Coward. Traitor. Judas.

'Who's that?'

Pico pushed himself from the wall to see Mani pointing down the street towards the house they were watching, nestled between shops. A large man with a thatch of brown hair had emerged from the door, a little white dog trotting out at his side. It was Wynter's man, Ned. He stood there for a while, looking up and down the street as though waiting for someone, the dog nosing in a pile of rubbish, before retreating back inside.

'Just one of the guards,' Pico murmured.

Mani nodded to the others. 'We'll take turns on watch. We go in at dawn.'

Amelot had been running since she left the city, feet pounding the rutted road, the few people she saw, mostly travellers hastening in before the gates were shut, staring as she sprinted past, head down and dogged. At first, her determination to keep up with the wagon – and the man inside it – had been her fuel, her legs eating up the miles. But, as the city walls fell back behind her, the bells ringing the curfew from the watchtowers, the land had risen ahead, gently at first, then more steeply, the road curving around hillsides dense with cypress. She was flagging now, lungs burning, muscles screaming.

Unable to go any further, she halted where the path tumbled away beside her into a valley of darkness, the glitter of firelight in distant villas winking like amber eyes. The air, green with pine, was filled with the hiss of branches in the wind. Rain, a fine mist at first, was falling harder now, dampening her face and hair. Somewhere in the wild heights an animal howled.

Having caught her breath, she bent and checked the trail. Her eyes had grown used to the gloom and in the pale shimmer of starlight, appearing and disappearing between ragged bands of cloud, she could see the tracks gouged in the path, made by wheels and hooves. Steeling herself, she ran on, down a long, sweeping hill, then up the punishing slope that rose almost immediately on the other side, but within another mile she was floundering again.

The forest was thicker here, shadows of trees rising all around, a harsh shriek and a flash of wings overhead. The clouds had covered the stars and rain needled her cheeks. She had been in cities surrounded by noise and people for so long that she had forgotten what it felt like to be out in the world. It made her think of her childhood, her family moving from one place to the next with the others of their company, the space between settlements filled with nights like these; jolting wagons and men's steady words, the snorts of horses, warm blankets and her mother's voice. At the thought a wave of loneliness engulfed her, cold and solid, threatening to drown her in emptiness. She fought back the tears for a few more paces, then collapsed against a tree, sliding down into the soft moss of its roots, sobbing bitterly. They had gone. Everyone had gone.

She wasn't sure how long she stayed there, eyes squeezed shut, shivering inside her cloak, but it had stopped raining by the time she looked up. The clouds had been scattered by the wind, leaving a sky dazzled with stars. There, visible in their frosty light, a figure was moving along the road, weaving slowly from side to side. Amelot's first instinct was to run and hide, but she was concealed enough by the shadows and the figure made her curious; all spindle-armed and ragged, like a scarecrow come staggering out of a crop-field. As she watched, the figure stumbled another few yards, then buckled and went down in the middle of the road. She could hear wheezy breaths, the odd mournful moan. After a moment, curiosity got the better of her and she slipped closer, using the trees for cover.

Drawing near, she saw it was an elderly man, his gaunt body clad only in a tattered tunic. He was lying on his side, groaning in obvious pain. Suddenly, he raised an arm to the sky as if flinging out a desperate appeal to the stars above him, and cried out. Amelot heard the words – a prayer, spoken in French – at the same time as she saw the old man's raised arm ended at the wrist. With a strangled shout she charged out of the undergrowth, swooping down on the man who yelped in alarm. Then, as his glazed eyes focused on her, he let out a cry of disbelieving joy, his good hand rising to touch her cheek, while she sobbed and cradled his face.

'Oh, Amelot. My dear, Amelot.'

She was smiling and nodding, weeping as she held him. But, then, she saw it: something protruding from his back, long and thin, low down in his side. Fear gripped her heart as her fingers trailed towards it. His tunic was black and wet with blood. His face creased with pain as her fingers glanced across it. It was the shaft of a crossbow bolt, the rest wedged deep inside him. There was a low drumming in the earth.

Amaury's hand tightened on her. 'They've found me! Go! *You must go!*'

Ignoring his protests, Amelot seized him under his arms and dragged him towards the trees, steeling herself against his agonised cries. The thud of approaching hooves filled the air like thunder. Five riders emerged from the trees on the forest road, along the same path Amaury had staggered. She threw herself on top of the old man, covering them both with her cloak. From the thicket, she glimpsed men's faces, the flash of bridles, bright gusts of torch flames. They hurtled on past, iron hooves kicking up stones, the trembling in the earth fading as they urged their mounts up the hillside, following the track towards the city.

Amelot waited until she could hear them no longer, then sat up, pushing threads of hair back from Amaury's sweat-slick face, anxiously checking him with her hands. He fumbled out, grasped her wrist. His eyes were half-lidded. There was a black stain on his lips.

'My dear,' he breathed. 'I must . . .' He swallowed thickly, but when his lips parted and he tried to speak again, only a stream of blood trickled out.

'*Papa.*'

Amelot spoke the word faintly, no more than a breath or a sigh, but Amaury's eyes flickered open at the sound, filling with wonder. He raised his hand to touch her face, but the effort was too much and his arm flopped back. He drew in one long, shuddering breath, then closed his eyes, his head lolling back on the grass. Amelot sank down with him, darkness enveloping them in its mantle, the stars flickering like a million cold candles above them.

39

They marched him through the grounds of the estate, wind whipping his hair, buildings looming, pale in the starlight. As Jack was led towards arched doors, he heard shouts at his back and twisted to see men fanning out in the darkness. Had they discovered Amaury's escape? The two guards holding him, ignoring the commotion, forced him through into a torchlit passage, cracked tiled floor and limewashed walls yellow with age.

Passing a doorway, which opened into a spacious chamber, Jack glimpsed figures congregated around a table, some seated, others standing. A few of them glanced up as he passed. He caught sight of Marco Valori, his cloak dark with rain. There were others he recognised, familiar faces from the Court of Wolves. Now the veil had been torn from his eyes, these men – daggers and swords at their hips, silver wolves pinned to their chests – no longer looked like a company of young men questing for wealth and opportunity, but a private army, waiting for orders.

Marched on down the passage, he was thrust inside a kitchen. A dying fire smouldered in a great stone hearth, illuminating trestles and boards scattered with knives and platters, vegetable peelings and rinds of cheese. The smell of food tormented him. He hadn't eaten in days. The guards sat him on the flagged floor, pulled his hands behind his back, binding them around the leg of a table, before trussing his ankles, the rope grazing his skin. When he was secured, one of the guards left the kitchen, while the other stood sentry. In the silence, Jack heard the fading throb of horses' hooves. He prayed Amaury would elude them.

Boots clicked off the tiles in the passage, several pairs, coming closer. Jack swallowed dryly, desperate for a drink. Three men entered first. One was the guard, returning. The other two were Lorenzino and Giovanni di' Pierfrancesco de' Medici. Behind them came Marco Valori, gripping a slim figure by the arm. It was Laora.

Shock flooded Jack as he saw the source of Valori's threat. 'You son of a bitch,' he murmured.

'I warned you, Jack,' replied the young man, his voice low.

Laora's face was pallid and her cropped hair clung damply to her head, but apart from a reddish bruise that coloured one cheek she seemed unhurt. As she saw him, bound on the floor, her hazel eyes widened, but as they led her closer he thought he saw relief there too.

Lorenzino di' Pierfrancesco came to stand before him, blocking Jack's view of her. The young man's sallow face was hard in the shifting firelight, his glassy eyes pensive. 'The priest will not get far.' He nodded as Jack's jaw tightened. 'Your only chance to leave here alive is to tell us what we want.'

'This is between you and your cousin,' Jack told him. 'It has nothing to do with me. Or her,' he added.

'Nothing to do with you?' Giovanni stepped forward beside his brother, mouth twisting. 'You, who pledged yourself to us falsely? Spied on us for the signore, seeking to undermine us? This has everything to do with you, you duplicitous bastard!' He stepped forward, tugging a dagger from his belt, but was halted by his brother's hand, planted firmly on his chest.

'You'll talk, Sir James,' continued Lorenzino calmly. 'Or there will be consequences.' His eyes darted meaningfully to Laora.

'She's the daughter of one of your own,' Jack reminded him.

'Franco Martelli betrayed us the moment he spoke to you in the Stinche.' Lorenzino came forward, crouched before him. 'Jack. May I call you that? I know you are used to dealing with my cousin – to half-truths and false promises, veiled threats and outright lies. My brother and I, we are not of the same mould. What we say, we mean.' He smiled humourlessly. 'What do you owe the signore, anyway?'

Jack's mind filled with Amaury's last words. It wouldn't just be Lorenzo's dream he would tear down. It was the priest's dream. His father's too. He tried to think of how he might lie, tell them something, anything other than the truth, but his head was fogged with pain and he couldn't keep his thoughts straight. 'How do I know you'll let us live?'

'Enough of this,' snapped Giovanni, who had stepped back at his brother's command, but had been pacing behind him, still clutching the dagger. Pushing Marco aside, he seized Laora by her hair and forced her to her knees. She gave a strangled scream as he yanked her head back and held the blade to her neck. 'Talk, or I'll slit her!'

'All right!' Jack shouted. He was shaking – shaking with fury, wanting to tear free of his bonds and rip Giovanni's throat out with his bare hands, but with fear, too. He wouldn't – *couldn't* lose Laora.

And so he spoke, answering Lorenzino's questions, telling the young men what they wanted to hear, giving away as little as he could, but forced at times – Lorenzino's shrewd eyes not leaving his face – to expand on his words, prompted by Giovanni's threats, Laora petrified in the young man's grip, a bloody nick on her neck where he'd started to cut when Jack had been reticent with details.

He told them about the map from the *Trinity* and the lost island of Atlantis Lorenzo believed it showed; told them this map was gone, taken by Harry Vaughan. He told them about Prince Djem, who they knew of from their pact with the pope – which seemed to have ended after the unsuccessful attempt to take the Turk – and he told them about Lorenzo's plan for peace.

'Peace?' Giovanni had spat, his face creasing with scorn. 'He wants peace with the infidel? *That* is his grand plan?'

'And trade, I would imagine,' ventured Lorenzino, glancing at his brother. 'Money is our cousin's first mistress, after all.' He looked back at Jack. 'This map – you saw it for yourself? This land it showed.'

'Yes, but as I said, the map is gone.'

After a few more questions, Lorenzino rose. Gesturing for his brother and Marco to follow, he left the room. Giovanni lingered a moment longer, eyes on Jack, then relinquished his hold on Laora, leaving her sagged on her knees, sobbing silently at the feet of the guard.

Jack tried to catch her eye. 'Laora?'

'Quiet,' warned the second guard, standing sentry by the fireplace.

Jack ignored him. 'Are you hurt?'

'I said quiet!' repeated the guard, stepping from his place.

Laora looked up, nodding in reassurance at Jack. *I'm all right*, her face told him, although her eyes were glazed, tears streaming down her cheeks.

Time dragged on; murmured voices in the passage, footsteps coming and going. At one point, Jack glimpsed the bald head and thickset frame of Amerigo Vespucci, the man's dark eyes flicking towards him while Lorenzino spoke quickly, quietly at his side. When Amerigo vanished and more hoofbeats drummed outside, Jack presumed something he'd said had roused them to action, although what that – or his and Laora's fates – might be, he could not guess.

He tried to stay alert, as much for Laora as himself, but exhaustion was creeping up on him, tempting him to close his eyes and rest his aching body, slip into sleep. He spent the remainder of the night caught between drifting and jerking awake. Then, in the chill of dawn, cold blue light seeping in through the kitchen windows, the men returned. Hearing footfalls and voices, Jack snapped awake. The guards, one leaning on the hearth's mantel, poking at the fire's embers, the other sitting at the table, picking at a bit of cheese, stood to attention. Laora, curled in a ball on her cloak across from Jack, sat up, fear quickening in her red-rimmed eyes.

Lorenzino and Giovanni entered with Marco and another man, short and slender with olive skin and black hair. Jack didn't recognise him, but the newcomer seemed to have some knowledge of him as he came forward, eyes keen with question.

'Your name is James Wynter?'

One look at Giovanni's narrowed eyes, his fingers hooked in his belt by his dagger, told Jack he had no choice but to submit. He nodded tightly.

'Your brother is Harry Vaughan?'

The man's Tuscan was perfect, but his accent was hard to place. 'Half-brother.'

'This map, from the *Trinity* – Vaughan took it from you? Did he know what it was?'

'I've no idea.'

'But he gave it to King Henry of England?'

'I believe so.'

'And you saw this map for yourself? Saw land in the Western Ocean?'

Jack nodded, his unease growing. He glanced at Marco, who avoided his gaze, then at Laora, who was kneeling stiff and upright, anxiously watching the exchange.

After a pause, the man turned to Lorenzino. Something passed between them and the men retreated once more into the passage to talk.

'What is happening, Jack?' murmured Laora.

'I don't know.' He wanted to tell her it would be all right, that he would protect her, but the words wouldn't come.

Marco was the first to return, nodding to the guards. 'Untie him.'

'What now?' Jack questioned, wincing as the guards slashed at the ropes that bound his ankles and wrists. They had to haul him to his feet, his body was so cramped with pain and cold, his limbs tingling like fire as the blood rushed into them. 'Will you let us go?' he demanded, when Marco didn't answer, but gestured Laora to her feet. 'I answered your questions!'

'Signor Gianotto is taking you into his custody.'

Jack guessed this was the stranger, but the news was bewildering. 'What? Why?'

Marco paused, glancing to the doorway. 'He and my masters have entered into a partnership,' he told Jack, his voice low. 'A new business venture. Signor Gianotto believes you have information that could prove of use to its success.' He shook his head. 'I'm sorry, Jack, but he is taking you with him. Both of you,' he added, glancing at Laora, some flicker of remorse in his eyes.

'Taking us where?' Jack demanded. 'God damn it, Marco! *Where?*'

'To Spain.'

Lorenzo stood in his study, his black robes draped with a mantle of purple velvet, lined with ermine. Earlier, opening the shutters of his bedchamber, he'd been greeted by a cold, clear dawn, the sky winter blue, the dome of Santa Maria del Fiore blood-red in the rising sun. He had ordered the servants to bring fresh baskets of logs and Papi was now hunched by the hearth, banking up the fire.

Reaching out, Lorenzo slid a hunting horn, decorated with gold, along the shelf to better fill the gap. There were spaces all over the grand display. It had been four days since the quake, when he and his family had been caught in the piazza outside San Lorenzo, Black Adam and his bodyguards throwing themselves on top of him as the earth heaved and his children screamed. While many items survived the fall from the shelves, some had not and Bertoldo had spent hours searching through the wreckage of splintered glass and chipped marble, trying to salvage what he could.

Still, Lorenzo reasoned, it could have been much worse, the palazzo sustaining only minor damage. His eyes alighted on his precious chalice, entwined with serpents and cradled with wings, safe behind the iron grille of the cupboard.

'Signore, shall I bring food?'

'Please, Papi. And summon Marsilio. And Rigo,' he added.

'Yes, signore.'

As the old man shuffled out, brushing ashes from his hands, Lorenzo limped to his desk. His toe, when he'd risen, had been swollen, an augur of the gout that troubled him more and more these days. Reaching into the drawer, he pulled out the ivory box in which he kept his grandfather's ring, a sapphire set in gold. The old man had suffered terribly from the affliction and his physician had recommended the healing properties of the jewel. Lorenzo slid his grandfather's ring on to his finger.

There was the usual pile of messages from his secretaries on the desk: requests for an assembly at the Signoria, invitations to banquets. Since Maddalena's betrothal – the plans for the wedding now set – and the announcement of his son's entry into the College of Cardinals, the messages had increased in volume and obsequiousness. He tried to focus on a few, but his eyes scanned the words without reading.

'Signore?'

Lorenzo looked up to see Rigo lingering on the threshold. His staff were used to being barred from this chamber and it was taking them time to adjust to his new openness, now Prince Djem had been moved. Wynter was still adamant that someone other than Franco Martelli and his daughter was responsible for the infiltration of his household and the collusion with Pope Innocent, but with Martelli in prison, Laora vanished, and no further sign of any attempts to interfere with his affairs, Lorenzo had begun to wonder if, as Adam Foxley had believed, Wynter had simply been blinded by love.

He gestured impatiently to Rigo, who came to stand before him. 'I take it there has been no word?'

'From James Wynter? No, signore. Not since he was here four days ago.'

'And you didn't see him leave?'

'No, signore, but . . .' Rigo shook his head apologetically. 'The quake. All was chaos.'

Lorenzo nodded after a pause. 'Get Black Adam for me.'

As Rigo bowed and left the chamber, Lorenzo sat back, twisting the ring on his finger. When Wynter hadn't shown up for their meeting, he had sent Black Adam to the safe house near San Marco. His bodyguard was the only man in his circle other than Marsilio who knew where he was hiding the Turk, although Poliziano, whom he'd grown close to again, now knew of the prince's existence. Black Adam had returned with news that all was well, but Wynter's men hadn't seen him since the quake.

As the sapphire glittered, catching the burgeoning fire, Lorenzo thought of his grandfather, sitting here behind this desk, wearing this very ring, while he stood at his side, half listening to his talk of the Signoria or his plans for the Academy, half revelling in being close to this man, the most powerful in the republic, perhaps even in Christendom itself.

Pater Patriae.

Dear God, but he had almost lost it all – the legacy that had been passed down to him. He couldn't risk any more failures. He needed to concentrate on strengthening what he'd managed to retain: rebuild the reputation of the Medici Bank, make certain young Giovanni would have a voice in the Vatican, cement his alliance with Prince Djem and seek out New Eden, teach his son and heir, Piero, what his grandfather had taught him. Set the Medici name in the stone of history.

Lorenzo looked up, hearing footfalls in the grand hall.

Rigo appeared, hastening through the bedchamber towards him. 'Signore! Wynter's men have come!'

'What?' Lorenzo rose.

'Something has happened and . . .'

Not waiting for explanation, Lorenzo strode from his study, out through his suite and down the wide staircase to the inner courtyard, Rigo following.

A small crowd of servants and guards had clustered beneath the bronze statue of David. Bertoldo was there, calling for water and cloths. In their midst were two figures. One, lying sprawled on the floor, was Ned Draper, the other, crouched beside him, was Valentine Holt. Both men were drenched in blood, although most of it seemed to be coming from Ned, pulsing out of a puncture wound in his shoulder, bright red spatters trailing across the marble floor from the doorway. A white dog was whimpering and yapping at his side. As Lorenzo descended, he scanned the rest of the crowd, but there was no sign of Djem. As Valentine Holt turned to him, Lorenzo knew – the prince was gone.

40

Harry Vaughan lounged in the shade of an orange tree, the wine he'd drunk with his food making him dozy. Autumn had tempered the Spanish sun, but the afternoons were still warm in the courtyard of the little house on the edges of the Jewish Quarter of Seville granted to him by King Ferdinand for his service in the fight for Málaga.

The clatter of dishes sounded as his slave, a quiet-voiced girl with spice-brown skin, who bobbed her head in acquiescence to everything he asked, busied herself preparing the evening meal. Already, he could smell it: lamb stewed with saffron and cinnamon, felt his mouth water. The muscles he'd come home from the war with were softening again at his stomach, forcing him to loosen his belt a notch.

Harry opened his eyes at the distant knock of the door. He sat up, hearing voices. Peter appeared, leading a visitor. It was Don Luys Carrillo. Harry rose eagerly to meet him. Carrillo had been in Córdoba with Queen Isabella for the past fortnight and he'd been awaiting the man's return with mounting impatience.

It was several months, now, since Harry had left the court, Ferdinand and Isabella travelling north after the fall of Málaga to take advantage of the temporary peace that had come with the city's demise to attend to other business in their realm. They had agreed the continuation of the uneasy truce with the emir, Boabdil, but while they set about replenishing their war-drained coffers with the sale of slaves, rewarding supporters and agreeing ransoms for the eminent Moors in their custody, they were making their battle plans for the last bastion of the enemy – the city of Granada.

Harry, worried the gains he'd made in the court might be affected by the monarchs' absence, had been appeased by the gift of the house and by Ferdinand's request that he make an enquiry to King Henry about the possibility of a future union between their daughter, Princess Katherine, and Henry's infant son, Prince Arthur. But even with his position as ambassador clearly established, he still had a task that remained incomplete and a master in England no less keen for news.

'Señor Luys,' he greeted. 'Peter, some wine.'

Don Luys shook his head at the offer. 'No, thank you. I'm heading on to my estates from here. I just wanted to inform you that the queen's commission have given their verdict.'

'And?' urged Harry.

'The commission have concluded that Cristóbal Colón's proposal is unfeasible,' said Carrillo. 'Impossible, several of them went so far as to declare.'

Harry bit back his triumph. As Peter stepped out to hand him the wine, he hid his glee in a gulp from the goblet. Already, in his mind, he was composing his message to King Henry. Of course, he would be sure to highlight his quick-witted thinking back at Málaga when questioned by Ferdinand, which had no doubt led to the commission's final decision and the thwarting of Columbus's plan. Henry would surely be delighted.

Word from England over the past year had not been good. There had been a coup against Henry that had sought to set a Yorkist pretender – a boy named Lambert Simnel – on the throne of England. The rebellion had been crushed and the ringleaders imprisoned, but Harry knew the king would welcome this news. In the last message he'd received, Henry had informed him that he'd replaced Thomas Croft, the Bristol customs official who had led the *Trinity* expeditions, with one of his own men; the first preparation for a voyage west.

'No matter,' Harry told Carrillo, with feigned disappointment. 'The sailor's notion was merely a passing interest of my lord's.'

'The sailor's plan may be ailing, but it isn't dead yet. More's the pity.'

Harry lowered his goblet. 'What?'

'Lady Isabella still believes it has potential, no matter the judgement of her commission, or the belief of her husband. She told Cristóbal Colón she will consider his proposal again, when the city of Granada has fallen.'

'I see,' said Harry, gritting his teeth.

'Have you heard any word? From your king?' Carrillo's face tightened at the question.

Harry shook his head. 'My lord king has agents hunting for Wynter, that I can assure you. God willing, they will find him.'

Carrillo studied his face, then nodded. 'If you hear anything . . .?'

'You will be the first to know.' The lie came easily to Harry. Carrillo would never know he'd not written to Henry about this. Wynter was long gone and good riddance. He would turn over no stone in search of the bastard.

'Well, I must be about my affairs. Good day to you, señor.'

'Good day.' Harry kept the smile on his face until Carrillo had gone, then cursed and poured himself another drink, wine sloshing over the rim.

Telling Peter he would sleep until dinner, he made his way up to his room.

As he pushed open the shutters, the chamber was flooded with the sun's golden glow. Sitting on the window seat, he looked out over a jumble of red-tiled roofs, past the lofty bell-tower of the cathedral, the Giralda, to the Guadalquivir. He cursed again and drained his wine. Columbus seemed to be a stain that wouldn't wash out.

Still, he told himself, there was no need to panic. It would be months, longer even, before the king and queen were ready to take on the might of Granada. King Henry would have time to implement his own plans. Harry sat back, feeling the warmth of the wine soothe him, eyes on the glittering waters of the wide blue river that wound its way down to the sea.

The hold was dark, the timbers slimed with sea and pitted with age. The odour was overwhelming, salt-sour brine and ocean-dankness. With the smell and the uneasy swaying of the ship, creaking and clunking against the harbour wall, Jack felt as though he were underwater. He could hear the muffled shouts of men on the docks of the Port of Pisa, the shrieks of gulls and the stamp of feet on the decks above him as more supplies were loaded on board the hulking caravel.

He shifted awkwardly, trying to find a position of relative comfort, the iron manacles that dragged at his wrists attached to a chain fixed to the low roof. There were other shackles, swinging empty all the way down the hold, he guessed for the slaves he now knew Gianotto Berardi traded in.

Jack had only seen the man once since he and Laora had been taken by wagon, five days ago, from Cafaggiolo to the port. The young man had been frank, telling him if he complied with his orders he and Laora would come to no harm. Jack had been told little of what these orders would be, or what the man expected of him, but he'd been told Berardi was involved with Christopher Columbus, the sailor Amerigo Vespucci had spoken of, and that Lorenzino and Giovanni di' Pierfrancesco had entered into a deal with these men, of which he was now part. What a terrible twist fate had made. He was heading west as planned, not with his friends to seek his fortune and future, but in the chains of enemies to a place where Harry Vaughan – his blood and his enemy – waited.

Jack assumed Berardi wanted him for his knowledge of the map and guessed Laora had been brought as leverage to ensure his compliance, but all the repeated questions about Harry had made him wonder. Did Berardi think he could influence his brother; even get the map back from King Henry? If so, he was surely going to be disappointed, although Jack hadn't said anything of these thoughts out loud. As long as Berardi thought he and Laora were of use it seemed they would be safe, for now.

His body was weak, ribs still painful to the touch, his skin mottled with bruises. His captors had given him water and bread, enough to keep him moving, but not enough to give him strength. Laora, at least, had been offered better treatment; a small cabin at the aft. But although he was glad she wouldn't endure this discomfort, he was deeply troubled by their separation, unable to protect her, alone with Berardi and his rough-voiced crew.

He had prayed Amaury had made it to Florence and warned Lorenzo of his cousins' conspiracy: that they were gathering an army against him in the Court of Wolves and intended to bring him and all his dreams of peace and empire to ruin. That the signore was now aware of his own plight at their hands. In fitful half-dreams, Jack imagined Lorenzo riding in with his forces, armed to the teeth; the throb of hooves and clash of swords, Laora safe in his arms, a glad reunion with his friends and Lorenzo's gratitude. But the ease with which Berardi had spirited them to the port had crushed his hope of rescue and he'd been plagued, instead, by the deepening belief that Amaury had not outrun those horses.

In these empty hours, the ship creaking against the harbour wall, the irons weighing heavy on him, Jack thought often of his comrades, wondering what they would think when he didn't return. Ned and Valentine had known he was going to the palazzo the day of the quake, but only Amelot knew he intended to search the upper storey for any sign of a link between the palaces and, even if she could explain that to them, would they tell Lorenzo? Would he even listen, blinded as he was by his belief in his own family? Maybe they would just assume he'd left the city, eloping with Laora, forgetting all about them.

Such thoughts tormented him. There were so many things left unsaid, unfinished. With his friends and Lorenzo, the Academy and Prince Djem, even Marco Valori and the Court of Wolves. But, most of all, with his father.

Amaury's words in the cellar had cracked open a fissure through which memories, packed-down and forgotten under the weight of confusion and doubt, had come seeping. It was true, he knew; these past years, in an effort to understand the man, he had been looking at his father only through the eyes of others – through half-truths and secrets, prejudice and dogma.

Who was he to you, James?

The answer to that was as clear as a new dawn. The man had been everything. His past and his present, and all his future hope. He should have believed in him, as so many others had: young Prince Edward who had doted on him as a father, King Edward who trusted him with the care of his son, his mother, Sarah, who had loved him through all the parting years. His anger and doubts had peeled away, leaving a painful kernel of grief, but something else too – something bright and hard that had taken root – a growing desire to protect Thomas Vaughan's legacy, a legacy that had been entrusted to him the moment his father passed him the map and sent him his ring, telling him to seek out the Needle.

Returning to Spain, where that journey had begun, Jack felt as though Fortune was turning back the wheel, giving him another chance. A chance to stop seeking the father he had always known and become the son he should be. As the gangplanks were drawn up and shouts sounded; a slap of ropes on water, the groan of timbers, he made a pledge that while he would do whatever he could to keep Laora and himself alive, he would not give these men what they wanted. That he would protect the legacy his father had left him.

The path before him – full of threat – was unclear, but there was some light at last, shining his way forward, with the rock of waves against the bow and the snap of sails unfurling.

AUTHOR'S NOTE

Although many of the characters, locations and events in this book are based in reality, history doesn't always fit perfectly into the plot of a novel and I've tweaked or changed some details to fit my narrative and for ease of reading.

Probably my greatest alteration is with the story of Prince Djem (also known as Sultan Cem). His background as portrayed here is true: in losing the war for the throne against his brother, Sultan Bayezid, Djem fled to Rhodes, where the Knights of St John took him into custody in exchange for a truce and an annual payment from Bayezid. Djem was later moved to a specially built tower in France, during which time several factions – including Pope Innocent VIII, the kings of Hungary and Naples, and the Republic of Venice – vied to take possession of this valuable asset in Christendom's struggle against the Ottoman Empire, following the fall of Constantinople.

In 1489 a deal was brokered between the Knights of St John and Pope Innocent and Djem was taken into papal custody in Rome, where Bayezid reportedly attempted to assassinate him. The prince's time in Lorenzo de' Medici's keeping is fictitious, although it has been suggested that Djem did indeed make the offer of a permanent peace between Christendom and the caliphate if he was supported in his bid for the throne.

Lorenzo de' Medici's Academy is very much based on the so-called Platonic Academy established by his grandfather, Cosimo: a circle of Italian artists, poets and philosophers, who promoted and advanced the tenets and ideals of humanism, including Plato's concept of a World Soul. Cosimo paid men to hunt down and recover ancient texts on astrology, philosophy, mathematics, alchemy and Hermeticism

– among them the *Corpus Hermeticum*, translated by Marsilio Ficino – gathering together a vast library of knowledge at his palace in Florence, on which the Vatican Library was modelled.

The secret map from the Bristol merchant ship, the *Trinity*, is my invention, although the vessel did undertake several mysterious expeditions in the early 1480s and it is thought its crew may well have spied the coastline of what would become known as North America. Soon after taking the throne, Henry VII replaced the customs official behind these expeditions, Thomas Croft, with a man loyal to him. Later, in 1496, England entered the race westwards with John Cabot at the helm, under Henry's authority.

To keep up the pace and avoid occasionally lengthy waits between action in this period, I've altered the dates or timing of certain events. Pope Innocent did allow Lorenzo's son, Giovanni, to enter the College of Cardinals as part of the marriage arrangements between his illegitimate son and Lorenzo's daughter, but this agreement was made a few years later than portrayed. In 1513 Giovanni de' Medici ascended the papal throne as Pope Leo X.

Giovanni Pico della Mirandola, a close friend of Lorenzo de' Medici, was accused of heresy by Pope Innocent for his unorthodox writings on humanism and fled to France before being arrested and brought to Rome for questioning. But his book, *Oration on the Dignity of Man*, as depicted here, was published after his death.

Loja fell to the Spanish in the early summer of 1486, while I have it occurring later in the year, and Queen Isabella met up with Ferdinand's forces at Moclín, not Loja, although she did visit Sir Edward Woodville, who was instrumental in the town's fall and badly injured, much as described. I've simplified the assault on Málaga; the Spanish were involved in several skirmishes with the Moors and an attack on Velez-Málaga before they reached the city, although I've kept much of the detail of the siege and surrender as is. Harry Vaughan was Sir Thomas Vaughan's son, but very little is known about him and his place as ambassador to Spain and attempts to thwart Columbus's voyage are fiction, although his father was an ambassador for Edward IV. His half-brother, Jack Wynter, is solely my creation.

Christopher Columbus arrived in Spain in the summer of 1485, where he met the slave trader Gianotto Berardi, with whom he began a partnership, and sought support and funding for his idea of sailing west to seek the Spice Islands. But it would be nearly five years before the council established by Queen Isabella to look into the feasibility of such a voyage – the Talavera Commission – gave their verdict, during which time Columbus returned to Portugal, where he'd spent several years, to appeal to John II to aid him in his dream. Columbus was thwarted in his ambition when the explorer Bartolomeu Dias sailed around the cape of Africa in 1488, opening up a new route and focus for the Portuguese. Columbus travelled back to Spain only to learn that the Talavera Commission had declared his voyage impossible. Queen Isabella, however, remained interested and promised to look into his idea again when Granada fell to her forces. She kept her word.

The Court of Wolves is my invention, although the backstory of its patrons, Lorenzino (whose name in reality was Lorenzo – Lorenzino was a nickname later used by a descendant of the family, but I've employed it here for simplicity's sake) and Giovanni di' Pierfrancesco de' Medici is based in fact. Lorenzo de' Medici was accused of taking his cousins' inheritance and was forced to settle the dispute with the transfer of his estates at Cafaggiolo. Giorgio Antonio Vespucci was employed as the cousins' tutor and his nephew, Amerigo Vespucci, was their clerk, although Lorenzo had clashed with other members of this family. His cousins later became enemies of his son and heir, Piero de' Medici, and the two branches of the family entered into a struggle for control of Florence during the invasion of Charles VIII of France in 1494.

Lorenzo's cousins, through the connections of Amerigo Vespucci, did enter into a business relationship with the slave trader, Gianotto Berardi, and his partner, Christopher Columbus, although slightly later than portrayed. It was, in part, Medici money as well as funds from the Spanish crown that helped finance Columbus's first voyage and although Amerigo wasn't the first man to set foot upon the New World that was 'discovered', the continent he later navigated and explored would come to bear his name.

Robyn Young
Brighton, March 2018

CHARACTER LIST

*(*Indicates fictitious characters or relationships)*

ABU' L-HASAN: *Emir of the Kingdom of Granada, father of Boabdil*

*ADAM FOXLEY: *brother of David, served under Thomas Vaughan*

*AGATA: *daughter of Franco Martelli*

*ALESSO: calcio *player*

*AMAURY DE LA CROIX: *French priest and member of the Academy*

*AMELOT: *ward of Amaury de la Croix*

AMERIGO VESPUCCI: *clerk to Lorenzino and Giovanni di' Pierfrancesco de' Medici*

ANGELO POLIZIANO: *poet and friend of Lorenzo's, member of the Academy*

ANTHONY WOODVILLE: *brother of Elizabeth Woodville, executed by Richard of Gloucester in 1483*

ARTHUR: *son of Henry VII and Elizabeth of York*

*BARTOLO: *guard at the Stinche*

*BATTISTA DI SALVI: *Monsignore under Pope Innocent VIII*

BAYEZID II: *son of Mehmet II, Sultan of the Ottoman Empire, half-brother of Djem*

*BERTOLDO: *chief steward of the Palazzo Medici*

BLACK MARTIN: *bodyguard to Lorenzo*

BOABDIL: *son of Emir Abu' l-Hasan of the Kingdom of Granada*

*CARLO DI FANTE: *former servant of Pope Sixtus, died in 1483*

*CARLOS: *Spanish nobleman and captain under Ferdinand*

CHRISTOPHER COLUMBUS: *Genoese sailor and business partner of Gianotto Berardi*

CLARICE DE' MEDICI: *wife of Lorenzo*

CONTESSINA DE' MEDICI: *daughter of Lorenzo and Clarice*

COSIMO DE' MEDICI: *ruler of Florence and head of the Medici family, died 1464*

CROOKED ANDREA: *bodyguard to Lorenzo*

*DAVID FOXLEY: *brother of Adam, served under Thomas Vaughan*

DJEM: *son of Sultan Mehmet II, half-brother of Bayezid II*

*DONNA SANTA: *wife of Franco Martelli*

EDWARD IV: *King of England (1461–70 and 1471–83), brother of Richard of Gloucester, father of the Princes in the Tower and Elizabeth of York, died 1483*

EDWARD V: *son of Edward IV and Elizabeth Woodville, succeeded his father as king in 1483 but was never crowned, assumed dead by autumn 1483*

EDWARD WOODVILLE: *English knight, brother of Elizabeth Woodville and uncle of the Princes in the Tower*

*EL BARBERO (THE BARBER): *Spanish soldier under Rodrigo de Torres*

ELIZABETH WOODVILLE: *wife of Edward IV, mother of the Princes in the Tower and Elizabeth of York*

ELIZABETH OF YORK: *queen consort of Henry VII, daughter of Edward IV and Elizabeth Woodville*

*ESTEVAN CARRILLO: *son of a Spanish nobleman, killed by Jack in Seville in 1483*

*FEA: *daughter of Franco Martelli*

FERRANTE I: *King of Naples*

FRANCESCHETTO CYBO: *son of Pope Innocent VIII, betrothed to Maddalena de' Medici*

*FRANCO MARTELLI: *wool merchant and former business partner of Lorenzo de' Medici, member of the Court of Wolves*

FERDINAND II: *King of Aragon and husband of Queen Isabella*

GALEAZZO SFORZA: *Duke of Milan, assassinated 1476*

*GARCIA: *royal official under Isabella and Ferdinand*

GIANOTTO BERARDI: *Florentine slave trader*

GIORGIO ANTONIO VESPUCCI: *priest, uncle of Amerigo Vespucci and tutor to Lorenzino and Giovanni di' Pierfrancesco de' Medici*

GIOVANNI DE' MEDICI: *son of Lorenzo and Clarice, destined to enter the Vatican*

GIOVANNI DI' PIERFRANCESCO DE' MEDICI: *cousin of Lorenzo de' Medici, younger brother of Lorenzino*

GIOVANNI PICO DELLA MIRANDOLA (PICO): *Italian nobleman, philosopher, friend of Lorenzo and member of the Academy*

GIROLAMO SAVONAROLA: *Dominican friar*

GIULIANO DE' MEDICI: *younger brother of Lorenzo, assassinated during the Pazzi conspiracy in 1478*

GIULIANO DE' MEDICI: *youngest son of Lorenzo and Clarice*

*GORO: *former henchman to Carlo di Fante, now serving Pope Innocent VIII*

*GRACE: *childhood sweetheart of Jack's in Lewes*

HARRY VAUGHAN: *son of Thomas Vaughan and Eleanor Arundel, *half-brother of Jack*

HENRY VII: *son of Margaret Beaufort and Edmund Tudor, King of England (1485–1509)*

*HERVEY: *Harry's manservant*

INNOCENT VIII: *pope*

ISABELLA I: *Queen of Castile and wife of King Ferdinand*

*JACK (JAMES) WYNTER: **son of Thomas Vaughan and Sarah Wynter, *half-brother of Harry Vaughan*

JOHN II: *King of Portugal*

KATHERINE (OF ARAGON): *daughter of Isabella and Ferdinand*

*LANDO: *member of the Court of Wolves*

*LAORA: *friend of Maddalena and Lucrezia de' Medici*

LORENZINO DI' PIERFRANCESCO DE' MEDICI: *cousin of Lorenzo de' Medici, older brother of Giovanni*

LORENZO DE' MEDICI (THE MAGNIFICENT): *grandson of Cosimo, ruler of Florence and head of the Medici family*

*LUCA: *Italian mercenary*

LUCREZIA DE' MEDICI: *eldest daughter of Lorenzo and Clarice*

*LUIGI DONATI: *member of the Court of Wolves*

LUISA DE' MEDICI: *daughter of Lorenzo and Clarice*

*LUYS CARRILLO: *Spanish nobleman under Isabella, friend of Rodrigo de Torres*

MADDALENA DE' MEDICI: *daughter of Lorenzo and Clarice, betrothed to Franceschetto Cybo*

*MANI: *mercenary*

*MARCO VALORI: *son of a silk merchant, member of the Court of Wolves*

MARGARET BEAUFORT: *Countess of Richmond, mother of Henry Tudor*

MARSILIO FICINO: *philosopher, priest, friend of Lorenzo's and founder of the Academy with Cosimo de' Medici*

MEHMET II: *Sultan of the Ottoman Empire, father of Bayezid and Djem, died 1481*

MUHAMMAD AL-ZAGAL: *brother of Abu' l-Hasan and uncle of Boabdil*

*NALDO: *manservant to Franco Martelli*

*NED DRAPER: *served under Thomas Vaughan*

NENCIA: *Lorenzo's mistress*

*ORHAN: *assassin*

*PACINO NARDI: *member of the Court of Wolves*

*PAPI: *manservant to Lorenzo*

*PETER: *Harry's secretary*

*PHILIPPE: *French nobleman*

*PIERA: *daughter of Franco Martelli*

PIERO DE' MEDICI: *eldest son of Lorenzo and Clarice*

RICHARD III: *Duke of Gloucester, brother of Edward IV and King of England (1483–85), died in battle against the forces of Henry Tudor*

*RIGO: *guard at the Palazzo Medici*

*RINALDO: *barber to Pope Innocent VIII*

ROBERT STILLINGTON: *Bishop of Bath and Wells*

*RODRIGO DE TORRES: *hidalgo and royal vassal under Queen Isabella*

RODRIGO PONCE DE LEON: *Marquis of Cádiz*

*SARAH WYNTER: *mother of Jack Wynter and *mistress of Thomas Vaughan*

SIXTUS IV: *pope, died 1484*

*STEFANO DI PARRI: *member of the Court of Wolves*

*SMILER: *North African soldier*

THOMAS CROFT: *customs official in Bristol, leader of the* Trinity *voyages*

THOMAS STANLEY: *Lord Stanley, husband of Margaret Beaufort*

THOMAS VAUGHAN: *royal official and chamberlain to Prince Edward, father of Harry and Ann Vaughan and *father of Jack Wynter, executed by Richard of Gloucester in 1483*

*TOM: *Harry's groom*

*VALENTINE HOLT: *gunner, served under Thomas Vaughan*

*VITO: *friar at San Marco*

BIBLIOGRAPHY

Baker, Timothy, *Medieval London*, Cassell, 1970

Ballerini, Isabella Lapi, *The Medici Villas*, Giunti Editore, 2011

Bergreen, Laurence, *Columbus, the Four Voyages, 1492–1504*, Penguin Books, 2011

Boyle, David, *Toward the Setting Sun: Columbus, Cabot, Vespucci and the Race for America*, Walker & Company, 2008

Brucker, Gene A., *Renaissance Florence*, University of California Press, 1969

Davies, Owen, *Grimoires: A History of Magic Books*, Oxford University Press, 2010

Ebeling, Florian (trans. David Lorton), *The Secret History of Hermes Trismegistus: Hermeticism from Ancient to Modern Times*, Cornell University Press, 2007

Edge, David and Paddock, John Miles, *Arms and Armour of the Medieval Knight*, Bison Group, 1988

Edwards, John, *The Spain of the Catholic Monarchs, 1474–1520*, Blackwell Publishers, 2000

Edwards, John, *Ferdinand and Isabella*, Routledge, 2013

Elliott, J.H., *Imperial Spain, 1469–1716*, Penguin Books, 2002

Evans, James, *Merchant Adventurers*, Phoenix, 2014

FitzRoy, Charles, *Renaissance Florence on Five Florins a Day*, Thames & Hudson, 2010

Fornaciai, Valentina, *Toilette, Perfumes and Make-up at the Medici Court*, Sillabe, 2007

Frick, Carole Collier, *Dressing Renaissance Florence: Families, Fortunes and Fine Clothing*, Johns Hopkins University Press, 2005

Goldthwaite, Richard A., *The Economy of Renaissance Florence*, Johns Hopkins University Press, 2011
Hale, J.R., *War and Society in Renaissance Europe, 1450–1620*, Sutton Publishing, 1998
Hibbert, Christopher, *The Rise and Fall of the House of Medici*, Penguin Books, 1979
Hibbert, Christopher, *Florence: The Biography of a City*, Penguin Books, 2004
Irving, Washington, *The Works of Washington Irving: Tales of a Traveller, a Chronicle of the Conquest of Granada*, Lea and Blanchard, 1840
Kirkham, Anne and Warr, Cordelia (eds.), *Wounds in the Middle Ages*, Ashgate, 2014
Lee, Alexander, *The Ugly Renaissance: Sex, Disease and Excess in an Age of Beauty*, Hutchinson, 2013
Mazzini, Donata and Martini, Simone, *Villa Medici, Fiesole: Leon Battista Alberti and the Prototype of the Renaissance Villa*, Centro Di, 2004
Mirandola, Giovanni Pico della (intro. Russell Kirk, trans. A. Robert Caponigri), *Oration on the Dignity of Man*, Gateway Editions, 1984
Najemy, John M., *A History of Florence 1200–1575*, Blackwell Publishing, 2008
Nicolle, David, *Granada 1492: The Twilight of Moorish Spain*, Osprey, 1998
Penn, Thomas, *Winter King: The Dawn of Tudor England*, Penguin Books, 2012
Ross, Cathy and Clark, John, *London: The Illustrated History*, Penguin Books, 2011
Spufford, Peter, *Power and Profit: The Merchant in Medieval Europe*, Thames & Hudson, 2002
Stapleford, Richard, *Lorenzo de' Medici at Home: The Inventory of the Palazzo Medici in 1492*, Pennsylvania State University Press, 2013
Strathern, Paul, *The Medici*, Jonathan Cape, 2003
Thomas, Hugh, *The Slave Trade: The History of the Atlantic Slave Trade, 1440–1870*, Phoenix, 2006
Unger, Miles J., *Magnifico: The Brilliant Life and Violent Times of Lorenzo de' Medici*, JR Books, 2008